The Dead Wife

Sue Fortin is the *USA Today* and #1 Kindle bestselling author of *The Girl Who Lied* and *Sister Sister*. She has sold over half a million copies of her books worldwide.

Sue was born in Hertfordshire but had a nomadic childhood, moving often with her family, before eventually settling in West Sussex. She is married with four children, all of whom patiently give her the time to write but, when not behind the keyboard, she likes to spend time with them, enjoying both the coast and the South Downs between which they are nestled. She is a member of the Crime Writers' Association.

@suefortin1
www.facebook.com/suefortinauthor
www.suefortin.com

Also by Sue Fortin

United States of Love
Closing In
The Half Truth
The Girl Who Lied
Sister Sister
The Birthday Girl
Schoolgirl Missing

The
Dead
Wife

SUE FORTIN

HarperCollins*Publishers*

HarperCollins*Publishers*
The News Building
1 London Bridge Street
London SE1 9GF

www.harpercollins.co.uk

This paperback edition 2019

First published in Great Britain in ebook format
by HarperCollins*Publishers* 2019

A catalogue record for this book
is available from the British Library

ISBN: 9780008294519
US ISBN: 9780008348069

Typeset in Birka by
Palimpsest Book Production Ltd, Falkirk, Stirlingshire

Printed and bound by CPI Group (UK) Ltd, Croydon CR0 4YY

MIX
Paper from
responsible sources
FSC
www.fsc.org
FSC C007454

To Ged and our first trip to the Lake District
back in the 1990s when we toured the area
on a motorbike. It rained a lot. We got very wet.
But, despite rotten weather, we still had great fun
and fell in love with the area and the fantastic scenery.

Chapter One

Two Years Earlier,
Conmere Resort Centre, Lake District, Cumbria

Everyone who visited, worked or lived at Conmere knew the lake to be both beauty and beast all at the same time. A water with two faces – the south shoreline the beauty, bathed in sunlight, the water sparkling and glistening as it gently lapped the pebbles around the edge. It was the jewel in the crown of the Conmere estate. By contrast, the north side was where the waters were dark and shrouded for most of the day in shadow cast by the Con Point Hills, which loomed large and jagged over the water. This was where secrets were drowned and silence prevailed.

It all happened in a matter of seconds, but to her, time stretched as her brain registered her body falling towards the water. So many more impressions filled her mind. The blackness of the water, that it was particularly deep at this point of the lake, that there was no gentle slope from shallow to deeper depths, and there was a tangle of weeds. She wondered if the weeds would soften her fall but then remembered she was wearing a heavy Barbour coat – one that Harry had

1

insisted she wear that morning because the weather had taken a turn for the worse overnight. Then, of course, there were her wellington boots – she wished she'd had time to kick them off before they filled with water.

Turning her face to the side, she impacted the lake with first her shoulder and then her hip and her feet. For a moment she thought the weeds had acted as a safety net but then her head went under the water and the cold water swamped her face, rushing up her nostrils. She kept her mouth closed, squeezed her eyes tight shut and blew out from her nose. Automatically her arms flew out as she tried to paddle water, but her limbs were heavy and it was difficult to move in the thick coat. The water had already soaked through her clothing and the cold and wet wrapped itself around her arms. She kicked her feet, but her boots had gulped in the water, making it impossible for her to move.

She flung her head up and her face broke through the surface. She gulped in fresh air. A deep, huge lungful before being dragged down again. She had to get the coat off and frantically she grappled with the press studs. She must remain calm. One press stud undone. She must concentrate on what she was doing. Two press studs undone. She mustn't panic. Three press studs undone. Her lungs were ready to burst. Four press studs undone. She grabbed at the zipper pull and yanked it down and, releasing the pin, with a Herculean effort managed to shrug the thick, waxy garment from her shoulders. Instead of falling away, it drifted almost motionless in the water. Her arms began to flap, trying to force her body upwards to the surface. The panic was taking hold now. She needed air. Lots of it. Her lungs were stinging – so painful.

She mustn't take a breath. It was an automatic bodily reaction but she knew she would only take in water if she did.

For the second time, she broke through the surface and gasped for air. She managed another lungful before she felt the pull of the water in her boots. She had the fleeting image of a figure standing on the bank. Her brain registered the sound of a dog barking.

Down again into the depths of the lake she sank. Her arms and legs were so tired and heavy, now starved of oxygen, she couldn't move them. Didn't they say that when a person drowned, their life flashed before them? Her lungs were once again at break point. In one last attempt she tried to move her arms to push herself to the surface but it was futile. She needed oxygen. She could no longer fight the urge not to breathe in and she felt the rush of water into her body.

Her last thought was, why hadn't anyone tried to save her?

Chapter Two

Instagram Story

Well, today I have been tasked by my illustrious boss at *Vacation Staycation* to spend the weekend in the Lake District at Conmere Resort Centre, which has been revamped by the Sinclair family – Pru and her three sons, Dominic, Harry and Owen. And, best of all, I get to meet them and sample the new facilities – can't wait! #BestJobEver

'What do you think?' asked Steph, as her friend read her Instagram post.

'I must say, you sound far more enthusiastic on Instagram than you do in real life,' said Ria, putting down her phone. They were sitting in the office at the back of the gallery, Steph having called in to her friend in her lunch break.

Steph looked at her across her cappuccino. 'I'm looking forward to it. I remember Conmere House from when I used

4

to live up there. You know, my dad was a delivery driver for the Sinclair family for quite a few years, up until he died, actually, which was soon after the three sons took it over.'

'And the sons have done the refurb?'

'As I understand it. They offer all sorts of outdoor activities now but aimed at the high-end market. Pretty expensive, from what I've seen of the price list. Anyway, it's not so much the resort I'm excited about, it's the scenery. I'm hoping I'll get a chance to take some photos for my portfolio.'

'Oh, yes, do,' encouraged Ria. 'Lakes and mountains always sell. Soon you'll be rich enough to leave your job at the travel agency.'

'Yeah, in my dreams. Don't get me wrong, I do like my job, but this is about as exciting as it gets. I'd like to get my teeth into something juicier.'

'Like what?'

'Oh, I don't know. Something that's a bit more serious and high profile. Current affairs or investigative journalism.'

'I thought you were going to say you'd prefer to do photography.'

'I would, but it doesn't earn me a regular steady income. It's hard-going being single. I thought after being divorced for over a year, I'd be more financially stable now.'

'I think you were too easy on Zac; you should have pushed for more.'

'Just because he had an affair? No, I was actually relieved when I found out. At least it prompted me to do something about it – to start afresh. We both knew our marriage was over long before that.' Ria didn't look convinced, but Steph had long since given up trying to justify her actions to her friend, as, no matter how well-intentioned Ria was, she hadn't been in that marriage. Ultimately it had been down to Steph and Zac to sort things out, which they had done amicably. Privately, Steph had admitted to herself, if Zac hadn't been the one to have an affair, it could so easily have been her. They had both been looking for love and affection, which sadly neither could provide the other with.

Steph cleared her throat in a bid to clear her mind. Zac and their marriage and divorce certainly didn't need revisiting. 'Anyway, back to my new assignment. I'm sure I can get some great photos up there in the Lake District and any extra money will be most welcome, especially at the moment. I just had to spend out to get my car through its MOT.' Steph's gaze dipped as she concentrated placing her cup onto her saucer.

'Hey, don't be so glum. You know you're a great photographer but it's a hard market, you know that,' said Ria, not saying anything they hadn't already said over the past few years. Ria gave Steph a sympathetic smile and then struck a cheerier note. 'And there's the bonus that you'll be back on your old stomping ground.'

'I'm not sure I'd describe that as a bonus.'

'You might be able to spend a bit of time with your mum, now that she's retired.'

Steph appreciated the delicacy with which her friend spoke the words. The relationship between Steph and her mum was difficult at the best of times, so she wasn't entirely sure spending time together was on the agenda.

'How is your mum enjoying her retirement?'

Steph could hear the genuine concern in Ria's voice. 'Hard to say, if I'm honest. She says in the end she hated working for the police, especially CID when she was promoted to DCI. There was so much paperwork and red tape that went along with the job, it just wasn't her thing.'

'It's a shame she feels like that. It should be something she looks back on with pride and affection.'

'You'd think so, wouldn't you?. She was more married to the job than she was to my dad.'

'Did she ever encourage you to join?' Ria picked up the cups and took them over to the sink.

'God, no. Besides, I didn't want to be overshadowed by the wonderful DCI Wendy Lynch. The one who was awarded a bravery medal, the one who cracked a child-trafficking ring, the one who went deep under cover and nearly paid for it with her life.' Steph shook her head. 'No, thank you.'

'Instead you opted for a career with no security, one that's full of uncertainty.'

Steph opened the Twitter app on her phone. 'If I can create a bit of a buzz about my new assignment, get the word out about the photography too, I might get some more work. I'm going to tweet it as well as putting it on Instagram and Facebook.'

'Good idea. I'll retweet it and share it, of course.'

Steph read the tweet aloud as she typed. 'Long weekend in Lake District to review Conmere Resort Centre. Can't wait! #Conmere #Sinclairfamily #freelance.'

'You need to word it so there is some sort of interaction,' pointed out Ria. 'Ask people to recommend places, then maybe you can approach those places for some promo work.'

'Excellent idea,' said Steph as she reworded her tweet before posting it.

'Look, I need to get back to work. I've got an American coming in looking for something special for his apartment,' said Ria, rinsing the cups and drying her hands. 'Don't forget it's Gareth's birthday meal a week on Friday. Eight o'clock. My house.'

'How could I forget? But no matchmaking. I don't want to be stuck with your husband's latest single male colleague he's rustled up from the depths of the corporate world's basement.'

'Don't be such a spoilsport,' said Ria.

'I mean it!' Steph gave her friend a hug before going on her way.

Brighton, Monday, 6 May, 7.23 p.m.

Throughout the afternoon, Steph's phone pinged intermittently with replies to her social media posts. Ria had been right about asking for people's recommendations; it had provided a wealth of answers. It would be even more exciting if one of those transformed into a new commission, thought Steph as she ran herself a bath. She really didn't fancy bar work but, judging by the balance of her bank account that afternoon, she wasn't going to have any choice in the matter. She had enough in her savings account to pay two months' rent and then that was it. The books weren't balancing; her income-to-outgoing ratio was tipping the wrong way. She'd have to come up with something soon because she sure as hell wasn't going to go begging to her mother for a sub. For a start, that would be admitting defeat – it would prove her mother right that travel journalism wasn't any better than the local reporting she'd done when she first left uni. All her mother's doom and gloom predictions could be soon fulfilled if Steph didn't get something sorted.

Having spent a good hour in the bath, dressed in her pjs, her hair wrapped in a towel and with a tub of ice cream in one hand, a spoon in the other, Steph opened her laptop to catch up on some box-set viewing. While she was waiting for the series to load, she checked her phone. The social media notifications had calmed down now, but when she opened the Twitter app she saw she had a direct message.

Hello, Steph. I saw your tweet about Conmere Resort Centre and the Sinclair family. My daughter was married to one of the Sinclair brothers. Check out my timeline and Google Elizabeth Sinclair. My daughter's death was NOT an accident. I'm looking for someone to prove this. I can pay well. Message me if you think you're up to the job. From Sonia Lomas.

Chapter Three

S teph read the message for a second and third time. It was probably the most bizarre message she'd ever received, and yet the most intriguing one too. It must be some crank, surely? Who in their right mind would DM someone on Twitter about looking into the death of their daughter? She went to close the app but her stomach gave a little somersault of excitement. What if this was true? What if there really had been a miscarriage of justice?

Steph allowed herself the luxury of taking the thought further. This could be her chance to change the trajectory of her career. If she discovered the death of this woman's daughter had been covered up, then what a scoop that would be. Not to mention the money she could earn from it. Perhaps she could even sell it to one of the nationals.

She looked at the TV screen as a box-set uploaded and, picking up the remote control, she pressed the pause button. She placed the ice-cream tub and spoon on the coffee table, her appetite for such delights now disappearing. She had to find out more about this Sonia Lomas and her daughter.

She logged on to Twitter via her laptop, the bigger screen being easier on her eyes at this time of the evening, and then scrolled through Sonia Lomas's timeline.

The screen was filled with picture after picture of a young woman, about Steph's age, smiling at the camera, her blonde, relaxed curls sitting on her shoulders, her make-up light and natural and her teeth white and straight. All with the hashtag of Elizabeth Sinclair. Every so often there was a different photograph of her: in one she was sitting on a wall in a pair of denim shorts, her tanned legs crossed at the ankles; in another she was leaning against the side of a yacht in a rather clichéd blue and white striped jumper, cropped chinos and bare feet. The images alone made it look like a photoshoot for a high-end outdoor-clothing chain. The words accompanying each tweet, however, painted a different picture.

HELP! @CumbriaPolice did not investigate the death of my daughter fully. Please sign the petition to have her case reopened. #JusticeForElizabeth

Elizabeth Sinclair, wife of Harry Sinclair of the Sinclair family, died in suspicious circumstances. @CumbriaPolice won't listen to me. I need your help to reopen her case. Please sign the petition. #JusticeForElizabeth

And so the tweets went on, each accusing Cumbria Police of not doing their job and each asking for the petition to be signed.

11

Steph clicked·on the link which took her to the petition, where she found more detailed information.

Two years ago, my daughter Elizabeth Sinclair was found unconscious in Conmere Lake on the estate of the Conmere Resort owned by the Sinclair family in Cumbria. She was taken to hospital but never regained consciousness and her life-support machine was turned off two days later. The coroner recorded a verdict of misadventure. Cumbria Police investigated my daughter's death but failed to consider other lines of enquiry which would suggest my daughter was, in fact, murdered. I have had an independent review of my daughter's death which recommends a further and fuller investigation. Despite countless requests to Cumbria Police to reopen my daughter's case, and letters from my solicitor, Cumbria Police have refused to do so, citing not enough new evidence to warrant the case being reopened.

As a mother, I cannot let this matter rest until it has been fully investigated again and I would urge you to sign this petition to help me gain the publicity I need to apply enough pressure on the police to reopen the case.

Thank you.
Sonia Lomas

Steph's stomach gave another roll of anticipation. This Sonia Lomas was serious; she wasn't a crank at all. She was a mother fighting for her daughter's memory. Steph couldn't help comparing her own mother to Sonia Lomas and instantly wished she hadn't. It struck a painful chord – Wendy was so out of tune with motherhood. Steph pushed the comparison away and typed 'Elizabeth Sinclair' in the search bar.

The story of Elizabeth's death was towards the end of the page and it gave a few more details. Steph picked up her pen and notebook from the coffee table and made some notes.

Elizabeth Sinclair
30
Married to Harry Sinclair
No children
Born in London. Mother – Sonia Lomas, Care
    Assistant, Hackney
No siblings
Father? Not mentioned
2 years ago – found unconscious – died later
    in hospital

She then searched the name Harry Sinclair. Steph knew the Sinclair family had a large estate in the north-west of England which was a holiday resort centre, and was aware of the backstory, how their great-great-grandfather had won another man's estate during a game of poker back in the early 1900s. The family had managed to hold on to their position, wealth and prosperity through two world wars and several recessions. The younger generation of the Sinclair family consisted of three brothers who had managed to turn what had become a failing business into a highly successful company. Max

Sinclair had inherited the home, which had been in disrepair after years of financial pressure. He had turned the fortunes of the Sinclairs around by developing the 150-acre site into a commercial high-end woodland-activity-type business. Max's vision had been much more upmarket, and the log cabins inspired by his time working on a ranch in Texas where he'd met his wife-to-be, Prudence Cutchins. When his sons had come on board their vision had broadened the estate further and encompassed not only all things outdoors but water sports, rock climbing, mountain-bike trails, hiking and a health spa.

This was as much as Steph knew from her time living in the Kendalton area and from her briefing with her boss, Tim, about her assignment. Now she needed to dig deeper with her research. The next person to check out was the husband himself, Harry Sinclair.

This proved harder than she expected. There was next to nothing on the internet about Harry Sinclair. There were a few photographs of him and his brothers, sometimes with his mother in shot, standing outside a stately-looking home which would be worthy of Downton Abbey status. The three brothers looked very striking, all sharing their mother's dark hair; the older two had theirs cut short, while Owen, the youngest brother, wore his a little longer, which reminded Steph of some sort of art-student type. Dominic and Owen were smiling, whereas Harry's expression was sombre. Steph checked the date of the photograph. It was six months ago, so that also made it a little over eighteen months since his wife had died, in which case he was excused for looking pretty miserable. Although, as she looked at the photograph again, she wasn't sure if miserable was the right word. He looked more . . . serious . . . moody even.

Steph read some of the articles about the resort the family had opened, but there was very little personal information.

Eventually, she came across an online local newspaper which had reported the death of Elizabeth Sinclair. It wasn't much, but it did give a little more information. It would seem Elizabeth had taken the family dog for a walk which was later found wet and covered in mud. It was assumed that the dog had gone into the water and Elizabeth had taken it upon herself to rescue the much-loved pooch but had become entangled in the weeds just below the surface.

After another half an hour of searching, Steph surveyed her notes.

Harry Sinclair
Middle brother – 35
Widower
Stays out of the limelight
No comments found concerning the death of his
   wife

Dominic Sinclair – named after GGG
Older brother – 37
Director
Driving force of the company
Attends lots of business and social functions
Divorced – 1 child – 15, boy – with former wife
Another child – 7 – with current partner –
   Lisa – together 10 years

Property in South of France
Lives in private lodge in the grounds of resort
Comment re death of SIL – Very much missed
   by us all. We are all in shock.

Owen Sinclair
Youngest of three brothers – 32
Director
Married – Natalie (27)
3 children – twin boys aged 3 and daughter
   aged 5

Pru Sinclair
Mother
Director – 68 years old
Widow. Husband died 2014
Formidable. Public speaking
Involved with lots of charities and local
   businesses
Comment re death of DIL – Deeply saddened.
   Elizabeth the daughter I never had.

It didn't scream murder to Steph but she knew she wouldn't be able to leave this alone now. Something was urging her on – journalistic gut instinct? She wasn't sure, but she wasn't going to ignore it.

She was about to close the article when the bottom paragraph caught her attention. The air was knocked from her lungs and her heart thudded against her chest wall.

'Bloody hell.'

She peered closer to the screen as if to make certain she was reading it correctly. She read each word with precision.

There had been speculation that Elizabeth Sinclair had been having an affair but police dismissed this notion. DCI Wendy Lynch of Cumbria Police issued a statement that there was no suggestion whatsoever that these rumours were in fact anything other than local tittle-tattle, which was completely insensitive to the family's current circumstances and in particular to Mr Harry Sinclair himself. Lynch went on to request that the family's privacy was respected at this difficult time.

Steph picked up the phone and called her mother – DCI Wendy Lynch.

Chapter Four

Frustratingly, Steph's call to her mother went to answer-phone. She left a brief message, asking her mother to ring her in connection with the death of Elizabeth at Conmere. Steph had decided to keep it brief; she didn't feel the need to elaborate, as her mother would, no doubt, recall the case.

She picked up the tub of ice cream, which had defrosted to the point that calling it ice cream was almost criminal, but nevertheless she managed to secure a spoonful of the cookie-dough mixture on the spoon. It struck Steph as strange that Wendy had never mentioned the Elizabeth Sinclair case. A death of a member of the Sinclair family was a little out of the ordinary and, although she knew Wendy wouldn't have gone into any detail, the fact that her father had worked for the Sinclairs made it more personal and worthy of a mention at least.

Steph sighed as she savoured the ice cream in her mouth.

Steph knew it had been passed down through several Sinclair generations.

She wondered again why her mum had never mentioned

Elizabeth's death, and as she tracked back over Sonia Lomas's timeline her idle curiosity morphed into something more insistent. She hoped her mum would talk about it, but Steph had long since learned that Wendy Lynch was a tough negotiator and not easy to move once she had made her mind up about something. In fact, Steph struggled to think of a time when Wendy had ever conceded.

Brighton, Tuesday, 7 May, 8.45 a.m.

Steph had to admit, twelve hours wasn't exactly a long time to wait for her mother to reply, but she had been barely able to sleep last night as she had repeatedly gone over the whole Sonia Lomas message and everything connected with it. Her imagination had certainly been fired up and her desire to find out what her mother could tell her was in overdrive.

'Ah, you're there,' she said when her mother answered the phone. 'How are you?'

'Hello. I'm fine. A little busy. Is everything OK, only I'm about to go out?'

Steph was used to her mum's brusqueness. Wendy Lynch had never quite been able to leave the formalities of the workplace behind. Even as a child Steph remembered their days being like a military operation. In fact, her mother would have been as suited to a military career as she had to a police one.

'Did you get my message last night?' asked Steph as she stirred her coffee and settled herself at the breakfast bar in her little apartment in Brighton. She didn't miss the slight pause her mother gave before replying.

'On the answerphone? It was a bit garbled, to be honest. I didn't really know what you were talking about.'

'Elizabeth Sinclair,' said Steph, trying to keep her patience. 'You know, the Sinclair family who Dad worked for and the wife who drowned in the lake on their estate.'

'Well, yes, I do remember her but it wasn't really much of a case. It was one of my last ones. She was out walking. The dog jumped in the water and she tried to save it. Got into difficulties and tragically drowned. That's all there is to it. Why do you want to know?'

'You didn't listen to my message at all, did you?'

'As I said, it didn't come out very clear and I am rather busy.'

Steph reined in her sigh and attempted to inject an affable tone into her voice. 'Work want me to go up to the Lakes and cover the new opening of Conmere Resort Centre. I'm going to be up there for the weekend and I tweeted about it. Then I got this weird direct message from Elizabeth Sinclair's mother. She said her daughter's death was not an accident. I've looked into it and I was amazed to see your name at the bottom of an article.'

Wendy gave an audible sigh. 'You really mustn't listen to Sonia Lomas. She's got mental-health issues. I mean, it's tragic, but the fact of the matter is, Elizabeth Sinclair drowned and it was an accident. The woman has been hounding Cumbria Police for the past two years about it. I can't really tell you much else, not because I don't want to, but there simply isn't anything else to say.'

Steph couldn't help thinking her mother probably knew more about it than she was letting on. It wouldn't surprise

Steph if her mother was purposely being light on detail. 'Do you think there's anything at all in the accusations? Is there even the slightest possibility it might have been anything other than an accident?'

'Now listen to me, Stephanie,' said Wendy. 'There is nothing at all in Sonia Lomas's accusations. What I suggest you do is concentrate on the task you've been given, i.e. report about the reopening of the resort and don't go poking your journalistic nose into matters that are purely fiction or don't concern you.'

'My journalistic nose is my business,' said Steph, rearing up at her mother's demand. It had been a long time since her mother had told her what she could and couldn't do. Steph wasn't going to start listening to her now. 'I was only asking if there might be any truth in it.'

'I meant it when I said don't go poking your nose in where it's not welcome. You'll be upsetting a lot of people, not to mention Mrs Sinclair herself, who would be quite within her rights to complain about you to your boss. And then where would you be? I'll tell you where: sacked. So think on.'

'I'll tell you what, Mum. Say what you think, don't pull any punches, honestly. Speak your mind.' Steph couldn't help coating her words with sarcasm.

'I've always been honest with you, Steph. Why wouldn't I be now? Anyway, like I said, I'm in a hurry and really must go.'

'Don't you want to know if I'm coming to see you when I'm in Cumbria?' asked Steph. 'I mean, I'm there for the weekend, it would make sense. That's if you want me to come over.'

Steph wanted her mother to say yes. She wanted Wendy to want her to visit. And yet, at the same time, the desire frustrated the hell out of her. She hated the fact that she still sought not only her mother's approval, but her affection as well.

'Of course I want you to come and see me. It goes without saying.' This time there was a softening in Wendy's tone.

'OK, good,' said Steph, acknowledging the morass of emotions she was experiencing. 'I'll message you Sunday evening when I'm leaving the resort and maybe I can come over and stay for a couple of nights? If that's OK with you.'

'Stop asking if it's OK. Of course it is. Now I really must go. Have a good weekend and I look forward to seeing you on Sunday, but remember, don't poke your nose in where it doesn't belong.' And with that the line went dead.

'Yeah, love you too,' said Steph, looking accusingly at the silent receiver. Disappointment washed over her. Here she was, practically begging to be able to visit her mother. Why did she always set herself up for a fall? Her mother was never going to change now.

Steph spent the next hour researching the Elizabeth Sinclair case some more. She phoned a contact she'd had from her days working in Carlisle for a local newspaper after graduating from uni. That placement had been far enough away from her hometown of Kendalton and her mother, to put a reasonable distance between them, so that any visits needed to be prearranged. It was an excuse that had worked for both of them.

Steph looked back fondly at her days with the local rag; despite the lack of action it had been a good starting point, and Adam Baxter had taught her everything he knew and had made the job so much more bearable.

While Adam had been happy to stay with the local paper, Steph had felt the need to explore other opportunities, and when the job with *Vacation Staycation* had arisen the lure of being based on the south coast tempted her to apply. She had been delighted to be offered the position and, with nothing to keep her in Cumbria, Steph had made the move five years ago. She had meant to keep in touch with Adam when she moved, but phone calls had been replaced by text messages, and over time the messages had become fewer and fewer. Steph wasn't sure when she'd last been in touch with Adam – two, maybe three years ago?

She searched through her phone contacts, locating her ex-colleague's name, and hoped he still had the same mobile number. She was in luck. Adam answered almost immediately.

'OMG! Well, if it isn't Stephanie Durham herself. What a blast from the past.'

'Hi, Adam. How are you?'

'Surprised but oddly pleased to hear from you.' She could hear him pause as he drew on a cigarette. 'Now, what do you want?'

'What makes you think I want anything?' said Steph, noting how easily they fell back into their old, comfortable ways with each other.

'Seeing as I haven't heard so much as a whisper from you in the last three years, call it journalist's intuition, but I'm guessing you want something from me. Either that or you pocket dialled me and are too embarrassed to hang up.'

Steph gave a laugh. 'OK, you got me. I pocket dialled.'

'Bollocks did you,' said Adam. 'What is it you want to know?'

Steph dispensed with any further preamble. 'Elizabeth Sinclair. What do you know about her death?'

'Elizabeth Sinclair . . . wait, let me think.'

Steph waited patiently, giving Adam time to raid his memory bank. He had a knack for being able to recall news events as if he had his own database in his head. 'Do you need a clue?' she prompted.

'Nope. Elizabeth Sinclair – I've got her now.'

'Like you didn't have as soon as I mentioned the name,' said Steph. 'You can quit humouring me now.'

'Right, here goes. Elizabeth Sinclair was married to Harry Sinclair from the highly esteemed, not to mention wealthy, Sinclair family who own the great big fucking house up near the Con Point Hills. Elizabeth drowned in a lake on the estate while trying to rescue her dog.'

'What else do you know?'

'Nothing.'

'Come on, Adam, you always know more than you let on. Did anything stand out as odd?'

'No, nothing. It was a family tragedy. Simply an accident.'

'So why has Elizabeth's mother been running a media campaign to have the investigation into her daughter's death reopened? She says it wasn't an accident. Have you not seen her Twitter feed?'

'Oh, you mean Sonia Lomas. She's a fruitcake. She's a mother who desperately doesn't or can't accept her daughter is dead.'

'What makes you say that?'

'Everyone knows it – she was like it before her daughter

24

died and she's got worse since.' Adam was beginning to sound bored with the conversation.

'What was she like before?'

'Highly strung. Emotional. That's what friends and family said anyway.'

Steph pushed on. 'If you were convinced your daughter was murdered and no one believed you, wouldn't that be enough to give you mental-health problems?'

'My point exactly, especially if you were a bit that way inclined beforehand. Anyway, why the interest?'

'I'm going up to Conmere Resort Centre to cover the reopening of the place since its major refurb.'

'Ooh, get you. All expenses paid, I hope.'

'Of course. Why do you think I left the *Carlisle Post*?'

'If you want my advice, which you probably don't, but I'm going to give it to you anyway,' said Adam, his voice taking on a more serious tone, 'you'll be best off just sticking to the assignment and not concerning yourself with Elizabeth Sinclair's death.'

'That sounds more like a warning than a piece of advice,' said Steph, doodling a lake surrounded by bulrushes on the notepad in front of her.

There was a significant pause before Adam answered. 'Look, Steph, the Sinclairs are a powerful family. They know lots of people, influential people. It won't do you or your career any favours if you come up here and start ruffling feathers about the death of one of their own.'

Steph gave a laugh, despite the seriousness of Adam's speech. 'And you must realise, as someone who once worked on a paper, I can't leave something alone when there's a whiff of a story.'

'Honestly, Steph, there's no story. Don't you think I would have been on it if there was?'

'True.' Adam was like a bloodhound when it came to sniffing out stories, but at the same time her own sense of intrigue wasn't quite satisfied. Both Adam and her mother were keen for her not to pursue the Elizabeth Sinclair story any further, and for some reason that troubled her.

'If you get time, why don't you give me a call when you're up here?' said Adam, changing the pace of the conversation. 'We could meet for a drink.'

'Yeah, I'd like that but I'll have to see how much time I get. I'm supposed to be visiting my mother too.'

'Good luck with that,' said Adam. 'Unless, of course, things have drastically improved between you two.'

'Not really,' admitted Steph. 'She retired last year and I thought we might see more of each other, but it's never really happened.'

'Look, if you get a chance, call me.'

'Cheers, Adam . . .'

'And forget the Elizabeth Sinclair story.'

'Don't know what story you're talking about,' replied Steph with exaggerated innocence.

Adam made a *humph* sort of noise, clearly not convinced. 'Look after yourself, Steph,' he said, before hanging up.

His parting words felt loaded with meaning but, far from putting Steph off, they only served to drive her on to find out more.

She opened the Twitter app on her phone and went to the direct message from Sonia Lomas.

Steph: Hi, Sonia. Would you like to meet up? Where are you based?

She received a reply within a few minutes.

Sonia: I'm in Croydon but can travel.

Steph: How about Arundel? It's about halfway between us. 12 tomorrow at The White Swan? We can meet for coffee.

Sonia: Yes, that works for me. See you then. And thank you.

For some reason, Steph didn't think Sonia Lomas was unhinged. Sad and depressed, yes, but not mentally ill in the way both her mother and Adam had implied.

Chapter Five

Harry Sinclair swung his BMW X5 into the private car park at the back of Conmere House and, taking his spot marked with a small wooden placard bearing his name, next to his brother's Range Rover, he cut the engine, letting out a small sigh as he did so. Just one week to get through and then he could leave all this behind him. It wasn't only the physical presence of Conmere House that troubled him, it was all the bad things in his life that it represented, not least the death of his wife.

As he stepped out of his car he was greeted by the sound of yapping – his mother's beloved trio of bichon frise dogs came scampering out from the pathway between the laurel hedges.

'Hello, girls,' said Harry, practically folding his six-foot frame in half to give the dogs a quick pat. His mother had borne only sons and he supposed Daisy, Flora and Rosie were her substitute daughters. Thank God he was a male, otherwise she would no doubt have adorned his hair with a ribbon as she had the dogs'.

28

'Harry! Oh, it is you, darling,' came his mother's clipped voice, with only the tiniest of remnants left of her Texan accent. Pru Sinclair walked down the path, waving to him over the hedge.

'Hello, Mum,' said Harry, greeting her with a kiss on each cheek.

'I was just wondering whether to phone you or not. I thought you were coming earlier.' She stood back and surveyed her son. 'You're looking very well; the French climate seems to be agreeing with you.'

Harry retrieved his holdall from the back of the car. 'A bit of simple living doesn't do the body or mind any harm.'

His mother gave a small raise of her eyebrow. 'Well, that's as maybe, but I'm glad you're home.'

Harry felt himself bristle but resisted the urge to correct her use of the word *home*. This place had never felt like home to him and, despite his mother's best intentions to subtly change his perception with her own version of cognitive behavioural therapy, Harry knew the sooner he was away from Conmere House the better he would be. The sabbatical in France with the design company was the perfect excuse to break the family ties. He followed his mother down the path that bordered the lush green lawn and through the open patio doors into the main living room. The three white fluffy hounds scampered back and forth along the path, excitedly announcing the arrival of Harry.

'Oh, thank God you're here. Mum was about to put out an APB, ring all the local hospitals and get the BBC to reconstruct your last known movements on a special edition of *Crimewatch*.'

Harry's older brother rose from the armchair he was

occupying and greeted his brother with a handshake and slap on the back.

'He's exaggerating. Take no notice,' said Pru. 'Now, I'll make us all a coffee. Are you hungry? I can make a sandwich or get something sent through from the cafe.'

'Coffee will do fine, thanks, Mum. I stopped on the way for something to eat,' said Harry over the noise of the dogs, who were building themselves up into a frenzy of whining and yapping.

'Oh, the girls are so pleased to see you,' laughed Pru as she headed out of the room.

Harry exchanged a look with his brother. A sadistic smile spread across Dominic's face. He looked down at the dogs and gave a swift kick to one of them, catching her bottom. The dog yelped. 'Now fuck off,' said Dominic, holding his arm outstretched. He hustled the dogs out through the patio doors. 'Jesus, they get on my nerves. They must be the most pampered pooches in the county.'

'I forgot what a compassionate soul you were,' said Harry. 'You'd better not let Mum see you do that.'

Dominic gave a shrug. 'Anyway, I'm glad you're here,' he said, walking over to the drinks tray on the walnut sideboard. 'I wasn't sure if we'd actually see you.'

'Really? Why's that?' Harry settled himself in the wing-backed armchair by the fireplace, a favourite spot of his late father's. Max Sinclair had always sat in that seat and woe betide anyone who had dared occupy it. Harry rested his hands on the arms and mentally gave his father a two-fingered salute. He hoped the old bastard could see him now and that he was turning in his grave.

Dominic paused with a bottle of gin in his hand and turned to give his brother a reproachful look. 'You really need me to spell it out? How many times have you been back to the estate since Elizabeth's accident?'

'I've been busy in France,' said Harry, noting the uneasy roll his stomach gave.

Dominic made a scoffing noise as he returned to mixing himself a G&T. He gestured with the bottle to Harry, who shook his head. Dominic sat down on the sofa with his drink. 'I'll tell you how many times . . . three. Christmas two years ago and twice for Mum's birthday.'

'I'm a dutiful son,' said Harry. 'Like I said, I've been busy. Anyway, I'm here now for the grand reopening. What's the problem?'

Harry knew what the problem was but acting ignorant somehow gave him an excuse, if only to himself. Of course, everyone knew what the real reason was for his absence but for the most part they skirted around it. Dominic, however, appeared to want to buck the trend. Harry eyed his older brother as he rested his forearms on his knees, his hands clasped around the crystal-cut tumbler.

'Mum misses you,' began Dominic. 'She worries about you.'

'She doesn't need to,' said Harry. 'I'm a grown man in my thirties; I don't need my mother clucking round me. In fact, I don't need anyone worrying about me.'

'Bit of a selfish attitude,' said Dominic, swigging the G&T down.

'She worries unnecessarily. It's suffocating. Why do you think I moved to France?'

Dominic sat back in his seat. 'OK, I'll level with you.' He gave a furtive glance towards the door. 'This is strictly between us.' He took a deep breath and Harry knew he wasn't going to like what he was about to hear. He steeled himself as his brother continued. 'Mum's not well. Not well at all.'

Harry's body gave an involuntary jolt. 'How unwell are we talking?'

Dominic rose and poured himself another drink and this time made Harry a neat Scotch. He passed it over and resumed his position on the sofa.

'Dom, how ill?'

Dominic gave him a steadying look. 'The cancer is back.'

Harry sucked in a breath so hard, he almost winded himself. 'Prognosis?'

'The worst. Months.'

'How many?'

'Twelve if we're lucky. Six if we're not.'

'We'll get a second opinion. I know some brilliant doctors in France,' began Harry, allowing his pragmatic approach to jump ahead of his emotions, a trait he'd learned at a young age when dealing with his father. 'She'll get the best treatment and fast.'

Dominic shook his head. 'It's too late. Don't you think I've made sure she's seen all the top oncologists? Nothing more can be done.'

'Radiotherapy? Chemo? Surely there must be something?'

'No. It's untreatable. Besides, she's refusing to go through chemo again.'

'On what basis?'

'On the basis of freedom of choice,' snapped Dominic, and

then became calmer. 'She wants to live her last months to their fullest. She doesn't want to spend them sick, recovering from treatment which to all intents and purposes is futile. You know how ill she was before. She literally can't face it again.'

'Fuck,' muttered Harry as his emotions finally surfaced. He downed the Scotch in one go and rested his forehead in his hand. 'Fuck.'

'Sorry, mate,' said Dominic.

Harry let out a long breath, composing himself before sitting back in his chair. 'But she looks so well.'

'You know Mum. She's a trooper.'

Prudence Sinclair had to be the most stoic woman Harry knew. For a start, when she was just twenty years old she had moved thousands of miles from her home in Texas after falling in love with his father, Max, who was working out there on the family cattle ranch one summer. Harry had never heard her once complain about her life in the UK, and to the outside world Max and Pru Sinclair had had it all – a wonderful life, consisting of a grand family estate and four sons, until tragedy had stepped in with the death of Elliot, the youngest of the boys, who had died at three months old from cot death. A turning point in their lives where nothing was ever quite the same. Not that the outside world would know, but inwardly, behind the imposing gates and high walls of Conmere House, the dynamics had shifted, and the once solid foundations had begun to subside. It was only Pru's underpinning that had saved them. According to Pru, Max had never got over the loss of their youngest son and had carried his heartbreak to the grave, although Harry had always been sceptical of this and privately assigned his mother's thoughts to wishful thinking on her part. Harry remembered his father as someone who was hard to please, someone around whom he and his brothers had tiptoed for fear of upsetting him. Max was someone who believed in strong discipline and especially so where his sons were concerned. Harry had long since replaced the 'strong discipline' mentality with that of a bully.

'Does Owen know?' asked Harry, his thoughts turning to his younger brother.

'Not yet. Mum doesn't want to tell him. She's worried he'll start drinking again.'

'He's been sober for a good eighteen months,' said Harry. 'Do you think he would?'

'Who knows? Owen and Natalie are going through a bit of a rough patch, from what I can tell.'

'That's a shame. Anything in particular?'

'I don't know the details – he doesn't say much to me – but reading between the lines, three-year-old twins and a five-year-old are putting a bit of a strain on their marriage. Natalie wants to move back to Norfolk to be near her mum. Owen doesn't.'

'Not if he's going to be part of the business,' said Harry. 'I mean, what else could he do? And Mum, she'd be heartbroken.'

'Exactly. Although that didn't stop you.'

'It's different. I'm a widower. I haven't got any kids. I've never wanted to be part of the business.'

'Mum was still heartbroken.'

'No, she wasn't. She was just sad about me going, but not heartbroken,' said Harry. 'Is Mum aware you're telling me?'

'No. She was adamant she didn't want anyone to know, including you.'

'So why are you telling me?' While Harry was glad Dominic had broken the news, he knew his brother well enough to know there'd be another motive behind the disclosure.

'Jesus, Harry. Why the fuck do you think I'm telling you?' hissed Dominic. The sound of their mother humming as she came down the hall filtered through into the room. 'Because you're her blue-eyed boy and nothing would make her last days happier than having you about.'

'She said that?'

'Of course she didn't but everyone knows that's true. You can't go back to France. You need to stay here.'

Harry eyed his brother as he considered the prospect of having to stay. It wasn't that he didn't want to support his mother, far from it, but Conmere itself held far too many bad memories for him. Memories he had escaped from when he'd moved to France. The idea of staying at Conmere any longer than a few days filled him with a sense of unease, but the alternative – leaving his mother when she had only months to live – was unimaginable and something he knew he couldn't do.

Chapter Six

Two Years Earlier,
Conmere Resort Centre, 10 August, 10.30 a.m.

Elizabeth took a final sip of her Earl Grey tea and, glancing down at the little dogs sitting expectantly at her feet, she picked up the croissant from her plate, broke it into three and chucked it onto the terrace. 'You can afford to get fat,' she said as the dogs eagerly gulped down the evidence.

She checked her watch for the fourth time. Surely the breakfast meeting Harry was attending with his mother and brothers was over by now. She looked at her phone in case she'd missed any messages from Harry, but there were none. Harry had said the meeting was primarily to discuss the sale of some land to a housing developer. The twenty-acre site on the edge of the estate was prime development land and, from what Harry had gleaned, outline planning permission for up to one hundred houses would be granted.

The land was worth in excess of 3.9 million pounds. Elizabeth couldn't understand the hesitancy of her mother-in-law. Pru Sinclair wasn't convinced about selling for any price, whereas both Harry and Dominic could see the potential. Naturally, pathetic little Mummy's boy Owen had taken his mother's side and the family were at an impasse. Elizabeth drummed her manicured fingernails on the bistro table. She hated being shut out of the business discussions like this.

'Morning!' came a voice.

Elizabeth turned her head and saw Natalie, Owen's wife, coming along the terrace with her three children in tow – the twin boys, Max and Oscar, in their double buggy and three-year-old Tilly on the buggy-board. Great, just what Elizabeth needed, the next generation of the Sinclair dynasty squawking around her. Yes, they were Harry's niece and nephews, and on the whole they were generally lovely and very cute, but that was when there were enough pairs of hands and the adults outnumbered the children with at least a 2:1 ratio. When the ratio was not in the adults' favour, Elizabeth struggled to find her charity.

'Hi, Natalie,' she said, plastering on a smile. 'And hello, Tilly. How are you?'

Tilly jumped off the buggy-board and headed towards Elizabeth, a sticky lolly positioned in her hand like a medieval jousting pole. 'Cuddle!'

Elizabeth eyed the lolly and noted the sticky face. Deftly, she managed to catch Tilly's wrists and avoid any direct contact with the sweet. God knows what Natalie was thinking, letting the child have a lolly this early in the day. Elizabeth managed the briefest of contacts before picking Tilly up and sitting her on the chair opposite.

'Are they still in the meeting?' asked Natalie, jiggling the buggy into place. One of the twins, Elizabeth couldn't work out which one, began to grizzle. Natalie rummaged in the changing bag and produced a ready-made bottle of formula milk. She offered it to the child, who immediately stopped complaining but whose cries were replaced by his sibling's.

'Here, let me hold that,' offered Elizabeth, feeling sorry for her sister-in-law as she struggled to fish out the other bottle.

'That's better,' said Natalie once twin number two was catered for. 'Thanks. I was hoping Owen would be out by now. We're supposed to be going to my friend's today.'

'What, and missing Sunday lunch? How did you manage to get a pass for that?' Getting out of a Sinclair Sunday dinner was equivalent to a Houdini escapology trick.

'It's my friend's birthday,' said Natalie with a wry smile.

'They've been in there ages,' said Elizabeth. 'I didn't think it would take this long.'

'Do you know what the meeting is about?'

Elizabeth raised an eyebrow in her sister-in-law's direction. Natalie was very sweet, but she either had no interest in the business side of things or, more likely, didn't have the time. 'It's about the twenty acres that Carter Homes want to buy. Hasn't Owen mentioned it?'

'Oh, that! Yes, he did tell me, but I was only half listening. I think he said Harry and Dominic thought it was a good price and they should sell, but Pru didn't agree and Owen backed her up. Is that it?'

'Pretty much.'

Natalie was distracted by Tilly's sticky hands and took a wet-wipe from the changing bag hanging on the back of the pushchair. 'I don't get too involved, but I think Owen wants to do something with the land; I'm not sure what though.'

'Hopefully it will get sorted out today,' said Elizabeth. 'I mean, 3.9 million pounds . . . that's nearly a million each.'

'How much? Wow! I didn't realise we were talking those kinds of figures.'

'It's not as if that part of the estate is used for much either, other than rambling or mountain biking. Even then, there are better trails on the south side of the estate. For the use it gets, plus the added costs of its upkeep, it's not worth it. It doesn't attract that much income per annum. Certainly not 3.9 million pounds' worth.'

'Gosh, you sound like you should be in the boardroom yourself.'

Elizabeth gave a small laugh. 'Oh, I intend to be one day.'

It was Natalie's turn to laugh. 'Yeah, like Pru would ever let that happen.'

'Don't forget, it's my background. I've come from the travel industry. I was head of PR. I do know my stuff,' said Elizabeth, withdrawing the bottle from the now dozing baby's mouth. 'I do actually have an official role here as PR Officer. I think they all forget that sometimes.'

'Ah, but not a shareholder. Not able to vote on anything,' replied Natalie. 'In effect, an employee.'

'For now,' said Elizabeth, unable to ignore the irritation she felt at Natalie's accurate summary of her position. 'Things do change, though, and, as frustrating as it may be, I simply have to be patient and bide my time until the opportunity arises. And it will.'

Chapter Seven

The White Swan, Arundel,
Wednesday, 8 May, 11.50 a.m.

Steph stepped off the train at Arundel and was glad she'd only brought a lightweight jacket with her, the warmth of the May sunshine hinting at the imminent arrival of summer. She arrived first at the pub, found a seat near the window and placed her notebook on the table. Steph's Twitter profile picture was a clear photograph of herself and it would be easy for Sonia to spot her.

Steph's gaze trailed the people walking past the pub. Arundel was a popular place with tourists and the clement weather had drawn them out. A woman walking across the bridge towards the pub caught her attention. Her dark hair was tied back in a ponytail and the red-framed glasses she wore looked stark against her pale complexion. She was wearing jeans and a T-shirt, a pair of lace-ups and a lilac fleece. Before the woman even appeared in the doorway, Steph was certain it was Sonia Lomas. The woman had an aura of sadness about her, and as she paused to scan the pub Steph could see the emptiness in her eyes, the slight droop in the shoulders of someone carrying the burden of grief. The woman met Steph's gaze, nodded and approached the table.

'Sonia Lomas?' asked Steph, albeit needlessly, as she stood up to greet her.

'Steph Durham?'

Steph held out her hand, which Sonia shook. 'Nice to meet you.' She gestured to the seat opposite. 'Can I order you a coffee or a tea?'

'Coffee, please. Black. No sugar,' said Sonia.

Steph returned a few minutes later with the coffee and sat down opposite Sonia. 'I'm glad you came,' she said. 'It's much easier to speak face to face than over social media.'

'I assume it was also to weigh me up,' said Sonia. There was no malice in her voice. 'Just to make sure I'm not some crazy woman who can't accept the outcome of the police enquiry.' The last words were spoken through gritted teeth.

'I'm interested in the truth,' said Steph. 'Whatever that might be.'

Sonia looked across the rim of her coffee cup. 'The truth is, my daughter was murdered.'

'Mrs Lomas,' began Steph. 'Sonia . . .' She looked at the older woman, waiting for approval at the use of her Christian name. Sonia Lomas offered no objection, so Steph continued. 'Why do you think Elizabeth was murdered?'

Sonia placed her cup carefully down on the table. 'She was frightened. Things weren't working out with her husband. She wanted to leave but was too scared.'

'She told you that?'

'She left me a voicemail saying as much.'

'Did you ever speak to her in person about it?'

'I didn't get the chance. I phoned her straight back but she said she couldn't talk. I tried again the next day and the day after but each time she said it wasn't a good time. Then she sent me a text message telling me not to worry, she knew what she was going to do and she'd be back home as soon as she could.'

'Do you still have the voicemail?'

'Of course,' said Sonia, a touch of indignation in her tone. She fished in her handbag and retrieved her mobile phone. 'Dial 121 and listen to saved messages.'

Steph took the phone and accessed the voice message. She listened to it twice. Elizabeth's voice was younger-sounding than she had imagined and Steph tried to match it to the image she'd retrieved from the internet. *'Hello, Mum, it's me. Look, I'm sorry to call like this and leave a message. I really wanted to speak to you in person but . . . things aren't too good here. I've got myself into something and it's way above my head. I don't like it. I have a bad feeling about it all. I need to come home. I'm going to leave this place. Leave Harry and come home. I'm not sure when, but it will be soon, just as soon as I've worked a few things out. Got to go. Speak soon.'*

'And you've no idea what this thing is that she said she'd got into?'

'I assumed it was her marriage.'

'Her marriage? I'm not sure that fits with what she's saying.'

'She shouldn't have married into that family. They are way above her pay scale. All that money and property,' said Sonia with a degree of disdain. 'I'm just a working-class single mother. Elizabeth was born in a council flat. We never had much money and I worked two jobs to provide for us. I was and still am proud of my background but Elizabeth, she was ashamed of her roots.' Sonia took a sip of her coffee. 'She was ambitious, she wanted to better herself, make a name for herself, and I did everything I could to ensure she lived her dream. Only now, I wish I hadn't.'

'There's nothing wrong with being ambitious,' said Steph, gently.

'If she'd never met that Harry Sinclair, then she'd still be alive today. I'm sure of that. I blame myself for telling her she could be anything she wanted to be.' Sonia looked down at her hands. 'I gave her permission to be ambitious. I empowered her but never did I think it would end in such a bad way. I sometimes think I should have encouraged her to be content with what she had.'

Steph paused for a few moments to allow Sonia to regain her composure. Personally, she thought empowerment and ambition were good things but it wasn't the appropriate time to challenge Sonia on this. She still had the phone in her hand. 'Did you let the police listen to this voicemail?'

'They weren't interested at all. Said it was just Elizabeth moaning about her husband and it neither proved nor disproved anything. You know, Harry Sinclair has stopped returning my calls. He stopped about six months after Elizabeth's death. He actually blocked my number recently.'

'You continued to phone him?'

'Of course! Even when he moved to France. He can't get away from what happened that easily. I'm not giving up.'

'May I send a copy of this voicemail to my phone?' asked Steph.

'I don't see why not. I play it sometimes, just to hear her

voice.' Sonia gave a small sniff and as she looked away from Steph two swollen globes of tears dropped onto her lap. She took a tissue from her pocket and wiped her eyes. 'Sorry about that. It still gets me.'

Steph reached out and touched her arm. She felt a compassion for this woman who clearly loved her daughter, something Steph could never imagine her own mother displaying. 'It's bound to. Take a moment while I sort this voicemail out. Would you like me to get you another coffee?'

'Thank you, that would be nice.'

It was certainly a strange message, but Steph wasn't sure it was referring to Elizabeth's marriage. However, she couldn't deny her interest was piqued even further, but before she committed herself to anything she needed to ask Sonia some more questions. Returning to the table, she slid another cup of coffee towards her.

'What was Elizabeth's relationship with her husband like?'

Sonia let out a sigh. 'On the face of it, they appeared happy, and they definitely were when they first got married, but once they were living up there at the Sinclair place things started to go wrong. I could tell from the way she spoke – she stopped telling me how wonderful Harry was and started complaining about him.'

'In what way?'

'Oh, just the usual. Working too hard. Never having time for her. They used to do quite a lot of things – holidays, weekends away, visiting friends – but that all fizzled out. I think Elizabeth was bored, to be honest. She had nothing to do and playing housewife all day really wasn't her thing. You know, she was very clever. She had a good business brain and I think she hoped it would be put to use up there, but it wasn't. All they did was give her a PR role, which basically meant updating the website and posting on social media.'

'It doesn't sound bad enough that someone would want to murder her though,' said Steph. 'I can't help thinking there must be more. What exactly did she mean when she said she'd got herself into something?' It was meant to be a rhetorical question, but Sonia answered anyway.

'Like I said, the marriage. She'd got herself married and was in too deep just to walk away. I suppose she wasn't able to support herself financially. She was scared of not having a future.'

Steph remained unconvinced. She placed the phone on the table. 'Do you think there could possibly be anything else she was scared of?'

'No. Oh, I don't know. Maybe there was, but I have no idea what it could possibly be. Believe me, I've played out every single scenario in my mind and I keep coming back to that wretched family.'

'I don't mean to sound harsh, but for you just to think something isn't enough. That's probably why the police came to the conclusion they did.' Now wasn't the time to mention her mother had been the investigating officer, Steph decided. She'd only mention it if it became an issue if she decided to take this job on. And at the moment, that was a big if.

'You see, I believe Elizabeth wanted a divorce and Harry was refusing to agree to one. Probably didn't want to lose any money in a divorce settlement, unlike his brother, who had to pay his ex-wife a fortune.'

'I know, but murder her? That's a bit extreme.' She saw the disappointment in Sonia's eyes.

Sonia picked up the phone Steph had left on the table. She scrolled through and passed the phone back to Steph. 'Listen to the next voicemail and you tell me you need more evidence.' She sat back in the chair, her arms folded across her chest.

Steph put the mobile to her ear and listened. It was Elizabeth again; her words were almost a whisper and there was a slight slur to them. *'It's me. Your daughter. The one stranded in the fucking middle of nowhere. Not for much longer. I tell you, Mum, I've had enough of this lot. I'm totally fed up with Harry. God knows why I ever married him in the first place. Anyway, the shit is going to hit the fan now. I'm going to tell the sorry lot of them about the affair. I can't wait to see the look on their faces. And then, I'm coming home.'*

The message ended abruptly. Steph looked at Sonia. 'Had she been drinking?'

'Possibly. Probably, but it doesn't matter. She wasn't that drunk and she said she was going to tell the others about the affair. She sent me that message the night before she died.'

'Why did Elizabeth leave voicemails? Why didn't she speak to you herself?'

'I was a care worker. I worked unsociable hours. Both times she left a message I was on a call-out. I can't always answer my phone when I'm working.'

'And she never discussed this with you in person?'

'No. This all happened in the week leading up to her death. Like I said, every time I tried to call back to speak to her, she was busy.'

'What about friends? Who were they? Is there anyone

there who could back up your suspicions? Someone she would have confided in?'

Sonia gave a small shake of her head. 'She didn't really have any friends there. That was half the trouble. She was so bored. She had her sister-in-law, Natalie – she was married to the youngest of the brothers. But outside the family . . . no, I can't remember her talking about anyone in particular. Well, I say that . . . there was someone she mentioned, someone called Camilla. I remember that because at the time I laughed and said what a posh name that was.'

'Has anyone spoken to Camilla? Do you have a surname?'

'I assume she was spoken to by the police – they did say they were speaking to everyone who knew her. I'm afraid I don't know her surname. She was a relatively new friend.'

Steph beat down a sigh. There wasn't much to go on at all. She passed the phone back to Sonia. 'And you've shown this to the police?'

'Yes, of course I did.'

'And what did they say?'

'That they'd look into it. I waited for nearly a week before I had to chase them. They said there was nothing to suggest anyone was having an affair, least of all Harry. They said that Elizabeth was clearly drunk and was probably referring to business matters. Harry seemed to think she was going to tell the rest of the family about him wanting to leave the business. She knew that would cause trouble. Elizabeth sent me an email telling me to ignore her voicemail. The police said it was proof Elizabeth hadn't been serious.'

Steph's throat felt dry and she took a swig of the remains of her coffee. 'Do you know the name of the officer that dealt with this?' She sat a little straighter and her body tensed as she waited for her mother's name to be mentioned.

'Won't ever forget it. Right snotty cow, she was. She headed up the investigation into Elizabeth's death. If you can call it an investigation. Took all of two days and that was that – they declared it an accident. DCI Wendy Lynch.'

Steph studied Sonia Lomas for any sign that she knew the connection. There seemed to be none, but was Sonia just good at acting? 'Why have you asked me to look into this? Why not someone else?'

'I would have thought that was obvious. You tweeted about Conmere. You're a journalist. You're going to be there on the inside, so to speak; you can ask questions the police didn't, find things out they couldn't. People are more likely to talk about it to someone other than a police officer. And now that a couple of years have gone by, people won't be so on their guard.'

Steph wondered whether it was because of her connection to her mother, but if it was, Sonia didn't let on. Steph wasn't sure if maybe Sonia did know and this was the real reason why she had chosen her. Tentatively, she tested the water. 'I'm sure the police have investigated this—'

Sonia cut her off. 'They didn't do their job properly. They didn't want to upset the influential Sinclair family. The whole of the Cumbrian police force is crooked.'

Steph swallowed. She found it hard to believe that her mother could be crooked; it just wasn't her style. Wendy had been dedicated to her job and had put it above all else, including her own family. However, Steph acknowledged the sweeping nature of Sonia's comment and she may well have a point, no matter how paranoid it was making her sound. 'That's quite an accusation,' she said, calmly.

Sonia gave a her a defiant *yeah, I know* look but didn't pass further comment on the issue, instead changing tack. 'There's one more thing,' she said. 'The email Elizabeth sent me, the one telling me not to worry . . . I don't believe it was from her. I think someone else sent that to stop me from worrying.'

A few taps on the screen and Sonia was pushing the phone back to Steph for her to read the email in question.

Hello Mum
  Please don't worry about me. Everything is fine. I was just feeling a bit fed up and had a little too much wine when I phoned you. Just ignore me. ☺ Will speak to you soon.
  Love
  Elizabeth

'What's the significance?' asked Steph, rereading the message.

'Because she signed her name Elizabeth. She never used her full name on emails or birthday cards to me. She always just put E.'

'And you think someone sent this, pretending to be her?'

'Yes. I think someone heard her on the phone to me, leaving me that voicemail. Whoever sent me that email is responsible for her death. They didn't want the truth getting out.'

'And you think that's Harry Sinclair?'

'Look, I'm not fooled by him. He comes across as the quiet one, the nice guy, the brother everyone loves, but you tell me, what other reason did he have to scoot off to France no sooner than Elizabeth was dead and set up some sort of design business over there?' Sonia frowned and sighed. 'Are you going to look into my daughter's death or not?'

'I'm not sure what I'll be able to find out,' began Steph, but then stopped herself. There was something about Sonia's undeniable love for her daughter that resonated with Steph. Something that Steph felt was so lacking in her relationship with her own mum. An unbidden wish that Sonia was her mother took Steph by surprise. She brushed it away, feeling disloyal to Wendy, and yet at the same time a sense of deep disappointment settled inside her. What did Sonia and Elizabeth have as a mother and daughter that she and Wendy lacked? Or was it a case of not what they lacked but who lacked what? Steph couldn't help feeling intrigued by Elizabeth – what was it about this woman that engendered this fierce belief and devotion from her mother? Steph couldn't imagine igniting such a reaction in Wendy and, if she was honest, it made her a tiny bit jealous.

'You'll have access to the resort like no one else has had— you'll be able to ask questions,' Sonia continued, drawing Steph back to the conversation. 'Please help me. Just think, if you force a new police investigation, then that's going to help your career a lot. You could end up working for a national paper. You could make a name for yourself.'

It was a tempting proposition, Steph had to admit. She knew her position at *Vacation Staycation* wasn't somewhere she wanted to be for the rest of her working days. She did have ambitions and Sonia was right, this could be an excellent opportunity to springboard her career. However, it would mean going back to where she'd grown up – not a place high on her wish list. It brought back too many sad memories, especially those of her father. Whenever she thought of Kendalton, the very next thought was of her father's funeral. Coupled with the emotional desert of a relationship she had with her mother, Kendalton was not her happy place.

Steph looked at the woman across the table. 'You and Elizabeth were obviously very close.'

Sonia looked slightly thrown by the statement but replied anyway. 'Yes. We were. We stayed in touch with each other as she grew up and moved away. We might not have seen each other as much as we would have liked, but we spoke often.' Sonia closed her eyes for a moment and then opened them, looking directly at Steph. 'I miss her dreadfully. I can't rest until I know she can rest in peace.'

Steph swallowed and blinked back her own tears. She couldn't help not only envy the relationship Sonia had had with her daughter but also admire the love. She reached out and squeezed Sonia's hand. 'I'll do it,' she said softly and then added, 'But I'm not making any promises. What I find is what I find, if I find anything at all.'

Chapter Eight

Conmere, Wednesday, 8 May, 2.15 p.m.

Harry dumped his bag onto his bed and, going through to the en-suite, splashed cold water over his face.

'Shit.' It was the only word he could think of to describe the past tortuous hour. One where he could barely look his mother in the eye yet could hardly stop looking at her. How could she be so ill and still look so elegant and well? Why wouldn't she confide in him? He wasn't sure he was going to be able to carry on as if he didn't know the cancer had returned. He wasn't exactly famed for Oscar-winning performances when it came to hiding his feelings.

Drying his face with the soft white towel, he went back through to the bedroom. It had been a hard decision to stay here in the lodge where he'd lived with Elizabeth or to stay at the main house, but in the end his desire to hide away from the painful memories was lost to his greater desire to face those ghosts. He hated the thought of anything having that sort of power or control over him. His mother had arranged for the lodge to be cleaned from top to bottom and, in her words, given a small makeover. Looking around the place, he saw that had meant new curtains, a new bedspread and some fresh cushions in the living room. Subtle changes, but they were enough to signify a new start. He appreciated his mother's thoughtfulness on this occasion. He didn't want to dwell on the past or the dark thoughts that inevitably followed.

He sat on the edge of the bed – his side of the bed – and stretched his hand out across the duck-egg blue duvet cover as he gave a small sigh. It wasn't that he'd never slept in this bed alone and, indeed, had done so for several months after Elizabeth's death, but being back here was stirring up more feelings than he had anticipated. A fleeting image of Elizabeth lying on the bed, propped up on one elbow, smiling at him while her fingers traced a path through the hairs on his chest came to mind. They hadn't been married very long and those early days were such happy ones. He closed his eyes as her smiling face was eclipsed by one of anger and rage. One of their arguments where she had shouted and screamed at him and, in frustration, thrown her hairbrush at him. It had caught him perfectly above the eye. He touched his right eyebrow as he remembered that day and how he'd come up with a fake story of missing an intended catch after asking Elizabeth to chuck the hairbrush to him. God, she was fierce when she was angry.

Absently, Harry pulled open the drawer of the bedside table and paused as he saw a photo frame face down in the drawer. He reached in and picked it up, turning it over. It was of his and Elizabeth's wedding day. They had been married in the grounds of the estate and this photo had been taken in the Rose Garden. Elizabeth's blonde hair had been fixed in a neat French pleat and her elegance was equal to that of a royal princess. He had loved her so much then.

Harry replaced the photo frame and pushed the drawer closed. He could feel his mood dipping and the last thing he wanted was to become morose. He turned his attention to his holdall and spent the next few minutes unpacking his clothes. He didn't have too much with him – he had only packed for a week – and living in rural France for the past eighteen months, where he only had to worry about himself, meant wearing a T-shirt twice wasn't out of the ordinary. He doubted his mother would approve but what she didn't know didn't hurt her.

He had just finished putting his toiletries in the en suite when the sound of voices from somewhere outside filtered through the open window. He wandered over to take a look. About fifty metres or so from the boundary to Owen's lodge, Dominic was standing by the entrance to the driveway, glaring at another man, who had his back to Harry. He could hear Dominic's raised voice, although he couldn't make out the words, but from the look on his face he was clearly angry about something. Harry didn't need to see the face of the other man – he knew instinctively it was his younger brother, Owen.

What the hell was going on with those two?

Owen's shoulders were slumped and his head bowed slightly as Dominic berated him. Then Dominic gave Owen a clip round the ear with the tips of his fingers and pushed him away along the track which led back to the resort.

It wasn't quite how Harry expected to see his younger brother, but there was clearly some issue between first and third born. Dominic was a bit of a hothead and Owen very much the baby of the family. The scene reminded Harry of ones he had lived through himself as a youngster where he had been at the receiving end of his father's wrath.

Whatever was going on between his brothers, he'd find out later. He felt a small pang of pity for Owen. He was never going to grow up if he was always treated as if he were ten years old. Harry wondered if Owen really *was* still sober these days. It wasn't something he could just drop into conversation when he called his mother. Pru was a strong woman, but having an alcoholic son was not something she liked to dwell on.

Harry turned away from the window. They were all due to have dinner together tonight – the whole Sinclair family, including partners and children. Feeling restless and unable to settle, Harry decided to go for a walk around the grounds. He might even bump into Owen, who had appeared to be heading towards the stables. Owen loved the horses and was responsible for looking after the animals they used at the resort. Horse riding in small groups, hacking around the lake and surrounding countryside, was where his brother was at his happiest.

Harry made his way towards the house, which was at the centre of the resort, and, following the path, he headed across the courtyard to the stables. He went through to the yard, the distinct smell of manure wafting in the air as the stable lad mucked out one of the stables. He gave Harry a look and a polite nod.

'Hi, is Owen around?' asked Harry as he neared the stable lad.

'He's in the office, I think. Do you want me to get him?'

'No. It's OK, I'll be fine. Thanks.'

Harry made his way along the row of stables, stopping as a big bay stuck his head out the half-opened door. 'Hello, Billy.' Harry rubbed the white blaze on the horse's face. 'Long time no see, eh? You're not looking bad for an old boy.'

'Same could be said for you,' came a voice, and Harry looked up and grinned at his younger brother.

Owen wore a V-neck jumper, cords and a checked shirt, and his dark blonde hair flopped down into his eyes. 'Unlike you, who looks like they're just about to do a photo shoot for *Horse & Hound*.' Harry strode over and shook Owen's hand, before giving him a brief hug. He realised as he did so he had taken a moment to monitor for any smell of alcohol on his brother. Old habits die hard, he thought, but was relieved that today Owen only smelt of aftershave. 'How are you, mate?'

'I'm good, thanks. You? Or should that be, *ça va?*' Owen said with a French flourish.

'Very good – you're practically bilingual.' Harry followed his brother into the yard office.

'Good to see you,' said Owen, giving a small sniff as he took his seat and plucked a tissue from the pack on his desk. 'You OK?'

'Yeah, a bit of hay fever, that's all.' Owen wiped his nose and dropped the tissue into the bin. 'Mum's really been looking forward to you coming home.'

Harry pushed his hands into his pockets. 'Yeah, so I hear. I'm not home though. This isn't my home any more.'

'You try telling Mum that.' Owen moved a riding hat from

the desk and picked up the diary. He spun it round so Harry could see. 'Look, she even made me cross today's rides out. *HARRY COMING HOME.* See, capital letters as well.'

'I'm here for the week, then I need to get back. Things to do.'

'Yeah, I know. Things to do.' He didn't want to alert Owen to the fact he was going to have to change his plan. 'People to see. Money to make.' Owen took out a pouch of tobacco from his pocket and began rolling himself a cigarette. 'Isn't that what the old man used to say?'

'Something like that,' said Harry, not missing his brother hurriedly poking a small plastic bag back into the pouch. 'Along with, don't answer me back, didn't you hear what I said and all the time I'm alive we'll do it my way.'

Owen gave a small rise of his eyebrows. 'If you can't say something nice . . .'

'Jesus, you're full of quotes today.' Harry blew out a long breath. 'Sorry, but that's what being back here does to me. Makes me bloody miserable.'

'Well, just keep up the pretence for the next seven days and that will keep Mum happy, eh? Then you can wave bon voyage and head off back across the Channel and not have to think about us for another six months. That's how it works, isn't it?'

Harry gave a shrug and turned to look out of the window at the stables. 'How's it all going with the yard?'

'Good. Really good.'

'Billy is still going strong, then.'

'I think he's a bloody donkey really. He'll outlive us all,' said Owen, standing up. 'Fancy a stroll? I can smoke this once we're out of the yard.'

'Natalie and the kids OK?' asked Harry as they walked across to the gardens at the back of the house.

'Yeah, they're all great. You'll see them tonight.'

'I'm looking forward to it,' said Harry honestly. 'Everything else OK? How's things with Dominic?'

There was a notable pause before Owen answered. 'How everything always is with Dominic,' he said eventually. 'He still treats me like I'm some junior employee. Really pisses me off at times. I want to get more involved with some of the other aspects of the business, but he keeps knocking me back. I don't think he can bring himself to even say what I want to do is a good idea, let alone agree to it going ahead. I've got a great idea for this place.'

'Like what?'

Owen lit his cigarette as they wandered around the formal gardens. 'We've got the water sports pretty much sewn up. We've loads of things going on there but I think we're missing a trick with the outward-bound things. Hiking and Nordic walking are both OK, but what about survival weekends? You know, proper boy-scout stuff for adults as well as kids. Spend a night out under the stars, learn how to start a fire, collect water and all that.'

'Sounds good to me,' said Harry. 'But Dominic's not inter-ested, I take it?'

'Not in the slightest. If it was his idea, it would be a different story, of course.' Owen scrunched his nose up and sniffed again.

'You want me to speak to him?' offered Harry.

'Would you? He's more likely to listen to you, and if you think it's a good idea then he can't really say no.'

'He probably could, but I'll give it a try. What does Mum think to it?'

Owen drew hard on his cigarette. 'She's not sure. Said she'd have to think about it, look at insurances, et cetera. Basically, she just agrees with Dominic.'

'If I get a chance, I'll speak to him.'

'Thanks. I appreciate it.'

'It will cost you, though,' said Harry, stopping and turning to face his brother.

'What's that?'

'Stop putting that shit up your nose and I'll back you one hundred per cent.'

Owen's eyes widened and he took a step to the side, the back of his hand automatically going to his nose. 'What? I . . .'

'Don't even try to deny it. I'm not stupid. I saw the little white packet in your baccy. And you've never in your life suffered from hay fever. The sniffles are from the coke.' He shook his head. 'You're such a fucking idiot at times.'

'It's not what you think,' said Owen, his eyes darting around. 'It's just now and again.'

'What, just like the alcohol was now and again?'

'Hey! That's unfair.' Owen looked embarrassed. 'Seriously, it's not really any of your business anyway. You don't even live here any more and you're only back because of Mum, so don't pretend you care about my well-being or anything.'

Harry sighed. Owen's sulky expression made him look like a kid again. He placed his hand on his brother's shoulder. 'You of all people shouldn't underestimate me or how much I care. Just because I'm in France, it doesn't mean I'm not here for you – if you need me, that is.'

Owen looked away and Harry gave him time to contemplate his response. Finally, Owen spoke. 'I'm sorry. It's just I've had Dominic on my back this morning already and now you. Look, I promise I'm not doing coke or anything like that. One of the guests left it in their lodge and one of the cleaners handed it in. Dom wasn't about, so I took it. I meant to flush it down the toilet, but I forgot I'd put it in my baccy pouch. I didn't want anyone to see it.'

Harry wasn't entirely convinced by his brother's story – after all, it wouldn't be the first time Owen had lied about his habits.

'OK, sorry if I jumped to conclusions,' Harry said, making a mental note to keep an eye on Owen while he was in the UK. They began walking again. 'What was the beef with Dominic?'

'Oh, nothing really. Just Dominic being Dominic. I think he forgets that I don't actually work for him and that we work with each other. You know, all equal.' Owen kicked at the gravel path. 'But going back to what we were saying – if you can speak to him about the survival-days idea, then I can get on with it and sort it all out. He doesn't even have to get involved.'

'I'll do my best,' said Harry, although he was pretty sure that wasn't what his brothers had been arguing about earlier.

Chapter Nine

Two Years Earlier,
Conmere, 19 August, 10.55 a.m.

'Damn that bloody woman,' said Elizabeth as she ended the call on her mobile. She was sitting in the coffee shop in the main shopping street of Kendalton, consoling herself with some retail therapy. Several boutique bags sat at her feet, but today the feeling of satisfaction wasn't there. She didn't really care for the £250 dress, the £300 boots or the £120 skirt she'd just acquired. It had been done out of spite, if she was honest. She'd used the credit card Harry had given her linked to his account which was supposed to be for emergencies, but Elizabeth had felt justified in using it today. After all, it was an emergency as far as she was concerned.

She'd come into town to get some legal advice on her position within the family business. She'd hoped there would be a loophole she could apply which would give her some sort of voting power or at least something she could use to apply pressure on the Sinclairs to allow her a vote on issues such as the sale of the land. As it turned out, there was nothing. It frustrated the hell out of her.

The call had been from Pru, asking her to be a darling and pick up her evening dress from the dry cleaners.'

Pick up her evening dress from the dry cleaners! Who the hell did Pru think she was talking to? Elizabeth wasn't some sort of PA!

Elizabeth eyed the garment bag from Jones' dry cleaners, which she had carefully laid over the chair next to her so as not to crease it. Pru wanted it for a dinner party she was attending that evening. Elizabeth drummed her acrylic nails on the table, and a small smile tipped the corners of her mouth. She sloshed some of her coffee into the saucer before reaching over and unzipping the garment bag. Taking the edge of the dress, she turned the pale blue fabric over and, making sure no one was paying her any attention, she dripped the coffee from the saucer onto the silk. The muddy-coloured latte bloomed to the size of an apple.

Elizabeth's smile broadened. That would teach the old bag a lesson. Pru probably wouldn't even notice it until she was getting dressed and turned to admire herself in the full-length mirror of her dressing room. The coffee would well and truly have dried by then and it would be too late for Pru to do anything about it.

Elizabeth would, of course, deny all knowledge and claim it must have happened at the dry cleaners. No one would suspect she'd do anything like that – why would they?

Zipping up the garment bag, Elizabeth returned to her coffee – God, that tasted even better now. A small victory, with the only downside being Elizabeth wouldn't be there to see the look on her mother-in-law's face when she eventually spotted the stain. It would, of course, be awful if she didn't spot it until she was already out. Yes, that would be dreadful.

As she sat back smugly in her seat she cast a glance out of the window, absently watching the people of Kendalton go about their business. Something – or, rather, someone – on the other side of the street caught her attention. She sat up straighter and there, hurrying along, was Owen Sinclair. Tracking his path, she watched him enter the shop across the road – a bookmakers'.

'Why, Owen, you are a naughty boy,' she said quietly to herself. Harry had told her about Owen and his gambling habits, how Owen had promised he wouldn't do it any more and had even taken counselling sessions to overcome his addiction. Clearly, they either didn't work or Owen didn't want them to work.

Elizabeth gathered up her bags and the dry cleaning and left the coffee shop. She could be jumping to conclusions. Maybe Owen had business in the bookmakers' and it was legitimately to do with the stables or the horses. Although something told her that she was probably being quite naive in thinking that. She crossed the road and slowed her pace, before taking her phone out and pretending to look at messages, but in actual fact looking in through the window of the bookmakers'.

She couldn't really get a clear view of Owen, but he was definitely at the back speaking to a cashier. Elizabeth opened the camera on her phone and took a couple of snaps. She wasn't quite sure what she was going to do with the pictures but a vague idea was forming in the back of her mind. As she looked up she could see Owen turning to leave and she scooted into the shop next door so he wouldn't spot her.

She waited patiently and a few moments later Owen walked past the window. She assumed he was heading back to wherever he'd parked his car.

Again, Elizabeth didn't have time to reason out her actions, but she stepped out of the shop and from a safe distance followed him down the road. Fortunately, it was market day in the town and both locals and holidaymakers were out in force, making it easy for Elizabeth to follow Owen without being seen. She assumed Owen had left his car down one of the side roads but was once again surprised to see him pause outside a pub, where he had a quick look to his left and right, before entering.

'You are being exceedingly naughty,' said Elizabeth quietly. No wonder Owen had driven all the way out here. He probably thought he was on safe ground and no one he knew would be over this way. Well, he hadn't banked on Elizabeth and her retail therapy, had he?

With the idea of what to do with this knowledge now taking a better shape, Elizabeth followed Owen into the pub. He was standing at the bar watching the barmaid pull him a pint of lager.

Excellent! This really was going rather well.

Elizabeth moved out of Owen's peripheral vision and waited patiently as he paid for his pint and then took a long swig from the glass. She didn't miss her opportunity and snapped him on her phone as he slugged the cold liquid.

As he put down the glass he rested his arm on the bar and half-turned to face the rest of the room. It was then he did an almost comedy double-take as he saw Elizabeth standing there. The expression of surprise was quickly replaced with guilt. He moved his body so that he shielded his pint and picked up the glass of orange juice which was sitting on the bar.

Elizabeth admired his tactic and foresight; it was just a shame the execution and delivery were poor. She smiled back at him and walked over. 'Owen! What a surprise. I thought it was you coming in here.' She air-kissed the side of his face. 'What on earth are you doing in Kendalton?'

'Hi . . . er . . . I had to come over on business,' he said, not meeting her eye. 'Can I get you a drink? I was just having an orange juice. Sore throat.' He gave a small cough and patted his neck with his finger. 'Think I'm getting a cold.'

Not a bad bit of acting, thought Elizabeth. She gave a sympathetic look. 'There's a lot of it going around at the moment. I'll have a white wine, thanks.'

Owen caught the attention of the woman behind the bar and ordered his sister-in-law's drink. 'What are you doing over here?' he asked as the glass of wine was placed on the bar.

With her forefinger Elizabeth traced a path through the condensation on the glass. 'Had some shopping to do and needed to pick up your mum's dry cleaning.' She took a sip of her drink. 'I was just having a cup of coffee when I saw you across the road.'

The uneasy look on Owen's face returned. 'Well, it's a nice surprise. Are you on your own, then?'

'Harry's back at the resort sorting out the new booking system. I'm surprised you're not there.'

Owen shrugged. 'Need-to-know basis, apparently.' He tried to look nonchalant, but Elizabeth could tell he wasn't very happy about it.

'It's terrible that they don't keep you in the loop with everything,' she said. 'It's almost like they don't value your opinion or input on anything.'

'That's exactly what it's like.'

'And, from what I can tell, you get outvoted on a lot of the decisions.' A small tide of red rose up Owen's neck. Elizabeth knew she was hitting all the right places with her comments. She continued. 'I thought it was a ridiculous decision not to sell the land for development.'

'It's not really any of your business.'

'I'm about to make it my business,' said Elizabeth.

'What are you on about?'

'You need to protect yourself.'

Owen straightened up, his face full of suspicion. 'Against what?'

Elizabeth cocked her head to one side and smiled sweetly at her brother-in-law. 'Having your naughty little secrets exposed.' She was loving the look on Owen's face.

'I still haven't got any idea what you're talking about.'

Elizabeth leaned round Owen and slid the pint along the bar, leaving it between them. 'This,' she said simply.

Elizabeth had to give Owen his due as he made a valiant effort to act surprised and then disinterested, as if he'd never seen the pint of lager before. 'That's not mine,' he said.

Elizabeth gave a patronising chuckle. 'Oh, dear, sweet Owen. You're a really bad liar.' She took her phone from her pocket and called up the photos, turning the screen so Owen could see. 'There's one of you definitely supping that pint. And here's another one of you in the bookmakers'. Now, I'm

66

sure neither Natalie, your mum or either of your brothers will want to see these pictures.'

'Are you for real?' Owen looked incredulously at her.

'Very real indeed.'

'Look, it's no secret that I have a pint now and again. Am I supposed to be worried that you've caught me?' He emphasised the last two words to underline how ridiculous she was. 'What exactly do you want, Elizabeth?'

'No wonder Dominic despairs of you at times. Do I really have to spell it out? You change your mind about the sale of the land and I don't send the photos. It's quite simple.'

'You're serious.' He laughed in disbelief. 'You're really fucking serious.'

'Deadly.'

Owen shook his head and defiantly took a swig of his pint. 'You're bluffing.'

'Try me.'

'You really expect me to agree to the sale of the land just because you have a couple of photos of me.'

Elizabeth smiled again. 'Yep.'

'You're crazy, you know that?' said Owen. 'And you really think I'm that worried?'

'I know that Dominic has threatened to cut your salary if he finds out you're drinking again.'

'Fuck off, Elizabeth. As I said, drinking isn't a crime. Dominic doesn't care as long as I'm not paralytic.'

'I still don't think they'd be happy to see you drinking during the day, in secret, which, to all intents and purposes, is what you're doing. And then there's the gambling. I know Harry is concerned enough about you to agree to your salary being cut.'

'You're some piece of work.'

Elizabeth was just about to thank him for the compliment when before she had time to react Owen snatched the phone from her hand and dropped it into his pint glass.

Elizabeth let out a screech and tried to grab the phone, but Owen was too quick and moved the glass out of reach, covering the top with his hand. She looked disbelievingly at the phone and could already see the screen had gone blank.

'You bastard!' She pulled his hand away and dipped her fingers into the glass, pulling out her phone, which dripped across the bar. Elizabeth wrapped it in a towelling beer mat. 'You've ruined it!'

'Oh, dear, that's a shame. I guess the photos won't be of any use now.'

Elizabeth rushed out to the toilets. Maybe she could dry it under the hand dryer before it did too much damage. 'For God's sake!' There were only paper towels in the ladies'.

Owen was leaning casually against the bar when she came back out, an orange juice in his hand. 'No joy?'

'Fuck you.' Elizabeth grabbed her bags and the dry cleaning. She could kick herself that she didn't have automatic cloud storage for her photos.

'Have a nice day, now,' said Owen.

'In case you didn't hear me the first time,' hissed Elizabeth, her face only inches away from his, 'fuck. You.' She spun round and marched out of the pub. He might think he was clever, and he might have got the better of her this time, but this only strengthened her resolve to get what she wanted. She'd think of another way, one that he couldn't get out of. God help her, she'd die trying before giving up.

Chapter Ten

Conmere, Friday, 10 May, 1.00 p.m.

Steph chose to drive up to Cumbria. Her Fiat 500 didn't miss a beat as she motored north, but all the same, it was with relief Steph saw the entrance to Conmere Resort Centre. She swung her car through the gates and followed the road, which filtered through trees and eventually opened up to reveal the imposing Edwardian building of Conmere House. Signs indicated that she was to follow the road past the main entrance and to a car park further along. There were already lots of cars in the car park and, looking at her watch, Steph realised she was cutting it fine to get to the welcome meeting.

The receptionist checked Steph in. 'Leave your bags here and the concierge will take them to your lodge. If you go through to the main reception room there on the left, the welcome talk is just about to start. You'll be given your room key at the end.'

'Thank you,' said Steph, now wishing she'd left just half an hour earlier. She hated the thought of being the last one to enter the room.

She was relieved to see it was a very informal affair in the reception room. There were probably another seventy-five to one hundred travel-agency PR people and reporters, all standing around in small groups chatting amiably and all with a drink in their hand. Steph was approached by a waiter with a tray of champagne and she gladly took a glass before making her way over to the buffet table and filling up her plate with as much food as was polite. She was starving and knew just one glass of alcohol on an empty stomach would be enough to make her want to curl up and sleep this afternoon. She had to make sure she paced herself and was able to write a full report. She also wanted to keep her wits about her so she didn't miss an opportunity to find out more about Elizabeth.

The clinking of a spoon against a glass brought the chatter of the room to an end and all the guests turned to the front, where three men and a woman were standing – the Sinclairs.

'Hello and welcome to Conmere Resort Centre,' began one of the men. 'It's great to see so many of you here. My name's Dominic Sinclair and this is my mother, Pru, and my brothers, Harry and Owen.'

Dominic was a natural speaker and came across as professional and charming. Steph tried to concentrate on what he was saying, but her mind kept drifting back to Sonia Lomas and her quest to find justice for her daughter. Steph looked at the Sinclairs – could one of them be a murderer, as Sonia had implied? Which one looked as if they could be capable of killing Elizabeth?

A round of applause from the other guests brought Steph back from her thoughts as Dominic invited everyone to enjoy the buffet and feel free to ask any questions as they mingled. The Sinclairs smiled at the guests, although Harry Sinclair's contribution was rather more lacklustre than the rest of his family's.

Steph finished her drink and exchanged the champagne flute for a bottle of sparkling water, making a show of examining the label as she surreptitiously kept an eye on her hosts. Pru was already engaged in conversation with one of the guests, standing slightly to one side, but her eyes every now and then scanned the room.

Dominic was holding court with a group of reporters; with his hands in his pockets, he looked at ease in their company, smiling and being particularly engaging, looking at the scale model of the resort in the centre of the room, identifying various points of interest. He was clearly in his element.

Aware that she should probably be speaking to at least one of the Sinclairs, Steph let her gaze seek out the remaining brothers. Owen was talking earnestly with two older men.

So that left Harry Sinclair – her person of interest. Not immediately seeing him, Steph casually wandered over to the centrepiece of the room, beside which Dominic was chatting. The model of the resort was under a glass case, labels showing the main attractions. The indoor swimming pool with jacuzzi, sauna and spa pool were at the heart of the park and fanning outwards were the other facilities with groups of lodges dotted around. It looked like a small town to Steph.

Something made her look up and on the far side of the room, standing almost in the shadows, was Harry Sinclair. They locked eyes for a moment. Steph's heart bumped hard in her chest and, for a second, all she could hear was the pumping of blood in her ears at the power of his gaze. And then a beat later he broke the brief but intense moment, his eyes returning to his phone.

Steph exhaled a small but controlled breath as she continued to watch him and was pretty certain he was purposely making himself appear unavailable to speak to anyone. As soon as someone looked as if they were approaching him Harry would raise his phone to his ear and mouth an apology to the approaching guest, accompanied by a smile, before looking down as if in deep conversation. Steph witnessed him do this at least three times, and it was quite amusing to watch.

After deflecting a fourth approach with this ploy he looked up and, again, looked over at Steph, who gave a small shake of the head in admonishment. He offered a blank look in reply.

A small laugh escaped Steph's mouth. This was too good an opportunity to miss. Milling her way through the guests, she headed straight for Harry Sinclair. As she neared him he looked up and put his phone towards his ear, with his by now well-practised don't-bother-me look. Steph was undeterred and came to a halt in front of him.

'That's a ten for presentation, ten for technical ability and a nine for artistic impression.'

Slowly, Harry lowered the phone. 'Only a nine for artistic impression? Where did I lose the point?'

'Repetition, darling. Repetition,' said Steph in a mock-showbiz voice. 'You can't pull the same stunt all the time – someone will get wise.'

'Such an amateur mistake.'

'I'd say.' She leaned in conspiratorially. 'However, your secret's safe with me.'

'Why do I get the feeling there's a catch coming?'

'Because I wouldn't be doing my job as a travel reporter if there wasn't.'

'True. Fire away.'

'Give me an exclusive on the resort and we'll say no more.'

'An exclusive? I'm not sure if I've anything exclusive to tell you.'

Steph knew she had to pace herself here and not get too carried away. 'Oh, I don't know, there must be power battles between three ambitious brothers such as yourselves. What really goes on in the boardroom?'

Harry gave a laugh, which Steph felt was forced. His eyes looked wary, although he tried to hide it. 'You've come to the wrong place if you want any scandal.' He paused and looked at Steph's lanyard. 'Ms Stephanie Durham.'

'It's Miss, just to clarify, and no one ever calls me Stephanie – it's just Steph.'

'Ah, fatal mistake,' said Harry. 'Never say you're just someone – it's so passive, which I suspect, with you, is a contradiction.'

'Definitely not. Proactive, I'd say.' Steph smiled broadly at him. He really did have the most sparkling eyes when he was joking. For a moment it hid the deep sadness that she sensed lay within. 'If there's no scandal, why don't you give me a guided tour?'

'There's no scandal and there's a guided tour in half an hour.'

Steph wasn't giving up so easily. 'What about if you show

me your favourite part of the estate later? After I've been on the official guided tour?'

Something must have caught Harry's attention. He looked over Steph's shoulder and his expression darkened.

'Shit,' he muttered.

Steph turned to follow his gaze. 'Shit,' she heard herself echoing. Sonia Lomas was heading straight for them. What the hell was she doing here? Sonia had never mentioned to Steph that she was coming to the resort. How was this going to play out in front of Harry? She turned and looked for a reaction, but Harry's gaze was fixed on his mother-in-law. Steph had a second to decide how to play this. She opted to say nothing and see how Sonia was going to react, but couldn't help feeling irritated at the unexpected appearance. It could ruin everything.

Harry stepped forward. 'Hello, Sonia,' he said, his voice the epitome of professional politeness. 'I didn't know you were coming.'

'I didn't tell you, that's why,' replied Sonia. She looked at Steph and then back at Harry. 'And who's this? Your new girlfriend?'

Steph silently thanked Sonia for the coded message.

'No. This is one of the guests.'

Steph held out her hand to Sonia. 'Stephanie Durham. *Vacation Staycation* website and magazine. I'm here to cover the reopening of Conmere Resort Centre.'

Sonia shook Steph's hand. 'Sonia Lomas. My daughter was married to Harry.'

Steph feigned a thoughtful look, followed by what she hoped was one of realisation. 'Oh, I see. Er . . . Elizabeth—'

Harry cut her off. 'Nothing that needs discussing here.' He turned to Sonia. 'Would you like to go somewhere more private, where we can talk?'

Sonia raised her eyebrows. 'No. I wouldn't actually. I'm quite happy to talk right here.'

Steph looked from one to the other. She had no idea what Sonia's game was. As far as Steph was concerned, she was supposed to be here to make discreet enquiries, but now Sonia had turned up it was clearly putting Harry on his guard. She felt she should excuse herself, but the professional side of her knew she should stay rooted to the spot to glean as much info as possible.

'I'd sooner we didn't,' said Harry, and then he turned to Steph. 'Would you mind excusing us?'

'Oh, yes, of course,' said Steph, although it was the last thing she wanted to do.

'Why don't you stay?' said Sonia. 'I'd prefer to have someone else here.'

Harry leaned closer to Sonia and said something in low tones that Steph couldn't make out above the buzz of the room. Sonia listened for a moment, her face hardening before she took a step back. 'Please, Sonia,' said Harry. 'Not here. Not today.'

'What? Are you worried I'm going to cause a scene? I don't suppose you want me to start reminding everyone about what happened here two years ago, do you?'

Steph looked at Sonia, who swayed on her feet, and she and Harry simultaneously put a hand out to keep the older woman from stumbling. It was then Steph got the whiff of alcohol from Sonia's breath.

'Get off me,' said Sonia, her voice rising enough to make the guests nearby turn around. There were tears in her eyes. 'Don't you care, Harry? Don't you care what happened to your wife?'

Before Harry could answer Dominic appeared, his manner rather more abrupt than his brother's. Steph could see the anger blazing in his blue eyes. 'What the fuck is she doing here?' Dominic hissed and then, noticing Steph, made a clear effort to regain his composure. 'Mrs Lomas, this afternoon is strictly for the press. I'm afraid you can't stay.'

'That's what you think,' said Sonia.

Dominic turned his head and wrinkled up his nose. 'Jesus. You're drunk,' he said. 'Honestly, Harry, you need to get her out of here before I call Security.'

'Go easy,' said Harry, eyeing his brother. 'I don't think we need Security.'

Dominic looked at Steph. 'And don't even think about reporting this,' he said. 'You do what you're here for. OK?'

Steph was rather taken aback at Dominic's aggression. She was about to pull him up for it, but Harry spoke first.

'No need for that.' He turned to Steph. 'Apologies; my brother didn't mean to sound so rude. Did you, Dom?'

Dominic took a moment to collect himself. 'No. Sorry. Very sorry. Please, let me get you a drink while Harry sees to his mother-in-law.'

Steph was pretty sure Dominic was anything other than sorry, but she accepted his apology all the same. However, she wasn't about to be bought off with a drink. Fortunately, Sonia started up again.

'Look, you two, don't try to silence me like you did my daughter. I'm not scared of either of you. Any of you.'

'No one wants you to be scared,' reassured Harry. 'Let's talk about this – somewhere else. Please, Sonia.'

Steph watched Harry put a hand on her arm and offer a sympathetic smile. He seemed genuinely concerned about Sonia. He had a kind and calming way about him. Hardly the reaction of someone who might have murdered his wife.

'Don't touch me,' snapped Sonia, clearly not ready to accept the olive branch.

Steph moved towards Sonia. 'Why don't you come outside with me?' She smiled warmly at the other woman. 'There's no need to cause a big fuss here. If you want to be taken seriously, there are better ways to do it.' She willed Sonia to agree to come with her.

'I don't know if that's a good idea,' said Dominic.

'It bloody well is if you want me to leave quietly, and just because I'm going it doesn't mean you've heard the last of me,' said Sonia. She linked her arm through Steph's. 'I'd like to leave now. With you. No one else.' Sonia looked defiantly at the older Sinclair brother.

'Just get her out of here,' said Dominic, glancing around the room. 'Quietly. There's a room directly across the hall. She can sober up in there. I'll get someone to bring in some coffee.'

'Thank you,' said Sonia as she staggered slightly on the turn and allowed Steph to lead her towards the door.

Steph glanced over her shoulder at Harry, whose eyes she was sure had tracked them the whole way across the room. She could see the brothers muttering to each other and then Harry give a slight nod in her direction.

Across the hall and in the sitting room, Steph sat Sonia down on the sofa. 'What are you doing here?' she whispered. 'I thought you were going to leave this to me.'

'I changed my mind,' said Sonia. She flopped back on the sofa and closed her eyes. 'I'm not drunk, by the way.'

'I'm not so sure about that.'

'I've had a couple of drinks, but that's all. A bit of Dutch courage.'

'I still don't understand what you're doing here though.' Steph was anxious to find out but Sonia was being vague. 'Look, if you want me to investigate your daughter's death, you've got to let me do it. You can't come gatecrashing. All that's going to do is put the Sinclairs on edge. I don't need them getting suspicious and giving them any clue that I might be working with you.' Sonia's eyes remained closed. 'Do you even understand what I'm saying?'

Sonia opened her eyes and looked at Steph. 'Truth be told, it was a spur-of-the-moment decision. I don't really know what I was hoping to achieve. I thought maybe I could cause a bit of a stir and get people talking about Elizabeth again.'

'You need to leave it to me,' said Steph. She could see the pain in Sonia's eyes and a surge of sympathy welled up in Steph's chest. 'Please, let me find out things my way. If you go for a full-on attack, they are only going to close ranks. I need to win their confidence, not put them on their guard.'

Before Sonia could answer, the door opened and Harry walked in carrying a tray with two cups of coffee on it. 'Thought you might like one too,' he said to Steph.

'Thanks.' Steph looked at Sonia, whose eyes were once

again closed. She could only assume Sonia was acting but she decided to play along with her for now.

'How is she?' Harry placed the tray on the side table and looked down at his mother-in-law.

Steph shrugged. 'Sleeping it off, I guess.'

Harry let out a long sigh. 'She never used to drink but I think what happened to Elizabeth has pushed her over the edge.'

'It's hardly surprising.'

'You obviously know about what happened to my wife?'

'Yes, and I'm sorry for your loss. I researched your family prior to coming here.'

'Well, looks like you've got yourself a nice, juicy story. One for the gutter press. Get a couple of photos and you can probably make yourself a few pounds.'

Steph inwardly winced at the remark. Despite how accurate it may be, the way Harry said it made it sound callous and uncaring and she found herself challenging his assumption. 'What makes you so sure I'm going to run a story on this?'

'I thought that's what all journalists did.'

'We're not all hacks. Some of us have integrity and, technically speaking, I'm here for PR and advertising, not scandal,' said Steph, inwardly blanching at her contradiction. She, of course, had a hidden agenda but she wasn't going to let Harry know that. She ignored the voice of conscience in the back of her mind.

Harry gave her a sideways look. 'I'll happily be proved wrong,' he said.

Sonia let out a small groan and opened her eyes. Steph admired her acting ability as she took a moment to focus and take in her surroundings. Her gaze rested on the cup of coffee. 'I suppose that's for me.'

Harry passed her the cup. 'Black, no sugar and a splash of cold water. Just as you like it.'

Steph noted that Harry still remembered how Sonia liked her coffee and realised that he was more thoughtful than she would have expected.

'Thank you.' Sonia sipped at the warm liquid.

'How did you get here?' asked Harry.

'Taxi from the station. I'd heard about the reopening and I found myself catching a train. I'm not sure why.' She dipped her head but not before Steph saw the tears welling up in the older woman's eyes.

Steph rummaged in her bag and pulled out a tissue, passing it to Sonia, who mopped at her eyes. Taking an audible breath in and releasing it slowly, Sonia placed the cup on the table and stood up. 'I need to go.'

'Where are you staying?' asked Steph. 'I could drive you back.'

'I'm not staying anywhere. I'm getting the train home.'

'Not in that state you're not,' said Harry. 'You need to sober up first.'

'I'm not drunk. I've had two drinks, that's all. God knows why I came here. It was a stupid idea. Might have known I'd hit a brick wall with you. I can't believe how uncaring and cold-hearted you are about my daughter. I thought you loved her but you clearly didn't.'

Sonia pushed past Harry and headed for the door. He looked shell-shocked and perhaps not without reason, Steph thought. He had been anything but uncaring and cold-hearted with Sonia since she'd turned up, but right now this wasn't Steph's main concern. She rushed after her and caught her up in the hall. 'Let me drive you, please.'

'No. I've got a cab waiting. I just wanted to say my bit and leave,' said Sonia as she strode towards the main entrance.

Steph followed her out. 'I will get to the truth,' she said. 'But, like I said before, I can't promise it will be what you want to hear.'

Sonia paused and eyed Steph intently. 'Just don't be taken in by them,' she said eventually.

'I've been around long enough not to do that.' Steph was slightly affronted that someone would think she was gullible. 'I'll find the truth even if it kills me.'

'Let's hope not,' said Sonia as she climbed into a waiting taxi. Her eyes never left Steph as the driver started the engine and the car pulled away.

Steph turned to go back inside but hesitated when she saw Dominic Sinclair standing at the top of the steps, his hands in his pockets, watching her. Despite the warmth of the afternoon, she gave a small shiver. His eyes were as cold as ice and his face unsmiling. She forced herself forward and smiled. 'She's going home now. Won't be bothering you again.'

'I'm glad to hear it,' said Dominic. 'Sorry, what did you say your name was again?'

Steph held up the tag on her lanyard. 'Stephanie Durham. *Vacation Staycation*.'

Dominic frowned. 'Durham. Stephanie Durham. Have we met before?'

Steph smiled, hoping to disguise the unease she was feeling.

'No, we haven't. I've just got one of those faces that everyone thinks they recognise.'

Dominic smiled back. 'I'm usually good with faces but even the best of us get it wrong sometimes.'

'Right, better get back to the reception,' said Steph, injecting false cheer into her voice. Her stomach gave an anxious roll. Something about Dominic Sinclair scared her and there was an undercurrent of danger to him that was unnerving. In Steph's profession this made someone particularly interesting, although she sensed she would have to be very careful around him.

Chapter Eleven

Conmere, Friday, 10 May, 1.50 p.m.

H arry sighed. Sonia Lomas turning up had been the last thing he had expected and the last he needed. He wasn't quite sure what she was hoping to achieve by her visit, but that wasn't what troubled him the most.

It wasn't the first time Sonia had appeared to remind him of Elizabeth's death and to imply it had been anything other than an accident. Actually, she never implied anything; she wasn't that subtle. No, Sonia said exactly what she thought – that Elizabeth had been murdered. But what had troubled him most today was that it had all played out in front of the reviewer from *Vacation Staycation*. Despite the lowly job title, she was still part of the press and Harry knew from past experience what they could be like. He'd better go and see that this Steph had managed to persuade Sonia to leave.

He stepped out into the hall and could see Dominic standing on the front steps of the house, just as the woman was coming back inside. He noted the small exchange between them and observed that Steph looked flustered as she came through the front door, unaware he was there.

'Fuck,' she muttered, not quite enough under her breath. She looked up and was obviously startled to see him standing in the middle of the tiled hallway by the centrepiece flower arrangement. 'You frightened me.'

Harry gave an apologetic smile. 'I was just coming out to check Sonia was OK.'

'Don't you mean, to check Sonia had left?'

'Both, actually. You, on the other hand, don't seem too OK.' He nodded in the direction of Dominic, who was still standing outside, taking the opportunity to smoke a cigarette.

She straightened up and smoothed out her hair. 'I'm fine. And you'll be pleased to hear, your mother-in-law is on her way back home.'

He could tell by the look she gave that she was less than impressed with the way things had been handled. 'I'm not as heartless as you think,' he found himself explaining. 'I used to have a very good relationship with Sonia, but she's taken her daughter's death – my wife's death – very badly. I'm in a position where I can no longer help her. She needs professional help and that's way out of my comfort zone.'

'When I was told I was coming here for the weekend and did my research, I was surprised that you were going to be here. It must be difficult for you too.'

Harry didn't answer immediately. He was surprised by his reaction to this journalist's questions. Normally, if anyone outside the family spoke about Elizabeth and her death he felt compelled to end the conversation there and then. Yet here he was, having to quell the urge to open up to her. Before he could form a response, the closing of the main door and footsteps on the tiled floor caught his attention. He looked beyond the journalist to see Dominic walking towards them, one hand casually in his trouser pocket, the other tucking his phone into his breast pocket.

'Sorry, am I interrupting anything?' said Dominic, a faux smile on his face. 'I hope you're not giving this young lady an exclusive.' Dominic gave a tight smile in an effort to hide his annoyance, but Harry wasn't fooled and, judging by the expression on Steph's face, neither was she.

She gave a quick smile at Harry. 'I'd better get back. I need to get one of those info packs before they all go.' She glanced at Dominic and then disappeared back through the double doors and into the hubbub of the reception.

'That was a bit unnecessary,' Harry said. 'I was just thanking her for seeing to Sonia.' OK, that wasn't quite the truth, but he didn't need to share everything with his brother.

'Do you know her?'

'No. I spoke to her for the first time about ten minutes ago. Why, what's up?'

Dominic gave a shrug. 'Nothing, probably. I just thought she looked familiar. Stephanie Durham from *Vacation Staycation*?' He looked at his brother.

'Nope. Still doesn't mean anything. Other than the *Vacation Staycation* site. They've got a good social-media presence – maybe you've seen her on Twitter or something.'

'Maybe,' said Dominic, not sounding convinced. 'I can't put my finger on it, but there's something about her that's bugging me. I might do a bit of investigating myself.'

Harry wasn't sure he liked the tone in his brother's voice or what might follow. 'I really don't think you need to worry about her,' said Harry, surprised at his reaction. 'She's just a feature writer, a reviewer, that's all.'

'Still a journalist, and I don't want anyone poking around looking for a story that's not there.'

'I think you're overreacting. No one is interested in what happened to Elizabeth.' He swallowed to relieve the dryness in his throat and took a breath. 'It's old news.'

'Don't underestimate anyone,' said Dominic. 'Especially not a pretty female.'

'You really think there's something to worry about?' The thought of Elizabeth's death being dragged into the limelight again was like a black cloud looming on the horizon. Too many bad memories of their marriage, too much doubt and too much grief for him to want to face it all over again.

'I don't know and I don't like not knowing, so I intend to find out. Keep your eye on her.'

Harry suppressed the sigh that was threatening to escape. He'd forgotten what it was like to be around Dominic for any length of time. The intensity, the brooding, the second-guessing and the need to be in control was tiring.

'Hey, what's going on?' Owen joined them in the hallway. He looked from one to the other and settled on Harry. 'Was that Elizabeth's mother I saw with you just now?'

Harry nodded. 'She's gone now.'

'What was she doing here? I don't remember anyone inviting her.'

'Of course no one invited her,' snapped Dominic. 'Why the fuck would anyone do that?'

Harry couldn't help but feel uncomfortable for his younger brother's embarrassment at being reprimanded by Dominic.

'Hey, it doesn't really matter; she's gone now and that's that. Just forget about it.'

'Let's hope she doesn't come back,' said Dominic, his annoyance still apparent. He turned to Owen. 'Do you know that bird from *Vacation Staycation?*'

Owen looked blank and shook his head. 'What bird, as you so nicely put it?'

'That one who took Sonia out just now.'

'I didn't see her. What's her name?'

'Stephanie Durham,' replied Dominic. 'Blonde hair. Wearing black trousers and a short-sleeved top.'

'Doesn't exactly narrow it down,' said Owen. 'But the name doesn't mean anything to me. Why?'

'It's nothing,' interjected Harry. 'Dominic thinks he knows her, that's all.'

'Probably some bird you had a one-night stand with,' said Owen, mimicking his brother's expression with a degree of disdain.

'Fuck off,' said Dominic impatiently.

'Gladly,' replied Owen. 'I don't know about you two, but I'm going back in. Mum will have a fit if she realises we're all out here.'

Harry stood by Dominic's side as they watched Owen go back towards the reception room. 'He has a point,' Harry said.

'Yeah, but he's a little prick at times.'

'Go easy on him, Dom. You don't give him enough credit at times.'

'Well, he is a little prick. It's all right for you, you don't have to see him practically every day of your life. You don't always have to be looking out for him, making sure he's not fucking things up.'

'Is that why you won't give him any more responsibility?'

'What's that supposed to mean?'

'Like let him go ahead with the outdoor-adventure thing he wants to do.'

'Jesus! You've only been back a couple of days and he's already been getting at you about that.'

'We were just talking, that's all. I asked him what he was up to and he told me about his idea. I personally think it sounds a great idea and will definitely draw a different demographic of guests in. One we've possibly not explored before. People want adventure but they want it in a safe environment. It would be good for Owen too – you know, give him something else to keep him busy.'

Dominic pursed his lips before speaking. 'Look, it's a great idea and I think it would work, but Owen isn't up to it.'

Harry winced. He had a feeling he knew what was coming next but he obliged with the question, 'Why's that?'

'He's not clean. He may have given up the booze, the gambling, the fags, but you know Owen, always got to have some vice. I wasn't going to say anything, what with you being in France, and I haven't, of course, said anything to Mum, but he's been doing drugs. Coke, to be exact.'

Harry blew out a long breath, resting his hands on his hips. 'You sure about that?' He had wanted to believe Owen when he said the drugs in his baccy pouch weren't his, but it wouldn't be the first time his younger brother had lied about his addictions.

'I caught him doing it. In the stables.'

'What an idiot. Kind of makes the gambling seem small-fry now.'

'Doesn't it just? That's the reason I won't agree to the outward-bound thing. He's got to get his head together, and fast. I can't keep it from Mum forever but, with the way things are for her health-wise, I don't want that little shit upsetting her.'

'You need to tell him about Mum.'

'No. I don't. I can't trust him. He won't be able to cope and he'll be no good to Mum.'

'But giving him an incentive might make him sort himself out.'

'Are you for real? He's got an addiction. He can't sort himself out. If it's not coke it will be something else.'

'Then let it be something else. Something not so harmful. Get him the help he needs.'

'I'm through with babysitting him all the time. Making excuses. Taking responsibility for him. That's why he's like he is. He's a baby. Never grown up. Always got someone else digging him out of shit.'

'But giving him responsibility might be the making of him. Instead of treating him like the baby of the family, treat him like an equal.'

'He's got the stables. It's not as if he has nothing to do.'

'And he makes a good job of that. Let him take on more.'

'Just shows how out of touch you are, Harry. I have to double-check everything he does over there. He doesn't know but I'm always checking up on him, making sure he's got the staff rota sorted, the hours covered, timesheets in, up-to-date with the vets and everything else that goes with running a stable. I can't trust him. He needs to prove to me he can be trusted.'

'Not that you're a control freak or anything.' Harry knew his brother liked to be in charge, but even by Dominic's standards this seemed a little over the top.

'I'm not just talking about work, though. That's just the tip of it. What I mean is, the sooner he takes responsibility for himself, the sooner he'll make something of himself. And don't look at me like that; you're just as bad as Mum. He needs tough love.'

'You sound like Dad.'

'Maybe that's not such a bad thing at times.' With that Dominic strode off back into the reception room, leaving Harry brooding over the predicament. He knew Dominic was right about a lot of things but he didn't agree that leaving Owen to fend for himself and shutting him out of stuff was the way to go about it. And as for Dominic's assertion that being like their father wasn't a bad thing, well, Harry certainly didn't agree with that.

Dominic halted at the doorway and came back over to Harry. 'You must have a short memory. Remember the shit-storm he caused before?'

Harry's chest tightened as he looked his brother in the eye. How could anyone forget that? Although Dominic was being rather magnanimous, as it had been Elizabeth who had been the catalyst of that shitstorm with her scheming to try to get what she wanted. All the same, he was taken aback that Dominic would bring it up. It was an unwritten agreement in the Sinclair household. No one spoke about that. Until now, it seemed. 'Why bring that up now?' Harry managed to say with a degree of control.

'Because Owen is a liability and I need to make sure he

doesn't get out of control again. I know you don't like talking about it, but what Elizabeth did to him just goes to show how susceptible he is. He's a weak man and no one, least of all you, wants that episode dragged up again. So, when I say keep an eye on that journalist and keep Owen under control, it's with good reason. It may not be so easy this time to keep our personal business out of the spotlight.'

Harry felt the old familiar feeling of irritation wash over him. Dominic could be dogmatic at times. Once he got an idea into his head, it was hard to get him to see it any other way. Now he had a bee in his bonnet about Steph and was trying to manipulate Harry's thinking by dragging up the past. Harry sighed. This time he didn't have the luxury of France for an escape.

Chapter Twelve

Conmere, Friday, 10 May, 2.00 p.m.

Steph was relieved to be back in the reception room, where she could lose herself among the other journalists and holiday reps. Even so, she kept one eye on the door, taking the stance that it was better to know where Dominic was at all times, rather than be surprised by him again. A few minutes later he came into the room, followed by Harry. The latter slunk back against the wall, while Dominic strode to the front of the room, stepping up onto the small stage.

'If I can just have your attention one more time, please . . . So, ladies and gentlemen, just to let you know that you are free now to look around the grounds either on your own or on one of our guided tours. Your rooms are ready, so if you could check in over here and grab a welcome pack, you'll see where your accommodation is. Please don't hesitate to ask any questions, and a reminder that the restaurant will be open from six o'clock this evening. There is also a less formal restaurant situated in the Old Barn, just behind the pool house.'

Dominic smiled broadly at his guests. There was no doubt about it, he was coming across now as everything you'd expect from a successful businessman, thought Steph – eloquent, charming, but rather different to how he had been to her outside after Sonia had left. Steph cast her gaze around the room and landed on Harry. He looked the part too but there was something missing, she could see it in his eyes. It wasn't grief, as she might have expected, even though it was two years since his wife's death. No, it was a disconnect. It was as if he'd rather be anywhere than where he was right then.

As Dominic left the stage, some of the guests began to head towards the check-in desk and Steph made her way over too. She wanted to get out of this room as quickly as possible and have a bit of time to herself in her accommodation. The receptionist furnished Steph with her welcome pack and handed her a key.

'Lodge 174,' she said. 'That's just behind the swimming pool.' She circled the building on the map.

'Thank you,' said Steph. She took a moment to study the map and then, with as much haste as she could get away with without looking as if she was about to break into a sprint, she left the reception room, crossed the terrace and trotted down the steps towards her lodge.

'Someone's keen!' another guest called out as she overtook them.

Steph looked back and gave a polite laugh but couldn't think of anything particularly witty to say in response. She reached the foot of the steps and had to physically restrain herself from breaking into a run. She didn't know what was wrong with her but she wanted to get as much distance between herself and the reception room as possible. As she turned the corner of the pool house, she glanced back up to the terrace. Her heart bumped hard against her breastbone. Dominic was standing on the terrace, tracking her with those piercing blue eyes of his. He tipped his head a fraction in acknowledgement.

'Shit,' Steph whispered to herself. Surely he couldn't be on to her already?

The lodge she had been assigned was a one-bedroom accommodation, situated at the end of a terraced row of five other lodges which curved around the main hub of the resort, shielded by trees. Each lodge had its own courtyard at the front, with a wall separating one from the other to give some privacy. They were painted a cream colour with oak doors and window frames. She could tell just from the outside that it was high-spec. But then, she expected nothing less at Conmere.

The interior didn't disappoint either. The door from the courtyard led into a large open-plan living room, with one wall papered with a scene from what Steph assumed was the Lake District. To the rear of the room was the kitchen, separated by a breakfast bar. A door at the back led to an outside eating area and ensured that at any given time of the day guests could sit out in the sun or the shade, as they desired.

A hallway led down to the bedroom and a large bathroom. It was all very tastefully furnished in a modern style with oak furniture throughout. The bedroom feature wall had also been papered with the landscape of a lake and hills in the background. She wondered if it was of Conmere Lake and made a mental note to ask Harry when she next saw him.

The thought stopped her in her tracks. She was surprised that she should think to ask Harry anything. She'd only had a brief conversation with him and yet she felt drawn to him. Unlike his brother, Dominic. Steph gave a shudder as she remembered how he had looked at her after she had persuaded Sonia to take the taxi home. How he had seemed convinced he knew her from somewhere.

There was no way he could possibly recognise her or even her name. Obviously, he would have met her mother when she had been the investigating officer into Elizabeth's death, but there would be absolutely no reason why Dominic would suspect Steph was related to Wendy. She didn't look like her mother, that was for sure, and Wendy had never taken her married name of Durham, but had instead kept her maiden name Lynch. Wendy had always maintained it was because she wanted to keep her family safe from anything that happened at work. Steph had never really bought this as she got older. She didn't know of any other police officer who went to those lengths. On a personal level, it had felt like another barrier between her and her mother, something that stopped them ever really belonging together. Steph had always felt like her father's daughter and never her mother's.

A small lump lodged itself in her throat as she thought of her dad. Oh, she missed him so much. His early death several years ago had left a huge hole in her life.

'Stop!' she said firmly. 'Keep it together.' She took a deep breath and forced herself to think of something different. Sometimes it was just too difficult to remember her father, and today was one of those times.

To distract herself, Steph took her notebook from her bag and jotted down a few of her first impressions of the accom- modation and then took a few photographs. *Vacation*

Staycation didn't have the budget for a full-time photographer and, as photography was one of Steph's hobbies, she was always more than happy to take the pictures herself. Plus, it earned her a bit of extra money.

Next, she took a look at the schedule. Her boss had instructed her to try out as many activities as possible so she could write a complete review on the facilities. The more things the article covered, the more likely they were to get the hits online.

Steph blew out a long breath as she looked at the activities she was expected to take part in. She checked her watch, and realized she had fifteen minutes before she had to be at the health spa, where she had a session in the thalassotherapy pool booked, which would give her a chance to use the indoor pool, jacuzzi and sauna room. After that she had a massage booked and then it would be time to get ready for dinner. That was the next couple of hours taken care of anyway.

Steph changed into her swimsuit, putting her active-wear on over the top, and headed over to the health spa, where she was rewarded with a white fluffy dressing gown and pair of white slippers. She thoroughly enjoyed the two hours of pampering and couldn't remember the last time she had been able to sit back and totally relax. It was at times like these when she loved her job.

She emerged from the massage room with her clothes in her bag and just her dressing gown on over her swimsuit. She felt so relaxed now, all she really wanted to do was go to bed, but her stomach had other ideas. The guests in her group had declared how impressed they were so far with the resort and that the recent refurbishment was stunning. Some remembered how it had been before, but, although Steph's dad had worked for Max Sinclair, she had never visited the house with either of her parents, who had both kept strict boundaries between their personal and work life.

It was then she had a sudden, rather unsettling thought. Dominic might not associate her with Wendy because their names were different, but would he have known her father's surname? Was that the connection he couldn't quite pinpoint?

As Steph walked out of the pool house, she was mentally working out the probability. Durham wasn't a particularly unusual name, but was it enough to jog Dominic's memory? And would Dominic have even known her dad? She wasn't sure of the timeline, but she thought her dad had passed away before Dominic had taken over. Lost in thought, she didn't notice Harry coming the other way until she almost bumped into him.

'Oh, I'm so sorry,' she said. 'I was miles away.'

'That's a shame,' said Harry. 'The idea of this weekend is to make you wish you were anything but miles away.'

Steph gave a small laugh. 'I was actually working out what I was going to write for the review of the health spa,' she said quickly.

'All good, I hope?'

'I'm sorry, but I'm not at liberty to divulge that information,' said Steph, with a grin. 'You'll have to wait and see.'

'Hmm, I guess I will. At least tell me how many marks the dressing gown gets.'

'It's OK. I do feel a bit *One Flew Over the Cuckoo's Nest* when I look around and there are quite a few people walking around in their dressing gowns too.'

Harry gave a snort of laughter. 'I'm not sure that's the image we were going for but I take your point.' He looked her up and down. 'Although I have to say, you are rocking the cuckoo look.'

'I'm not sure if that's a compliment or an insult,' said Steph as she felt her stomach give a little tumble at their banter.

'Oh, it's a compliment,' said Harry.

'I might just wear it for dinner tonight, in that case.'

'You might be able to get away with it, but if it starts a trend and they all follow suit, it's going to put some people off their dinner.'

They stood there grinning at each other for a moment, before self-awareness and embarrassment caught up with them both.

'I'd better get going,' Steph said. She waved her hand in the direction of her lodge.

'Yes, of course,' said Harry and then, seemingly reverting to his business-like self, 'Is everything all right with your lodge? Is there anything you need?'

'Everything's fine,' said Steph, making a conscious effort to sound professional. 'I'm very impressed with it.'

'Good. Right, I'll see you later.'

'Yes. Bye.'

Steph walked off to her lodge, cringing at herself for the flirty banter and for the feeling of embarrassment that had followed. What was she thinking, flirting with Harry Sinclair? And there was no doubt about it, he had flirted back! And, while she had to admit she did find him very attractive, she couldn't be sure it was the same for him. Maybe he was going around and using the same sort of patter with all the female guests here this weekend? By the time Steph had reached the safety of her lodge, she was convinced she had just made an utter pillock of herself.

She had just over an hour before dinner. Perhaps it would be best if she didn't go after all. At least that way she wouldn't have to see Harry again today, and then if she bumped into him over the next two days she could just be very offhand and act as though what just happened hadn't taken place.

Her stomach gave a growl of disapproval. No, this was silly. She couldn't hide away in the lodge. It was best if she just got ready and acted professional when she next saw him. She'd make a conscious effort not to go all giggly and flirty around Harry Sinclair.

Steph looked at her clothes in the wardrobe. She had two evening outfits. A clichéd little black dress, which she had envisaged wearing tomorrow night for the gala dinner the Sinclairs were laying on for their guests, and a pair of tight black velvet trousers with a floaty chiffon top for tonight. As she wriggled herself into the trousers, another thought struck her. What if she did get close to Harry? She might be able to gain his trust a little and he might open up about Elizabeth if she asked him some questions. She was, after all, here for a reason other than just to report on Conmere Resort Centre. If she was going to find out anything more about Elizabeth Sinclair, then who better to ask than her husband? She side-swiped the little voice of warning in the back of her head that if Elizabeth had been murdered, then it was quite possibly Harry who had done it. Wasn't it a fact that wives were more often murdered by their spouses? And yet he had been so kind and considerate to Sonia when she had gate-crashed the reception, tagging him as a murderer seemed ridiculous.

Steph gave herself one final look-over in the mirror of her room. The trousers were pretty snug, but she felt comfortable in them and ready to face the Sinclairs.

The restaurant was in the west wing of the house, just off the main entrance hall, and she was ushered to her seat by the maître d'. Steph found herself on a table with several other tour-guide representatives and three local business people who were providing outside services to Conmere.

'It's great the way the family support the local community,' commented one guest.

'How are you associated with the Sinclairs?' asked Steph, genuinely interested. She had no idea about this side of the business.

'I'm a local produce grower. Tina Eames of Eames Farm. This is my husband, George. We're based about five miles away, just on the other side of Conmere.'

'And they order their fruit and veg from you?'

'Yes, the lot. They've saved our business, if we're honest. We just get priced out of the market by the big supermarkets. We can't survive on the kind of money they're prepared to give us and I hate to feel like we're being bullied by the big boys.'

'I had heard it's quite cut-throat,' said Steph. Her estimation of the family notched up a little. 'Fair play to the Sinclairs.'

'They've been good to us as well,' said a man sitting on the other side of Tina and George. 'We're an independent brewery. We make craft beers and the Sinclairs always order in bulk from us to stock their bar.'

'That's fantastic,' said Steph. She looked at the local entre-
preneurs. 'Is it kind of quid pro quo?' She kept her tone
casual, as if it was the most normal thing in the world to
ask.

The guy from the brewery looked a little uncomfortable
at the question, as did George, but Tina was less perturbed.
'Well, although there isn't any formal agreement, as such,'
she began, 'I think I speak for most of the local businesses
who work with the Sinclair family that the loyalty they offer
us is the same sort of loyalty they expect back.'

Steph pondered the answer. She wanted something more
specific. 'How do you mean exactly?'

'I suppose we are supportive of their business as much as
they are supportive of ours. They wouldn't do anything to
jeopardise what we might want to do, and equally we wouldn't
stand in their way.'

'So, hypothetically speaking, if you wanted to extend your
greenhouses, they wouldn't object and, still hypothetically
speaking, you wouldn't object to any planning applications
to expand Conmere?' suggested Steph.

'Hypothetically speaking, yes,' interjected George. 'Anyway,
what about you? Are you a reporter?'

'I work for a digital-first holiday company, *Vacation
Staycation*. I'm a feature writer and deal with PR for the
agency,' replied Steph and went on to explain a bit more about
the business to George. She probably wasn't going to get
much more out of Tina right now, but give it a couple of
hours and a few glasses of wine and then she was sure Tina
would give her some more gossip about the Sinclair family.
A local who was willing to divulge information was the ideal

person to chat to, and Tina was bound to know something about Elizabeth Sinclair.

Her hunch was proved right, and by the time the main course had been cleared away Tina was really quite drunk. Steph had surreptitiously topped up Tina's glass regularly and had kept the conversation light so as not to draw any suspicion from George. He was more relaxed himself now and talking earnestly to the beer-brewing guy again. Steph decided this was her best chance to engage Tina in conversation about Elizabeth.

'So, Tina, you've lived locally all your life, have you?'

'Yes, that's right. I was born and bred in Kendalton as were both my mother and my father.'

'Wow, a proper local. I bet you've seen some changes over the years.'

'You can say that again. I don't think my mum and dad would recognise the place these days.'

'What about Conmere? That's undergone some changes?'

'Oh, yes, it has, and all for the better. When Max Sinclair was in charge it was all a bit old hat and dated. The house was in need of repair and the grounds were beginning to look a bit unkempt, but he was as tight as a witch's earhole and never wanted to spend a penny. Mean old bugger, he was.'

'I didn't realize that,' said Steph. 'I lived here when I was younger but moved away when I went to uni. I must admit, I didn't pay much attention to this place.'

'Since the brothers took over, it's undergone a real transformation. Of course, this reopening is the biggest of all. I think after what happened . . .' she lowered her voice '. . .

you know, to Elizabeth Sinclair, well, they needed a fresh start, so to speak.'

'I've heard about her death. So tragic. She wasn't a local girl, though, was she?'

'Oh, no. Harry met her in London, I think. She was very glamorous.'

'Did you know her at all?'

'Not really. Only when I'd come up here with a delivery or she'd sometimes be in the village pub with Harry, but I can't say she was a friend or that I knew her.'

'Did she have many friends here?' asked Steph.

'You must be joking.' Tina drained the last drop of wine from her glass and Steph topped it up again.

'Why's that?' Steph felt she was on the brink of finding out something about Elizabeth as her stomach fluttered with nervous excitement.

'She was a bit stuck up. She was very good at making enemies.'

'Enemies? People in the village?'

Tina gave a snort. 'I think she upset most people at some point or another.'

'Like who?'

Tina tapped her chest with her forefinger. 'Me. She wanted some fancy exotic fruit one day and put it on the order. When I came up and explained that I couldn't get it, she was very put out. As I was just completing the paperwork with the kitchen, I heard her saying to Harry that they should think about a different supplier who could get some different fruit in.'

'What did Harry say to that?'

'Told her that he was very happy with us and there wasn't the demand for dragon fruit, or whatever it was she wanted.'

'I see,' said Steph, and she couldn't help feeling a little disappointed that there wasn't more of a story there.

'Do you think Elizabeth was happy here?' she asked, going for a different angle.

'It wasn't really her scene, from what I heard. She was a city girl who liked to party. The brothers used to hold some big parties from time to time and apparently Elizabeth was in her element then.' She gave a quick glance towards her husband. Tina leaned closer. 'There was a rumour once that Elizabeth was having an affair with someone in the village.'

'Who?' This was more like it, thought Steph.

'Cameron, who runs the pub. He's a bit of a ladies' man and fancies himself something rotten. He would never confirm nor deny the rumour, but he spent a lot of his time teaching Elizabeth yoga.'

'Yoga?' Steph almost spluttered her drink out of her mouth.

'Yes, he's a yoga fanatic. Does Reiki, Indian head massage and all that business.' She grinned at Steph. 'I know it sounds a bit odd. You'd expect a barman to be pot-bellied, smoking and drinking, but not Cameron, he's not like that at all.'

'Do you think she was having an affair with him?'

'I'm not so sure. She might have flirted with him. She did spend a lot of time there but I don't know if they ever . . . you know.'

'Had sex?' supplied Steph.

'Exactly. I think she stopped going because it was causing a bit of tittle-tattle in the village. Harry wasn't very happy either,' said Tina.

'What happened?' asked Steph when it looked like Tina wasn't going to elaborate.

Tina's gaze flicked around the table before she spoke. 'Apparently, he confronted Cameron about it. In the pub. In front of all the customers. Cameron. After that, he was really pissed off and said he couldn't give a shit about her.'

'Why the sudden change of heart?'

'I wouldn't be surprised if Harry said something to him or possibly stopped asking him to supply the craft beer or holding his yoga classes up here at Conmere.'

'I thought . . .' Steph inclined her head towards the beer-brewing man.

'That's only in the last eighteen months. Before that, Cameron used to supply them,' explained Tina.

'That must have been a blow for the pub,' said Steph.

'Definitely. You can imagine how much a place like this spends a week on alcohol. It would have been a very big blow to Cameron but . . .' She hesitated.

'But what?'

'I shouldn't really say this, but it was almost like a warning going out to the locals who did business with the Sinclairs.' Tina glanced around again as she spoke, her voice barely audible above the noise in the hall. 'Mess with the Sinclairs at your peril.'

Steph sat back in her chair as she mulled this over. It seemed the Sinclairs really liked to get their claws into people and then keep hold of them tightly, and woe betide anyone who upset them.

Chapter Thirteen

Two Years Earlier,
Conmere, 23 August, 2.30 p.m.

Elizabeth shuddered as the front door to the lodge slammed shut. She was sitting on the patio at the rear of the house, making the most of the warm afternoon and spoiling herself with a vodka, lime and lemonade.

'Elizabeth!' Harry called as he stomped his way through the house.

Elizabeth sighed and looked up over her sunglasses at her husband, now standing in the doorway. 'You don't have to shout,' she said. 'I'm not deaf.' She took another look at him and with a sinking sensation realised Harry was in a foul mood – it practically oozed from every feature on his face and every tense and tight muscle in his body.

'We need to talk,' he said.

Elizabeth pushed her glasses up on her head and took a long sip of her drink through the straw, before placing the glass on the table and turning to look at him again. 'What's wrong?'

'The name Cameron mean anything to you?'

Elizabeth gave what she hoped was her best puzzled expression while wondering how the hell Harry had found out about Cameron. 'I don't think it does, no,' she said after a moment's thought.

'Bollocks.'

She raised her eyebrows at him. 'Pardon? For a moment there I thought you swore at me.'

'Cut the wounded-lady crap,' said Harry. He paced back into the living room and Elizabeth could hear him pouring a drink. She got up and followed him into the lodge, watching him down the whisky in one and then pour himself another. He looked back at her defiantly as he downed the second shot in the same fashion.

'I take it that's not the first drink of the day,' she said, noting his eyes weren't quite focusing as sharply as normal.

'What of it?' With a heavy hand, he plonked the glass back on the sideboard. 'Not every day you find out your wife's been shagging the local barman.'

'I take exception to that,' snapped Elizabeth. 'I don't know who you've been talking to, but it's untrue.'

'Not according to half the pub.'

'What exactly does that mean?'

'Just admit it, you're having an affair.'

'Why would I admit something that's not true?' Technically speaking, it wasn't true. Yes, she'd had a little thing going on with Cameron, but that had finished weeks ago. Harry was speaking as if it was still happening. 'Who's been winding you up with idle gossip?'

Harry glared at her intently before speaking. 'Someone said something to Dominic.'

Elizabeth gave a burst of laughter. 'Dominic. Seriously? You're listening to village gossip via your brother? That's insane. I thought you were above all that.'

'He seemed to take it seriously.'

'He would,' said Elizabeth, as if she was already tired of the conversation. In reality she was seething underneath her calm and nonchalant exterior. Wait until she saw Dominic; she'd rip him to shreds. She forced a smile and moved towards Harry. 'I promise you, I'm not having an affair. It's just nasty rumours. Yes, I've spent some time with him practising yoga but that's all. Honestly, Harry, you really shouldn't believe everything you hear, and Dominic should know better.'

Harry appraised her through narrowed eyes. 'Don't mess with me, Elizabeth.'

She didn't like the way he delivered the line, but she ignored the underlying threat. 'I'm not. Honest. Look, I know things haven't been great between us lately but it's not come to this yet, has it?'

'I don't know; you tell me. I'm certainly not the one rumoured to be having an affair.'

'Not with a woman anyway,' said Elizabeth. 'You are with your job, though. And what makes it even more insulting is that you don't even like your job that much.'

Harry slumped onto the sofa. 'You really hate the set-up here, don't you?'

'I'm bored, that's all. There's nothing to do. I'm a good businesswoman and I had a good job before I came here. I want to put my brain to work.'

Harry groaned. 'Not all that again. You know it's not possible.'

'I don't see why not. Just because your family are stuck in the dark ages and won't let an outsider into the inner sanctum, it doesn't mean you have to agree with them. Besides, it's no different to your mum working.'

'It is different. It's her company. In fact, it's more than that, it's her baby. You know how she is about Conmere.'

'You are all so frustrating,' said Elizabeth, following up her comment with a growl of frustration and clenched fists. 'What does it take to make you, any of you, change your mind?' She marched out of the room and stamped her way up every stair, slamming the bedroom door shut behind her as a grand finale.

Chapter Fourteen

Conmere, Friday, 10 May, 7.00 p.m.

Harry took his seat at the table with some guests his mother had arranged to dine with him. They were all probably hoping for some dynamic conversation like they'd expect from Dominic or even Owen, but Harry just couldn't feel the love for the place or its inaugural relaunch. The magic of Conmere had long since worn off. Not only since Elizabeth's death, but long before that he had become disillusioned with his way of life here and with the whole Sinclair dynasty. It was one of the things that had put a strain on his marriage. Elizabeth had thought she was marrying into some rich family and it would be all Hollywood glamour, but the reality of it was far different. It was hard graft, business meetings, talking to suppliers, organising staff, looking at spreadsheets and bank balances – all pretty boring really. No wonder Elizabeth hadn't been satisfied.

'It's so wonderful what you've done here,' said one of his guests, breaking into his thoughts. 'It's as if it's had new life breathed into it.'

'That was the intention,' said Harry. 'I'm glad you like it.

The introduction of the health spa and the thalassotherapy pool have been a major investment and we're delighted with the results; we're hoping to offer guests the whole package and deliver on all fronts.'

It was rehearsed patter Dominic had briefed him with ahead of the weekend. Harry did indeed think it was a great asset to Conmere but he was also aware the passion in him for the place had pretty much died out. He looked over to where his mother was sitting, talking enthusiastically to her table guests, and his heart filled with both pride and sadness. She was an amazing woman, so strong, so determined to make a success of the place. She wouldn't let anything get in her way, least of all cancer. And with this new knowledge, his planned visit – SAS-style, in and out under the radar – wouldn't hold out. He was going to have to stay now until . . . until the end.

He mentally went through the arrangements he'd have to make in France. He could manage some of the design work here at Conmere. He'd have to take a flying visit back to France to tie up a few loose ends but for the most part he could work away from the office. He'd have to do this all without making his mother suspicious, although he kind of felt she'd realise something was going on and soon make the connection that he knew about her illness. So be it, he thought; he would rather it was out in the open anyway. He hated the way his family kept secrets all the time.

He realised his guest was still speaking to him, enthusing about the accommodation he was staying in. Harry nodded encouragingly and thanked him for his thoughts. 'I'm glad you like it. You're in one of the executive suites; we're hoping to attract the business clientele and offer them a different sort of stay to one they might get at other resorts.'

'Oh, definitely. I was thinking that myself.' The guest waffled on some more about the company he worked for and where he saw Conmere sitting within the market. All of which Harry politely listened to, although he wasn't really taking it in. His attention had been caught by the table off to his left, where he'd noticed Steph sitting. He'd wanted to thank her properly for dealing with Sonia and had meant to earlier when he'd seen her coming out of the spa, but he'd been distracted by their banter.

Waiting for an appropriate pause in the conversation, Harry made his excuses to his guests and threaded his way through the tables, his gaze on Steph. She looked up as he approached, smiled and looked away. When he arrived at her side, he could tell she was startled by his appearance and blushed a little, which amused him.

'Sorry to interrupt,' he said, acknowledging the rest of the table, whose conversations ended abruptly. 'I just wondered if I could speak to you for a moment?'

'Me?' said Steph.

'If you don't mind.'

She put down her napkin and Harry moved her chair away as she rose. 'Am I in trouble?' she asked as he guided her towards the bar.

'Not at all. I just wanted to thank you for earlier with the Sonia Lomas situation.'

'Situation? You make it sound like a military issue,' said Steph with a smile, and then more seriously, 'I hope she's OK. Have you spoken to her at all?'

'Not yet,' admitted Harry, suddenly feeling rather guilty for not considering Sonia. 'I'll phone her tomorrow.'

'Will you?'

Harry felt the weight of her gaze. Would he call Sonia tomorrow? He hadn't planned to but he had suddenly felt compelled to say it was on his agenda. 'I will. It's not as black and white as you think.'

'I don't suppose it is,' she replied, her tone softening. 'Family rarely is, and before you say anything, I know she's not strictly family but you know what I mean.'

'You sound as if you speak from experience.' He felt intrigued by this woman and he had to admit it was probably the first time since Elizabeth's death that he'd been interested in a female for anything more than a passing fling or one-night stand.

She shrugged off his comment. 'I won't bore you with the details but yes, my mum and I struggle a bit with each other.'

Harry ordered them both a drink at the bar and then nodded towards the terrace. 'Let's go outside; it's less noisy.'

The evening was cooler than he'd thought, and he noticed Steph shivered as they stepped out through the bifold doors. 'Wait right there,' he said, placing the glasses on the edge of the wall, and nipped down the steps, returning with a soft fleece shawl. He wrapped it around Steph's shoulders. 'We keep these shawls and blankets dotted around the outdoor-seating area in the evenings.'

'Thanks; it's so hot in there you forget that it can be a bit chilly in the evenings.'

'So, how have you enjoyed your first day at Conmere?' he asked.

'It's been good. Ten out of ten, so far.'

'That's good to hear. The health spa is our big investment. What have you got planned for tomorrow?'

'I thought I'd go on a wild walk,' she replied. 'I'd like to explore the grounds and maybe get some photos.'

'You take photos as well as write the reports?' he asked.

'The photography is a hobby really, but my boss wants me to get a few shots while I'm here.'

'I'd be interested to see those,' said Harry. 'What wild-walk route were you planning on taking?'

'I quite like the sound of the two-hour hike mentioned in the brochure. The one that goes up by the lake.'

Harry felt his stomach muscles tighten a little. 'The lake? You can get some nice shots up there.'

'I thought I'd get some angles that hadn't been covered on the website or in the brochure,' she said.

'You need to be careful up there,' he said, concerned she might not realise how challenging parts of the lake area could be. 'The north side of the lake isn't a good place for an inexperienced walker. In fact, the official path doesn't even go that side of the water. We highly recommend guests keep to the south side.'

'That's exactly my point,' she said. 'I want shots that you can't get by being the usual guest. I'll bear your advice in mind though.'

Harry got the distinct feeling that Steph probably did what she wanted to do most of the time and didn't take the advice offered. 'I'm serious – you can't just go walking alone in places like that.'

'I haven't got anyone to come with me,' she said.

Harry knew he probably shouldn't say what he was about to but he was going to anyway. 'Why don't you let me come with you? That way I can make sure you're OK.'

'Thanks; if you have time, I'd like that.'

He didn't really but he'd make time. 'It's not a problem.' God, it was a long time since he'd been up to the lake – in fact, it was something he had avoided. He'd been up there twice since Elizabeth had drowned. It wasn't a nice place to be and it made him feel small, lonely and isolated. The vastness of the Con Point Hills stretching behind like an overbearing watchdog only added to the sense of deep apprehension whenever he was there. Despite all this, his mouth had engaged before his brain and was now offering to go with Steph on her walk.

She reached out and rested her hand on his arm. 'You don't have to come if you really don't want to.' She spoke so quietly he had to concentrate to hear her. 'I know what happened up there. I'll be careful.'

He was touched by her thoughtfulness and surprised all at once. He offered a small smile of gratitude. 'That's very kind of you and I appreciate it, but I'll be fine.'

'Only if you're sure.'

'Positive.'

'OK, but if you change your mind at all, it really won't matter.' She returned the smile and then the thoughtful look settled again and he could tell she was going to ask another potentially delicate question. 'Why did you come back here?'

He frowned. 'For the reopening, of course.'

She took her hand away and turned to lean on the wall, looking out across the pool. 'It's just, I get the impression that you're not entirely comfortable with it. And I don't mean because of what happened to your wife. Is there another reason?'

She was perceptive, he couldn't deny that, and she sounded genuinely concerned. He was aware he was on the brink of answering sincerely when he remembered she was a journalist. He could easily say far too much and then God knows what sort of trouble that would bring them.

'You ask too many personal questions,' he said, aware his tone and manner had changed. He felt like Jekyll and Hyde. 'The last thing I want is my personal life splattered across a tabloid paper.'

She stood upright, her body rigid as the shawl slipped from her shoulders, and there was a flash of anger across her face. He could see her make a conscious effort to control her reaction.

'I'm offended you'd even think that, let alone say it,' she said stiffly. 'I was actually asking you person to person. I have my own personal and professional integrity and, despite what you think, I wouldn't consider selling a story to a tabloid when you've told me something in person, off the record. I'm here to report on Conmere Resort Centre.'

'Hey, hey, I'm sorry,' he said quickly. 'I didn't mean to offend you. I just have to be careful, that's all.'

An uneasy silence stretched between them. Harry picked up the fleece and offered it to her.

'Thank you,' she said, wrapping it around herself once again. 'I didn't mean to jump down your throat then, but I was genuinely just asking. It certainly wasn't to sell a story.'

'Sorry, I take back what I said,' replied Harry. 'It gets me like that sometimes. I overreact.'

'I'm surprised you came back here at all, then,' she said.

This time he could tell there was no malice in her voice. 'Me too,' he admitted ruefully. 'But I didn't have a lot of choice.'

'I suppose you can't wait to get back to France.'

'Actually, I might be here a bit longer than I planned,' he found himself saying. Shit. There he was again, close to telling her things he shouldn't really be telling a journalist, but her concern sounded genuine.

'I expect your mum likes you being here,' she said.

His stomach clenched again. Steph, of course, had no idea about his mother's health and how it was the only thing that would be keeping him here. He forced himself to answer and push the cancer from his mind. 'Yeah, she likes me being here, but I guess it's a mum thing.'

'Your brothers must like it too.'

He shrugged. 'I don't know. You'll have to ask them that. Anyway, about this walk tomorrow – what time are you heading off?'

'Early. Straight after breakfast.'

'OK. I'll meet you at the gate at the back of the pool house at ten.' He was encouraged by her smile.

'It's a date,' she said.

The sound of someone calling his name made Harry turn towards the restaurant area. It was the head of Housekeeping, Heidi. 'I'm sorry to bother you, Harry,' she said, glancing at Steph. Her voice sounded urgent.

'It's OK. What's wrong?' He saw Heidi throw another look at Steph.

'I'll leave you to it,' said Steph. 'I need an early night anyway.'

It was nice talking to you. See you in the morning.' She slipped the fleece from her shoulders and folded it over the wall.

'Yeah, sure,' replied Harry. He watched her go and acknowledged the slight disappointment he felt that he wouldn't be seeing her any more that evening. Then, remembering Heidi was still standing there, he focused his attention back on the head of Housekeeping.

'There's been a problem in the laundry room,' said Heidi.

'What sort of problem?' Harry wished she would get to the point. He looked beyond her at the disappearing figure of Steph.

'Two members of staff, Antonio and Jerome – they've had a bit of a bust-up and Jerome has walked out. We're going to be short staffed tomorrow.'

'Wouldn't it be best if Dominic or Owen dealt with this?' he said. 'I'm not really too involved with the business these days.'

'Owen told me to tell Dominic, who in turn said he's busy with some important clients and to tell you about it. He said you were on duty tomorrow so you'd need to know.' Heidi looked awkwardly down at her feet.

Harry reined in a sigh and reminded himself not to shoot the messenger. However, he could easily throttle both his brothers right now. 'Don't worry. These things happen, especially at the start when there are teething problems. Thanks for letting me know. Just sit tight and we'll wait to see what happens in the morning.'

After Heidi left him, Harry took the opportunity to enjoy a brief moment of solitude. He was out of practice with the socialising these types of events required and was reminded just how tiring it was being nice to people all the time. Although, on reflection, the one person who it hadn't been a trial to be nice to was Steph. He'd happily be even nicer to her. This thought he then knocked back into shape by reminding himself that she was a reporter and he needed to keep an eye on what he said and an eye on what she did. For some reason Dominic was suspicious of her. Despite this, Harry found himself wanting to prove his brother wrong, and what better way than getting close to Steph?

Chapter Fifteen

Conmere, Saturday, 11 May, 7.00 a.m.

Harry woke up the next morning and for the first time since arriving at Conmere actually felt in a good mood. He stretched out an arm to silence the alarm clock and thought about the day ahead. It was then the reason for his good mood struck him. Steph Durham. He was meeting her that morning for a trek up to the lake.

The lake wasn't the ideal place from Harry's point of view. He swung his feet onto the floor and rubbed his face. He mustn't dwell on what had happened to Elizabeth. It was too dark a place to go and he certainly didn't want it to hang in the air while he was up there with Steph. He might even try to persuade her to go somewhere different. There were other nice places on the resort; admittedly, the lake was the centre-piece, but even so, he might be able to take a detour elsewhere.

He showered and went down for breakfast, looking out for Steph in the dining room. He didn't think she was there at first, but as he scanned the room for a second time he caught sight of her sitting by the window at a table with several other guests. She looked up and gave a brief smile before returning to her conversation. Harry went out to the reception area.

'Good morning, Mr Sinclair,' said Raymond, the head of Reception.

'Good morning, Raymond,' replied Harry. 'Could you look up one of the guests' details for me, please?'

'Certainly. And the name?'

'Steph Durham.'

'She's a popular lady. Your brother, Dominic, was just asking about her too.'

Harry felt himself tense. He didn't like the sound of Dominic taking too much interest in Steph. It didn't bode well. 'Really? What did he want to know?' He hoped he portrayed only a mild interest.

Raymond hesitated with an awkward look on his face. 'Er, I'm probably speaking out of turn.'

Harry gave an encouraging smile. 'Not at all. It doesn't matter, I can ask him myself if you'd rather not.'

'He just wanted to see her booking information. Name, home address, telephone number, vehicle registration, who she worked for, that's all. There isn't anything else on the booking sheet.'

'That's all I want too. If you can print me off a copy.' Harry waited patiently and took the printout, giving it a quick glance-over before folding it up and putting it in his pocket. Thanking Raymond, he went into the private rooms, where his mother was sitting at the dining table eating scrambled egg on toast.

'Ah, there you are,' said Pru. 'Are you going to join me for breakfast?'

Harry grabbed a slice of toast and gave his mother a kiss on the cheek. 'I'll just get some coffee. Won't be a minute.'

Leaving his mother, he went out to the kitchen, and while he was waiting for the coffee machine to do its stuff he took out his phone and the piece of paper Raymond had given him. After noting her number and storing it on his phone, Harry sent Steph a quick text message. He wanted to be sure she would still turn up.

Looking a bit grey out there today. Might need a waterproof. See you at 10.

It was probably needless. He was sure she would be well equipped for the day. All the same, it would be a good excuse to text her and to ensure she had his number.

He took his coffee back through to the dining room and sat down with his mother.

Pru had finished her scrambled eggs and was now sipping her tea. She looked over at his black coffee. 'Aren't you going to have anything proper to eat?'

'A bit early for me. I've had a slice of toast. To be honest, I prefer brunch.'

'I suppose that's a habit you've picked up in France. I thought the French loved their breakfast. Fresh croissants, hot chocolate . . .'

He knew she was teasing him a little and it made him smile. He still found it hard to believe that she was ill. She looked so vibrant and healthy, sitting there with her Earl Grey tea and scanning the daily newspaper. 'So, what have you got planned for today?' she asked, turning the page of the paper.

'Need to check in with Heidi in Housekeeping. Apparently one of the staff walked out. Not sure if we're going to be short-staffed or not.'

Pru looked up at him. 'Trouble?'

'No. Nothing I can't sort out. Although I'm not sure why I've been left to deal with it.'

'One of you has to, I suppose,' said Pru.

Harry wasn't sure if he was being set up by his family or not for some ulterior motive, like making him become involved and hoping he might change his mind about going back to France eventually. Sadly for them, they were mistaken. He had walked away eighteen months ago, and he was as sure today as he had been then that he'd made the right decision. The only thing that was keeping him from rushing back was his mother.

His mobile phone bleeped an incoming text message. Harry looked at the screen.

Will take more than a drop of rain to put me off. In fact, it's my favourite kind of weather. See you at 10.

Harry slipped his phone back in his pocket, aware his mother was watching him from over the top of her reading glasses.

'You look happy with yourself,' she said.

Harry could feel a smile tugging at the corners of his mouth and wanted to kick himself for giving anything away to his mother, who never missed a thing. 'Anything happening in the world today that we should know about?' he asked, nodding at the newspaper in an attempt to deflect the comment. He certainly wasn't going to give his mother an insight into his text message.

'Hmm,' she said, looking speculatively at him. Then she flicked the paper closed and folded it in half. 'Becoming more like a gossip magazine than an informative paper.' She stood up. 'Must take the girls for their walk. What are you up to today?'

'Not sure yet,' said Harry. 'Might take a walk out along one of the hiking paths. Risk assessment.'

Pru placed her hand on his shoulder. 'And would that be on your own?'

Harry patted his mother's hand. 'You're a terrible snoop at times,' he said fondly. 'Now, don't go overdoing it.'

'You make me sound like an old woman,' protested Pru. 'There's life in this old dog yet.'

Harry smiled as his mother left the room, but once the door was closed he pinched the bridge of his nose. He'd have to speak to Dominic again. He was over the shock of the news and decided in that moment he wasn't going to sit back and let the disease take hold of Pru. If there was something that could be done, he'd make sure it was done, and if that meant staying indefinitely to see it through, then so be it.

Harry went out to the housekeeping office in search of Heidi. He tapped on the open door and popped his head round. It sounded as if she was just finishing a phone call and she waved him in. Once she had hung up, she slumped back in her chair.

'Do you want the bad news or the bad news?' she said.

'Like that, is it?' Harry sat in the seat opposite her.

'Jerome has definitely left. I went up to see if I could speak to him first thing but he'd already packed his stuff and left. Must have gone late last night.'

'And the other bad news?'

'Molly, one of the cleaning crew, has gone too. Apparently, they were best friends and where one goes, the other follows.'

'Ah, so we're now two down on housekeeping,' said Harry.

'I'm afraid so and I won't be able to get anyone in at short notice for the weekend. I could try an agency and see if they've got anyone, or I'll have to advertise, and it's going to take a couple of weeks to sift through the applications, interview and appoint.'

'I know Dominic prefers not to have agency staff,' said Harry. 'It costs us a lot of money long-term to have temping staff in.'

'I can get an ad on the website first thing Monday morning,' said Heidi. 'And I can go through the list of applicants we had when we advertised last month. See if any are suitable and if they are still looking for a job.'

'Sounds like a plan,' said Harry. 'It's a shame it couldn't have been next week when we haven't got all these reporters here, analysing our every move.'

'Exactly.' Heidi flicked through a file. 'I'll give a couple of the girls a call who weren't rostered to work this weekend. Hopefully one of them can come in.'

'OK. Thanks. I'll check in with you later and see how you've got on.'

Harry spent the next hour and a half checking his watch and milling about the main house making sure everything was running smoothly and all the guests had everything they needed. It was the personal touch which he hoped they would appreciate, although really it should be Owen or Dominic making themselves more accessible – they were, after all, the ones who were going to be running the show.

Although the weather had been good the past week, the forecast today wasn't looking so promising, and Harry nipped back to his lodge and grabbed his hiking jacket and boots. He had a small rucksack with him containing bottled water and some protein snack bars, together with his phone and binoculars. There was a lot of wildlife to be found up by the lake and he hoped they'd be lucky today and he could show Steph some of the natural inhabitants.

Steph arrived promptly at ten. 'Someone's keen,' she said as she approached.

'I'm always early,' replied Harry. 'I hate being late for anything.'

Steph looked at her watch. 'Good job I'm dead on time, then.'

Harry was pleased to see she had dressed appropriately for a hike down to the lake. 'It's only a twenty-minute walk,' he said as Steph fell into step beside him. 'But if we're going around the north side, we've got to allow for a good ninety minutes. Or we could go somewhere else if you prefer a shorter walk.'

'Not at all. It sounds great,' she replied without hesitation. 'Did you bring your camera?'

'Yep. It's in my rucksack,' said Steph. 'I can't wait to get up there and take some shots.'

'How long have you been into photography?' Harry asked, genuinely interested.

'It's been a passion of mine since I was about twelve years old and my dad bought me a camera,' said Steph. 'He was into photography too. Not on the scale I am, but he always loved taking photos and in those days it was a traditional film which had to be developed. He had a dark room set up in the garage and I was sometimes allowed to go in there and watch him develop the pictures. It was like magic.'

'What sort of things did he take pictures of?' Harry noticed how her eyes lit up as she spoke.

'He loved birds. He'd go out and sit for hours in a hide, just waiting to capture a picture of one particular type of bird. He took an amazing photograph of a kingfisher diving into the water once and it actually won an award in a national magazine. I have that photo in a frame at home.'

'Does your dad still take photos?' He noticed the light in her eyes disappear and a sadness take its place.

'No, he passed away a few years ago,' she said.

Shit. He wanted to kick himself for being so clumsy. 'I'm sorry. I didn't mean to upset you.'

'It's OK. You didn't know, and yes, it does still make me sad, you know, catches me out now and again, but I like to talk about him. It makes me feel close to him, like he's not forgotten.' She smiled at him.

'You're lucky to have such nice memories of your father.'

'You say that as though you don't.' Her voice was soft and there was no accusation in her tone.

Harry gave a shrug. 'I wasn't that close to my father,' he said simply.

'I'm sorry,' said Steph.

'Don't be. I'm not.' Harry was surprised at his candour. He didn't usually speak to anyone about his relationship with his father, and here he was, swapping stories with a woman he barely knew. Make that a reporter he barely knew.

Harry pulled his zip up higher as they walked. The wind had picked up and the track they were taking was more open to the elements.

'Looks like we might get wet,' said Steph, looking up at a grey cloud above them.

'There is a hide at the lake – we might be able to get there before it rains.'

'That's on the north side, isn't it?'

'You've been doing your homework.'

'I wouldn't be doing my job if I didn't check things out beforehand,' said Steph.

'You say you're a feature writer,' he said. 'Have you done any other sort of reporting?'

'Like what?'

'Investigative journalism?'

She shook her head. 'Nothing serious,' she said. 'I did move to Carlisle and take up a job with the local newspaper. In those days, I had high hopes of one day moving to London and working for someone like the BBC, but it never really happened. Anyway, I saw the job I'm doing now advertised and, on a whim, fuelled mainly by the thought of living by the sea, I applied and got the gig with *Vacation Staycation* based in Brighton. That's where I met my friend, Ria, who frames and sells my pictures for me.'

He was surprised, but also impressed. 'You must be pretty good at it.'

'Thanks. I'm hoping she's managed to sell a couple this month, as the money would come in very handy right now.'

'I suppose the income can vary a lot each month.'

'Yeah, it's very unpredictable.'

'I find that with the design work I do in France. Feast or famine.'

'What exactly do you do out there?'

'Graphic design mostly. Most of my customers are UK based, but because it's all digital these days I can work anywhere I want.'

'Have you always been interested in design?'

'Very much so, especially when I was younger, but it wasn't something I pursued as an adult.'

'Why was that?'

Harry cast her a sideways look. 'You ask a lot of questions.'

'I'm interested, that's all,' she replied with a smile.

'It wasn't something I was encouraged to do. My career was already mapped out for me . . . here, at Conmere.' He thought back to his father telling him design work was all right for a hobby but it wouldn't make him any money. It was one of the few occasions he'd wished his father were still alive so he could prove the old man wrong.

'Do you have a portfolio?' asked Harry, moving the conversation on and away from memories of his father.

'Back home, not with me,' she replied. 'But I do have some on my camera.'

'I'd like to have a look. I might be able to put some business your way.'

'Really?'

'Yes. I'd like to get some local scenes printed and framed up. I was thinking this morning that the breakfast room might be a nice place to have some.' He hadn't been thinking that at all, but as he said it, it did sound like a good idea. 'I'll pay you properly, of course,' he added, wanting to be sure she saw this as a business opportunity.

They chatted for a while about what sort of pictures he was looking for and Steph agreed to take some for him to look at. 'The only thing is,' she said, 'would you mind not mentioning this to my boss at *Vacation Staycation*? He might want to take a percentage, as technically I am working for him this weekend.'

'Sure. No problem. We'll keep this just between the two of us,' agreed Harry.

'Thanks, I appreciate that.'

They walked on along the track, gradually leaving the organised and landscaped area of the resort behind them.

'It's certainly beautiful scenery here,' said Steph as they walked through a bank of trees and out into the more open landscape, where Conmere Lake was just ahead of them.

As they walked, Harry pointed out some of the landmarks and gave a brief history of the place.

'The lake is nearly ten square kilometres, one of the largest in the Lake District. It's not very well known though because it's in the private grounds of Conmere House. The largest lake and probably the most well-known is Windermere. That's over ten miles long.' He waved his hand out towards the trees. 'Woodland covers about twelve per cent of the Lake District.'

'You sound like you really love this place,' said Steph. 'Or is that just your sales patter?'

Harry gave a wry smile. 'You've caught me out,' he admitted. He stopped himself from saying how he'd used to love the scenery but now he couldn't see any beauty in it, not since it had claimed Elizabeth's life. Now it was a place he associated with dark memories and death.

'Do you miss not living close to your family?' she asked. He was grateful for the tactful sidestep in conversation, although he wasn't altogether pleased with the new direction.

'You're not afraid of a direct question, are you?' He gave her a sideways look. 'I see I'm going to have to watch what I say.'

'Sorry, wasn't prying. Just interested,' said Steph, and she looked down at her feet as they walked. 'I was just asking because I'm always fascinated by other people's relationships with their immediate family. I don't get on with my mum that well. What I mean is, we get on OK, but there's no big display of affection or any talk of feelings. I always feel we're holding each other at arm's length.'

He was touched by her openness and genuinely interested. 'Do you live near to your mum?'

'No. She lives up here in the Lakes, actually. Kendalton.'

'Are you from here originally?'

'Yes. I moved away when I was eighteen to go to uni.'

'And you've never come back to live?'

'No, not in Kendalton anyway. Nothing to come back for. As I said, me and my mum aren't exactly close. I used to come back more often when my dad was alive.'

'You were closer to your dad?'

'Yeah. I miss him a lot.' She gave a big sigh. 'What about you and your dad? Were you close?'

'Not especially,' Harry found himself confessing. 'And all this is off the record, right?'

'Of course! Like I said last night, I have my own personal integrity and I'm not here to report on your relationship with your dad. You have to trust me or, if you can't, then change the subject. We can talk about the scenery again, if you like – it's a safe subject and at least you can't sue me.'

Harry gave a laugh. 'OK, I do trust you.' He wasn't sure if

he should trust her, but he realised he actually did. Maybe it was her honesty about her own difficult relationship with her mother and the easy nature of their conversation. 'Like you and your mother, my father and I didn't have a great relationship. I didn't fit into the Sinclair mould. Fortunately, I had an older brother who did and a younger brother who wanted to, and, largely, I could slip by without too much attention.'

'So, what made it not great?'

'I'm not some privileged silver-spoon kid who is just stamping his feet.'

'I didn't say you were.'

'But you were thinking it.'

'Make me think differently, if, hypothetically speaking, I was.'

Harry had a whole fund of examples, and he tossed a few around in his mind. There was the time his father had made him stand outside and eat his dinner at the patio table for being ten minutes late home one evening, which in itself would have been fine, but it was pouring down with rain at the time. There was also the time when Max had heard him telling Dominic to fuck off. He had been thirteen and totally fed up with his brother for teasing him about a girl at school. Max had dragged him to the bathroom and washed his mouth out with soap. There were many occasions like that but the one which stayed with Harry the most was the time when he was ten and they had this gorgeous Labrador puppy. Owen was always making a fuss of it and one day had forgotten to close the kitchen door properly. The puppy had got into Max's study and chewed the leg of a chair and crapped under Max's desk. Owen had been told plenty of times before about letting the dog out, and after discovering the damage Max had been furious. Owen had been so scared of his father that when they heard Max shouting Owen had peed himself. Harry had taken the decision to take the blame for the puppy and gone straight down to his father to confess.

Max Sinclair wasn't a stupid man and not easily fooled. He had listened to Harry and spoken to Owen, who was too scared to say anything different.

'So it was definitely Harry who let the dog out and not you?'

Owen had nodded, barely able to speak, let alone look at his father.

'It was definitely me,' Harry had insisted, although he could hear the waver of fear in his own voice.

'Right,' their father had said. 'Owen, what's your favourite toy?'

Owen had looked confused, and he'd shot a look at Harry, who had given the slightest of shrugs. He'd had no idea why his father was asking him that.

'My model plane,' Owen had stammered.

'Go and fetch it, so I can see it.' Max had squeezed Owen's shoulder and sent the youngster off to get his prized possession. The next few minutes had been almost unbearable as Max had stood looking at Harry with a small smile on his face. Owen had returned a few minutes later with the plane.

'Put it on the floor,' Max had said, and then without batting an eyelid had stamped on it, crushing the plastic toy.

'No!' cried Owen, which had only made Max stamp on it

again. Owen had known better than to say anything else, but the tears ran down his face.

Harry had felt sick to the stomach. He knew his father hadn't believed him and that by punishing Owen he was punishing Harry in a way that was worse than a beating. Harry would recover from the physical pain of a slap or a thrashing with the belt, but he'd find it hard to recover from the hurt inflicted on his brother.

In the end, Harry opted to tell Steph about the mouth-washing incident as the lesser of the evils.

'I'm sorry,' said Steph, not for the first time.

'I don't want any pity,' said Harry. 'I'm long past that stage. In fact, I ought to be grateful to him for being such a bastard.'

She raised an eyebrow questioningly. 'How's that?'

'I now know exactly how not to behave if I ever have any children. Basically, all the tactics my dad employed I shall totally ignore and do the complete opposite. That way my child won't fear me, won't hate me, won't try to avoid me and won't secretly wish they had been born to another family.'

'Wow. That's quite a confession.'

He hadn't meant to say so much, but somehow she was drawing it out of him with the casualness of her conversation, as if the questions were perfectly normal between two friends who were comfortable with each other, but then, of course, she was a reporter, so maybe it wasn't surprising.

They walked on in silence for the next ten minutes and as they rounded the track they got their first glimpse of Conmere Lake.

They walked down to the edge of the lake and sat on a wooden bench. Harry looked across the water; the breeze was causing small, wave-like ripples across the surface. It was a grey-blue colour today, with the clouds overhead shielding it from the sparkle of the sun. The Con Point Hills on the north side of the lake looked down on them like an oppressive bodyguard, hunched and ready to swoop at the first sign of danger. Years ago he had nicknamed them Pru, Dominic and Owen. Defenders of the Sinclair name.

Harry ran a hand down his face. 'Elizabeth was rescued from the water,' he said, his thoughts taking him back to that day. 'It was my mother who first saw her and raised the alarm. Elizabeth was flown to hospital and fought for another forty-eight hours. But she died, surrounded by family, by nursing staff; everything was done to save her, and when we were told there was no way back everything was done to make her comfortable.'

'That must have been so difficult for you.' Steph rested a hand on his arm.

Harry gave a slight nod. 'The most difficult thing I've ever had to deal with in my life.' He closed his eyes to regain some control of his emotions as the memory of those last few days of Elizabeth's life stung like a scab picked from a healing wound.

'Do you know how she came to be in the water?'

'You've read the reports, no doubt. You should know.' He suddenly felt suspicious of Steph and all her questions.

Her eyes looked wary. 'I thought there was a suggestion that she was trying to rescue her dog, but I didn't know if that's what was concluded. Sorry, I didn't mean to upset you.'

He weighed her up for a moment. She certainly looked sincere. Maybe he was overreacting, but Dominic's caution whispered in his ear. He had learnt a long time ago not to pay attention to Dominic, the hothead of the brothers, but to trust his own instinct, which oddly enough was sending out ambiguous signals. 'She'd taken my mum's dogs for a walk. They were all on the bank when my mum came along, but one of the dogs was wet, so it was assumed that's what happened. That Daisy – that's the dog – went into the water first, and Elizabeth went in after her and got into difficulties.'

'I can only imagine how awful that was for you and, no doubt, continues to be,' said Steph.

Harry didn't want to talk about it any more. He could feel his mood sliding and if he dwelled on it for too long it would be a struggle to come back from it. He was relieved when she took out her camera without asking any more questions about Elizabeth.

'Shall we go around to the north side?' asked Steph after she had spent ten minutes taking some photos of the lake and the surrounding area. 'I think the light will be really effective over there.'

'Sure.'

Harry led the way along a narrow footpath that cut through brushes and undergrowth, gradually inclining as it curved its way around to the north side. Underfoot the path became more stony.

'Mind how you go,' said Harry as they passed a particularly uneven patch of ground. He looked back over his shoulder, hoping he would see Steph struggling, which would give him the excuse to insist they turn back, but she was right behind him, barely out of breath. The trek was clearly not a challenge for her.

'Don't worry about me,' she said, as if able to read his thoughts. 'I'm a lot tougher than I look.'

He didn't doubt that, but he got the distinct impression she was tough on the inside by necessity rather than desire.

'Does anything faze you?' he asked as they climbed over a stile. He offered his hand to help her down, but she used the post to steady herself instead, before jumping down, either ignoring or oblivious to his gesture. He pushed his hand in his pocket.

'Oh, stand there, just like that,' she said suddenly, twisting out of the straps of her rucksack. 'No, don't move.'

Harry did as he was told, while Steph took her camera from her bag and framed up a shot of him. The shutter clicked several times. Steph took some more shots but from different angles. 'Perfect!'

'Can I see?' asked Harry, moving towards her.

'All in good time,' she said, turning off the camera. 'I want to vet them first and then show you my favourite.' She slung the camera onto her shoulder.

The path made its way further up the incline and then ran parallel with the lake. There was a five-metre drop from the path down to the water's edge.

Harry came to a halt and looked out across the lake. The vastness and stillness of the water seemed to capture him, paralysing him.

He felt the cold nip in the air on his face, and as his gaze travelled back to the murky water below he felt his body sway. It was as if the water had a kinetic force of its own and was drawing him in. Not for the first time he wondered if Elizabeth had felt that same pull. Was that why she had come up to the lake so often, her subconscious drawing her towards danger?

'Hey! Careful.'

Steph's voice brought him out of his trance, and he looked down at her hand on his forearm and the other holding tightly to his upper arm. He took a step back from the edge.

'Sorry, I was miles away there.' He blinked rapidly and concentrated on his surroundings.

'I thought you were going in for a moment,' said Steph. Her voice was light, but Harry could see concern in her eyes. 'Thought I was going to have to jump in after you.'

'You wouldn't want to have to do that,' said Harry. 'Not here. Not this side.'

He could see she knew instantly what he meant. This was the spot where Elizabeth had entered the water. He shivered, not able to decide if the air temperature was the cause or not.

'Shall we walk on?' Steph let go of his arm. 'Or would you prefer to go back? I can use the shots I took earlier.'

He could tell she didn't really want to cut short her walk and he had a feeling she would only venture out here again if they went back now. He didn't like the thought of Steph being out here on her own – this side of the lake was too dangerous.

'It's fine. I'm fine,' he reassured her.

The next hour sped by. Steph looked to be in her element. Eventually, they came upon the hide.

'Couldn't be better timing,' said Harry, holding his hand out as several drops of rain landed.

'Hopefully it's just a shower,' said Steph, 'although I can get some pretty spectacular pictures in this weather.'

Harry groaned and hurried her along as drops of rain began to speckle their jackets. 'At least let's have something to eat and drink before we venture out and get soaked.'

'Spoilsport,' said Steph, and laughed. The specks of rain grew into globs, pattering on the leaves of the bushes. She matched his pace as he broke into a run. 'Race you!'

They bundled into the hide and laughed as they flung themselves down on the bench, panting hard.

'I think I won,' said Harry, pushing back his damp hair.

'You did not! I think I won that. Come on, admit it, I beat you.'

'To save my embarrassment, let's just call it a draw,' said Harry.

'Oh, the male ego. You owe me now,' said Steph, nudging her shoulder into his.

'Is that right? And what exactly do I owe you for?'

'My silence. You will have to pay for it.'

She was facing him now.

'I know a different way to silence you,' Harry heard himself saying, his voice low.

The smile slipped from her face and the look which now invaded her eyes he was sure reflected his own. Harry leaned forward and his mouth locked onto hers. There was no resistance, no moving away. He looked her in the eye and this time she instigated the kiss. His whole body hardened as she took the kiss deeper and unfastened his jacket, and, tugging his T-shirt out of the way, her hands touched the bare skin of his stomach. He let out a small groan as her hands travelled downwards and then they were both hastily removing and moving clothing out of the way. It wasn't the first time he'd been with a woman since Elizabeth's death, but it was the first time he'd felt no guilt. He searched for it, but it just wasn't there.

'Stop.' It was Steph who spoke, her hands pushing against his chest as she moved her mouth from his. 'Stop. I'm sorry. This isn't right.'

Harry let his arm fall immediately and took a step back. She had beaten him to it by half a beat. It didn't feel right, not here. 'OK. It's fine. I'm sorry. I read the situation wrong.'

'No, you didn't. You read it perfectly.' She dipped her head and fastened the button on her trousers. 'I just think it's not the time or the place. I don't usually . . .'

'Please, Steph, you don't have to justify yourself. It's OK to change your mind.' Harry knew that and of course respected that, but his mind was a little bit more understanding than his body. He turned away and adjusted his clothing, giving Steph space to do the same. Then, not wanting to feel as if he was snubbing her, he turned back and tipped her face up so that she could look at him. 'Honestly, I'd hate for you to do something you're not happy with, and, to be honest, you're right.' He looked around the hide. 'Not exactly the most romantic spot.' He smiled and dropped a kiss on her forehead. And now, with the heat of the moment extinguished, he could think of much nicer places to have sex with Steph. It suddenly felt cheap and almost disrespectful to Elizabeth's memory.

Chapter Sixteen

Conmere, Saturday, 11 May, 11.45 a.m.

'Look, I don't mean to sound crass or anything,' said Harry, 'but I have to get back soon for a meeting.' He genuinely felt bad just saying it. This wasn't how he'd like to leave things at all. 'What are you doing later?' he asked, his hand on the wall above Steph's shoulder.

'I need to look at my pictures and see if they're up to your high standards.'

'Maybe you want some help with that?' he replied, relieved the confident banter was back between them.

'Maybe I would,' Steph replied as she ducked out from under his arm. 'But isn't there the small matter of the gala dinner tonight?'

Harry groaned. 'Don't remind me.' All sorts of notions ran through his head of what he'd rather be doing than sitting at a gala dinner later. 'You'll be there, won't you?'

'Of course. I've bought my LBD especially.'

Harry raised an eyebrow in question. 'LBD?'

'Little black dress,' offered Steph.

'Now, that I'd like to see,' said Harry, pushing himself away from the wall.

'You will, at around seven-thirty tonight.' She picked up her rucksack and walked out of the hide.

Harry looked at the empty doorway for a moment. Had all that really just happened? He hadn't planned it at all, not that it hadn't crossed his mind just how attracted to Steph he was. He'd like to get to know her better. The thought that she'd be gone in around twenty-four hours spurred him into action. He jogged to catch up with her.

'Hey, I was thinking,' he began. 'Don't take this the wrong way but you know what you were saying about needing to earn a bit more money – I wondered if you had anything planned for the coming week?'

She stopped walking and looked cautiously at him. 'No, I don't, as it happens,' she said slowly.

'We're one short in Housekeeping. Actually, we're two short, but if you fancied a week's work, I can arrange it for you.'

'Housekeeping?' She looked sceptical.

'I know it's not very glamorous, making beds, sorting out linen, and that sort of stuff, but the pay's not bad. We offer well above the minimum wage.' He stopped. He'd offended her. Shit. That wasn't his intention at all. 'Sorry. Forget it. I shouldn't have asked. You've got much better things to do.' He dragged his hand across his chin in agitation at himself. It had been an impulsive offer, which, for a start, was out of character for him, but he really disliked the thought of Steph heading back to Brighton before they'd got to know each other better. He didn't suppose Dominic would be particularly happy about the offer, but as far as Harry was concerned that was neither here nor there.

'No. It's fine. It was nice of you to think of me,' she replied. 'I must admit, housekeeping isn't exactly at the top of my ambitions list.'

'No, I realise that. Honestly, I'm sorry for mentioning it.'

'Wait. Let me finish. While it's not top of my ambitions list, I'm not so precious that I won't roll up my sleeves and get stuck in. To be honest, anything is better than nothing. And the money really would be handy.'

He felt a small stirring of relief. 'You don't have to do full-time hours if it doesn't suit. I know you've got your photos to sort out, but it's there if you want it.'

'Thank you. I'll take it.' She smiled broadly.

The walk back towards the resort seemed to be far quicker than when they had left a couple of hours ago. Harry was disappointed that they were parting company so soon. They stopped outside Steph's lodge.

'When do you think the photographs will be ready to see?' he asked, pushing his hands into his pockets to stop himself from kissing her again. She was intoxicating. He felt bewitched. He couldn't remember feeling like this before and suddenly an image of Elizabeth entered his mind. Had he ever felt this way with his wife? He was sure he must have done at some stage of their marriage, but his feelings for Elizabeth had quickly changed.

The sound of people chattering as they walked along the path broke the moment. Harry looked up and smiled, saying hello and asking them if they were having a good weekend. To which he got very positive replies.

'Much as I would love to go inside with you right now, I really need to get to this meeting.'

'I'll see you this evening at the gala dinner.' Steph smiled as she let herself into her lodge and closed the door on him.

As he walked back to the main house, he replayed the morning in his mind. Harry wasn't quite sure what he was getting himself into. Part of him felt he should steer clear of Steph – after all, she was a reporter and she'd asked a few questions about Elizabeth, which should be ringing alarm bells, but he was aware he was making a point of ignoring them. He was sure Steph wouldn't find anything out and, besides, he really liked her. His gut feeling was she was genuine and that was important to him. As he walked, he realised it was something that had sadly been missing in his marriage for a long time.

When he arrived at the house, he went into the sitting room, where his mother was resting in a chair by the fireplace. Harry crept in and took the rug from the back of the other chair and placed it carefully over her knees.

Pru opened an eye. 'I'm not that old. You don't have to treat me like you've come to visit me in a retirement home.' She smiled at him.

'I thought you were asleep,' said Harry, assessing her appearance. It wasn't like his mother to rest during the day. He wondered if it was a new symptom of her illness. She went to get up. 'Stay there, Mum. Can I get you anything? A cup of tea?'

'That would be nice.' She looked him up and down. 'Nice walk, was it? You know, your risk assessment?'

'Yeah. All good.' He avoided eye contact with her. He could

tell when his mother was fishing. She hated not knowing what was going on with every aspect of Conmere, including the private lives of her sons.

'Dominic was looking for you a little while ago.'

'What did he want?'

'I don't know. Just said to tell you he was looking for you.'

'I'll do your tea and then I'll go and find him.'

Harry returned to Pru a few minutes later with a cup of tea and a couple of biscuits. He dropped a kiss on his mother's head and went off to Dominic's office across the hall. The door was closed and he knocked, opening it a fraction to peer in. Dominic was on the phone, but he waved Harry in and pointed to the chair as he wound up his call.

'Mum said you were looking for me.'

Dominic leaned back into his deep padded chair, hooking one ankle over the other knee. 'Where have you been this morning?'

'You're as bad as Mum, wanting to keep tabs on me,' said Harry. 'I just went for a walk.'

Dominic looked speculatively at him. 'A walk?'

'Yes. A walk. Anyway, what did you want?'

'You just went on a random walk? On your own?'

'Jesus, Dom. What's the big deal? I went for a walk with one of the reporters because she wanted to go down to the lake.'

Dominic shook his head. 'You went for a walk with a reporter? It wouldn't be Steph Durham by any chance, would it?'

'Can you get over this, please?' said Harry impatiently, bored at Dominic's obsession with what Steph was doing or not doing.

'And you went to the lake? What the fuck did you go there for?'

'She wanted to see it. She's a photographer. She wanted some different shots. In fact, I might be buying some to put up in the breakfast room. And while I'm here I might as well tell you that I've given her a job for the week. To cover the two members of staff who walked out this morning.' He gave his brother a challenging look, knowing Dominic would hate this, but Harry didn't care. It was a small, possibly petty, victory, but satisfying all the same.

'What?' Dominic sat up in his chair. 'That was very good of you,' he said, clearly put out by Harry's decision-making. 'Not bad for someone who swans into the place twice a year only and spends the rest of the time holed up in some old house in the middle of the French countryside.'

'Seeing as I'm not going back to France for a while, I took the initiative. I had a problem and I've dealt with it. Now can you get on with what you wanted to see me about.' Harry could feel the old tension rising between himself and his brother. He had always had to defend his decisions and actions to Dominic, who had, in Harry's opinion, too readily taken up where their father had left off. It was no wonder Owen was totally pissed off with Dominic.

'It might have been better if you'd run it by me first,' said Dominic, his brow furrowing. 'What I wanted to talk to you about was actually Steph Durham.'

Dominic had his attention now. Harry shifted uneasily in his seat. He'd seen that look in his brother's eye many a time. It was one where the scent of blood was strong, and Dominic was preparing to mount his attack. Harry inwardly steeled himself for what Dominic was about to say about Steph as a somewhat unexpected desire to protect her rose.

'What about her?'

'I did a bit of digging. There was something familiar about her and I couldn't place it,' said Dominic. 'I was certain I'd seen her before.'

Harry held out his hands in an impatient gesture. 'And . . .?'

'You know I have a good memory for faces,' said Dominic. 'I'd seen her at a funeral. Her dad's funeral. I should have made the connection as soon as I heard the surname.'

'What?'

'Yeah, a few years ago I went to Mick Durham's funeral. Nice bloke. Married to a local police officer from CID. In fact, you know her. She was the one who investigated Elizabeth's death – DCI Wendy Lynch.'

Harry felt sure the colour had drained from his face as he stared at his brother. Both of Steph's parents were connected to Conmere and her mother in the worst possible way. He could hardly believe it. 'Fuck,' he said at last.

'Yes, fuck indeed.'

Harry took a moment to digest the information. 'Are you sure about that?'

'Positive. As I say, I was at the funeral. Wendy Lynch was the grieving widow; despite the different surnames, the two of them were married. Mick Durham knew Dad. They went back a long way. Durham worked for Dad and then when Dad died I inherited him. You must know who I mean?'

'What sort of work did he do?' asked Harry, with a certain amount of trepidation. 'Or do I not want to know?' He knew both his father and his brother sometimes sailed close to the wind when it came to their business activities. Harry had purposely taken a step back from the business on this basis; he didn't want to be involved with anything under-hand. He'd made his feelings well known to Dominic and, although he had tried to persuade his brother to move away from their father's business tactics, his words had fallen on deaf ears.

'He did some driving for us. Just deliveries. Sometimes he'd drive Dad down to Manchester or London on an ad hoc cash basis.'

Harry fought down the ball of anger that was rolling around in the pit of his stomach. Steph hadn't mentioned her dad working for the family and, more worryingly, she hadn't mentioned the connection with Wendy Lynch either. He wanted to cut her some slack, but he was having trouble summoning up the generosity.

'You were never really interested in what went on here, even when you were a kid,' said Dominic. 'I think most of it passed you by.'

'I had my reasons.'

'Yeah, well, let's not drag all that up now,' said Dominic. 'That's all water under the bridge. We need to focus on what's happening now, and that we've got a reporter who is related to an ex-employee and the DCI who headed up the enquiry surrounding Elizabeth's accident.'

'I don't actually think there's anything to worry about,' said Harry as he contemplated the new information. 'We have nothing to hide.' He looked pointedly at his brother. Something about the way Dominic's gaze shifted away from his bothered him. 'Or do we?'

Dominic rattled his pen between his teeth before speaking again. 'Has this Steph Durham been asking any questions?'

Harry thought back to earlier. 'Not especially. We chatted, but not in detail about anything. Surprisingly, what happened to Elizabeth isn't my favourite topic of conversation.' Despite this statement, Harry wondered now if their conversation had been as innocent as he had originally thought.

'Did she mention her mother at all?' Dominic pushed on.

Harry didn't want to betray Steph's confidence. She had told him some things that he got the distinct impression were very private, things she hadn't spoken about to many people. Harry shook his head at his brother.

Dominic pursed his lips. 'Are you shagging her?'

Harry sighed and gave a roll of his eyes. 'What sort of question is that?'

Dominic gave a shrug of indifference. 'If you are, she could be playing you.'

Harry made a conscious effort to keep his facial expression neutral. He'd be pissed off if she was. He repositioned himself in his seat and decided to ignore his brother. 'How did she end up being invited? Who organised the guest list?'

'Who do you think? Our baby brother. I knew I shouldn't have given him the task but it seemed so straightforward. Invite one hundred of the most influential clients in the tourism industry for a freebie weekend. Might have known he'd cock it up somewhere.'

'I think that's a bit harsh. From what I know, it seems like a legitimate invite. Anyway, he would have invited the company – it's up to them who they send, not us.' Harry couldn't help feeling a little sorry for Owen. He was Dominic's scapegoat at times.

Dominic spoke again. 'We could use this to our advantage. Get to know her real reason for coming here.'

'It's just to do the feature. Relax. What exactly are you frightened of, Dom?'

'I just don't want any more bad publicity. Elizabeth's death was bad enough, but I don't want anyone digging around to see what Owen has been up to recently; it's bad for business and bad for Mum.'

'What exactly has Owen been up to recently?' asked Harry, purposely shifting the conversation away from both Steph and Elizabeth. 'I saw you two arguing outside your place yesterday.'

'You don't want to know.'

'The drugs,' interjected Harry, despondently.

Dominic turned his palms up to the ceiling. 'Now you can see why I don't want anyone poking around.'

'Nothing to do with your side-lines?' Harry ventured, watching his brother's face for a reaction. 'You're not helping him in any way?'

Dominic's eyes narrowed, his nostrils flared and he pressed his lips together. 'Not in the way you think.'

'And what way is that? Not like you haven't before,' Harry shot back without flinching. Gone were the days when he was intimidated by his brother, or even looked up to him. Christ, that had been a long time ago in their childhood and the big-brother admiration Harry had once felt had gradually waned during their adult lives. Sometimes Harry wondered how the hell they were related. Sure, he loved his brother, but he didn't always like Dominic and he sure as hell wasn't worried about upsetting him these days.

Dominic pointed a finger at Harry.

'Oh, no, you don't,' he said, his lip curling in the way it did when he was fighting to keep his anger in check. 'Don't play that card. You're not so innocent. All that stuff before was recreational and you know it. Christ, even your wife indulged at times.'

'Elizabeth?' He swallowed hard at the thought.

'Unless you've got another wife somewhere. Jesus, Harry, surely you knew?' Dominic sat back in his chair and gave a laugh, then leaned forwards again. 'Better it came from me, where it was clean, than some shitty street dealer where it'd been cut with talc and God knows what else. Same goes for Owen. This way I can control it and manage him.'

'You bastard.' Harry clenched his fist. Right now, he wanted nothing more than to punch his brother's smug face. Sure, Harry had suspected that once or twice Elizabeth had taken something more than alcohol at one of the parties, but he had never suspected his own brother had been the supplier. How had he missed that?

'Don't be so hard on yourself,' said Dominic. 'It was only a couple of times and I made sure she was OK.'

Harry pinched the bridge of his nose. The foundations on which he'd built his memories of his marriage and Elizabeth were crumbling. He'd thought he knew everything there was to know, but maybe he'd got that wrong. Maybe she'd kept more secrets from him than he realised. He drew breath . . . Had one of those secrets led to her death?

Harry forced himself not to say anything more about

Elizabeth. It wasn't constructive and didn't change anything. He needed time to think this through.

Owen, however, was another matter. He'd always felt sorry for his younger brother. He was weak – one big walking Achilles heel. 'You should be getting Owen help, not feeding his addiction.'

'You can lead a horse to water and all that.' Dominic gave a shrug. 'I keep an eye on him. I keep him out of Mum's way. I look after him. I make sure it's all kept in-house. Not for my sake, or even for his, but for Mum's. Surely you appreciate that.'

'You're doing it for yourself. You've always looked after number one.'

'I've looked after all of you.' Dominic's superior look had returned to his face. 'You may not know it, or like it, but I've always made sure everyone is protected. If you don't like my methods, tough, but I've never had any complaints about the outcome.'

A shudder ran through Harry. How far was his brother prepared to go to protect the family? Dominic was pretty ruthless and conscience-free when he had to be, but . . . Harry hardly dared think it:' had Elizabeth known something that had given Dominic reason to step in? . . . He looked up and met his brother's eyes.

'The means justifies the end, is that what you're saying?'

Dominic returned his gaze with equal intensity. 'Something like that.' And then, rather more dismissively, 'Anyway, you've not been here, so it's not really any of your business.'

'That's where you're wrong,' said Harry, unswayed by his brother's attitude. 'Anything that involves Conmere has a direct impact on Mum and by default that makes it my business, especially as she's not well.'

'Then you had better make sure that Steph Durham doesn't cause any trouble.'

Was that a threat? Had Elizabeth been a threat? Before Harry had a chance to answer there was a knock at the door, which opened at the same time, and Owen appeared in the office. 'Hey, how's it going? I've just been accosted by . . .' He stopped speaking, looking from one brother to the other. Slowly he closed the door behind him. 'What's going on?'

'Nothing; I was just checking with Harry if there was anything that needed doing for the gala dinner,' Dominic answered smoothly. 'Did you want me for anything?'

Owen didn't look particularly convinced but said nothing. 'Just to say one of the guests complained their room hadn't been serviced this morning,'

'Well, sort it out, then. Get someone over there sharpish,' snapped Dominic.

'I have,' replied Owen, scowling. 'I was just mentioning it. I spoke to Heidi, and she said she had already spoken to Harry about being short-staffed.'

'That's right. I've got it sorted now,' replied Harry.

'Yeah, he's got one of the reporters staying on for the week,' said Dominic in an incredulous tone which told Harry he still wasn't fully on-board with the idea.

'A reporter?' questioned Owen.

'Don't,' said Dominic. 'Anyway, nothing for you to worry about. Haven't you got some horses that need feeding or whatever it is you do with them?'

Harry once again felt sorry for his younger brother.

Dominic was so dismissive of him and almost seemed to revel in belittling him. 'Thanks for sorting the problem out, Owen,' he said.

'Yeah. No worries. Nice to be appreciated by some.' Owen emphasised the last word and looked at Dominic before he glanced back at Harry. 'Catch you later,' he said and left the room.

'You're too hard on him,' said Harry. 'You're not his father, you know.'

'Don't start all that again. He's fucking useless most of the time. Sometimes I can't believe I'm actually related to him.'

'Like I said before, you don't give him enough credit.'

'Honestly, Harry, now's not a good time to start telling me about Owen. You only see him once in a blue moon. I have to see him every day and manage him every day. We've got more important things to discuss.'

'And, as I said, I don't think there's anything to worry about,' said Harry, and then, really just to pacify Dominic, added, 'but I'll keep a closer eye on her.' He hid the smile that threatened to creep across his face and give him away. He fully intended to keep a closer eye on Steph, but maybe not in the way Dominic envisaged.

'Just making sure we're on the same page,' replied Dominic.

Personally, Harry wasn't sure he wanted to be in the same book as Dominic, never mind on the same page, but he left without further retort.

'You sure know how to pick them,' said Dominic as Harry reached the door. Harry threw him a blank look. His brother elaborated. 'First there was Elizabeth, who was always stirring up trouble, and now you've got yourself involved with someone else who could be doing the same thing.'

A rush of anger surged through Harry's blood. 'Fuck off,' he snapped. 'You know, I had hoped the apples had fallen a bit further from the tree, with all of us. Seems I was wrong about you.' He went to leave, but stopped and added, 'And, like I said before, leave Elizabeth out of this.'

Dominic looked amused. 'Touchy. A bit too close to home, was it?'

'Fuck off,' said Harry again and left the room. He'd had a gutful of this place already. It brought nothing but disharmony and bad memories.

Chapter Seventeen

Two Years Earlier,
Kendalton Green Hotel, Kendalton, 1 September, 3.30 p.m.

'So, let me get this right, you want to do this to see if your husband is cheating on you?'

'Yes, that's right.' Elizabeth looked at the woman sitting opposite her in the foyer of Kendalton Green Hotel. She was probably in her late twenties, although she had the air of a much more experienced woman and had clearly been doing her job for a long time. Elizabeth didn't like to use the word *prostitute*; it sounded coarse and common. She much preferred the term escort, and not just any escort, but a high-class escort. The agency she'd contacted had assured her they had someone perfect for what Elizabeth was looking for and had set up the meeting here at the hotel. 'It's Camilla, isn't it?' said Elizabeth.

'That's right.'

'I want a divorce but he won't agree to my terms. I need something that will change his mind. I made the mistake of letting him hold all the purse strings, and out of spite he won't co-operate. I can't leave unless I've got some money.'

Camilla shook her head. 'Rule number one – never rely

on a man for anything. Didn't your mother teach you that? I've drummed that into my daughter since she was just a kid. Some people may disapprove of my chosen profession and say I'm letting men take advantage of me, but I'll tell you now, that is not the case. I earn enough money to support myself and my daughter. And as for taking advantage of me, it's the other way around. I'm using them to support my lifestyle, which isn't cheap.'

'No, I can see that,' said Elizabeth. It was obvious from the moment she had first seen the woman that she liked to buy and wear the top brands, but it was an understated sophistication which actually made her even more sophisticated. 'I actually admire you for that.' Elizabeth didn't really admire her, but it was the right thing to say to get Camilla on her side. When Elizabeth had called the agency and explained what she wanted she had been told her it was down to the woman in question whether she wanted to take the job or not, and Elizabeth was now on the charm offensive. She smiled at Camilla. 'I wish I'd had the same foresight as you. I feel like I've lost myself since I've been married. I've gradually disappeared, and now I've finally found the courage to leave, he still wants to control me, and the only way he can do that is by cutting off my finances.' She took a tissue from her bag and dabbed at her eyes, hoping to garner some sympathy.

Camilla rested her hand on Elizabeth's arm. 'Don't feel guilty. It's not your fault. It took me a bad relationship before I truly worked it out. We'll get this bastard of a husband and you can walk away from your shitty marriage. Trust me. I know what I'm doing.'

'Oh, you're so kind. I'm sorry about getting upset. I don't

usually,' said Elizabeth. She smiled at Camilla. 'I really appreciate you agreeing to this. Your employer tells me you've actually done this before.'

'Admittedly, it's not my usual task, but in answer to your question, yes, I have done this before. I'm not as innocent as I look.'

'I'm sure you're not,' replied Elizabeth. She leaned forward and lowered her voice. 'You don't have to go the whole way and have sex with him if you don't want to. I just need proof that he was about to, that the intention was there. You don't need to show your face or anything like that. I'll set the camera up so that it's aimed at the bed. I'll put it on the dressing table, hidden in plain sight.'

Camilla laughed. 'This is like a spy movie. I'm actually quite excited by the prospect.'

'After he's gone, message me and I'll come in. If it's good, then there's some extra cash in it for you.'

'I like your style. I think we'll make a good team.'

Elizabeth took a photograph from her pocket and passed it over to her accomplice, together with a piece of paper. 'Here's what he looks like, and he'll be here on Friday afternoon. I've booked a room upstairs.'

'How do you know he'll be here? What if he doesn't turn up?'

'He thinks he's meeting a potential client. Someone who wants to do business with him,' explained Elizabeth. She'd gone to a lot of trouble to set this up and everything relied on her plan working.

'So, I'll text you once I've got his attention and then you'll message to cancel the appointment?'

'That's right, then he's all yours.'

Camilla looked at the photograph. 'Not a bad-looking man, your husband. What's his name? Not that I'll use it, of course, until he tells me himself, I'm just curious.'

'Owen. Owen Sinclair.'

Elizabeth couldn't help smiling to herself as she drove back to Conmere that day. This was a fail-safe way of getting something on Owen. She had gone to Kendalton the week after she'd seen him at the betting office and then the pub – she'd wanted to see if he was there but she'd obviously spooked him enough to put him off returning. No doubt he had changed his whole routine and found another day and another town to feed his gambling and drinking habit, but Elizabeth had been unperturbed. This time he wouldn't even know he'd been caught with his trousers down until she showed him the film, and before that she'd make sure she had made several copies of the footage. There'd be no dropping it in a pint of lager this time. She fully intended to ensure there would be no wriggle room for Owen.

Two Years Earlier
Kendalton Green Hotel, Kendalton, 9 September, 4.10 p.m.

The following week couldn't come soon enough for Elizabeth. There had only been a few times in her adult life when she had felt this excited. One such time was when she'd first met Harry at a dinner party and, after sitting next to her for the evening, he'd asked if he could see her again. That night she had felt as though she was walking on air. Not only was Harry very good-looking, charming, knowledgeable and engaging, but he was also extremely wealthy. It wasn't until she had done a bit of digging in the ensuing week that she had realised quite how wealthy he was. Yes, she'd been excited then.

Another time was when Harry had proposed to her while they were on holiday in Canada. And her wedding day, of course. That day had been pretty exciting. It was weird how someone who had once had such a dazzling effect on her now seemed dull and boring. What was the saying? All that glitters is not gold. Well, she'd discovered that. Being married to a Sinclair brother had turned out to be more on the bronze side of things, certainly not gold – silver had slipped by too. Still, she couldn't deny, today was exciting. Today she was going to catch Owen literally with his pants down and the consequence would certainly put a bit of sparkle back into her life.

Elizabeth parked her car several streets away from the centre of town and after a few minutes' walk was standing at the reception desk of the Kendalton Green Hotel.

'Elizabeth Sinclair. I have a reservation.'

'Yes, of course,' replied the receptionist.

Elizabeth waited patiently while she was assigned a key card and given directions to her room.

The room was a reasonably sized double which over-looked the street, something she had specified when making the booking over the telephone earlier in the week. It was perfectly arranged too. The bed was in the centre of the room and on the opposite wall was the television with a small writing desk below it. This would be the perfect place to site the spy camera.

She had ordered the camera online and, although a little sceptical at first, she had been impressed with it when it had arrived. It was a super-small camera which actually looked like a TV remote control. She had practised with it during the week, setting it up in her own bedroom at home. It was so simple to use that all Camilla would have to do was press the red button and the device would start to record. As far as Owen would know, it was just another remote control. With any luck he'd be too interested in Camilla to bother with his surroundings.

Elizabeth lined everything up and pressed the red button to check it was working. She sat on the bed and rolled around to make sure the whole of the bed was in shot and then returned to the device, pressing the yellow button to switch it off. Then, lifting it up, she turned it over and slid what looked like a battery cover off, which was in fact a tiny screen where she could replay the recording. Yes, it was working, and in fact it not only got the bed in shot, but most of the room to either side as well. She was very happy with her purchase. She replaced it on the writing desk and smoothed out the bed. Oh, she was enjoying herself.

Several minutes later Elizabeth settled herself down in the window of a small café, from where she had a good view of the main street. The hotel where she had set up the supposed meeting with Owen was almost opposite. Taking out a newspaper and ordering a sandwich and a coffee, she pretended to read while keeping an eye on the hotel. Soon after, Camilla came and joined her at the table.

'I'm glad you turned up,' said Elizabeth.

'Why wouldn't I? It's a job. We had an agreement,' said Camilla simply. 'And besides, I want to stitch that mean bastard up nearly as much as you do.'

Camilla was wearing a jersey wrap-over dress which revealed quite a lot of cleavage and clung seductively to her hips. A pair of high-heeled natural-toned shoes added at least another four inches to her height, and her blonde hair had been curled into big waves which she had scooped to one side of her neck, trailing over her shoulder. Her make-up was light apart from her lipstick, which was pillar-box red, accentuating her full lips. She looked sophisticated and extremely sexy.

'Owen is going to love you,' said Elizabeth.

'Let's hope so. Have you got the room key?'

Elizabeth slid the key card across the table. 'Room 54 on the first floor. It overlooks the street, just up there. Second window from the left.' She pointed to the building opposite. 'When you're in the room, close the curtains and I'll know everything is going to plan.'

'I'll ring you once the deed has been done. Don't worry if I take a little longer than expected. I might actually enjoy this one.'

Elizabeth raised her eyebrows at her partner in crime. 'It's up to you, but I'm paying a flat rate, not by the minute.'

Camilla laughed. 'I'll bear that in mind.'

'Oh, look, there he is,' said Elizabeth. Both women looked across the road as Owen Sinclair walked along the pavement and entered the hotel.

Camilla gathered up the key card and her handbag. 'Right, I'd better get to work.'

Elizabeth ordered herself another coffee and, waiting patiently, eyed the hotel window across the street. Within ten minutes, a text-message alert sounded from her phone. It was a pay-as-you-go cheap disposable one that she had bought for this. She didn't want Camilla to have her usual phone number. She read the message on the screen.

Having a drink with O.

Excellent. So far, so good. Elizabeth called up the fake email account she had created and sent an email to Owen, apologising that the fictitious client wouldn't be able to make their appointment today and would call later. That should clear the way for Owen to spend some time with Camilla now.

Elizabeth felt like she had been sitting there for ages and there was still no sign that Camilla had persuaded Owen to go up to the hotel room with her. She toyed with the phone. Should she send Camilla a message and ask her what was going on, or would that ruin Camilla's game? She decided to give it another half an hour. If Camilla hadn't got Owen upstairs by then, the chances were it wasn't going to happen.

Finally, her patience was rewarded as she saw the figure of Camilla come to the window of the hotel room. She appeared to pause for a moment before reaching out and taking a curtain in each hand, then drew them together.

OMG! It was actually working. Owen had fallen for Camilla's charms!

It felt slightly voyeuristic even imagining what stage Camilla and Owen were at, but Elizabeth couldn't think of anything else. She was desperate to get her hands on that recording – not that she was looking forward to seeing Owen having sex, but the consequences of his actions were her ticket to getting her hands on some of the money for the land.

It was another forty-five minutes before she got a further text message from Camilla to say the deed had been done and Owen was just leaving. Elizabeth sat tight, monitoring the door, and sure enough, a few minutes later Owen exited the building. She watched him head off down the street and shortly afterwards Elizabeth left the coffee shop and went over to the hotel.

Camilla let her into the room. The window was open, but Elizabeth was sure she could still detect the faint smell of bodies and sex. She looked over at the writing table, where Camilla had made a cup of tea. She was a very cool customer, that was for sure. She passed the camera over to Elizabeth.

'There you go. Hope it's come out. Although if it hasn't, Owen did leave me his number. It seems he quite likes me.'

'Really? And will you call him?'

'Not if I don't have to. I mean, I'm sorry he's cheating on you but he's really not my type.'

Elizabeth had to remind herself that she'd told Camilla she was married to Owen. 'Cheating bastard,' she said as she opened the back of the device and pressed play.

Sure enough, there were Camilla and Owen entering the room. Owen hadn't wasted any time in getting himself comfortable on the bed. Elizabeth inwardly winced as she watched Camilla go over to him and within a few minutes they were both naked and writhing around. Camilla was either very good at her job or genuinely enjoying herself. She glanced at Camilla with a raised eyebrow as she saw Camilla perform oral sex on Owen.

Camilla looked over her shoulder. 'Ah, yes. That was just a teaser. I did think I'd stop there but then I thought he really needed to have sex so he couldn't worm his way out of it. I hope you don't mind.'

'Mind? Of course not. I've got the cheating bastard now.' Elizabeth continued to watch, feeling decidedly uncomfortable, but she needed to see it all so she could blackmail him properly. 'It's a bit awkward watching,' she admitted.

'Do you want me to fast-forward to the sex bit?' asked Camilla. She took the device from Elizabeth and returned it to her a few moments later.

Elizabeth watched the recording and there was Owen, first lying down while Camilla was on top and then flipping her over and thrusting away at her. Her stomach gave a little turn of disgust as she had a full view of his white arse bobbing up and down.

Elizabeth switched the recording off and put the device safely into her bag. She couldn't help feeling rather seedy and wanting to wash her hands. Instead, she took out an envelope, which she passed to Camilla.

'Two hundred and fifty bonus for you,' she said.

Camilla looked inside the envelope and slipped it into her bag. 'Nice doing business with you,' she said. 'Let me know if you need me again. Here's my number.'

Elizabeth shouldn't have been surprised that Camilla had her own business card, but the white card with Camilla's name and phone number in gold lettering was every bit as sophisticated as she was.

'Thank you. I'll keep that in mind,' said Elizabeth.

She waited in the room after Camilla had left and played out in her mind how she was going to take great pleasure in blackmailing Owen with this recording. First, though, she needed to make sure she took multiple copies and kept them safe. If Owen tried anything clever, as he had with her phone that time, then she'd be ready for him. She leaned back in the chair and smiled. She really was enjoying herself.

Chapter Eighteen

Lodge 174, Conmere,
Saturday, 11 May, 5 p.m.

Dry-slope skiing, Steph decided, wasn't really her thing, and after falling over four times she'd given it up as a bad idea. Now, as she showered, she inspected her body for any grazing or bruising, of which there appeared to be none, thankfully. As Steph washed, she couldn't help thinking about what had happened that morning. If anyone had said to her she would be on the brink of having fast and lustful sex in a bird hide with Harry Sinclair, she would have either laughed in their face or been totally mortified. She let the water run over her body as she thought of Harry Sinclair – she really should be careful. It probably wouldn't be her best move to become involved in some sort of relationship with him, not when she was trying to find out what happened to his wife. However, a small voice in the back of her head was quietly reminding her that becoming involved with Harry Sinclair might be an advantage when it came to finding out more about Elizabeth and what had happened here two years ago.

Conmere, Saturday, 11 May, 7 p.m.

Steph took extra care with her appearance that night and was thankful she'd packed the LBD rather than another pair of trousers. She certainly felt much more feminine than she had last night.

Walking over to the main house, she kept an eye out for Harry, half expecting him to meet her at some point, and couldn't help feeling a little disappointed when she arrived in the dining hall and he was nowhere to be seen.

This evening she was at a different table with different guests who didn't appear to be local but were from further afield. Steph tried to concentrate on the various conversations but her gaze kept wandering, trying to seek out Harry. It wasn't until right on 7.30, when the food was being brought out, that she saw him slip into the room. He looked over in her direction immediately and she assumed he must have checked out the seating plan beforehand. He gave a nod and a small smile, which sent her stomach into a spin but for all the wrong reasons.

There was something different in his face tonight. The smile was there but there was no warmth with it, and his eyes didn't sparkle as they had earlier that day. She looked down at her glass, embarrassed that she had expected anything else. She'd made a fool of herself earlier, that was certain. She was so bloody stupid sometimes. He was probably after a different conquest tonight. She could feel the burn of embarrassment in her face. She would just have to play it cool and not show that it bothered her.

As she looked up with what she hoped was more

composure, she was surprised to see the maître d' at her side.

'Excuse me, Miss Durham?' he said. 'I'm very sorry but there has been some mistake with the seating plan this evening.'

'What?' Steph looked at the man in bewilderment.

The maître d' placed his hand on the back of her chair and indicated for her to leave her seat. 'If you could come with me, please.' He looked at the other guests. 'Would you please excuse Miss Durham?'

Steph looked apologetically at the other table guests and rose from her seat before following the maître d' through the tables. To her surprise, he led her straight to Harry's table and sat her next to him.

'Thank you, Antonio,' said Harry. He smiled at Steph, and this time his expression seemed a little warmer. 'Sorry about that. They were supposed to change the seating plan earlier. Let me get you some wine.'

'It's a very nice surprise,' replied Steph.

Harry leaned in towards her. 'You look stunning. I love the LBD.'

'Is the right response,' said Steph. Her stomach gave another jump but this time for the opposite reason. However, she warned herself not to get carried away. 'How was your afternoon?' she asked, changing the subject to safer ground.

'Don't ask,' said Harry. 'A bit crap, if I'm honest.'

'Oh, sorry.' She'd put her foot in it now and the tension from his body was undeniable.

'How did the skiing go?'

'Don't ask,' she said, echoing his earlier reply.

'That good, huh?'

'Nothing to do with facilities,' she added quickly. 'More a case of my mind being more capable than my body.'

Harry gave an indistinguishable grunt but said nothing more. They sat in silence for a moment and Steph was beginning to wish he'd never brought her over. It was obvious he didn't really want her there. Or did he? She felt confused. So many mixed messages were coming from him. Sod it, she'd just have to ask.

'Look, Harry, please don't feel you're under any obligation with me just because of what happened this morning,' she said in hushed tones. 'I'm not going to go to pieces or have a hissy fit or anything like that. I'm a grown woman and I can take it. In fact, I'd sooner you were honest with me, rather than feel sorry for me or awkward for yourself.'

Concern entered his eyes. 'What? God, no. Don't think that,' he said hastily in a low but insistent voice. 'I'm sorry, I'm just a bit preoccupied with work. I didn't mean to seem off with you. That's the last thing I want to do.' He held her gaze with his own.

'Anything I can help you with?' asked Steph, aware of the relief at his words and yet scolding herself at the same time for being such a pushover.

He looked as if he was really considering what she'd said and that he wanted to say something, but in the end he just smiled at her. 'I'm sure you're quite capable of solving my work-related problems, but I wouldn't bore you with the details.'

At that moment the waiters appeared with the starters. 'I'm a good listener,' she said. 'If you ever want to sound off or get something off your chest, then I'm your girl.' It was intended as a subtle signpost, that Harry could talk to her about anything – including Elizabeth – but she couldn't deny that it was first and foremost meant out of genuine concern.

'Thank you,' he said, with a sincerity Steph hadn't heard before. 'Actually, before I forget, I meant to ask you if you need accommodation for the week – that's assuming you still want to work here?'

'Absolutely. I can't afford to turn down that sort of offer,' said Steph, suddenly anxious that she might not only lose another source of income for the week but she might also lose a line of enquiry. And another week with Harry, came a little voice at the back of her mind. 'And yes, if I could stay here at the resort, that would be really handy.'

'That's not a problem, although I have to confess the staff accommodation isn't anywhere near as upmarket as your lodge.' He looked more serious again. 'I just didn't know if you wanted to stay with your mum at all? You did say she lived nearby.'

'I'm not that desperate,' said Steph. 'We get on better when we're not under each other's feet.' She didn't add that she wanted to keep as much distance as she could between the Sinclair family and her mother, in all senses of the word.

'Was it different when your dad was still alive?'

She considered his question. It seemed an odd sort of thing to ask and something she hadn't ever really thought about before. 'It was different when my dad was at home. We had a lot in common. If I'm honest, Mum was probably a bit of a bystander and I don't think that helped strengthen any sort of bond between us.'

'What did your dad do? For work?'

Again, a slightly off-kilter question, but she reasoned it was the sort of thing you asked someone when you were getting to know them. She took a sip of her drink to buy some time and settle the little flutter of unease in her stomach. 'He was a builder, but he retired early because of a bad back. He was too young to sit around and do nothing, so he used to spend most of his time running around for other people. He was always taking someone to hospital or to the shops or to the airport. All for free. He said he liked the company and it helped other people by saving them the taxi fare.' Something made her hold back on confessing her dad had worked for Max Sinclair. She wasn't yet ready to reveal to Harry all her connections to his family in case it put him on his guard.

'That was very generous of him.'

Steph smiled fondly at the memory. 'That was the type of man he was. Always trying to help someone else. When he died there was very little incentive for me to return home. Most holidays I managed to wrangle an invite to one of my friends' houses. It was better than sitting at home alone while Mum was at work.'

She felt an unexpected lump hit her throat as she thought of her dad. She hated the way grief could take her by surprise, often at the most awkward moments. She looked down at her hands and then up across the room, trying to prevent the tears from pooling in her eyes.

'Hey, I'm sorry,' said Harry. He reached out and squeezed her hand. 'I didn't mean to upset you.'

Steph ran the tip of her finger under each eye and forced

a smile. 'It's OK. Not sure where that came from. I'm usually quite good at keeping it together.'

'Do you want to get some fresh air?'

'No. Honestly, I'll be OK.' She poked at her starter some more and then, feeling her appetite dwindle, placed her fork on the side of the plate. Forcing a brighter tone to her voice, she changed the subject. 'What time did you want to come over in the morning to see the pictures? I've been through the set this afternoon and uploaded some of the better ones to my laptop.'

'I was rather hoping I could see them tonight,' said Harry under his breath as the waiter appeared to clear their plates.

Steph smiled and thanked the waiter as he took her plate away. She could read the subtext and, if she was honest, she was flattered and excited by the idea of sleeping with Harry. 'Tonight? Sounds like a good idea.'

'Excellent,' said Harry. 'And I'm sorry if I appeared a bit distant earlier.'

'It's fine. I appreciate you must be busy, especially on a weekend like this where you want everything to run like clockwork.'

They exchanged polite chit-chat with the rest of the table guests throughout dinner, but Steph couldn't help herself from thinking ahead to when they would be back at her lodge. She was under no illusion there would be the remotest interest paid to her pictures tonight. A voice of warning whispered in the back of her mind. If Sonia's belief surrounding Elizabeth's death was true, then Harry could potentially be involved. Steph pushed the warning away.

When they had finally finished their dessert, Steph excused

herself to use the ladies'. As she got up she felt a little light-headed. It must have been all the wine she had consumed. She had tried to match one glass of wine with one glass of water, which usually worked well for her, but with her glass being constantly topped up, she must have got lost on the ratio.

As she came out of the toilets, across the hallway she could see Harry in deep conversation with his brother Dominic. She really didn't fancy going over there just now. She didn't like Dominic. He made her nervous and she didn't know why, which in itself was unsettling. Instead, she opted for a breath of fresh air, hoping that would clear her head a bit before she returned.

As she crossed the hall towards the breakfast room, where she could slip out onto the terrace without being noticed, she rubbed her face, forgetting she had rather more make-up on than usual.

'Bugger,' she said. Looking back, she saw a mirror tucked away around the corner and hurried over to inspect her make-up. As she dabbed at her eyes with a tissue to try to remove the smudges, she became aware of different voices coming from the hallway. Hushed voices. Both male.

'Have you got it with you?' said the first voice.

'Yeah, of course. I said I would,' came the reply.

'Come on, then. I want three g.' The first voice sounded impatient.

'This isn't on credit.'

'When have I ever asked you for credit?'

Steph inwardly winced. She couldn't leave her spot around the corner – they would know she'd heard them talking and it was obviously a clandestine meeting. She'd just have to stay put until they were finished. She held her breath, not daring to move.

'There – £300,' said the second man. 'Hurry up.'

Steph could hear the first man taking his time counting out notes. She got the distinct impression he was being slow just to wind up the other bloke. Finally, she heard him say, 'It's all there.'

'Good, and there are three little bags for you. Oh, don't snatch. Didn't your mother teach you any manners?'

'Fuck off, Dean.'

'Now, now, Mr Sinclair, that's not very becoming of a man in your position.'

Steph stiffened at the mention of the name Sinclair. She'd been alert before but now she was super-alert for very different reasons. It sounded like she'd just heard a drugs deal take place involving one of the Sinclair brothers. It certainly wasn't Harry but whether it was Dominic or Owen she couldn't tell. She wasn't tuned in to their voices and wouldn't be able to recognise them just from hearing their welcome speeches yesterday. God, she wanted to know which one it was. She knew who her money was on . . . Dominic.

'Nice doing business with you, Mr Sinclair. See you again soon, no doubt.'

She heard footsteps recede and then whichever brother it was utter a pretty crude insult directed at the other guy. Very slowly, she leaned back just so she could see around the corner. She really didn't want to move her feet, frightened her heels would make a noise on the tiled floor.

As she peeked around the corner she could see a man standing with his back to her, looking at something in his hand. From his build and hair, she was pretty sure it was Owen. He began to walk back towards the hall and Steph breathed a sigh of relief and dropped her shoulders, which had been hunched up as she'd stood undetected. Unfortunately, her hand caught the corner of the wall and the mascara brush she was holding was knocked from her fingers, hitting the floor with a small but unmistakable clatter.

She stooped to pick up the mascara, aware that Owen had stopped walking. She sensed rather than saw him turn to see where the noise had come from.

'Bloody thing,' she muttered out loud and then looked up with faux surprise. 'Oh, sorry, didn't see you there,' she said, trying her best to look embarrassed at swearing.

Owen eyed her with suspicion. 'Where have you come from?'

'I've just come out of the toilets,' said Steph, putting the make-up back in her bag.

Owen's eyes darted from Steph to the toilet door on the other side of the hall. 'Just now?'

'Yes,' said Steph, injecting a defensive tone to her own voice. 'Is that a problem?'

He walked back towards her and Steph felt her heart beginning to hammer hard against her breastbone. 'Were you standing there just now? When I was talking to someone?'

'No.' She didn't like the look in his eyes. The pupils were dilated and there was a slightly glazed look about them. She'd seen it before when someone was high, and she guessed Owen had already taken drugs tonight. The thought made her nervous. 'If you'll excuse me.' She went to walk past him, but Owen moved in front of her.

'Are you sure you didn't hear me talking to someone just now?'

'Positive. Now, please, can you move out of the way?'

'Owen!'

Steph looked up. To her relief, Harry was standing in the hallway. He closed the space between them in four strides. 'All right, mate?' he asked, putting his hand on his brother's shoulder.

Owen turned to face his brother. 'Yeah. I was talking to . . .' He waved his hand as if he could pluck the name from the air.

Harry looked at Steph. 'You OK?'

She smiled. 'Fine. I was just going back inside.'

Harry studied her for a moment and then moved his brother aside. 'Let our guest through,' he said.

Owen stepped back and shrugged Harry's hand away. Steph heard him say something in response to Harry, but she hurried off through to the dining hall before he could catch up with her. The last thing she wanted was to be confronted by Owen Sinclair again.

A short time later, Harry joined her at the table. 'Are you really OK?'

Steph was touched by his concern. 'Yeah. But, and this is off the record, I think your brother is high. You need to speak to him or get him out of here because other reporters might not be so generous with keeping such information to themselves.'

'What do you mean?'

'I was just fixing my make-up around the corner and heard him and some other bloke do a drug deal.'

'Idiot.' Harry pushed a hand through his hair. 'I'm sorry. Really sorry.'

'Look, I don't know what's going on here with Owen but drugs are not my scene and I don't want to be anywhere near them,' she said. 'I think it will be best if I just meet you tomorrow during the day some time and bring my pictures to you.'

He looked genuinely hurt at what she was saying, which made her feel even worse than she already did, but there was no way she was getting involved with someone who had anything to do with drugs. She might be doing Harry a disservice but she'd had too much to drink to think it through properly, let alone get into any discussion about it. Much as she liked Harry, and God knows she really did like him, she wasn't prepared to become involved with the drug scene. She'd seen too many people in her line of work use drugs socially on a regular basis and she'd seen the devastating effect of the use turning to abuse and the dependency just to function on a day-to-day basis that followed.

'Can we at least talk? Will you let me explain?' asked Harry. 'I promise you, it's no reflection on me.'

'I don't know, Harry,' said Steph, fully aware she could so easily be swayed if Harry said the things she wanted to hear. 'Not tonight anyway.'

He looked as if he was going to say something else, but then changed his mind. 'OK. It's your call,' he said gently. 'I'm not in the business of putting pressure on anyone. We can talk tomorrow. At least allow me that.'

'Yeah, sure.' Steph gathered up her bag. 'I'm going to turn in now.'

'Let me walk you back to your lodge.' Harry rose at the same time as her.

'Thank you.'

They walked in silence back to Steph's lodge, where she found herself once again standing on the doorstep with Harry, wishing she didn't have to leave him. She hoped he wouldn't try to persuade her to change her mind, as she knew she wouldn't put up much of a protest.

Harry leaned forward and kissed her on the forehead. 'Sleep well,' he said and then turned and walked away without looking back.

Steph let herself into her lodge. 'Bollocks,' she groaned as she locked the door behind her. Tonight had not ended how she had planned it to at all. She contemplated making herself a cup of tea but decided against it. The easiest way to get over the disappointment of tonight would be to go to sleep. She washed the make-up from her face and stripped off, slipping into a T-shirt and fresh underwear.

She was just drifting off to sleep when a scraping noise jolted her back into consciousness. It was a brief sound but it had been out of the ordinary and enough to startle her. Steph lay very still in her bed, concentrating on listening for any other sound.

There was nothing and she was just beginning to think she had imagined it, or even dreamt it, when she thought she heard a gentle creak, almost like floorboards. Was it just the building softly groaning in the night or was someone actually inside the lodge?

She mentally replayed her movements before she'd come to bed. She had definitely locked the front door and, although she hadn't checked the patio doors at the rear, she knew she hadn't opened them. She chided herself at overreacting. This was a wooden lodge in the middle of a forest, there were bound to be all sorts of noises.

Steph slipped out of bed and stepped out into the hallway. The night-light was on, casting a soft yellow glow down the passageway towards the living area. She padded along the tiled floor and into the kitchen.

A movement in her peripheral vision made Steph look round just as a large, dark figure lunged towards her from the shadows.

She didn't have time to move out of the way, to run or even to scream. An instinctive reflex had her half-turning away from the intruder, her hands went over her head to offer protection and she hunched forward. The next thing she felt was the impact on her back which sent her off-balance, making her stumble forward.

A sharp, shooting pain pierced her head and the last thing she felt was the hard, tiled floor as she hit the ground.

Chapter Nineteen

Lodge 174, Conmere, Sunday, 12 May, 1.00 a.m.

'Steph, Steph? Are you OK?'

The voice sounded distant, as if her name was being spoken through a handkerchief or from the other side of a closed window. Steph moved her head and winced. It felt like a bowling ball slamming around inside her skull. 'That hurts,' she mumbled.

'Steph? Open your eyes. It's me, Harry.'

This time his voice was clear and she did as he requested, seeing his face peering down at her, his eyes filled with concern. 'Hey, you had me worried there for a moment.'

She went to raise her head, but it hurt too much and she lay back down, gradually becoming aware of her surroundings. She was lying on the sofa of her lodge, a pillow was under her head and Harry was perched on the coffee table next to her. For a moment she couldn't think what had happened and then the memory rolled to the front of her mind. She gave a gasp and her eyes frantically scanned the room. 'Who's here?' she said, looking back at Harry.

'It's OK. It's just me and you. No one is here.'

'You sure?'

'Yeah. Just us. What happened?'

'More to the point, what are you doing here?' Despite the thudding in her head, Steph sat up and leaned back into the sofa, pulling her hand away from Harry's. 'How did you get in?'

Harry sat back with his hands in a surrender position. 'It's all right, Steph. I'm not going to hurt you. I found you on the floor. I thought you'd passed out or something.'

Steph wasn't convinced. 'But you went . . . you left me. Why did you come back?' She looked at her watch. 'It's one o'clock in the morning.'

'I walked you back to your lodge, remember? You came in and I went back to the gala dinner.'

'Yeah, so why did you come back?' she repeated. She remembered that and she remembered going to bed. She also remembered with clarity what had happened next.

Harry looked a little embarrassed. 'I felt bad about how we'd left things. I suppose, in my wisdom, I thought I could try to explain things better so you'd realise that I wasn't as bad as you thought I was.' He drummed his fingers on his knee. 'It seemed like a good idea at the time, but, now I'm saying it out loud, it sounds rather lame.'

'So you came back, but how did you get in?' Steph asked, keen to get back to the facts.

'Your door was ajar. I called out your name and when I got no answer I came right in. Saw you flat out on the floor.'

'Someone was in the lodge,' she said. Her voice wavered as the realisation of what had happened to her came into sharp focus.

Harry reached out and held her hand. 'What?'

'Someone was here in the lodge while I was sleeping. Something woke me up, a noise from out here. I came out and then . . . I don't really know what happened next . . . I think someone pushed past me and I slipped.' She touched the side of her head with her hand. 'Ouch. I must have knocked my head on the breakfast bar as I went down.'

'Are you sure there was someone in here? Did you leave the door unlocked?'

Steph wiped away a tear as she tried to recall the chain of events. 'I'm certain I locked the door. I'm pretty good with that sort of thing.'

'How did they get in, then? Did you leave a window open?' Harry looked around the room and then got up and methodically checked all the windows in the lodge. 'They're all closed,' he said, before going to inspect the front door. 'And it doesn't look like anyone has forced the lock.' He sat back down on the coffee table.

'I didn't imagine it,' said Steph firmly, her shock making way for anger at the thought of an intruder being in the place. 'There was definitely someone in here.'

'You had been drinking; could you have simply tripped and fallen?'

'No, I wasn't drunk,' insisted Steph, annoyed that he should imply she was too drunk to know what she was doing. Gingerly she touched the side of her head where a lump had already formed.

Harry moved her hair to take a look. 'You need that looked at.'

'No. I'll be OK. It's not bleeding. Just sore.'

Harry didn't look entirely convinced. He got up and plucking a clean tea towel from the kitchen drawer, he proceeded to run it under the cold water, before squeezing it out and folding it into a pad. 'At least put this on your head,' he said, coming back over and offering her the compress.

'Thanks,' said Steph, wincing as she placed it to her head. 'There was someone here, Harry.'

'Did you see what they looked like?'

'Not really. It was dark. I didn't put the main light on, just the passageway light.' She closed her eyes as she tried to envisage the intruder. 'They were taller than me, I think, but I couldn't see their face. I think they had a hood up. Other than that, I can't tell you anything.'

'Shit,' muttered Harry and then took her hand again. 'I'm so sorry, Steph.'

'It's not your fault,' she replied, allowing her hand to be held.

'I feel responsible. You're here as my guest and then something like this happens. We should report it to the police.'

'Maybe,' she said, although in reality she had no intention of getting the police involved in case the connection to her mother was exposed. He looked at her questioningly. She continued, 'Unless something has been taken, let's not. I'd sooner not get the police involved; it's pointless. Besides, it probably won't do much for publicity.' She didn't add that her mind was already racing ahead and making possible connections. If the intrusion was anything to do with her being here on Sonia's behalf, then it suggested someone had something they wanted to keep hidden and were trying to warn Steph off. Bringing the police in would only make whoever it was even more on their guard.

'You're being very generous about this,' Harry said. 'We could do without the police turning up and drawing a lot of the wrong type of attention to the place. Obviously, I'm concerned there's someone on site who is going around trying to break in and steal stuff. I'll speak to Security and get them to up their rounds. But first, can you check that nothing has been stolen?'

'I'll look properly in the morning, but my laptop is there on the table where I left it and my phone should be in my bag.'

Harry rose and picked up her bag, passing it to her. 'Have a quick look.'

Steph opened her bag and retrieved her phone. 'Yep, that's here, and so is my purse and . . . yep, all my cards are still in there with the bit of cash I had. Nothing has been taken.'

'That's something at least,' said Harry, once again resuming his position on the coffee table. 'How are you feeling? Do you want a coffee or a sweet tea for the shock?'

'I would really like to get some sleep. I've got a raging headache. I think there is some paracetamol in my bag. I'll take a couple of those.'

Harry got up and ran Steph a glass of water.

'Thank you,' she said, taking the glass and swallowing two pills down. She let out something between a sigh and a groan.

'I don't think you should be on your own. I can stay with you tonight,' said Harry, and then added quickly, 'I can stay here on the sofa.'

'I'll be fine,' she said, although the thought of having someone else in the lodge for the night was appealing, even if the idea of coming across as a weak woman who needed looking after annoyed her.

'I would sooner not leave you on your own,' said Harry, this time more firmly. 'I'd like to get the locks looked at in the morning. It's too late to get anyone out tonight.'

'OK, you can stay on the sofa,' said Steph, and couldn't help feeling relieved. Whoever had broken in here tonight had either wanted to scare her or warn her. Her mind went straight to Owen and what she'd seen him doing. Could he have broken in to warn her off? And how did that relate to Harry? She wished she could isolate the incidents. She wasn't naive enough to think that, just because Owen was into drugs, Harry was too, but his reaction to his brother had been neutral.

'That's fine,' said Harry. 'I'll be right out here if you need me, though. Just shout.'

'Thank you,' said Steph, pushing herself up from the sofa. She purposely avoided his outstretched hand. She didn't trust herself to make physical contact with him. 'Goodnight, Harry.'

Once inside her bedroom, Steph closed the door and leaned back against it, letting out a sigh. Tentatively she climbed into bed, resting her head on the pillow. She didn't know how long she lay there before she finally went to sleep but images of the person in her lodge wouldn't leave her. She didn't think they had been there to do her any harm, otherwise they wouldn't have fled as soon as she'd knocked herself out. The more she thought about it, the more she was sure they hadn't meant to push her. They had simply been trying to flee. But what did they want? Maybe she had just disturbed them before they'd had time to search the place. Thank goodness her laptop was still there, although out of habit she always backed her work up on a memory stick and that was securely in her purse.

Eventually she felt herself beginning to drift off and her mind wandered back to the lake and kissing Harry. Knowing he was just metres away on the other side of the wall was both reassuring and frustrating.

Lodge 174, Conmere, Sunday, 12 May, 10.00 a.m.

When Steph woke in the morning she instantly remembered what had happened the previous night. There was no gentle drift of events into her consciousness; the memories were there immediately. She sat up and, although her head still hurt, the pain definitely had eased over the last few hours.

Steph hoped Harry was still there. She hated to admit it, but she felt a little nervous after last night. Sitting still, she listened for any sign of him, then she got up, wrapped her dressing gown around herself and ventured out.

'Good morning,' he said, rising from the sofa, on which he looked to have been studying his phone. 'How are you feeling?'

'Hi. Not so bad. I wasn't sure if you'd still be here.' She let out a small breath of relief to have him there.

'I was hardly likely to go off and leave you, not after what happened.'

'I know, but I thought you might have work to do.' She moved into the kitchen area and filled the kettle.

Harry was at her side. 'Here, let me do that; you go and

sit down.' He took the kettle from her and set about preparing the tea. 'I've checked in with Dominic and Owen. All is well, and it's times like this when a smartphone is actually the best invention. I can do all the things I need to sitting right here.'

'Thank you for staying; I appreciate that.'

'I've arranged for someone to bring over some breakfast.' He checked his watch. 'In fact, your timing is impeccable, as I told them ten-thirty.'

'You didn't have to,' she protested half-heartedly.

'I wanted to,' countered Harry. 'Someone is also coming over to change the locks. I know you're technically leaving this lodge today but, seeing as that's not until later, I wanted you to feel safe.'

'You're really thoughtful, aren't you?' said Steph, taking the cup of tea he passed over to her.

'I try to be. Now, once you've drunk that, can you double-check that everything is here?'

Steph looked round the room. 'I'm sure nothing has been taken,' she said. 'I think I probably disturbed whoever it was before they had time to grab anything.'

'How's your head? I still think someone should look at it.'

Steph touched the side of her head. 'It's OK. There was quite a big lump last night, but it's gone down now.'

'If you feel dizzy or sick, you must let me know. I'll take you straight to the hospital.'

'Thank you but I'm sure I'm OK.' She drank her tea, touched by his concern. It had been a long time since anyone had looked after her. Her ex-husband, Zac, had been attentive once upon a time, but that ship had sailed long ago. In fact,

Steph always saw it as the first indicator that her marriage had been on the rocks. She tossed the unhappy thoughts from her mind. 'Do you want to see the pictures now you're here?'

A knock at the door interrupted the conversation. Harry got up and went to open it. Steph could hear him speaking to the maintenance man who had come to change the locks.

'That was quick,' she commented, once he had carried out the task.

Harry handed her a new key. 'Hold on to that for now. I've got two spares, which I'll take over to Reception in a minute.'

She took the key and placed it in her bag. 'Does your maintenance department have a skeleton key for the lodge?'

'I should imagine so,' said Harry. 'What are you thinking? That someone has got hold of the master key?'

Steph shrugged. 'I don't know what I'm thinking really, but it's a possibility.'

'Which would mean they could still let themselves in.'

She was more scared than she cared to admit. What if the person decided to come back? Would they take such a risk? It was impossible to answer with any certainty. 'I suppose if I dead bolt the door, that should help.' She spoke with rather more confidence than she felt as her imagination got the better of her.

'Do you want to move lodges? Go into staff accommodation? Or . . . I can stay here with you.'

It was a tempting offer, there was no denying that, but she felt on edge – was it such a coincidence that Harry had turned up just after the intruder had fled? She needed time to process her thoughts and that meant space from Harry.

'I'll feel safer in the staff accommodation in the main house, if I'm honest,' she said.

Harry gave her one of his thoughtful looks, one that she couldn't quite read, before offering a small smile. 'Sure. I understand. Let me know if you change your mind.'

'Thanks.' And then, wanting to take her mind off what had happened, she asked, 'Shall we look at those pictures now?'

'I'd love to.'

They spent the next hour poring over the laptop, Steph calling up the best of the shots she had taken. Even though she was no longer on her own and Harry was there, the photos had an unsettling effect on her. The water from the south side looked so tranquil and peaceful, it was certainly a place where you wanted to spend time, just to sit and appreciate the hills behind it. But on the north side the water took on a totally different character. It was dark and moody, the water unwelcoming, and the shadows from the hills behind it cast themselves across the water like a cloak.

Harry hadn't said anything as they'd looked through her shots, and when she took a look out of the corner of her eye to gauge his reaction she saw an expression as dark as the water in her photo cross his face. He was lost in his own thoughts, somewhere far away from where they were now.

He must have felt her gaze, as he blinked a couple of times and looked at Steph, then back to the laptop screen. He gave what sounded like a fake cough. 'They're all great in their own way,' he said, clearly trying to recover his composure. 'I love how natural they are. No filter.'

'No smoke and lights,' said Steph. 'Everything in plain sight. That's just how I like it.'

She didn't look at him as she flicked back through the photos, but she was aware of his gaze on her this time. She wondered if he had experienced the same eerie and unsettling sensation that she had from the photographs. And, if he had, was it simply from the atmosphere she'd captured or was it because of what had happened to Elizabeth there?

Her mobile phone ringing broke the silence and Steph picked it up from the table. The name Sonia Lomas flashed up on the screen. Hurriedly she declined the call and placed the phone face down on the table next to her. She half expected Harry to say something, but it appeared he hadn't seen who was calling her.

'Didn't you want to take that?' he asked, his own eyes still fixed on the computer screen.

Steph swallowed. 'No. Not important. Just a friend.'

'A friend?'

Her palms felt sweaty as she reached out and clicked through to some more pictures. 'Sort-of friend. As I say, nothing important.'

Harry studied the photos again. 'They are all great,' he said, after a while. 'I was thinking . . . I could buy some of these from you and put the rest up for sale in the shop as well – that way, you get to make money twice: once from me, and once from anyone who wants to buy one as a memento of their stay, or just because they love the beauty of the lake. You say what you want to make on each picture and we'll stick a little bit on top by way of commission. How does that sound?'

'I'm flattered.'

'Don't be. It's a sign that you undervalue your own work.

You've got a talent for taking photos and you should be proud of it – know your own worth.'

Steph gave an embarrassed laugh. 'Point taken.'

There was an awkward silence between them for a moment and it was Harry who spoke first. 'Steph, about Owen,' he began. 'I promise you, what you saw last night was nothing to do with me. I'm not into any of that.'

'You didn't seem very surprised by it,' Steph replied.

'Owen has his own demons. I didn't know about this latest one until I came back. I've already decided I'm going to try to help him, if he'll let me.'

'You're a good brother,' she said. 'What are your demons?'

He didn't speak for a long time, and when he did his voice was soft and full of sadness. 'Guilt.'

'For what?'

Harry shook his head. 'I'd better go.' He stood up abruptly. 'Are you going to be OK on your own until checking-out time?'

He had switched so suddenly to business mode that it took Steph by surprise. She had really felt he was going to open up to her, but he had managed to hop from one mood to another in the blink of an eye.

She stood up too. 'Yeah, sure.'

'When you go to the office, if I'm not there someone will show you where your staff accommodation is,' he said. Before she could reply he was walking out of the door.

Steph went to call after him but changed her mind. What the hell had just happened there? She'd thought they had something between them just then, but now she just didn't have a clue. Was it something to do with what they had discussed? He'd said his demon was guilt. What exactly did he feel guilty for? Betraying his wife's memory by being with Steph? Or betraying his wife by having some involvement in her death? Steph didn't think Harry was a murderer, not that she had anything to base this assumption on, but from what she'd seen of him, he was a good man, kind and considerate. But then, what about the other side she'd seen last night, his acceptance of his brother and the drugs? Could Harry turn a blind eye to people doing bad things? He might not have had a hand in Elizabeth's death, but had he been a bystander? Steph closed her eyes – she really didn't know what to think.

The sound of her phone ringing took her attention. She picked it up and saw it was Sonia Lomas again. She'd totally forgotten Sonia had called earlier.

'Hello, Sonia. What's up? Why are you ringing me? We said no contact.' It wasn't the most gracious way to open a conversation but Steph's head hurt, she was tired and she felt cast adrift.

'It's important,' said Sonia. 'I need to speak to you.'

'What's happened?'

'Meet me today at one-thirty at the Fox & Hounds. It's a pub in the village. About a mile away from Conmere.'

'OK, but can you give me some idea what this is all about? Are you OK?'

'I think I'm being followed. I'll talk to you properly when I see you.'

Before Steph could ask anything more, the line went dead.

Chapter Twenty

Two Years Earlier,
Conmere, 10 September, 10.45 a.m.

Elizabeth checked the camera was in her handbag and, leaving the lodge, made her way over to the stables, where she knew Owen would be. If nothing else, he was a creature of habit. Harry had already headed over to the offices at Conmere House, as he and Dominic were interviewing for a new chef that morning. Elizabeth knew it pissed Owen off that he wasn't invited to these meetings, but Dominic was adamant he and Harry were best placed to deal with it.

As she walked across the stable yard, she could see the back of Owen's head as he looked at his laptop screen. He turned at her approach, her low-heeled boots announcing her arrival.

'To what do I owe this pleasure?' He emphasised the last word to make it clear this was anything but a pleasure.

'Don't worry, I'm not stopping long. And I assure you the pleasure will be all mine.'

Owen narrowed his eyes. 'Get on with it. I'm a busy man.'

Elizabeth looked at her watch. 'I was going to say the pub's not open yet, but I don't suppose that will bother you. I expect you've got something stashed away somewhere.'

'Oh, do piss off, Elizabeth. This is really very boring now.'

Elizabeth placed both hands on the desk and leaned towards him. 'The fun is only just beginning.'

Owen gave an exaggerated eye-roll and leaned back in his chair, steepling his fingers together. 'As I say, I'm busy. I haven't got much time.'

'Well, since our last chat about selling the land, I've had a little rethink.'

Owen threw back his head and gave a loud laugh. 'Oh, for God's sake, you're not still harping on about that, are you?'

'I don't give up. When I want something, I keep going until I get it.' She was actually enjoying this and the prospect of Owen being totally fucked was positively thrilling. 'Just be quiet and listen. You won't be laughing in a minute.'

'I'm all ears.'

'I understand you had a little trip yesterday for a meeting at Kendalton Green Hotel.'

The colour drained from Owen's face and he shifted in his seat. 'That's right.' His voice was steady.

'A little bird tells me that the meeting was cancelled.' She paused as Owen swallowed hard. 'But you had a meeting of another kind. A different sort of bird – a blonde one.'

'You're talking bollocks.'

Elizabeth held out the memory card to Owen. 'Am I?'

Owen snatched the memory card from her. 'What's this?'

'A short film. Why don't you have a look?'

Owen eyed her with pursed lips, before slotting it into the side of his laptop. He clicked on the play button.

Elizabeth didn't need to look; she could hear the muffled voices of Owen and Camilla. She winced slightly at the moan Owen gave. She knew what point of the recording he was at.

'What the fuck?' demanded Owen, sweat beading on his brow and above his top lip. 'What the actual fuck?'

'Good choice of words,' said Elizabeth, as she sat in the chair and looked at her brother-in-law's obvious distress.

He slammed the screen down, snatched the card from the laptop and jumped to his feet. He leaned over the desk, waving the memory card at Elizabeth. 'Where did you get this from?'

'That doesn't really matter, does it?'

'That bitch must have set me up.' Owen thumped the lid of the laptop and shoved the memory card into his pocket, with a small look of triumph.

Elizabeth laughed. 'Oh, really, Owen. You think I'm that stupid to just have one copy of your little show.'

'You were behind this?' Owen's face was bright red with rage. 'You give me the other copy. Now! Do you hear?'

'Or you'll do what? Why don't you take a deep breath, count to ten and sit down?' Elizabeth's voice grew hard. 'And get a grip of yourself. You weak, pathetic excuse for a man.'

Owen looked as if he was going to explode. He swiped his hand across the desk, sending the telephone and a pot of pens across the floor. 'I'm not messing around,' he shouted. 'Give me the other copy.'

Elizabeth made a big huffing noise. 'Honestly, Owen, just

sit down and shut up so we can work this out amicably.' She spoke to him the way she would to a naughty child who was in the middle of a temper tantrum. It was no wonder Dominic didn't trust him with anything other than a few old nags.

Owen slumped down into his chair, the effort to control his temper very much apparent, but he made a valiant endeavour and his natural pallor returned. Only his deep breathing gave him away.

'What is it you want?' he said finally.

'Excellent, we've come to the nub of this little exercise.'

'Just get on with it.'

Elizabeth smiled. 'It's very simple: you tell Dominic and Harry you've changed your mind about selling North Meadow and then the three of you can tell your dear mother and she'll have to abide by the majority voting rule and sell the land.'

'What? Are you serious?'

'Never been more so. It's not a big deal, Owen. We all win that way. You four will split the profits equally, which means, as Harry's wife and having joint accounts, I can have access to the funds too. That's all I want. It's not illegal.'

'It might not be but it's definitely immoral.'

'I don't think you're in any position to preach to me about morals.' Elizabeth inclined her head. 'I don't think Natalie will be very happy to know what your morals are.'

'You wouldn't . . . !'

'Try me.'

Owen's finger tapped rapidly against his leg. He was the one bluffing and Elizabeth knew, out of the two of them, she had the balls.

They eyed each other across the desk. Owen wasn't as strong as he liked people to think he was. He'd buckle. She knew it. Still, she applied a bit more pressure. 'I'll give you a chance. You keep saying no and I'll send this to Dominic first. See what he makes of it. Personally, I don't think he'll be very impressed and more than likely furious with you for getting yourself into this predicament. My betting is he'll take even more power away from you. That would be rather humiliating, wouldn't it? I mean, at this rate you'll end up as a stable lad, answering to someone else running the yard.'

The redness returned to his face. 'You're one evil bitch,' he said. 'When Harry first brought you home, I was convinced he had fallen on his feet with someone beautiful on the outside and the inside too. How wrong could I have been? You are rotten to the core.'

Elizabeth yawned uninterestedly. 'Stick and stones, sticks and stones.'

'Well, fuck you.' Owen almost spat the words out.

'I'd sooner you didn't.' She waggled her little finger at him. 'I'm used to a real man.'

She hadn't banked on his reaction and as he flew round the desk and grabbed her by the throat, sending the chair flying backwards, Elizabeth realized she'd gone too far. Jesus Christ! He was going to strangle her!

She grabbed at his wrists, trying to prise his hands away from her throat, while at the same time she writhed on the floor, twisting her body one way and the other, attempting to get away from him. As she twisted to the side, she brought her knee up swiftly and caught him straight in the side of the ribs. Owen let out a moan. She did it again. And again.

The pressure was released from her neck and she pushed him away. Owen rolled over, clutching his side and groaning. 'I think you've broken my ribs.'

On her hands and knees, gasping for air, Elizabeth crawled to the other side of the office and sat on the floor, leaning back against the door. She held one hand to her sore neck. The bastard would have killed her if she hadn't managed to catch him with her knee.

'You ever do anything like that again,' she spat, 'then I swear to God I will kill you myself.' She pulled the remote-control spy camera from her pocket. 'I've got all that recorded.'

Owen, now sitting on the floor, propped against his desk, looked over at her. 'Total fucking bitch,' he muttered.

After a few moments, Elizabeth hauled herself to her feet. She felt light-headed and had to hold on to the desk to steady herself.

Owen stood up too and righted the chair. He indicated for Elizabeth to sit and walked round to his side of the desk, taking the opportunity to pick up the telephone and pens he'd knocked over in his temper. Elizabeth took a moment to study him. The fight had definitely left him. The coward had frightened himself. She judged it safe to sit back down and resume their discussion.

'Not sure how I'm going to explain the bruising to my neck,' she said.

'Oh, I'm sure you'll think of something,' said Owen, with no trace of remorse.

He was probably only sorry he hadn't finished her off, thought Elizabeth. She cleared her throat. 'You know what needs to be done and it needs to happen by next Friday, otherwise I'll be sending a copy off to everyone; that includes the press and anyone you know on social media. So are you going to do it or not?'

'Doesn't look like I have much choice in the matter.'

'No, it doesn't.' Elizabeth stood up. 'Mind you don't lose that memory card, now.' This remark sent Owen into a panic as he tapped his pockets and frantically scanned the floor before swiping up the device from under his desk. Elizabeth gave the most saccharine smile she could muster. 'See you later, Owen.' She couldn't resist waggling her little finger at him again.

'Fuck you!' shouted Owen.

Elizabeth slammed the door behind her to deflect the paperweight Owen had thrown after her. It hit the door with a thud. She poked her head back round the door. 'Temper, temper.' Then this time, leaving the door open, she sauntered back across the yard to the house.

Chapter Twenty-One

Conmere, Sunday, 12 May, 1.10 p.m.

Steph took a quick shower and, once dressed, packed the rest of her clothes into her suitcase. Although she didn't have to be out of the room just yet, she wasn't taking any chances by leaving her possessions unattended again. She just didn't feel comfortable in the lodge now, despite the change of locks.

As she hurried along the path towards the car park and rounded the corner of the main house she glanced up, and saw Pru Sinclair standing at the French windows that opened out onto the lawn. Pru smiled and waved in her direction and Steph returned the gesture. As she did so Harry appeared at the windows next to his mother. He gave a small frown and nodded towards her case.

'I'll be back later!' she called. Without breaking stride, Steph carried on out of range of the watchful eyes and into the car park. She had just loaded her car and put the keys in the ignition when Harry appeared at the driver's door. Steph let out a small yelp of surprise, before opening the door.

Harry put his hand on top of the door. 'Changed your mind?'

'Not at all,' said Steph. 'I've just got to nip into town and thought I'd clear my room while I was at it. Save me having to do it later.'

'Are you sure you should be driving after that knock to your head?'

'Absolutely,' she replied. Her headache had subsided and she didn't feel groggy any more. 'I feel fine.' She went to tug on the door but his grip was firm.

'Maybe I should drive you,' he suggested.

'Not at all,' said Steph quickly. She could hardly meet Sonia with Harry in tow. 'Besides, I don't know how long I'll be.'

A frown creased his forehead. 'Aren't you supposed to still be working?'

'I'll make the time up later,' she replied, slightly irritated at his tone. He wasn't her boss – not yet. 'Don't worry, Conmere Resort Centre will get a full and glowing report, if that's what you're worried about.'

'I wasn't actually,' said Harry tersely. 'I was thinking more about you getting into trouble with your boss for skiving off.' He let go of the door and stepped back from the car. 'Enjoy your trip.' He gave the door a push and turned on the spot, before marching across the car park and towards the house.

Steph let out a sigh. She wasn't quite sure what had happened just then. There was an underlying tension between them since last night which kept rising to the surface.

She put the car into gear and headed out of the resort, her mind still occupied by Harry. Perhaps what happened yesterday at the lake should be put down as a one-off with no strings attached and no expectations from either of them. It certainly seemed to be the way Harry wanted to play it. Perhaps he was regretting their kiss now but didn't know how to tell her he wasn't interested in taking it further. She was an adult; she didn't need treating with kid gloves. She'd tell him once again it was OK, she didn't expect anything else from him and they could put yesterday behind them. She certainly wasn't some sort of bunny-boiler.

Twenty minutes later Steph was parked in the pub car park. She opened her phone and scrolled through her messages and emails. There was one from her editor asking when she would be able to deliver the report and could they have it asap as he wanted to get ahead of the curve and be one of the first, if not *the* first, to publish a report on Conmere. Steph tapped out a reply, confirming she'd have it with him before six that evening. She knew her boss would be working on a Sunday, as the website and the company were his baby, meaning he rarely took time off.

There was a text message from her ex-colleague Adam Baxter.

Hey, Miss Marple, how's it going? Solved the Mystery of The Dead Wife yet?

Steph sent a succinct reply.

Piss off!

She got a response almost immediately, as she thought she would.

Touchy! Seriously, I don't know if you're ruffling feathers over there already but we've had someone ring up asking about you.

Steph reread the text message and her heart gave an extra beat. Someone had been asking about her? She didn't wait to ponder the question any further and hit the call button. Adam answered straight away.

'Thought that might stir you up.'

'Are you being serious?' she asked, dispensing with any niceties.

'One hundred per cent.'

'Who was it?' she asked, looking round for any sign of Sonia.

'I didn't speak to them, Ian did. He seemed to think it was someone from Conmere House.'

Steph tried to remember if she'd even told them of her employment history. She might have mentioned it to Harry when they were chatting on the terrace on Friday night, but she certainly hadn't given him any authority to speak to anyone. 'What did Ian say to them?'

'That he couldn't discuss anything without a formal written request from them and confirmation from you.'

'Thank goodness for that,' said Steph, realising too late that she'd spoken the words out loud.

'What's going on?' asked Adam, the mildly amused tone having now left his voice.

'Nothing's going on.' Even to her own ears she sounded cagey.

'Are you sure? Are you OK?' Adam persisted.

'Yeah. Positive. I don't know what that was all about. I'm doing some work here at Conmere, housekeeping stuff, for the week, just to earn a bit of extra money, but that's all. Maybe it was to do with that.'

'You're not poking around into Elizabeth Sinclair's death, then?' Adam at least made an attempt to sound casual, when Steph was aware he was dying to know really.

'No, I'm not. Nothing to report, as far as I can see,' she lied, aware that she didn't want to share anything with him, partly because she wasn't entirely sure herself what was going on and if anything that had happened actually had any bearing on Elizabeth Sinclair's death.

'Not sure I believe you,' said Adam. 'But I'll let you know if we have any more calls about you.'

'Thanks.' She cancelled the call, trying to decide if she should be concerned or not. She looked around to see where on earth Sonia was. She'd give her another ten minutes and then send her a text. In the meantime, feeling agitated by Sonia's lateness and Adam's call, she decided to call Harry. She'd confront him while she was in the mood for it.

'Hello, Steph,' said Harry. 'Everything OK?'

'Not entirely. I just had an interesting call from one of my ex-employers.' She paused, letting the words hang in the air.

'Right,' he said slowly.

'Apparently, someone from Conmere has been making enquiries about me,' she said, not hiding the annoyance in her voice. 'I am grateful for the job this week in Housekeeping, but I don't remember signing any forms or agreeing to anyone contacting my former employer.'

'Hang on a minute,' interrupted Harry. 'I have no idea what

you're talking about. No one, certainly not me, has called your former employer. What makes you say that?'

She felt her earlier bubble of confidence deflate. 'My old newspaper in Carlisle rang to tell me someone was checking up on my employment history . . .'

'And you automatically assumed it was me?'

'It wasn't?'

'No. It wasn't.' Harry sounded very put out. 'The job is just a one-off – I was doing you a favour as much as you were doing me one. I had no intention of getting in touch with your current or former employers. Do you really think I'd do something like that without asking you first?'

'What about someone from the office?'

He let out a sigh of frustration. 'I haven't told anyone where you worked; it hasn't come up in conversation . . . it hasn't been necessary. I'm telling you, Steph, it wasn't me.'

'Oh, God. I'm sorry,' she said. He sounded genuine and her gut instinct was telling her the same. 'I just assumed.'

'Yeah, well, you know what they say about that.'

'Sorry.'

'Would it have been such a bad thing to get in touch with your former employer? Would they have told me what a hothead you are? How you jump to conclusions? How you're impulsive?' he said and then, dropping his voice, 'That you would be a distraction?'

'Me? A distraction?' She laughed out loud. She was relieved they appeared to be back on good terms.

'I honestly don't know anything about it,' he said. 'I can ask though. Just to put your mind at rest. Maybe it was someone wanting to hire you. Maybe someone had something they wanted you to review or investigate – I don't know.'

It was a good job Harry couldn't see her face; she felt the smile drop like a stone at the apparently casual comment. 'Yeah, maybe,' she said. 'Look, I'd better go. The friend I'm meeting will be here any minute now.'

'OK. I'll see you later.'

God, she felt so confused around him. She couldn't work him out at all. She definitely needed to speak to him later. But before any of that, she needed to know what was going on with Sonia. Steph decided just to phone her instead of messing around with text messages. She pressed the screen on her contact list and the phone began to ring at the other end.

'Steph. I'm sorry I'm not there,' said Sonia, and there was an urgency in her voice. 'I'm about ten minutes away.'

'Is everything OK?'

'Not really. I was followed but I think I might have been able to get away without them noticing.' Her voice was hushed. 'I'm in a taxi. I'll explain once I'm there.'

It was another fifteen minutes before a taxi carrying Sonia Lomas pulled up alongside Steph in the car park. After paying the fare and watching the taxi depart, Sonia jumped into the passenger seat next to Steph.

'What's going on?' asked Steph; she could see from the look on the other woman's face she was frightened. 'What's happened?'

'Ever since I made contact with you, I've had the feeling that someone is watching me. Sometimes I think I'm being followed. I'm getting paranoid. The other day I came home, and I don't know what it was but I just knew someone had been in the house.'

'Was anything taken?'

'Not that I could see. Everything looked exactly how I had left it, but it was just that feeling. Do you know what I mean?'

Steph considered Sonia for a moment. Yes, she did know what she meant. She was sure even if she hadn't come into contact with the intruder in her lodge last night, she would have instinctively known someone had been there. 'I do know what you mean.'

'Have you found anything out?' Sonia looked anxiously out of the window and then turned to look out of the rear window.

'I've only been there a couple of days,' said Steph. She hated admitting she was beginning to think that maybe there was nothing to report after all and Sonia was just desperately grasping at straws. That, over time, the loss of her daughter had sent her into the realms of conspiracy theories, the need to explain her daughter's death properly so great it was clouding reality. However, she wasn't quite ready to dismiss the older woman yet. 'I'm staying on for another week,' she explained. 'I'm hoping to find out some more things then. It will give me a chance to have a look around and ask other people who worked there at the time. That sort of thing.'

'Good, and thank you for believing in me.'

'Is that all you wanted?' asked Steph, thinking it could easily have been said over the phone.

'I came to give you this.' From her bag, Sonia pulled out a hardback notebook, with roses printed on the cover.

'What's this?' asked Steph, taking the notebook Sonia offered her.

'It belonged to Elizabeth. We met one day for lunch. Everything seemed fine. We chatted and left each other afterwards. When I got home, I found this notebook in my bag. I couldn't think where it had come from. When I opened it, I recognised Elizabeth's handwriting straight away.'

Steph looked down at the open book and flicked through the pages. It appeared to be a book where Elizabeth kept reminders for herself, to-do lists, places to go, almost like a filing cabinet but in no particular order. 'What's so important about this?'

'When I phoned to tell her I'd found it, she asked me to look after it. She said it was important to her, but she didn't want it back just yet. I think whoever was in my house was looking for it,' said Sonia. 'It's the only personal item I have of Elizabeth's.'

'Did you show the police this?'

'Yes. I did. And they weren't interested. CID had a look through it and dismissed it. They gave it back to me the next day.'

Steph's stomach gave a roll of unease at the mention of CID. It was highly probable it had been her own mother. She wondered now whether she should come clean and tell Sonia about Wendy. Would Sonia be OK about it or would she think Steph was more likely not to want to find out the truth? Undecided, she looked back at the book. 'Can I keep this?'

'Yes. I think you should. You need to go through it and find out what's in there that's so important.'

Steph had to admit she was a little sceptical that this

notebook would hold the key to Elizabeth's death, but she also knew she couldn't ignore it either. She tucked the A5-sized notebook into her own bag. 'I'll look at it tonight.'

'I know you probably think I'm crazy, but I'm grateful for all you're doing,' said Sonia. 'Not many people are willing to listen to me any more.' She squeezed Steph's hand and her eyes filled with tears. Sonia fumbled in her pocket and found a tissue to wipe her face with. 'I'm sorry. I'm not one for tears, but every now and again I can't help it. I miss Elizabeth so much and even though she wasn't an angel, she was my daughter, my flesh and blood, and I loved her more than anyone else could.'

Steph was struck by the sincerity in Sonia's words and she felt her own throat constrict with emotion. Sonia clearly loved her daughter no matter what sort of relationship they had had or what Elizabeth was like; she could only hope that it was the same for her own mother. She so wanted Wendy to love her the same way. She didn't have to say it, just show it one time; that was all Steph was looking for. She felt an overwhelming wave of empathy towards Sonia and silently vowed that she would do everything in her power to find out what had happened to Elizabeth. Maybe Sonia Lomas could finally lay her ghosts to rest.

'Would you like me to give you a lift back to the station or wherever you're staying?' asked Steph.

'If you don't mind. I didn't ask the taxi to wait as it costs so much and I'm not exactly flush. Elizabeth left me some money, but it wasn't a huge amount.'

'She left her money to you? That was nice of her,' Steph said as she turned the key in the ignition.

'I was surprised and I did offer it back to Harry but he

wouldn't hear of it. My solicitor advised me that Harry had topped the money up himself.'

'Really?'

'Yes. At the time I thought it was hush money, but now I think it was given in the true sentiment of his love for Elizabeth.'

'And you truly believe that?' Steph pulled out of the car park and onto the narrow road which wound its way through the countryside.

'I think there was a certain amount of guilt attached to the money. He said that he wished he could have kept her safe. It was an odd thing to say but at the time I was so full of grief, I didn't really pay it much attention.' Sonia fastened her seat belt. 'Grief does strange things to people and I must admit, I find Harry difficult to read sometimes. Or I used to. When Elizabeth was first married to him, I used to visit and sometimes he'd be happy and other times distant. He was never really at home at Conmere like his brothers and mother were. Elizabeth used to tell him off, said he should be grateful and people would give their eye teeth to be in his position. I always got the impression that Harry felt guilty.'

Steph considered what Sonia had told her and she had to admit, she found Harry difficult to read herself. She wasn't always entirely sure what he was thinking. Sometimes he hid his true emotions and thoughts behind those pale blue eyes of his. What Sonia had said wasn't far off what Harry himself had said about Conmere. Steph knew he didn't feel at home there and he certainly didn't feel comfortable about being back, but why was this? Was it just because of the unhappy memories it stirred up, or was there guilt?

'What do you think Harry feels guilty about?' Steph asked.

Sonia gave a half-laugh. 'What do you think? Either directly or indirectly, he played some part in Elizabeth's death. And if he wasn't responsible, then he should have protected her, he was her husband. He should . . .' she paused to wipe away a tear '. . . he should have loved her more.'

Steph didn't know what to say so she simply reached out and gave Sonia's hand a comforting squeeze, allowing Sonia time with her own thoughts and emotions.

Steph took the road at a steady pace – she wasn't familiar with this part of the Lakes and was relying on her satnav to guide them back to Kendalton Station. She looked in her rear-view mirror as a car came up fast behind them.

'Bloody hell,' muttered Steph. 'Does he want to get in my boot?'

Sonia immediately turned in her seat to look at the car behind, and then back the way they were going. 'He's very close,' she said and Steph could detect an apprehension in her voice.

'I'll pull over when I can and let him by. He's obviously in a hurry.'

She alternated her gaze from the road ahead to the rear-view mirror. The car following them was a black Audi but apart from that Steph didn't know what sort. The sun visor in the Audi was down, partially obscuring the top of the driver's face, while a pair of sunglasses and a scarf hid the rest of it. Steph couldn't even tell if it was male or female but the driver was edging the Audi closer and closer to her. Steph scanned the road ahead for a passing spot, but there was nothing. Suddenly, there was a crunching sound and her car jolted forward.

'He's bumped us!' exclaimed Steph, touching the brakes. 'What an idiot.' She began slowing down but the Audi bumped them again. 'What the . . .?'

'Don't stop!' yelled Sonia. 'Drive faster!'

Steph took one look at Sonia and the expression of pure fear made Steph obey the command. Concentrating solely on the road ahead, she accelerated hard. Her little Fiat 500 wasn't exactly geared up for racing and certainly not for rallying around the Lake District. She was fully aware the road was now climbing higher above a lake on their left. On one side were the hills and on the other an ever-increasing drop down to the water.

'Do you recognise the driver?' shouted Steph as she threw the Fiat around a sharp left-hand bend. She felt the back wheels lose grip for a moment and the tail-end slide but then the ABS kicked in and the tyres found traction.

Sonia turned to look behind them again. 'No. I don't know who they are. Can't you go any faster?'

'I'm doing my best!'

Steph felt another shunt and the Fiat jolted forward; she yanked the steering wheel to the right to avoid the drop. For God's sake, the driver was going to run them off the road, right down the hill and into the water. The road ahead began to open up and she knew the Audi would easily be able to overtake them.

Sure enough, the Audi came alongside them. Steph tried to get a look at the driver but the 4x4 was much higher than her car and she couldn't afford to take her eyes off the road for more than a couple of seconds at a time. She didn't know what to do – sheer power, size and probably skill were too superior for her and her Fiat. There was an almighty scraping noise, followed by Sonia screaming as the Audi swung in towards the Fiat. Steph felt her car bounce off the 4x4 and the wheel jolting out of her hands. She looked up and could see the road was bearing off to the right again but the other car wasn't giving them any room. The Fiat was heading straight for the clump of trees ahead of them. At the last minute the Audi took the bend, but it was too late for Steph. She slammed on the brakes and the car skidded across the verge, throwing itself towards a tree as Sonia screamed for a second time.

Chapter Twenty-Two

The Lake District, Sunday, 12 May, 2.05 p.m.

Steph groaned and, lifting her head, slowly opened her eyes. She was still strapped into the seat and thankfully by some miracle they had missed the trees, the Fiat 500 coming to rest in the small gap between two large conifers. She looked across at Sonia in the passenger seat.

'Are you OK?'

'That was close,' whispered Sonia, her eyes flitting between the trees which shouldered them. 'I thought we were going to hit them.'

'Do you hurt anywhere?'

'I don't think so. Just a bit shocked.'

'Me too.' Fortunately, none of the airbags had deployed, although the engine had cut out. 'Do you want to get out for a moment? I need to inspect the damage.'

Steph walked round and examined the car. Both the door and the rear panel were crumpled where she'd come into contact with the Audi. A big gouge ran from one end to the other and the wing mirror was smashed. Her boot was damaged too. 'Ouch,' said Steph. 'My poor car.'

'Is it still drivable?' asked Sonia, standing alongside Steph.

'I think so. If we can get back onto the road, we should be OK. Are you sure you're not hurt?'

'Just shaken up. I told you someone was following me. You being here has definitely got someone worried.'

Steph looked around; the road was deserted and there was no sign of the Audi. 'We should leave as soon as possible,' she said. 'Do you want to go to the police?'

'No!' Sonia almost shouted the word. 'No, not the police. I don't trust them.'

'But this . . .' Steph gestured to her car. 'This is at least intimidation and dangerous driving, and at worst attempted murder.'

'The police won't want to know. They never have.'

'But there might be different officers now.'

'No, we can't take that risk.'

'Are you saying you think the police are involved somehow?' Steph shivered at the thought, knowing the implications of this.

'I don't know but I don't want to go to them. Not yet, anyway. Look, I can pay to have your car fixed so you don't have to claim on your insurance.'

Steph did appreciate Sonia's offer, but at the same time she wasn't entirely comfortable with accepting it either.

'Please, I insist,' said Sonia, as if understanding her reservations. 'Get it to a garage, get a quote and let me know. I'll transfer the money into your bank account and you can get it all done.'

'It's really kind of you,' said Steph.

'It's the least I can do and it's a small price to pay for my peace of mind, knowing that we must be getting close to finding out the truth about Elizabeth. If there was nothing to hide, then none of this would be happening.'

Steph couldn't deny Sonia had a point and it was one she had been sifting through herself while she was standing there. 'OK, let's see if I can get the car back onto the road. Fingers crossed it will start.'

It seemed the damage was to the bodywork only, as the Fiat started on the first turn of the key, and after a tricky bit of manoeuvring to get out from between the trees Steph was able to drive the car up the bank and onto the road, where Sonia once more sat in the passenger seat.

They arrived at Kendalton Station twenty minutes later and Steph pulled up into a drop-off bay. 'Will you text me when you're home safe?' she asked as Sonia opened the door.

'Yes, and I want you to do the same when you're back at the resort.'

'Stay in touch,' called Steph as Sonia closed the door and headed into the station. Steph remained in the parking bay for a moment, her head resting back as she watched through the railings for Sonia to appear on the platform.

Had that altercation with the 4x4 really happened? Had they actually been purposely run off the road? It seemed so surreal and frightening too. She blinked back a few tears which were threatening to tip from her eyes. She was OK. Sonia was OK. As Sonia said, they must be on to something, otherwise that would never have happened. She didn't think for one moment the Audi episode was a one-off incident, caused by someone being reckless. It had the air of a targeted attack and either she or Sonia were the target, or possibly both of them. Surely, it had something to do with Elizabeth.

There couldn't be any other explanation, could there? She mulled this over. There was, of course, Owen and what she'd assumed was a drug deal taking place, but was that enough to warrant such a serious attack? Were the Sinclairs that ruthless?

Steph saw Sonia walk along the platform and give a small wave. A few minutes later the train pulled into the station and was then on its way. With the platform now empty and Steph reassured that Sonia was safe, she reversed the car out of the space and turned in the direction of Conmere House.

Conmere House, Sunday, 12 May, 2.55 p.m.

Driving into the resort car park, Steph was grateful she didn't have to pass too close to the front of the house. She really didn't want to draw attention to the dented and grazed side of her car. If she was lucky, she'd be able to find a parking spot in the corner and tuck her car away where no one would notice.

Fortunately, she was able to nab a spot bordered by a box hedge. She took her handbag and case from the car and made for the house. She needed to find someone at Reception to tell her what room she was now in. As she entered the main hall, her heart sank: standing at the desk in conversation with the receptionist was Dominic. He looked up as she approached.

'Ah, Miss Durham,' he said, with a smile which looked anything but welcoming. 'We were just talking about you.'

'All good, I hope,' said Steph with little conviction.

'Of course.' Dominic took the key which the receptionist passed to him. 'I'll show you to your room. It's really good of you to stand in like this at such short notice and also when housekeeping isn't a particular glamorous job.'

'I didn't have anything else to do this week and it doesn't matter what the job is – the money is all the same at the end of it.'

'I like your philosophy.' Dominic led her out to the main corridor, and instead of turning right they turned left and went through an open archway. 'Harry told me what happened to you last night. Are you OK?'

'Yes, thank you. I hit my head, but nothing serious.'

'I'm so sorry for what happened,' said Dominic. 'We take security very seriously here and I've instigated a full investigation into how someone might have got onto site and broken into your lodge. Although, from what Harry said, there weren't any signs of a break-in.'

'No, that's the odd thing. I locked the door, so I wondered whether someone had got hold of the master key?'

'Highly unlikely. We don't keep master keys lying around for anyone to pick up,' replied Dominic. 'I know you're adamant you locked the door, but I can't think of any other way someone would gain access.'

'I absolutely did lock the door,' said Steph firmly.

'It's odd that they should just target your lodge,' said Dominic in response. 'But, as I say, we are treating it very seriously and looking into it. Please accept my personal and sincere apologies.'

'Thank you,' said Steph, although she wasn't entirely convinced by Dominic's corporate approach to the whole incident.

They continued along the flagstone flooring and Steph guessed this was an area where the public didn't usually have access. A wooden flight of stairs wound its way to the second floor. 'Just along here,' said Dominic, leading her deeper into the rear of the building. He looked at the key fob. 'There we are. Room 15.' He held the key out for Steph and opened the door for her to step in.

It was a double room with two single beds separated by a bedside table. A double wardrobe stood on the side wall, together with a matching dressing table. It was all very white and clean-looking. Steph opened a door on the opposite wall and poked her head in. 'Oh, an en suite. That's nice.'

'We do try to make our staff feel as comfortable as possible,' said Dominic. 'It's all part of the ethos. Treat our staff with respect and don't make them do anything we wouldn't do ourselves, or indeed sleep or live in any sort of accommodation we wouldn't. There's a communal living room at the end of the corridor and a small kitchen.'

Steph put her case down by the bed. 'Am I sharing with anyone?'

'No. This is empty, so you have it to yourself. Again, we try to give staff their own rooms where possible.' He went over to the window and drew back the curtains. 'I'm afraid it's not much of a view, just the car park. Bloody hell, is that your car down there?'

Steph felt her heart sink. She went over to stand by him at the window and, sure enough, her car could be seen from this wing of the house, the box hedging not tall enough to disguise the damage. 'Yes, that's mine.'

'Is that recent?'

'I did it this afternoon, actually,' said Steph. She had already planned what to say in case anyone asked her. 'I skidded off the road on some mud and managed to side-swipe a wooden fence.'

'Are you OK?'

'Yes, I'm fine but, as you can see, my poor car isn't.'

'Whereabouts did it happen?' asked Dominic, still looking out of the window.

'Round by one of the lakes, on the other side of Con Point Hills.'

'That's a bit out of the way; what were you doing up there?'

'I met a friend and we thought we'd do a bit of sightseeing. My mistake.'

'You need to be careful. The roads round there can be deadly.'

She wasn't sure she liked the way he said the word *deadly* and the way his eyes fixed on hers. 'I misjudged it. I should have slowed,' she said, looking away, not wanting the fear in her own eyes to betray her.

'Sure it wasn't that knock on the head from last night?'

'No. Like I said, mud on the road.' She moved away from the window and hoped Dominic would take this as his cue to leave.

'Is there anything else I can help you with?' he asked, as he walked towards the door.

Steph was about to say no but changed her mind. 'There is actually. You didn't ask anyone to get references from my old employer, did you?'

Dominic looked surprised. 'No, nothing to do with me. I assumed Harry had that all under control – after all, he was the one who offered you the job. Why? Did someone contact them?'

'Yes; it might not have been from here though. I just wondered, that was all.'

'Best speak to Harry.' Dominic paused in the doorway. 'Oh, and tomorrow morning it's an early start. Seven-thirty in the laundry room. Heidi will tell you what you're doing.'

Once Dominic had finally gone, Steph unpacked her case with the few clothes she'd brought, having originally planned just to be here for the weekend. Maybe she'd be issued with a uniform tomorrow; if not she'd have to wash out her jeans. She didn't really want to spend too much money on clothes that she might not wear again.

Next, she plugged in her laptop and opened up a word document. She had promised her boss that she'd have the review to him by that evening and she needed to get it sent off within the next couple of hours if she was to stand any chance of being paid this month.

Conmere House, Sunday, 12 May, 5.10 p.m.

Steph spent the next two hours tapping away at the keyboard and putting together an article her boss would be able to upload onto the *Vacation Staycation* website and a shorter version he could push out to other online places. She also needed to find out if Harry was going to buy any of her photos, otherwise she'd get in touch with her friend Ria to see if she could put any in her gallery.

Once everything was completed, Steph leaned back on the

sofa and let out a whoop. All done and – she checked her watch – well within the deadline. She rolled her shoulders and then her neck; both felt stiff and she wasn't sure if it was from the car accident earlier or from being hunched over the laptop on her bed. A nice walk to clear her head and to loosen up her joints would do her the power of good, she decided, but before that she wanted to take a quick look at the notebook Sonia had given her.

Steph made herself comfortable on her bed and began flicking slowly through the pages. On some of them Elizabeth had jotted down a date, her writing bold and rounded with long tails and carefree dashes. Steph was no handwriting expert but the fluid and confident strokes across the page didn't give her the impression that Elizabeth was a shrinking violet. Her handwriting appeared to match up with the picture of Harry's wife she was now building in her mind.

Steph looked closely at the dated pages and realized these were the weeks leading up to her death. Surely, she wouldn't have given it to Sonia unless it held significant information and maybe something that someone else didn't want to be revealed. There must be something in amongst all the notes, the names, the phone numbers and the things to do that was important. Steph spent the next twenty minutes scouring through the pages. Elizabeth Sinclair had seemed to live her life by appointments at the hairdressers', the spa and dinner dates, the latter usually with Harry.

Steph drummed her fingers on the notebook. Sonia was convinced it was important and that someone was trying to get their hands on it. That made sense to Steph in light of what had happened on the road with the 4x4.

She shivered involuntarily as she replayed the whole car-ramming incident in her mind. It wasn't until now she could fully take on board exactly what had happened. Her stomach clenched and bile rose in her throat. She dashed through to the bathroom and retched over the toilet bowl. When she was convinced she wasn't going to be sick, Steph slumped on the floor, all her energy zapped from her. She cowered in a ball as first her hands, then her arms and finally her whole body began to shake violently for several seconds.

Shock. She knew it was delayed shock. And who could blame her? She made a conscious decision not to fight the physical reaction and waited for the shaking to subside. Carefully, holding on to the sink for support, she got to her feet. Her legs felt wobbly, but she made her way back into the bedroom and flopped down on her bed.

She lay there for some time, allowing her thoughts to wash over her. She wished she could work it all out. This incident had only served to convince her someone out there didn't want her at Conmere. They were trying to frighten both her and Sonia Lomas off.

Admittedly, it was tempting to pack her bags and head off back to the security of Brighton and her undemanding job at *Vacation Staycation*, but Steph knew she couldn't. There was no way she could let this go now. She felt some deep-rooted loyalty to Elizabeth, which was strange, considering they had never known each other. Maybe Sonia was the connection? Steph gave a half-laugh. God, a psychologist would have a field day with her. They'd say she was imprinting on Sonia, that Sonia was the mother she had always craved and now she didn't want to disappoint her or let her down.

Steph sat up and let out a sigh. The sad thing was, there was probably some truth in that self-analysis.

Steph's gaze rested on the notebook. She picked it up, more for a distraction than anything else, and thumbed through it again. The last page was dated 30 August, not long before Elizabeth's death. Steph scanned the handwritten notes.

Saturday 8.00 Dinner with Harry, Owen &
    Natalie
Tues, 10.15 Nails
Cam . . . 230 . . . 2206
01228 404404
Pick up dry-cleaning
Email re massage
Check out flights to Italy & villa

One entry in particular had been circled several times in red biro: *Cam . . . 230*. She couldn't quite read the word, as the handwriting was a little messier than Elizabeth's usual style. She studied it again. Cameron? Wasn't that the name of the man from the pub whom Elizabeth was supposed to be having an affair with?

She flipped the notebook shut with a frustrated sigh. She needed to be proactive. Cameron seemed as good a place as any to start. She'd drive down to the next village and see if she could speak to him. He might be able to give her an insight or some useful bit of info about what had happened when they'd met up that day. She wasn't entirely sure what she was going to ask him, but she'd work on that on the way. At least she was doing something now, and it was certainly better than sitting around, getting herself all worked up over the incident earlier. She needed to toughen up if she wanted to be an investigative journalist.

Steph was about to put the notebook safely away in her case, when she changed her mind. Someone might be desperate to get hold of this and if they managed to steal it she'd have no record at all.

It was a laborious task, but one that needed to be done, as Steph methodically took a photograph on her phone of each page and, one by one, emailed them to herself, then opening each email and downloading the contents to her drop box. That way she would still be able to access a copy. For good measure, she also copied them onto a memory stick.

'Talk about covering all bases,' she muttered to herself as she then hid the memory stick in the bottom of her case.

Before she left her room, Steph made sure her laptop was back in its bag and tucked away in the wardrobe. She took her handbag and her memory stick with her. She could easily replace the laptop if it was stolen, but not the work. Although, tucked away up here in the staff quarters, anyone trying to break into her room would have to be pretty brazen, she thought as she locked her door and tested the handle several times. She put the key into the inside pocket of her bag and zipped it up.

Chapter Twenty-Three

The Nag's Head Pub, Sunday, 12 May, 6 p.m.

The pub had that lazy Sunday evening atmosphere to it. The hustle and bustle of the lunchtime trade was now over and a more relaxed feel had settled, with the quiet conversation of a few customers mingling with the sound of the background music. It was comfortable and welcoming, Steph thought as she picked up a bar menu, not because she was hungry but to give her a little longer to take in her surroundings and suss out the bar staff.

There was a man and a woman serving behind the bar. The woman looked to be in her mid-twenties and the man older, possibly late thirties. They didn't look like a couple and Steph wondered if the man was Cameron. She had no idea what a typical pub landlord cum yoga instructor was supposed to look like. The man looked up and gave her a nod of acknowledgement as he pulled a pint and placed it on the bar for a customer.

'Cheers, Cam,' said the customer, taking a £5 note from his wallet and passing it over.

So he was Cameron, Steph thought. He was good-looking,

she decided as she took a closer look at him; his blond hair was cut short at the sides and a little longer on the top. He had good cheekbones and, as he turned back from giving the customer his change, he smiled at Steph, giving her the full benefit of his white teeth and notably green eyes.

'What can I get you?' he asked, coming over, fixing his gaze on her in such a way that Steph could feel herself almost blush and was then immediately annoyed with herself for such a reaction. She wondered if Elizabeth had been flustered at just the sight of Cameron. It probably hadn't been difficult to flirt a little and then for one thing to lead to another. In that one look, Steph got the distinct impression that Cameron, or Cam, as the man had called him, was permanently on the prowl.

'Diet Coke, please,' she said, realising he was waiting for her response.

'Ice?'

There was that smile again; it was almost cheeky. How could anyone make a simple question seem as though they were already sharing a private joke?

'Please,' Steph replied, hoping her flush hadn't reached her face.

He placed the drink in front of her. 'What else can I do for you?' he asked, resting an arm casually across the pumps. He now somehow managed to add a mischievous twinkle to his eyes.

Get a grip, girl, Steph scolded herself. She took a sip of her drink. 'Actually, I'm looking for Cameron,' she said, realising she had no idea of his surname. She gave a smile, hoping it would have the same hypnotic effect as his.

Cameron raised an eyebrow. 'Who's asking?'

'I'm a friend of Elizabeth Sinclair,' said Steph carefully, and instantly registered the slight change in his demeanour. The muscles in his jaw twitched and his shoulders tightened.

'And?' he said after a long pause.

'And I wondered if I could talk to you about her? You are Cam, aren't you? You look the way she described you,' she said, hoping flattery was his Achilles heel.

'How might that be?'

She'd guessed right. She gave a small giggle and dropped her gaze briefly, while simultaneously running her fingers through her loose hair. God, she was making herself cringe, but Cameron seemed to be buying into the act. 'Blond. Good-looking. Great eyes. She also mentioned other attributes, but I can only go by what I can see.'

'We could remedy that,' he said, moving to the side of the pumps and resting both arms on the bar.

Steph smiled and took another sip of her drink. If he thought this was going to go any further, he'd be disappointed, but until then she needed to capitalise on her position. 'Look, I'll be straight with you,' she said, acknowledging that she actually wasn't going to be. 'Elizabeth did talk to me about you, told me you were her yoga teacher, but she also said she knew you well, if you know what I mean – that you two were close.'

'It was a couple of years ago now. I'm really sorry about what happened to her but . . .' He paused and lowered his voice. 'Yes, we were close, but it was just a bit of fun. It certainly wasn't worth all the hassle it caused.'

For some reason it annoyed Steph that Cameron was dismissing Elizabeth so easily, as if she wasn't very important.

'She thought it was a bit more than that. She risked quite a lot.' OK, she didn't know that for a fact, but Steph had an overwhelming urge to fight Elizabeth's corner, and a little liberty with the truth wasn't the end of the world.

Cameron straightened up. 'Why are you asking all this?' A frown creased his forehead. 'What did you say your name was?'

'I'm Steph. I'm asking because I miss her, that's all. I came up here with the intention of going to see her husband, Harry, but I know they weren't getting on that well and I'm not sure I'd be welcomed by the Sinclairs.'

Cameron gave a snort. 'Yeah, they're not exactly the most welcoming bunch.'

'I tried to phone Harry but he didn't want to speak to me. I just wanted to talk about Elizabeth, that's all.' She ran her finger around the edge of her glass. 'You don't sound like you're their biggest fan.'

Cameron eyed her, this time without his Casanova gaze. 'Not exactly. Now, do you want to cut the bullshit and tell me what you're really doing here?'

Steph knew the game was up and kicked herself. She might as well come clean. She had nothing to lose and so much to gain. Cameron was hardly likely to go blabbing to the Sinclairs either. 'OK. Elizabeth's mother, Sonia Lomas, asked me to do some digging. She's not convinced her daughter's death was an accident. I'm sure you know that anyway.'

'I'd heard.'

'Well, I'm here to report on the reopening of the Sinclair resort and Sonia convinced me to have a look into Elizabeth's death.'

'You're a reporter?'

'Travel reporter. I'm just doing this for Sonia. I'm not working for a newspaper or anything.' She took out her *Vacation Staycation* identity badge and showed it to Cameron. 'Your name was in Elizabeth's notebook and really I'm just trying to get another opinion on what happened, or what you think might have happened, or what sort of people the Sinclairs are.'

'A bunch of bastards, that's what sort they are,' said Cameron. He glanced back at the bar. 'Holly, look after the bar for ten minutes?' He nodded towards a booth on the far side. Steph noticed he walked with a slight limp.

'Thanks,' said Steph as she sat down in the booth opposite him.

'I haven't got much to say,' began Cameron. 'But those Sinclairs think they're above the law. I've never come across such an arrogant family.'

'All of them? Even Harry Sinclair?'

'Him especially. They're a bunch of control freaks for a start. Dominic makes out he's all for the community and giving something back to the local economy, but that's only when it suits him. Yeah, he'll scratch your back and all that, but you have to give the biggest scratch – it's not a fair exchange.'

This wasn't a particular surprise to Steph. She'd already decided Dominic was the most scheming of all the brothers. She hadn't quite worked out Owen's angle, but he was an instantly dislikable character and she was certain drugs were only the tip of the iceberg. Harry, though . . . she was surprised he was being tarred with the same brush. 'Harry

Sinclair didn't much like you, from what I hear,' she said, steering the conversation.

Cameron gave a laugh. 'You can say that again. He thought there was something serious going on between me and Elizabeth but like I said, it was just a bit of fun.'

'That's not what she said.' Steph was beginning to feel a little frustrated at the lack of forward motion in the conversation.

'Like I said, we were close. She was bored. Lonely. I was single. I didn't go looking for anything; she came to me. I actually felt sorry for her.'

It was the first time anyone, apart from Sonia, had shown any compassion or empathy for Elizabeth. Not even Harry had said anything like this, and Elizabeth had been his wife. Steph wondered how close to rock bottom their marriage had sunk. 'It can be quite isolating being up at Conmere day and night.'

'Exactly. Elizabeth could go for days without speaking to anyone outside of that family. It's like a fucking cult, that place.'

'How long were you both close to each other?' ventured Steph, clear they were both using shorthand.

'About eight weeks. Personally, I would have been happy for it to be a few more weeks but I'm not young and naive enough to think it's as easy as that. It wasn't what Elizabeth really wanted. I was just an escape from it all.'

'Did she call your . . . friendship off?'

'Only because she had to. Harry wasn't keen on her coming over.'

'What happened with Harry?'

'The bloke's a bloody nutcase. It's the quiet ones you have to watch.'

'Really?'

'Yes. Really. He went ballistic. Came down to the pub – he'd obviously been drinking. He was shouting and a bit unsteady on his feet but it didn't stop him trying to drag me across the bar. Grabbed hold of my shirt and punched me right in the face.' Cameron touched the bump in his nose. 'I have a permanent reminder.'

Steph looked at him in disbelief. 'I can't imagine him doing that.'

'Then you don't really know him.'

Cameron had a point, she thought, but tried to console herself with the fact that Harry might not be the same man now that he had been back then. It was supposed to be a comforting thought, but by the same token, it was quite possible, back then, that the 'old Harry' was capable of being more violent. 'Did you fight back?'

'What do you think? I was too busy trying to defend myself, and look at me – I'm not built for fighting. I'm not a muscle-bound gym junkie. I'm all about stretching and relaxation. Or as much as I can do these days.' He patted the top of his leg.

It was true, Cameron was slight and flexible-looking, not really a match for Harry. 'What happened to your leg?' asked Steph, sensing it was relevant in some way.

'Hit-and-run,' said Cameron. He pursed his lips before speaking again. 'Same night as Harry Sinclair attacked me in the bar, as it happens. Funny, that. His brothers were there and they pulled him off me in the end and I thought that was that, it was all over. Harry's ego had been restored. I had a bloodied nose, but nothing that wouldn't heal.'

'What happened?' Steph's arms pricked with goose pimples. She was sure she wasn't going to like the next bit.

'Locked up that night. Walked the barmaid home. Oops, sorry, I'm probably not allowed to say barmaid these days, am I? Anyway, walked my female colleague home, as I didn't like the thought of her walking home alone in the dark and she didn't have a fella. As I was coming round the corner of the lane, this car came from nowhere and mowed me down. Right in the middle of the street.'

'Oh, my God. That's awful. Did they stop?' Steph swallowed hard. Despite the question, she was pretty sure she could guess the answer.

'Nope. Drove straight off. Left me lying in the road with a fractured thigh. That was my warning to leave Elizabeth well alone.'

'You think . . .' She couldn't bring herself to say out loud what she was thinking.

'Yes. I do. And, just so we're clear about this, I'm one hundred per cent certain it was Harry Sinclair, either directly or indirectly.'

Steph gulped down an eruption of fear at the thought of Harry committing such a horrific act of premeditated violence. If Cam was to be believed, then he could easily have been killed that night. 'Did you go to the police?' Her voice still harboured a note of incredulity.

'They weren't interested. Yeah, they made all the right noises but it was a half-hearted attempt at catching whoever it was. They said without a witness or registration plate they had no chance of questioning anyone.'

'What about CCTV?'

'Well, there's the thing. Turns out the only CCTV in that part of the road belongs to one of the local residents, who has a camera angled at their garage. And that particular night it wasn't working. Convenient, that.'

'You think they—?'

'I don't think,' interrupted Cameron. 'I know. I just can't prove anything.'

'The police officer who dealt with this – do you remember their name?' The goose pimples crept across her neck and swept down Steph's spine.

'I can't remember her name but she was a right sourpuss from CID.'

It had to be Wendy, surely. Steph gripped her glass to stop her hand from shaking. Wendy had warned her off getting involved. At the time Steph had thought it was for her own safety, but now it seemed increasingly likely Wendy was trying to protect herself. Just how much was her mother involved with the Sinclairs? 'Weren't there any witnesses in the pub who could have spoken up for you and made the police take the hit-and-run more seriously, or at least question the Sinclairs?'

'No one wanted to come forward. Basically, no one wanted to cross the Sinclairs. To add insult to injury, the family cancelled my beer contract with them and the yoga classes I used to run up at Conmere.'

'Just like that?'

For the first time Cameron looked a little embarrassed. 'Well, I took some compensation from them.'

'They paid you off?' The words came out unchecked.

'Keep your voice down,' hissed Cameron, giving the pub

a quick glance. 'Put it this way, they made me an offer I couldn't refuse,' he said in an adopted New York City gangster accent.

They fell into a small silence as Steph contemplated Cameron's revelation. At a push, she could imagine Harry being angry and possibly confronting him in the pub, but the idea that he'd punched Cameron didn't sit that comfortably with her. It was hard to imagine Harry doing such a thing; he seemed so in control of his emotions, or at the very least kept his emotions in check. What little she knew of him, he didn't strike her as someone who flew off the handle. So the idea that he had purposely run Cameron down in his car was verging on the ridiculous. Or was that because she didn't want to believe it of him? She tried to nudge her own personal feelings to the side. Was the Harry of two years ago a different man to the Harry of today? Had the death of his wife changed him? Or was it just a different side of him she hadn't yet witnessed? She hadn't seen the vindictive side of him, the side where reprisal didn't just mean at the public humiliation of a beating but also a premeditated and chilling act of violence, a potentially fatal action. And, as if that wasn't enough, to pay for Cameron's silence too. Was Harry capable of this? If he was, did it also make him capable of murder?

'Look, I need to get back to the bar,' said Cameron, breaking into her thoughts.

'Yeah, sure. Thanks for talking to me,' said Steph, standing up. 'Oh, sorry, just one more thing.' She rummaged in her bag and withdrew her notebook, flicking to the page where she'd made notes of some of the things in Elizabeth's book. 'Does Cameron 230 2206 mean anything to you?'

Cameron craned his neck to look at the page. He shook his head. 'Nope. Should it?'

'Elizabeth wrote it in her notebook.'

'Sorry, can't help you there, but she never called me Cameron, always Cam.'

'OK, thanks.' Steph put the notebook back in her bag. Elizabeth's handwriting had looked a bit rushed to Steph when she had copied it down. She'd go back and have another look at it.

'Mind how you go,' said Cameron. 'You seem like a nice person.'

'Oh, don't worry about me. I'm tougher than I look.'

'All the same, watch your step.'

Conmere, Sunday, 12 May, 6.55 p.m.

When Steph arrived back at Conmere, the evening sky was clear and the residual sun still strong enough to warm her face. She loved evenings like this usually but tonight her enjoyment had been tainted by thoughts of Harry and the alleged attack on Cameron. No matter how hard she tried, she couldn't imagine Harry doing such a thing.

Parking her car, she decided to go for a walk rather than back to her room, hoping the fresh air would help her think straight. With no particular destination in mind, Steph took a stroll through the resort. The car incident had certainly shaken her up, more than she had let on to Sonia and certainly more than the impression she had given Dominic. He would probably tell Harry, and Steph wondered if that would spur him into coming to see her. She was finding it hard to keep her burgeoning personal relationship with Harry separate from her undercover investigation into Elizabeth's death. Her journalistic brain was telling her that statistically Harry would be the one most likely to have harmed Elizabeth, and yet the Harry she knew, the man she had spoken to on the terrace on Friday night, the Harry she'd spent time with on Saturday and the same Harry who had looked after her last night, was not one she could associate with killing anyone, let alone his wife.

There was, of course, the Harry who confused her. The one who blew hot and cold in the time it took to say those words. She wanted to believe it was because he might be feeling guilty that he was betraying his wife's memory, but there was also the possibility that the Harry she liked was fake and every now and then his mask slipped.

She tried to set the facts out logically in her mind.

He was the one who had found her in her lodge.

He had access to a spare key.

He was a prime candidate for having something to hide.

He had known she was going out for a ride in the car today.

He might be playing her. He might not actually be interested in her at all. She had to admit, this last notion hurt. She didn't like the idea that he was using her to find out what she knew or whether she had an alternative agenda here. Which, of course, she did, but she didn't want him to know that. She also acknowledged the double standards here.

She couldn't make sense of Harry, not yet.

As she walked along the track which led towards the north

of the resort she saw a lodge set back into the trees. It looked far grander than the regular lodges in the park. It was much larger and there was a veranda which ran across the front of the property. It reminded Steph of something she'd seen on American TV. She half expected an old-age pensioner to be sitting there on a swing seat, smoking a pipe.

'Hello, can I help you?'

Steph started at the voice behind her. She turned and saw a woman roughly her own age with a child of about five years and a double buggy with twin toddler boys.

'Oh, sorry,' said Steph. 'I was just admiring this lodge. I'm a guest here – well, I was for the weekend, but now I'm staying on for the week to help out with housekeeping.'

The woman's face relaxed and she smiled. 'Oh, you must be Steph. I was told about you.' She put the brake on the buggy. 'My name's Natalie Sinclair; I'm married to Owen, Harry's brother.'

'Pleased to meet you,' said Steph, holding out her hand. She noted that Natalie had added the caveat of Harry's brother and obviously knew that she and Harry were on good terms. She wondered how much Harry had told his family about their relationship.

Natalie shook her hand. 'This is where Owen and I live with this little gang,' she said. 'It's close to the main part of the resort but far enough away to feel like we're not living on top of his mother.'

'I didn't realise that. I assumed you lived in the main house or off-site,' said Steph, once again admiring the facade of the property.

'No. We've all got our own lodges. Dominic's is over there,

a bit behind ours, and Harry's is the other side. Although Harry doesn't like being in his too much since . . . since he's been widowed.'

Steph couldn't believe her luck at the opening Natalie had given her. 'Yes, it's terrible what happened to Elizabeth. Of course, she was your sister-in-law; were you two close?'

'We got on well,' said Natalie. 'There was a certain camaraderie between us. We were the interlopers into the family – the outsiders who became the insiders.' She laughed. 'I'm exaggerating, of course, but you know what I mean. It's not always easy marrying into a tight-knit family like the Sinclairs with Pru at the helm.'

'But you get a beautiful home in beautiful surroundings,' said Steph, hoping to keep Natalie at her ease. She was easy to talk to and willing to talk. In the few minutes they had spoken to each other, Steph had got the impression that Natalie was a bit lonely and was enjoying the chance to have a friendly chat. Cameron had already told her that Elizabeth had felt lonely – had she been desperate for a friend in the weeks and months before she died?

Steph looked down at the twin boys in the buggy and the older child, a girl, who was crouched down investigating something in the dirt. 'You look like you have your hands full.'

'Oh, they keep me busy all right,' said Natalie. 'The boys came along rather sooner than anticipated and at double the number than anticipated.' She spoke warmly about the children and Steph could see just from her expression how much she adored her family.

'Have they got any cousins?' asked Steph, already knowing the answer.

'Dominic has a teenage son from his first marriage who lives with his mother, and he's got a daughter, who's seven, with his partner, Lisa. Their daughter is a great playmate for Tilly.' She nodded in the direction of her daughter.

'Harry doesn't have children?'

Natalie threw a look that told Steph she was surprised by the question. Steph quickly covered herself. 'I'm assuming he doesn't, as he hasn't mentioned them.'

'No, he doesn't,' said Natalie, with what sounded like a touch of sorrow. 'He would have made a good dad, but Elizabeth wasn't too keen.' She stopped and suddenly looked embarrassed. 'I'm sorry, you'll have to excuse me, gabbling on like that. Owen is always telling me I talk too much.'

'Oh, it's OK,' said Steph, touching Natalie's arm as if they were old friends. 'I won't tell if you don't.'

The sound of a diesel engine made both women look round and Steph saw a taxi coming to a halt in front of them. Owen Sinclair emerged and looked at her. Then, walking over to them, he kissed Natalie on the cheek and made a fuss of the children before saying hello to Steph.

'I was just taking a walk,' said Steph. 'I was admiring your house when I bumped into your wife.'

Owen nodded but his face was unsmiling.

'What are you doing in a taxi?' asked Natalie as the car performed a U-turn and drove off. 'Where's your car?'

'Bloody thing,' said Owen. 'Something to do with the electronics. Managed to disable itself. Someone from the garage is going to look at it.'

Natalie gave a sigh. 'And they say German cars are supposed to be some of the most reliable cars.'

Steph tensed at this comment. German? The car that had run her off the road had been an Audi. Owen's car was in the garage needing fixing – apparently it was the immobiliser – but could it be an Audi? She looked at Owen, who glared back at her. 'Actually, my car needs to go into the garage too,' she said, hoping she sounded light-hearted. 'I had a bit of trouble with it this afternoon. I managed to slide off the road and hit a fence. The bodywork needs repairing.' She watched Owen's face for any sign he knew what she was talking about.

'Oh, no,' said Natalie. 'I hope it doesn't cost you too much.'

'I hope so too,' said Steph.

'I need to make a few calls about the car,' said Owen, taking Tilly's hand. He nodded a goodbye at Steph and walked off towards the lodge.

'I'd better go in too,' said Natalie, twirling the buggy round. 'Nice talking to you. Might see you again in the week.'

'Yeah, that would be nice,' said Steph. She watched them walk away, unsure what to make of Owen. He wasn't like either of his brothers, who came across as confident, possibly over-confident at times. Owen was more . . . she scratched around for the right word . . . timid. He showed great bravado but it was just a show, she was sure. She'd seen the way his eyes were always darting around as if he was some sort of prey and danger was hot on his heels. The little tic he had running his hand across the back of his neck – she'd noticed him doing that more and more.

Chapter Twenty-Four

Conmere, Sunday, 12 May, 7.05 p.m.

Steph still felt unsettled as Natalie and her family unit disappeared into their home. She turned and continued walking through the woods, finding herself navigating in the vague direction of Dominic's house. She wasn't sure what had made her do so, but it wasn't long before she came upon another super-lodge, which could only belong to Dominic.

It was a Colonial-style house and looked as if it should be in the glossy pages of *Vacation Staycation* as a luxury home to rent for those families with an equally luxurious income. It was more modern and certainly more ostentatious than Owen's. It was bigger, for a start, and if the size of the picture window in the staircase was an identifier as to rank within the family, then Dominic's won hands-down. The porch didn't just sit at the front of the house as his brother's did, it wrapped itself around both sides of the property. There was also a matching first-floor balcony and two sets of double doors opening onto the front of the balcony from either side of the feature window. The driveway swept in a loop around a central grassed area and there was a double garage on the far side.

Wow. It looked like serious money here.

Keeping to the path and away from the boundary fence which marked Dominic's private residence, Steph worked her way around the perimeter, but the high fencing and heavily planted shrubs and bushes ensured this part of the house was kept extremely private.

The trees at the back of Dominic's house were denser and the height of the trees blocked out much of the light, leaving Steph feeling somewhat colder than before. As she left Dominic's house behind her, she knew she was now consciously seeking out Harry's house. She was dying to know what sort of property he and Elizabeth had lived in, not necessarily because she thought it would help with her investigation, but because she wanted to know what Harry's tastes were like. She wanted to know as much about him as she could. Even to her own mind, it sounded borderline stalking, but she was so drawn towards him, it was unnerving.

The crack of a stick made Steph spin round. She half expected to see someone walking along behind her, but there didn't seem to be anyone there. She completed a 360-degree turn, scanning the forest for any sign of movement. One tree blurred into another as she completed a second turn. No one and nothing was there. All at once, she felt unexpectedly afraid.

The need to get out of the forest and back onto the main part of the resort meant Steph having to abandon her idea of finding Harry's lodge. She picked up the pace, calculating that retracing her steps would take significantly longer than trusting her sense of direction and heading further round in a circle towards the resort. She estimated she had almost completed a semicircle around Dominic and Owen's houses.

Another crack of a branch and a rustle of the leaves had Steph looking back over her shoulder again. The forest seemed even darker now and she wondered if another bout of rain was about to hit. A movement in her peripheral vision had Steph whirling round. A dark shape darted behind a tree. Her breath caught in her throat, memories of the intruder from the night before orbiting to the fore. There was another noise, indistinct, coming from the same direction and she thought she saw something move again.

Steph spun on her heel. She could feel panic taking over, forcing her to break into a run. She didn't know where she was going but she was running as fast as she could away from whatever it was. Then there came a thudding noise that sounded like feet hammering the earth. She threw a look over her shoulder as she continued to run.

From out of the foliage sprang a deer, followed by another and then another. They galloped across the path, disappearing for a few moments, before appearing again as they wove their way in and out of the trees.

'Deer!' cried Steph in relief. 'It's only deer.' She slowed her pace and as she turned to see where she was going she ran straight into someone. This time she let out an ear-piercing scream as two hands grabbed her shoulders.

'It's OK. Steph! It's me, Harry.'

Steph took a moment to compute the words and to register the voice. She gave in to the struggle and focused on the face before her. 'Oh, God. I mean, thank God.'

Harry's grip loosened on her arms. 'What was all that about?'

Steph took a deep breath and slowly got her breathing under control. 'I was being silly,' she said, feeling embarrassed now. 'I heard something behind me back there. I thought someone was following me. Turned out to be deer.'

'Ah, the deer. Yes, we've got quite a lot of them in the forest. I thought you knew that?' He smiled with amusement.

Steph felt even more silly now. 'I knew that, I just spooked myself, that's all.' She gave a look which dared him to challenge her. 'Anyway, what are you doing creeping around in the woods?'

He chuckled. 'Not exactly creeping around.' He turned and pointed over to his left. 'That's my house right there. I was coming out to top up the bird feeder when I saw you running right this way.'

Steph looked beyond him and sure enough, there was another lodge-styled house sitting in amongst the trees, this one smaller than the other brothers' houses, but one whose finish stood out above those for holidaymakers on the resort. There was a laurel hedge and a wooden gate opening out onto the forest from the back garden.

'Have you been here all afternoon?' she asked.

'No. I was out with Owen earlier.'

'Owen?'

'Yeah. We went into town. A bit of time together. I haven't seen him for several months. It was good to catch up, just the two of us.'

'Actually, I saw Owen and Natalie a little while ago. He said about his car.' She purposely didn't expand, waiting to see what Harry had to add.

'His car?'

'Yeah, his car.'

'The one that decided to trigger its own immobiliser?'

Steph felt a glimmer of relief. Owen could possibly be telling the truth, or, of course, they could both be sticking to a story they'd concocted between themselves. 'He said it had to go into the garage.'

'Fortunately, it's just the old Audi we all share,' said Harry. 'It used to belong to my dad. Mum didn't want to get rid of it, so we kept it, and now if anyone just wants to nip into town we take the Old Bastard.'

'The Old Bastard?'

'That's what Dad used to call it. He didn't like it but he'd already spent the money and, Dad being Dad, was too pig-headed and too tight to trade it back in for something he did like. In fact, I think he liked hating it. He liked hating a lot of things.'

'One old bastard deserves another, I suppose,' said Steph.

Harry grinned. 'Something like that. Anyway, the car had been left in town earlier this morning. Mum had gone in to meet a friend for coffee and they went off in her friend's car, and then Mum was dropped straight home. So Owen and I went in to get it.'

Steph felt the earlier relief slide away. 'The car was in town on its own all day, then?'

'I suppose so. Why?'

'Nothing. It doesn't matter.' She couldn't say out loud what she was thinking, that one of them could have been driving the car that ran her off the road. She forced a reassuring smile.

'Anyway, I hear from Dominic that your car needs a bit of TLC.'

'You could say that. I don't know what happened; I slipped on some mud on the road and the next thing the car was sliding off onto the verge and hit a fence.'

'As long as you're OK, that's the main thing,' said Harry. He dipped his head to look at her. 'You are OK, aren't you?'

'Sure.' She wanted to say that physically she was OK but mentally she was bruised. Her head hurt and that wasn't from the bump last night, more from trying to figure out what on earth was going on in this place.

'Actually, Steph, I'm glad I've caught you . . . both literally and figuratively,' began Harry. 'I wanted to talk to you.'

She met his eyes head-on. 'I've been wanting to talk to you too.'

'I'm guessing it's probably about the same thing.'

'Probably.'

'Us.'

She nodded. 'That will be the one. I have to admit I've been a bit confused after what happened yesterday morning,' she said, deciding to get straight to the point and make it easier for him. 'I'm not expecting anything from you or anything more than what happened yesterday. Like I said, I've got no hidden agenda to try to trap you. I know you're probably still grieving for your wife and being back here is probably making it very difficult for you.'

'Stop. Stop right there.' He took her hands in his. 'I agree with everything you've just said.'

'You do?' She couldn't help feeling a touch deflated. He could have cushioned the blow a little.

'I do,' he continued. 'I haven't been able to stop thinking about you. You've been on my mind constantly. You have no idea how much restraint it took me last night to sleep on the sofa.'

'That's kind of you to say.'

'Jesus, Steph, I haven't just complimented you on a dress or your hairstyle. Stop being so matter-of-fact about it all.'

She winced at his words. It wasn't the first time she'd been accused of being stand-offish and shutting off her emotions. It was something she was aware she did by way of self-preservation, possibly to counter her feelings of rejection by her mother. 'I'm sorry,' she said eventually. 'I'm not very good at relationships, in case you hadn't gathered. Shit relationship with my mum. An even shitter one with my ex-husband, hence the ex-tag.' She gave a self-deprecating shrug.

'I'm pretty shit at them too, if I'm honest,' said Harry. 'Have avoided them like the plague since Elizabeth died.'

'So why exactly are we having this conversation?'

He paused and when he spoke his voice was no more than a whisper. 'Because I really like you.'

Steph let out a long, slow breath to steady her rapidly beating heart. It was true, something was different this time. Something she didn't recognise and something that frightened her yet excited her at the same time. Something which made her want to throw caution to the wind. So much so that when he drew her towards him and planted his lips on hers she didn't hesitate to respond, despite a voice in her head trying to warn her that this was dangerous. Harry was dangerous. The whole Sinclair family was dangerous. Yet, right at that moment, it was as though he had some mesmerising hold over her and there was nothing she could do to fight it, nothing she wanted to do.

When they broke for air, more from necessity than desire, Harry nuzzled her neck and breathed in deeply. 'Let's go inside,' he said.

The few seconds it took to get indoors were all that was needed to break the moment. Stepping inside, Steph felt self-conscious and awkward. Harry closed the door and turned to kiss her, but something about her demeanour must have alerted him. He gave a long appraising look which was followed by a small smile.

'Tea? Something stronger?' he said.

Steph felt the tension in her body dissipate and she was grateful for his subtlety. 'Tea would be nice.'

As Harry went into the kitchen to make her a drink, Steph took in her surroundings. The decor was calm and soothing, soft greys, warm whites and the odd splash of colour here and there. She was in the dining area, which was open plan to the living room at the front of the property. Oak furniture and oak flooring brought the lodge feel of the property into focus.

'It's a bit spartan,' said Harry, coming out of the kitchen with two mugs in his hand. He nodded towards the living room.

'I like the minimalistic look,' said Steph. Although, to be fair, he had taken it to the extreme with just one sofa and a chair.

'I got rid of a lot of stuff. I thought I wouldn't be coming back here again once I left the business side of things,' said Harry.

'You never properly answered my question the other day – what made you come back?' Steph asked. 'If you don't like it here and technically aren't involved with the business any more, what was it?'

'Because my mum asked me to come for the reopening. She wanted to put up a united front. It's what the Sinclairs do.' He gave a roll of his eyes. 'I wouldn't be here if she hadn't asked. I try to spend as little time here as possible.'

'Because of what happened?'

'What do you think?' He gave her a look which said she really didn't have to ask.

'Sorry. I didn't mean to sound insensitive. It must be awful.' Steph went to say more but changed her mind. She wanted to know so much more about his life here before Elizabeth had died, but at the same time she didn't want to hurt him by digging up painful memories. It wasn't exactly the mark of a good reporter, she acknowledged, but her conscience prevailed.

Harry hadn't missed her hesitation. He put the mugs down on the coffee table. 'What were you going to say?'

She thought of Sonia and the pleading look in her eyes. She thought of Elizabeth – there was so much more to know. She reached out for his hand. 'Do you miss . . . do you miss what you had before?'

'Elizabeth?'

'Was it a happy marriage?'

'You're quite direct when you want to be. Is this the reporter in you?'

'No. It's the woman in me.'

His thumb stroked her knuckles. 'Elizabeth and I were very happy when we first married. It was a bit of a whirlwind romance, as they say, but I thought after ten months we were both confident about how we felt for each other. We married eighteen months after first meeting.'

'Did anyone say anything about it being too soon?'

Harry let go of her hand and with a small sigh sat down on the sofa. 'In our eyes it wasn't too soon but, yes, they did. My mother was particularly vocal about it. Not in front of Elizabeth though, which I was grateful for. It's hard enough coming into a tight-knit family without the knowledge that more than one member of the family isn't exactly happy about it.'

'Who else? Dominic?' asked Steph, sitting down next to him.

'Owen, actually. Dominic was in no position to talk. He was divorced, had been through numerous girlfriends in quite quick succession, and was living with Lisa, who was the mother of his daughter. Lisa was there by default more than anything else, but they have a stable relationship now.'

'What was Owen's problem, then?'

'He had a long, and I mean long, engagement with Natalie. Something like five years, before he finally asked her to marry him. I think he was making sure she'd put up with him before tying the knot, only to have it unravel at some point.'

'Do you think Owen and your mum had reason to be cautious?'

Harry didn't answer immediately, but when he did his tone was more sombre. 'Elizabeth and I had a lot of fun in the early days. We did lots of things together, but after the wedding I had to knuckle down. The business was going well and we were really busy, trying to expand. Work took up a lot of my time. And when I say a lot, I mean it.' He blew out a long breath. 'I spent all hours working and I didn't see it at the time, but it meant I neglected my marriage. Elizabeth found other ways to amuse herself. But deep down I knew she wouldn't settle for just being someone who stayed at home. I knew she wasn't like Natalie.'

'Didn't you want children together?'

He gave a small rise of his eyebrows and she wondered for a moment if she'd asked too much, but he answered after a moment's pause. 'I did, but at some point in the future. Elizabeth agreed, it's just that her point in the future was a lot further away than mine. She still wanted fun and excitement. Elizabeth always wanted more. I thought I could keep up but I took my eye off the ball.'

'It takes more than one person to make a marriage.'

'But only one to break it.'

'It doesn't sound like that was you.'

'Depends how you look at it. Just because I didn't pull the trigger, it doesn't mean I didn't load the gun.'

'I think you're being very harsh on yourself,' said Steph. She thought back to what Cameron had said about Harry's temper. She still couldn't reconcile his version of Harry with the version before her. 'You sound very calm about it all.'

'Time does that to you.'

Her heart beat a little faster as she realised this was her chance to find out from Harry his side of the story. 'Did Elizabeth have an affair?'

The silence stretched before them and she could see the look of indecision on Harry's face as he debated how to answer. She resisted the urge to fill the gap.

At last he spoke. 'I think she did. She denied it and so did the bloke, but I found it hard to believe either of them.'

'You confronted them?'

'Hmm. You could say that.'

'What did you do?' she pressed. She needed to hear it from him.

'Honestly, I really don't want to talk about it. Let's just say, I wasn't a particularly good husband and I didn't respond well.'

'And now? What are you now?'

'I don't know. I've never tested myself again.' He looked earnestly into her eyes. 'That doesn't mean I don't want to. I've just never felt the need . . . until now.'

Steph sidestepped the last comment. She wanted to know more about this man. 'Have you come to terms with what happened to Elizabeth?'

'Yes. I have. Look, it's hard to explain but I did love Elizabeth very much in the beginning and I think her affair was a wake-up call. Yes, my pride was hurt, and I reacted in a way I'm not particularly proud of, but it was a wake-up call in the sense I realised my feelings for Elizabeth had changed. I didn't love her. I knew she didn't love me any more. It was after that we started to talk about divorce. It was complicated, though. We had a pre-nup but she wanted to contest it.'

'You would have had a lot to lose.'

'It doesn't mean I wanted any harm to come to her.' Harry's voice was prickly.

'I wasn't implying anything,' said Steph, realising she'd hit a nerve. She was fascinated by Elizabeth and fascinated by her marriage to Harry. She wanted to know more for her own personal reasons than she did for anything else.

'If Elizabeth hadn't died then I would have faced a lengthy and expensive divorce, no doubt about it. But if you think for one minute her death was convenient, then you're barking up the wrong tree,' snapped Harry. 'Christ, I'm not sure how the conversation got to this place.'

'Sorry, I didn't mean to pry. I only asked in the first place because . . . because I don't want to assume anything or rush anything if you're not ready.'

He kissed her hand. 'It's me who should apologise. I'm a bit defensive about it all, but just to reassure you, the fact that I've opened up so much to you already says a lot.'

He kissed her tenderly and Steph allowed herself to sink into his arms. It felt so reassuring and comforting. She missed having someone to hold and someone to hold her. It was probably the only thing she missed about Zac and about being married.

'Have you ever thought of moving back to the area?' asked Harry.

'I don't think so. Yes, my mum lives here, but I think we work better with distance between us.'

'What does your mum do again?'

'She's retired. She's busy doing her own thing; I don't think she's any more worried about our living several hundred miles apart than I am.'

'What did she used to do?'

The question sounded casual, but Steph felt something in Harry's body tighten. 'She was in the civil service.'

'Doing what?'

Why the in-depth questions? If she avoided them, it would seem odd. If she answered them Harry was bound to make the connection. 'Honestly, my mum is the last person I want to talk about right now,' she said. 'It rather spoils the moment.'

'I'm just interested.'

Harry's phone rang out, coming to her rescue. He pulled an apologetic face. 'Sorry, I'd better answer it, just in case it's my mum. She's not been feeling too well,' explained Harry, extracting himself and taking his phone from his pocket. He walked out onto the front porch, closing the door behind him.

Steph wandered over to the bank of photo frames adorning the wall to the left of the chimney breast.

The photographs were family shots which, judging by the look of them, had been taken at various times over the years. One of the older photographs caught Steph's interest. It was of Pru standing at the edge of a lake with three young boys, who Steph assumed were Harry and his brothers. They were all wearing wetsuits.

Harry came back into the room. 'Just work stuff,' he said, dropping the phone onto the sofa. He came to stand beside her. 'Rogues' gallery. This was my mother's touch. She replaced all the photos of me and Elizabeth that used to be here.'

'Wow. That was a deep clean of family history. Although, to be fair, I didn't keep my wedding photos up after my divorce.' Steph winced at her lack of tact. She went to apologise but Harry spoke first.

'My mum meant well. At the time I was grateful not having to look at all those happy memories that had turned so sour.' He gave a small sigh. 'I really should look at sorting the photos out myself, or maybe just taking the whole lot down.'

'Was this taken here?' asked Steph, pointing at the photograph of Pru and the boys.

'Yes, up by the lake. We used to swim up there a lot when we were younger.'

'Your mum as well?'

'Yep. She used to love wild-water swimming. She used to go up to the lake every day and swim for about half an hour. It was her love of water sports that kickstarted the more recent changes. My father had it running as a country retreat, where men could fish and women could enjoy the walks or sitting by the lake. He was rather traditional sometimes, whereas my mother was always looking for ways to improve it and bring in a wider demographic of guests. She had the real vision.'

Steph noticed the affection with which Harry spoke about his mother. 'What about your dad? Was he into the water-sports thing?'

'God, no. He only had a financial interest in it,' Harry said drily. 'It was Mum's passion for the outdoor life that drove it forward. At one point, Dad wanted to sell up – this was when we were kids – but Mum wouldn't hear of it and stood her ground. He even threatened to leave her, but she stubbornly refused to go along with the sale.'

'And your dad gave in?'

'Probably the one and only time he had ever considered anyone else in his life,' said Harry.

'Sounds like my mum,' said Steph and then felt like kicking herself for bringing the conversation back to Wendy.

Harry put an arm around her shoulder. 'You do know you can talk to me about anything.'

'Thanks.' She continued to look at the photographs, more to avoid looking at him in case her eyes betrayed her. She slipped out from under his arm. 'I'd better get back. I've got an early start tomorrow and I don't want to get the sack.' She had tried for a joke but it fell flat.

'I'm sure your boss would forgive you,' said Harry. He caught her arm and gave her a brief kiss. 'You can trust me, you do know that, don't you?'

Steph swallowed. 'Of course.'

'The same way I can trust you.'

'Absolutely.' She smiled, gave him a peck on the cheek and was gone before she crumpled under the weight of her lies.

Chapter Twenty-Five

Harry's Lodge, Conmere,
Sunday, 12 May, 7.20 p.m.

Harry closed the door as Steph left and gave a big sigh. He had given her the chance to confess about her mother, but she hadn't taken it. She had chosen to deceive him, to keep the knowledge to herself. To say he felt disappointed was an understatement.

He thumped the closed door with the side of his clenched fist. 'For fuck's sake, Steph!' he shouted. He was reluctant to think she'd come to Conmere with the intention of digging around in his past and yet everything seemed to be pointing straight to that. How the hell had he let himself become involved with her?

He took a quick shower and was towel-drying his hair when there was a loud rap on the front door. Harry opened the door expecting – or was that hoping? – to see Steph there. He was disappointed. Instead, his older brother marched in.

'Don't stand on ceremony. Just come right in,' said Harry sarcastically, pushing the door closed.

'It's not like you've got any visitors,' said Dominic.

'As far as you know.'

'I just saw Steph Durham go by my place,' said Dominic. 'I take it she was here.'

'None of your business,' said Harry.

'That's a yes, then.' Dominic flopped down in the chair. 'What did you find out?'

'About what?' Harry knew what Dominic meant, but his brother's attitude was pissing him off.

'About what she's doing here,' said Dominic, with a trace of impatience. 'Did you ask her about her mother?'

'There is nothing to find out,' said Harry, still feeling a loyalty towards Steph. 'I'm certain she's here for genuine reasons. She's here as a travel writer, a photographer, that's all.'

'I don't know what I've got to do to convince you she's up to no good,' said Dominic.

'What exactly is your problem?' Harry was beyond tired with Dominic's seeming paranoia.

'I've told you before. I don't want her poking around. Bringing up stuff that's bad for business and bad for Mum with the way she is right now. And you would do well to remember that.'

'Don't you dare try emotional blackmail on me. What are you frightened of?'

'Did you know Steph met Sonia Lomas today?'

'What?' Harry's body tensed.

'Thought that might create a response.' Dominic sat forward. 'Mum spotted Sonia being dropped off at the station. She only noticed her because she saw Steph's car. It's all dented down one side. That's what caught her attention.'

'And Steph was driving?'

'Mum didn't see who was driving, but she said it was definitely Sonia in the passenger seat and you must've seen Steph's car. If not, take a look.'

'She said she was meeting a friend today.'

'Guess Sonia is the friend. Now do you believe me? It's no coincidence – Wendy Lynch's daughter, Sonia Lomas's friend. I'm not being paranoid but she's here for a reason and it isn't to report on the resort. She needs talking to.'

'I'll do it,' interjected Harry. 'I'll speak to her, not you. Understand?'

Dominic held out his hands. 'Hey, mate. Don't get so het up. It's best you know now, but if you can't sort this out then I'll have to.'

'Leave it to me. You stay away.' Harry was aware of the hostility in his voice, and the flicker of surprise on his brother's face suggested he was too.

'It's cool. Just make sure you do.' Dominic rose from the chair. 'In the meantime, I'm going to pay Wendy Lynch a visit.'

Harry wasn't sure he liked Dominic's comment, but he was too consumed with anger to question him.

Harry threw on his jacket and, grabbing his keys, wallet and mobile, stormed out of the house, barking at his brother to lock the door on his way out.

Just what the hell was Steph up to? He had been totally mugged off by her. This time he wasn't going to let her avoid the questions. He was going to have it out with her once and for all. Direct and straight to the point the way he should have been in the first place.

261

Harry reached the house in double-quick time, only just remembering to acknowledge Heidi's greeting as he marched through to the back of the house and ascended the wooden staircase, taking the steps two at a time.

By the time he reached the second floor, he kind of wished he had been less petulant and taken the lift, but anger was a great motivator and he only paused for breath once he was outside Steph's room, and even then it was only a matter of seconds before he hammered at the door.

Steph opened the door with a look of caution and then a smile, which quickly became an air of concern as she registered his expression.

'Harry . . .' she began.

'Who was the friend you met today?' he demanded.

'What?'

'The friend that you met today. What is her name?'

'I . . .'

He cut her off again. 'And your mum. What's her name, while we're at it?'

He watched as Steph studied him and he allowed her time to process the implications of her potential answers.

Finally, she spoke. 'You'd better come in.' She stood aside and opened the door wide. He stepped in, glad they wouldn't have to continue the conversation in the corridor. She closed the door behind him and the small bedroom seemed to shrink even smaller.

Harry glanced at her bed and saw her bag and phone. He also noticed some clothing. Steph's eyes followed his gaze. 'I was just about to get dressed,' she said. It was only then Harry registered she was wearing a dressing gown and her hair was damp, presumably from the shower. She pulled the belt tighter around her body. 'At least let me get some clothes on if this is the hostile visit I sense it to be.'

Steph snatched at her clothes and went into the en suite. She reappeared a minute later in jeans and T-shirt, her hair tousled from the towel. She picked up a hairbrush and ran it through her hair – all the time watching him. Harry said nothing.

'Do you want to sit?' She indicated the spare bed.

Harry gave himself a mental shove, refocusing on his reason for being there. 'Your friend?' he reminded her, declining to sit.

Steph turned and placed the hairbrush on the dressing table. She paused for a moment before turning back to look at him. Harry's patience was wearing thin but at the same time his initial spike of anger was subsiding. He hated to feel so angry; it reminded him of both Dominic and their father.

'My friend,' began Steph, 'was Sonia Lomas, but you know that already, right?'

'Right,' said Harry. 'Your mother?'

'Again, I suspect you know she is Wendy Lynch or, as you probably know her better, DCI Lynch of CID, Cumbria Police.'

'Right again,' said Harry. 'Why didn't you tell me?'

She had the decency to look embarrassed. 'I didn't want to blur any lines.'

'Blur lines? What the hell do you mean? Let's do this one thing at a time. What's the deal with Sonia Lomas?'

'I can't discuss it,' she said.

'What? Of course you can!'

'Harry, before I say anything else, I want you to know that

my feelings for you are genuine. I don't know how you feel about me, whether you really like me or if you're just trying to find out about me, I don't know.'

'You've got a bloody cheek,' snapped Harry. 'It's me who should be asking you if you're genuine, but how can I actually believe anything you say when you've already lied to me?'

'I have not lied to you,' she snapped back. 'I avoided answering your questions for that very reason, because I didn't want to lie to you.'

'That's very noble of you.' Harry slow handclapped. 'I'm supposed to be thankful, am I?' He took a step closer to her. 'You may not have lied, but you've not told the whole truth and you've purposely deceived me. In my book, that's just as bad.'

'OK, I didn't want to tell you about my mother because of everything that was associated with her. If I told you I only found out myself last week that she was involved with the case, you probably wouldn't believe me.'

'Why didn't you tell me earlier when you had the chance?'

Steph looked away, but not before he caught a glimpse of a tear in her eye. He wanted to pull her into his arms and tell her it didn't matter, but the truth was, it did matter. It changed everything.

'I was avoiding telling you,' she said quietly. 'I knew I should, but I didn't want it to affect things between us. That's the same reason I didn't tell you about Sonia Lomas either.'

'I want to believe that, Steph, I really do. But I'm having a hard time doing so. Look at it from my point of view: you came here already friends with Sonia and your mother was the investigating officer into Elizabeth's death. And you're a journalist – what am I supposed to think?'

'I'm not actually a journalist,' said Steph. 'I'm a travel writer and a photographer.'

'You're just splitting hairs. And you're not denying it.'

'It's not looking very good for me, I know,' said Steph. 'But believe me, you and me, it's genuine and separate to everything else.'

'You may be able to separate the two, but I don't think I can.' He wanted to pace the room, but there wasn't enough space. 'How come you and Sonia were in the car together?'

'She wanted to talk to me.'

'About Elizabeth?' he asked, knowing it was the only possible answer. 'Just answer me, please.' He was giving her the chance to tell the truth, to be honest with him, but she was refusing his offer. What was wrong with her? He tried a different tack, hoping to throw her thoughts off-balance. 'Did you let things happen between us to get more information about Elizabeth's death so you could write a story with the help of Sonia?'

Well, that certainly caused a reaction. Her eyes blazed with anger.

'Did you want to sleep with me to find out what I was doing here?' she countered.

The remark hurt him, his reaction taking him by surprise. They stood their ground, staring at each other. Harry gave way first. 'No,' he said. 'No, I didn't.'

'I didn't either,' she replied.

He was relieved to hear her say that and, judging by the look on her face, she was equally relieved at his response.

'I'm glad you said that.' He wanted to stroke her face, to push her hair from her eyes, but he forced himself not to, and instead he made sure his voice was softer when he spoke. 'Steph, please, tell me what's going on? I can't just ignore it.'

The tears were back in her eyes and she blinked hard. Then, taking a deep breath, she straightened up and he saw the softness in her features tighten. 'Do you have any doubt about what happened to your wife? Do you know one hundred per cent it was an accident?'

Harry resisted the urge to yell indignantly at her. He couldn't remember anyone other than Sonia asking him such a direct question. It was like being punched in the stomach. 'No one knows for certain what happened at the lake but it was thoroughly investigated, by your mother, and there was nothing to suggest it was anything other than an accident.'

'So you can't be certain it was an accident? That's all I'm saying.'

'Why would anyone want to kill Elizabeth?'

'Divorce is expensive, you said that yourself.'

'Wait a minute . . . do you really think . . .? Fucking hell, Steph. I thought we'd been through this.' He pushed his clenched fist against his head in frustration. 'I thought you got that it wasn't about the money. It's not enough to make me want to murder my own wife.' He blanched at his own words, which sounded so harsh when he spoke them out loud. 'Money is not my stimulator, which is why I'm usually living in France with none of the Sinclair trimmings.' He moved a little closer to her. This time he did stroke her face. 'You don't have to be scared of me, Steph. If I didn't already care about you after just a few days, I wouldn't be here trying to convince you I'm not the bad guy and I have nothing to hide.'

'I believe you but I'm sorry, I still can't break client confidentiality.' She took his hand from her face but held on to it. 'Look, I just need a few days to finish what I'm doing. Maybe after I'm finished, we can see each other again – I mean, as in have some sort of relationship – but in the meantime we should perhaps put it on hold.'

He gave a snort of disbelief and snatched his hand away. 'Is that your idea of a trade-off? I honestly don't know what to say to that. I don't think keeping secrets about something like this is a good basis for a relationship. And we're going round in circles here. So no, that doesn't work for me.' He could feel his anger coming back. He needed to be away from Steph. He didn't want her to witness his fury. 'Look, you can keep the job for the week but I'll be watching you. You stay out of my business, do you hear?'

She looked startled, nodded and went to speak.

Harry held up his hand. 'Don't say anything.' He was only just managing to keep his anger at bay. He needed to get out of there. He turned and within a couple of strides was at the door. 'You need to tread carefully. Not everyone is as concerned about your wellbeing as I am.'

Harry stormed his way down the two flights of stairs and across the hall into the family's private living room. He was pleased to see it was empty – his mother was probably having supper over at Owen's, as she usually did on a Sunday evening. Harry went over to the decanter on the stand, poured himself two fingers of whisky and drank it down neat. He gave a small gasping noise of satisfaction as he placed the empty glass on the tray and poured another. This one he took more time to savour as he went to stand at the patio doors overlooking the gardens.

He couldn't get his head around Steph or why he felt so drawn to her. She was clearly up to something with Sonia and it was obviously concerning Elizabeth's death. On reflection, he probably shouldn't have flown off the handle the way he had as there was no way she was going to tell him anything now. He should have taken it easy and kept her on side, then he might have been able to draw her into his confidence, so much so that she would willingly share what she was doing and what she knew. At least that way he could keep Dominic at bay. Damn it! He hadn't handled it at all well.

Maybe he should apologise and try to smooth things over. He finished his drink, enjoying the small burn of alcohol as it travelled down his throat and into his stomach. He needed to think this through and work out a strategy.

Chapter Twenty-Six

Steph felt self-conscious going into the housekeeping room that morning wearing her Conmere cleaning uniform, which Heidi had just given her to change into. The uniform consisted of a bottle-green shirt and matching trousers, the Conmere logo of a lake and a tree embroidered in cream on the breast pocket.

'Look at you,' said Heidi, not unkindly. 'One of the staff now. Right, if you come with me, I'll take you on a quick tour of the house and tell you where you'll be working today and what you have to do.'

Steph spent the next hour going through the formalities with Heidi and learning the layout of the main house. A lot she was already familiar with, but when Heidi took her up to the first floor she had to hide her excitement as she was shown Elizabeth Sinclair's room.

'When I say it's Elizabeth's room, what I mean is, it's where all her things are kept,' explained Heidi, her hand wrapped around the door handle.

'What sort of things?' asked Steph.

'Some personal possessions that Harry didn't really know what to do with at the time.' Heidi had lowered her voice. 'Things that Mrs Sinclair Senior had sifted through and things that Mrs Lomas – that's Elizabeth's mother – wasn't offered.'

'Oh, I see,' said Steph, trying to hide her impatience as she willed Heidi to open the door.

'We don't go in here, though,' said Heidi. 'But you can have a quick peek in.' She opened the door and, remaining in the doorway, allowed Steph to poke her head into the room.

There was a double bed covered with a cream-coloured eiderdown, a wardrobe and a chest of drawers. The curtains, which were drawn, were a heavy, pale blue jacquard, shutting out the light from the window. A door to the side of the bed was slightly ajar and Steph could see through to the bathroom. There was a slight musty smell to the room but it was the heavy stillness which felt the most overpowering.

'Does anyone ever come in here?' she asked.

'Once a week to dust and open the curtains and windows for a while to let a bit of fresh air in.'

'Was it Elizabeth's private room?'

'She and Harry stayed in here while the lodge was being refurbished just before their wedding.' Heidi put her arm past Steph to reach for the door handle and Steph moved back into the hallway. 'I think Mrs Sinclair Senior would like to open up the room again, but Harry's never been about long enough to go through the rest of the things. Can't say I blame him, really.'

'When is the room next due for a clean?' Steph tried to sound casual.

'Friday. The rooms up here on the first floor are for guests who don't necessarily need a lodge and just want a room. More for those who are here on business or for the spa facilities.' They reached the foot of the stairs. 'Right, that's all the formalities done. I'll take you over to Greenway Lodges and pair you up with Eva – she's been with us a couple of years now and will look after you. I'll probably leave you with her for most of the week.'

Steph spent the rest of the morning cleaning, bed-stripping and bed-making, cushion-plumping and fridge-stocking. She was surprised at how fast the next few hours went and that they had finished the lodges and were now back at the main house, signing out for the day.

'Well done, Steph,' said Heidi. 'Eva tells me you did well today. See you in the morning.'

As Steph made her way up to her room, she couldn't help thinking about Elizabeth's room. She'd love to get in there for a closer look around and wondered if there would be the opportunity to slip in at some point that week. She wasn't sure what she would be looking for and what, if anything, she'd find, but it was too good an opportunity to pass up.

Primrose Close, Kendalton,
Monday, 13 May, 1.05 p.m.

Steph pulled up outside her mum's house. It was a two-bedroom bungalow sitting on the side of a hill overlooking the town of Kendalton. It was an unassuming property which blended in with all the other bungalows in the road. There was nothing about it which was notable and that was, no doubt, the way Wendy liked it. For Steph, growing up, everything had been very modest, from their home (a three-bedroom, 1960s semi), their family car (a Ford Sierra) and their clothes (bought from supermarkets) to holidays in a caravan in Dorset. Wendy was all about blending in and going unnoticed. In her younger days, Steph had often imagined her mother to be a secret spy who was living a double life. She couldn't believe her mum was really that dreary. It was only her job as a police officer that was mildly exciting.

As it turned out, Wendy Lynch hadn't lived up to any of Steph's expectations as a super-spy, rather as she hadn't lived up to Steph's expectations as a mother.

Steph made a conscious effort to shrug off those thoughts and feelings of disappointment. She hadn't seen her mother for over six months now and had spoken to her probably no more than three times, but maybe this time Wendy would be more relaxed. No longer a serving police officer, perhaps retirement had made her a warmer woman. Steph acknowledged that this was probably a high expectation, given her mother's usual conversational style, which Steph had often likened to a blunt-force trauma.

She rang the bell and waited patiently for her mum to open the door. 'You're early,' Wendy said, stepping aside so Steph could enter.

Steph checked her watch. 'Only by ten minutes.' She walked inside, not stopping to kiss or embrace her mother. It had never been something Wendy had done and by default something Steph didn't think about doing. In fact, it was only her father who would show any type of affection. She had often wondered how her parents had become a couple – they had just never seemed a good fit, and their union remained a great mystery to her. 'How are you?' she asked as her mother closed the front door.

'Fine, thank you. I've got a visitor. Someone you might remember.'

Steph gave her mother a quizzical look as she wracked her brains wondering who it could be. It certainly wouldn't be any family. Her grandparents on both sides had passed away and Wendy was an only child, so there were no aunties, uncles or cousins. On her father's side, there was a brother who lived in Australia, but she couldn't imagine him visiting. They only kept in touch via an annual Christmas card.

Steph followed her mother into the living room and immediately recognised the visitor as Rob Lacey, her mum's old work colleague from her days in the force. 'Hello, Rob, this is a nice surprise. How are you?'

'I'm good, thanks, Steph. You're looking very well. I haven't seen you since your father's funeral. Your mum has kept me up-to-date with what you've been up to though.'

Steph hid her surprise. She had no idea her mum kept up-to-date herself with Steph's life, let alone shared the information with anyone else.

They spent the next half an hour or so chatting generally about what they had all been up to, especially now Rob had retired too. He told them about his plans to go travelling now he had both the time and the money, and before it was too late, as he put it.

'I wish Mum would do something now she's retired,' said

Steph as Wendy took the cups out and washed up. 'I don't think early retirement was a good thing for her. From what I can work out, she doesn't do very much. Hasn't joined any clubs or anything. I'm sure she could have stayed on in the force for a few more years.'

Rob's brow furrowed and he leaned across the arm of the chair, pushing the room door closed. 'Retirement? But your mum never took retirement.'

Steph returned the frown. 'Yes, she did. Eighteen months ago.'

The crease deepened between his eyes. 'It wasn't retirement, not voluntary anyway. She didn't have any choice in the matter.'

'What? No. She retired. You must be getting muddled up with someone else.' She looked at Rob's apologetic expression and realised he wasn't joking. 'I don't understand.'

'Sorry, I shouldn't have said anything. She obviously didn't want you to know. She has her reasons, no doubt.'

'It's too late now.' Steph threw a cautionary glance towards the door. 'Tell me, Rob, if she didn't take retirement, what happened?'

'It's not my place to tell you.' Rob squeezed his bottom lip between his finger and thumb.

'OK, I'll ask her myself,' said Steph. She'd rather not, but now she'd been given this grain of information she couldn't just brush it off. Why had her mother been lying?

Rob let out a frustrated sigh. 'If I tell you, you mustn't let on that you know.' He waited while Steph nodded her agreement before continuing. 'She was asked to tender her resignation. She didn't have any choice. It was either that or be dismissed, which would mean no pension and a tarnished record.'

'What the hell did she do?' It was hard to believe Rob was talking about Wendy; this all sounded so out of character.

'There had been an investigation by Internal Affairs. I don't know the details but there was some sort of cover-up. Rumours were rife that someone, i.e. your mother, hadn't followed correct procedures and, although the word corrupt was never used, there were implications that something was bad in CID.' Rob spoke quickly and in hushed tones.

'My mother was corrupt!' Steph managed to bring her voice down to an astonished whisper.

'Not your mother, but something in CID was wrong. It was a general consensus of opinion that your mother was the scapegoat.'

Steph glanced towards the door again. 'Of all the things Mum is, I can't honestly believe she was corrupt.'

'Nor could anyone else. And that's why she wasn't made an example of.'

'Bloody hell,' muttered Steph. 'And you've no idea what it was all about?'

Rob Lacey shook his head. 'I'd moved to a different station by then.'

'Didn't you ask anyway? Didn't you even ask her?'

'She would never speak about it. I did try.' Rob looked apologetically at Steph.

The door opened and Wendy came through with her jacket over her arm. 'What are you two looking so guilty about?' she asked, although there was humour in her voice.

Rob gave a laugh. 'We were just debating the best pubs around here for a bite to eat. I'm starving.'

'So am I,' said Steph, thankful for Rob's deflection.

The King's Arms, Kendalton,
Monday 13 May, 1.45 p.m.

Lunch was a pleasant affair and, although Steph found her mind wandering back to Rob's revelation that her mother had been forced to resign, she did actually enjoy herself. Wendy seemed much more relaxed than Steph had anticipated. Maybe it was because someone else was with them, or was it the someone else that was making her relaxed? As Wendy laughed at something Rob said, Steph noticed a lightness in her mother's features.

Rob drove them back to Wendy's house later that afternoon.

'That was nice,' said Steph, after they'd said their goodbyes and Rob had driven off.

'It was indeed,' said Wendy as they went inside. 'And before you say anything, no, there is nothing going on between myself and Rob. We are just good friends.'

Steph let out a laugh. 'I wasn't going to say a word.'

'Oh, yes, you were, I can read you like a book.' Her mother actually smiled at her.

Steph couldn't help grinning as she settled herself in the conservatory. With the sun shining through the glass, if she closed her eyes and concentrated she could imagine herself on a beach soaking up the heat somewhere on the Adriatic coast. The glass of wine at lunchtime was making her feel quite heavy-eyed. She had anticipated leaving after lunch, but she was enjoying being in her mother's company right now. It was a rarity for them to share a joke and relax with each other.

'I heard Sonia Lomas turned up at the reception party at Conmere,' said Wendy as she took her seat opposite.

'How did you know that?' asked Steph, surprised her mother should know already.

'Bad news travels fast.' Wendy looked at Steph. 'You didn't have anything to do with that, did you?'

'Of course not! I don't know why everyone is so hostile towards the woman. Even Harry didn't seem very pleased to see his mother-in-law.'

'He has good reason. You're not to get involved with any of that, do you hear me?'

Steph felt herself prickle at her mother's tone. 'I'm not a child any more. I can make my own decisions.' So much for the relaxed atmosphere with her mother lasting.

'For once, if you never do anything else for me in your life, just promise to not get involved.'

Steph would have laughed if Wendy hadn't looked so serious. She put down her cup. 'Mum, what are you so worried about?'

'When are you going home?' Wendy asked instead.

Steph felt her whole being deflate. She hated feeling like this. She hated the fact that all she wanted was her mother to show some sort of concern or consideration for her, but she never did. Why Steph put herself through this she didn't know. Wendy had never been a hands-on, cuddly mum. It seemed that not even retirement had thawed the original ice-queen. She met her mother's gaze. Well, what Steph was about to tell her should make up for the disappointment Steph felt. Wendy was going to love this. She smiled at her mother. 'I'm not going home just yet,' she said.

'What do you mean?'

'I've got myself a job at Conmere.' Steph sat back, taking comfort from the look of horror on Wendy's face.

'Are you serious?'

'Absolutely. They were shortstaffed for the week and I was offered a job, plus Harry Sinclair had asked me to do some promo photos for the interior of the house and said he could put some in the shop to sell. I get paid for both, so it's a win-win for me. I didn't have any work this week and I need the money, so it would have been stupid to turn it down.'

Gosh, she wished she had her camera now to take a picture of the look on Wendy's face. It was somewhere between horror and anger, with a touch of disbelief thrown in, but it was fleeting and in a matter of seconds Wendy had regained her composure.

'I don't know what you're up to, Steph, but you're playing with fire,' she said.

'Don't be so dramatic. If there's something I should know, something that you're worried about, then you should tell me.'

Wendy looked undecided – not a common expression her mother wore, but she definitely looked to be in some sort of internal dilemma. 'There are things I can't tell you, Steph,' she said at last. 'I may be retired from the force but I'm still bound by the Official Secrets Act.'

'Sorry, but that's not good enough. I need something more concrete than that.'

'You're just going to have to take my word for it.'

Steph huffed in frustration. Aargh! She felt like throttling her mother. She was so bloody stubborn at times. She decided to try a different tack.

'Why did you retire?'

Wendy's shoulders and body tensed. She looked at Steph. 'Because I wanted to still be able to enjoy life. I didn't want to retire and be stuck in an old folks' home straight away.'

'So why haven't you done anything since you retired?'

'What do you mean?' Wendy's eyebrows darted together.

'You've just stayed at home, doing nothing, as far as I can tell. Are you going to follow Rob's example and do something exciting, like travelling?'

'I don't know. I might.' Wendy's shoulders relaxed but her eyes were still fixed on Steph.

'Don't you miss the force?' Steph knew she was being pushy but she was cross with her mum and didn't know when she'd feel brave enough to ask her about the police again. As it was, she knew she was approaching it in a roundabout way. She should be direct. Just ask the question.

'Mum . . . did you leave the force because you wanted to?' Steph asked the question as delicately as she could, her soft tone implying she knew more.

Wendy opened her mouth to speak and then closed it again. She put her cup on the table and placed her hands on her knees. 'Rob's a gossip,' she said at last. 'He shouldn't have told you.'

'He didn't mean to tell me. I kind of forced him.'

'Nonsense. He's come up against tougher interrogators than you.'

'Maybe he thought I should know for some reason.'

'A good idea would die of loneliness in his head sometimes,' said Wendy.

'So, what really did happen? Did you have to leave the force?' Steph pushed on.

'It was by mutual agreement,' said Wendy. 'I did nothing wrong. I was doing what I was supposed to be doing but sometimes when there's a change at the top of the food chain, it's those lower down who pay the price.'

'Mum, please stop talking in riddles all the time. Just be straight with me,' pleaded Steph.

Wendy sighed deeply. 'The new guv'nor didn't like the way CID was operating. I had been doing things the way I'd always done everything. The guv'nor didn't like it. He thought I was stuck in my ways and not keeping up with a modern-day police force. He didn't think I would fit into his vision for the department.'

'What were you doing that was so wrong?'

Wendy tapped one foot against the other in agitation before speaking. 'He didn't appreciate the work I put in behind the scenes fostering good working relationships with the local communities. He wanted results. Crime rates cleared up. He wasn't interested in making connections that might one day pay off. We reached an impasse and the only way for me was out. He put me on a disciplinary for not completing my paperwork on time.' She was clearly still angry about this. 'He wanted every minute of my shift accounted for on a timesheet. It was embarrassing and humiliating. I was doing nothing wrong. I was merely spending time with the local community.'

'He sounds like the old-fashioned one,' said Steph.

'Well, whatever, we didn't get on and when he suggested I leave I didn't exactly put up a fight. I wanted to protect my pension and my reputation.'

'You didn't think you could go to the union?' asked Steph. She was surprised by her mother's response to a man like that. It wasn't like her at all. Wendy was renowned for standing her ground, standing up to people. Steph found it hard to imagine her mum doing anything less, certainly not kowtowing to a bully. It seemed so out of character. Certainly not the Wendy Lynch she knew.

'I did think about the union, but that would have taken ages to go through and it would have meant my whole career being picked over and analysed. I didn't want the entire station to know that my policing methods were under scrutiny. I didn't want to be talked about in hushed tones whenever I came into a room. I didn't want people to talk about me behind my back and essentially become judge and jury. I also didn't want to have to call upon any of my colleagues to stand up for me. It could make things difficult for them too. I didn't want to put them in that position.'

'Had this man just singled you out or had he targeted other officers?'

'He had it in for me and me only. I don't know if it was because I'm a woman and he felt threatened by me but, whatever his real reasons, he didn't want me about.'

'Rob said something about people thinking the whole of the CID department was corrupt.'

Wendy raised her eyebrows. 'Corrupt? He used that word?'

'Only quoting what others had said.'

'I'm so glad to be out of that place,' sighed Wendy. 'Talk about Chinese whispers. No one in CID was corrupt as far as I know. Now, I really don't want to talk about it any more. I've said far too much and we've somehow managed to get off the topic of what you're doing up there.'

'Just working.'

'I don't believe you for one minute,' said Wendy. 'You be careful, Steph. Those Sinclairs won't hesitate to get rid of you if you're not up to scratch or they think you're being too nosy. They like their privacy.'

Steph might have used the word secrets but she didn't argue with her mother. She didn't know what it was, but everything about that family felt out of step and they seemed to be able to reach out and unsettle everything they came into contact with . . . Elizabeth, Cameron, Sonia, Wendy and even herself.

Without warning there was an almighty crashing noise of glass breaking from the front of the house. Both Steph and her mother jumped in fright.

'What the hell . . .?' said Steph. She sprang to her feet the same time as her mother.

'Let me go first,' commanded her mother, pulling at Steph's arm and making her wait behind her. Wendy pushed open the door to the living room and poked her head around it. She let out a sound somewhere between an exasperated sigh and an angry huff. 'It's the window. It's been bricked.'

Steph went into the room after her mother to see a house brick lying on the floor in the middle of the room, surrounded by shards of glass. One of the vertical blinds had been ripped and the sofa in front of the window was covered in bits of broken glass too.

'Bastards!' said Steph. She ran out of the bungalow and onto the street, looking up and down, but the road was deserted.

'Everything OK?' came a voice.

Steph whirled round and at the end of the garden path of the house next door was an elderly lady. 'I heard something crash.'

Steph marvelled at the neighbour's hearing. 'It was my mum's window,' she explained, walking over. 'Someone threw a house brick at it. You didn't see anyone, did you?'

'Oh, how terrible. I'm sorry, I was just closing my front door. I've been to the shops, you see. I heard the noise.'

'But didn't see anyone?'

'Not really. I came out onto the path and saw a car drive off.'

'Did you see who was driving or what sort of car it was?'

'It was too quick for me to see anyone inside. They went down that way. I think it was one of those big four-wheel-drive cars. It was black.'

God, it sounded all too familiar, thought Steph with a shudder. 'Number plate?' she asked but with little hope.

The neighbour shook her head. 'Sorry. Is Wendy all right?'

'Yes. Fortunately, we were in the conservatory. Maybe it was just kids messing around,' said Steph, not wanting to alarm the neighbour too much.

'Could have been. There's the footpath just along there. Kids could have run off or been on pushbikes.'

'Thanks anyway,' said Steph. 'I'd better get back and help Mum.'

When Steph went back into the living room, her mother was already picking up shards of glass and dropping them into a cardboard box.

'I just spoke to your neighbour. She heard the window smash but didn't see anyone. Although she did say a 4x4 car drove off as she looked out of the door. A black one.'

'That doesn't narrow it down. No plate number, I take it?'

'No. Do you think it was a deliberate attack or just kids?'

Wendy stood up and looked at her daughter. 'What do you think?'

'I don't know; that's why I'm asking.'

'Put it this way, it's a bit of a coincidence – you turn up interested in the Elizabeth Sinclair death, and while you're here, quizzing me about stuff from the past, I get a brick through the window.' Wendy shook her head. 'I suggest you quit that job and get yourself back down to Brighton sharpish and forget you ever heard the name Elizabeth Sinclair.'

'Mum, stop!' Steph was surprised by the command in her voice and it seemed her mother was too. Wendy blinked a couple of times but remained silent. Steph played to the advantage. 'I need to know exactly what happened. I can't leave this alone, especially not now.'

Steph waited while Wendy appraised her for what seemed like the longest time. Wendy let out a resigned sigh. 'There's not really much I can tell you; I told you I'm still bound by the Official Secrets Act.' She held up her hand to silence Steph's anticipated objection. 'I've never asked much, if anything, of you, Steph. I've never demanded anything of you, not as an adult, but this one time, I am. Please stay away from all this. Don't go stirring up things concerning Elizabeth Sinclair's death.'

Steph let out an exasperated huff. She really thought for a moment there Wendy was going to open up. For fuck's sake! A bubble of anger shot through her. 'Are you telling me Elizabeth's death wasn't an accident?'

'There are some questions you shouldn't ask.'

'There are things I can't leave alone.' Steph's temper finally snapped.

'If you pursue this, if you take the Sinclair family down, it won't end there. It will be like a pebble being thrown into the water. The ripples will reach wider than you can imagine and touch people you least expect them to.'

'You're doing it again! Stop talking in riddles!' Steph's voice rose, her temper finally getting the better of her as her words came out unchecked. 'Are you protecting someone? Oh, God . . . it's you. You're protecting yourself.'

'Get a bloody grip,' spat Wendy, her own temper being let off the leash. 'I'm protecting other people. There are folk in this community who depend on the Sinclairs for their live-lihoods. Without the Sinclairs buying in local produce, half the businesses round here would fold. You will do more harm than good.'

'But what about the truth?' insisted Steph. 'As a police officer that's your duty, first and foremost.'

Wendy broke eye contact and looked down at her shoes, before lifting her head and reconnecting with Steph's gaze. 'When Rob told you I was asked to leave, he was telling the truth. I can't go into detail about why exactly but it was to do with Elizabeth Sinclair's death – the investigation.'

For the first time Steph could see not so much a chink, but a fault line in her mother's tough exterior. 'What did you do?' she asked, her tone softer.

'It wasn't so much what I did, but what I didn't.'

'Mum, please . . . tell me.'

The fault line closed up. 'Look, all you need to know is that Elizabeth's death was an accident. It was recorded as such. The verdict was sound. It was what everyone wanted.'

Steph tamped down the urge to scream in frustration at Wendy's refusal to tell her anything meaningful. 'You say it's what everyone wanted, but does that include Sonia Lomas? I don't think so. She wants the truth, not just some convenient half-truth that's been created.' The words came out in a flurry of infuriation which only served to rile Wendy.

'You've got your priorities wrong. You're more concerned about Sonia Lomas than you are for your own mother.'

'Sonia Lomas loved her daughter without compromise or condition. She deserves loyalty. She deserves to know the truth.' Tears stung the back of Steph's eyes and she blinked furiously. She was not going to cry in front of Wendy, no matter how much the truth in her own words hurt her.

'And I don't? Is that what you're saying?' demanded Wendy.

'I would say, how could you be so cold and unfeeling? But actually it's no surprise,' continued Steph, rejection spurring her on. 'It's how you've always been – detached and devoid of empathy. You don't get Sonia Lomas because you don't get that real feeling of love and emotion.' For a moment, Steph took comfort in the shocked and – dare she say? – hurt look on her mother's face. It was a small victory; she'd actually broken through that hard exterior and the fault line had once again opened.

'That's not true.' Wendy's voice was low but forceful. 'You have no idea how much I sacrificed for you or how much I . . .' The sentence died on her lips.

'Go on, say it . . . You can't, can you? You've never been able to say you love me.'

Wendy jerked her head ever so slightly as if fending off a physical blow. 'Actions speak louder than words,' she said stiffly.

'Yeah, well, you need to work on that.' Steph grabbed her bag and marched out of the house. It wasn't until she was driving away that she let the tears fall unchecked.

Chapter Twenty-Seven

Conmere, Tuesday, 14 May, 6.20 a.m.

Steph woke the next morning before her alarm went off and let out a groan as she went to sit up. Her head was throbbing. She'd had an awful night's sleep, her mind suddenly awake at midnight, wanting to replay the unnerving events of the last couple of days. Car accidents, broken glass, the Sinclair family, the notebook and images of Elizabeth and Wendy all mingled with each other and made no sense whatsoever. It was certainly a reflection of her state of mind, she thought, tentatively standing up. She was bound to have some paracetamol or suchlike in her bag and hoped it would do the job of shifting her headache. It was a shame she didn't have anything that would shift the anxiety that had pitched up in her stomach last night.

She felt a pang of guilt as she remembered her parting words to her mum yesterday. Steph should have kept her mouth shut; there was no taking them back now, she thought as the image of Wendy's hurt expression hovered in front of her. Steph had been hurt and she'd made sure Wendy felt the pain too.

Swallowing down the two tablets with a glass of water, Steph sat on the edge of the bed and allowed her mind to gently sift through what she knew, or didn't know, about Elizabeth and what had happened then and now. She was still missing pieces of the puzzle. She had lots of clues but no way of fitting them together to see the big picture.

Her heart gave a flutter as she went over the car incident. She and Sonia had come very close to a serious accident or worse. They were both very lucky not to be in hospital right now. And as for the window-smashing incident – had that been aimed at Steph or her mother? Were the two episodes connected? Her gut instinct was telling her they had to be related. It was too much of a coincidence for them not to be and they were definitely linked with the notebook which, by default, meant it all had something to do with Elizabeth's death. She was rattling someone, that was for sure.

Much as it unnerved her, she knew she wasn't going to give up now. She refused to be frightened off.

Conmere, Tuesday, 14 May, 10 a.m.

Steph climbed the grand staircase at Conmere House, trying to act casual and carrying a pile of clean towels in her arms. If anyone were to stop her, she'd say she was putting the towels out in the guest rooms.

She hadn't spoken to Wendy since their argument. A couple of times she had picked up her mobile to ring her but hadn't quite had the nerve to do so. Steph was still angry at Wendy's unwillingness to help but she could get over that; what was worse was the rejection she felt. Wendy was still keeping her at a distance, just as she always had. A couple of times yesterday Steph had thought she was getting through to her mother, tapping into some sort of feeling or emotion, but each time Wendy had closed her down and it hurt massively.

And then there was Harry, someone else she'd fallen out with, but this time there was no feeling of anger or hurt, just one of regret. Despite this, she still couldn't see how she would be able to tell him the truth about why she was here. She should have told him when she'd had the chance.

She reached the top of the stairs, the red carpet soft under her feet, and walked along the main corridor, stopping at Elizabeth's room. Checking no one was about, she turned the porcelain handle gently. There was no resistance and the door opened with ease. Steph entered the room, closing the door behind her.

There was a small gap in the curtains and the morning sunlight cut through the tall Georgian windows, casting a mosaic of rainbow colours onto the floor. She drew in a breath as a small pang of jealousy nudged at her. She didn't like to think of Elizabeth and Harry sharing this room. She eyed the bed accusingly while simultaneously scolding herself for her reaction. She had no right to feel jealous of a dead woman, least of all Harry's wife.

Placing the towels on the bed, Steph walked over to the dresser and opened the first drawer. Inside were three cosmetics bags. Steph took each one out and had a quick look at the contents. Elizabeth sure liked her make-up and none of it was cheap stuff, as far as Steph could see. She replaced the bags and opened the second drawer. This contained another bag, but slightly bigger than the others. A quick look informed her it was full of hairbrushes, curling tongs and straighteners.

On top of the dresser was a shoebox. Steph carefully lifted the lid and was surprised to see it was full of perfume bottles. Some appeared to be hardly used, while others were obviously favourites. It seemed odd that all of Elizabeth's belongings had been packed away. Steph wondered who had done this. For some reason, she didn't think it had been Harry. She was sure he would have given more attention and care to his wife's things.

Steph moved on to the wardrobe. There was a small key in the lock which turned with ease, and the mahogany door opened without protest. A dusty smell of lavender mothballs and traces of expensive perfume filtered out. Chanel No 5, if she wasn't mistaken. There had been a small bottle of it in the shoebox.

Steph wasn't surprised to see the wardrobe stuffed with what she assumed was Elizabeth's clothing. She ran her finger-tips across the fabrics – cottons, silks, velvets, cords – creating a kaleidoscope of textures and colours. Numerous shoeboxes were stacked at the bottom of the wardrobe, some larger than others which probably contained boots, Steph decided. She knelt down and lifted the lid of one of the boxes. Inside was a cloth bag, and when Steph looked further she could see it contained a pair of nude-coloured shoes with a bright red insole and bright red sole and heel. She replaced the lid and stood up.

'What secrets you could tell if only you could speak,' she whispered at the clothing as her gaze lingered on them. A brightly coloured winter coat hanging from the rail, squashed at the end, caught her attention. Steph managed to pull it out from the other clothing. It looked beautiful. It was made of silk and the fabric was handprinted with dragonflies. It had an oriental look to it. Steph adored dragonflies and this coat looked exquisite. She had a sudden and overwhelming desire to try the coat on, just to see how it felt being Elizabeth Sinclair for a moment.

She slipped it from the hanger and slid her arms into the sleeves, pulling it across her chest. It was a little tight and she guessed that Elizabeth Sinclair had been a smaller size than she was, at least across the bust anyway.

There was a full-length mirror at the side of the bed and Steph couldn't help admiring the coat. She felt glamorous and chic – was that what Elizabeth had wanted to feel? She remembered Sonia saying how they'd come from nothing and Elizabeth's ambition was for wealth and success. In just this one item of clothing, Steph could feel that achievement, but had that been enough for Elizabeth? Had she wanted more and had that led to her death?

Steph slid her hands into the pockets and twirled around, admiring the coat from all angles. It was then she felt a hole in the lining of the right-hand pocket. She wiggled her fingers – yes, it was actually quite a big hole. Steph held the coat open and inspected the lilac silk lining. The pockets were sewn between the outer fabric and the inner fabric. As the light of the sun shone onto the lining it highlighted something small and rectangular inside the coat that must have fallen through the hole in the pocket. With a bit of dexterity Steph managed to pull it out back through the pocket.

It was some sort of business card – white, plain on one side and on the other, written in gold, was the name Camilla and underneath it a phone number. The card was bordered with a rose in the corner and an elegant scroll of gold around the edge. It looked as though it were a place card for a wedding, and if it hadn't been for the phone number Steph would probably have dismissed it as such. After all, the coat was gorgeous enough to wear to a wedding. Something about the card was bothering her, but she couldn't quite pin down the thought.

'Steph! Stephanie!'

The sound of her name being called made Steph whirl round in a panic. It was Pru.

Steph hastily shrugged off the coat. Her hand was shaking as she slipped it onto the coat hanger. She didn't have time to do the buttons back up or to squeeze it in at the end of the wardrobe where she'd found it.

'Have you seen Steph anywhere?'

Pru's voice was right outside the door.

Steph had no idea who Pru was talking to, but as quietly as possible she closed the wardrobe door. She was about to turn the key when she saw the door handle move.

She leapt away from the wardrobe and snatched up the towels before turning around to face the door just as it opened.

'What are you doing in here?' Pru's voice was harsh. Her eyes bored into Steph's.

Steph swallowed hard. 'I was just bringing these towels up to one of the rooms, but I think I've got my bearings all wrong.'

'You're not supposed to be in here,' said Pru, her gaze now touring the bedroom and coming to settle back on Steph.

'I'm sorry. I was just thinking I'd got it wrong.'

'Why didn't you answer me when I called you?'

'I only just heard you. I was about to come out.'

Pru opened the door wide and stood to one side. 'Well, don't come in here again. This was Elizabeth's room and Harry would be furious if he knew you'd been in here.'

'I honestly didn't realise,' said Steph, hoping her nerves at being caught would be read as nerves for being told off. 'I'd hate to make him angry. It was a genuine mistake. It must be very difficult for you all.'

Pru's face softened and she let out the smallest of sighs. 'It is. Such a beautiful young woman in her prime. Harry was devastated. We all were. I know it probably sounds a cliché, but she was the daughter I never had.'

'I really am sorry for the intrusion.'

'That's enough now.' Dominic's voice interrupted their conversation and he too stepped into the room. 'We don't need to dwell on Elizabeth's death. Come on, Mum.' He put his hand on his mother's shoulder and steered her towards the hallway.

Steph followed and Dominic closed the door behind them.

'What did you want me for?' Steph asked Pru.

'Oh, yes. I wanted you to get the Daffodil Room ready. We've had a last-minute booking from one of the travel companies who are very influential in the industry. I want it perfect for when they arrive.' She looked at her watch. 'Which is in two hours.'

'Leave it with me. I'll do it straight away,' reassured Steph.

'Thank you.' Pru paused. 'I'm sorry if I sounded cross just now.'

'It's fine. I'm sorry. I got muddled up with the rooms. My fault,' replied Steph.

'Right, I must get on. Come and find me or Dominic when the room is ready, just so we can give it a quick once-over. I'll be in my study.'

As Steph watched Pru disappear, she was aware Dominic was still standing next to her. She turned and went to step past him but he caught her arm.

'Can I have a word?' he said.

Steph looked down at his fingers wrapped around her forearm. She looked back up at him and although she was unnerved she wasn't going to let him know that. 'Would you mind not holding on to my arm?'

Dominic looked down at his hand, and for a moment Steph wasn't sure if he was actually going to let go, but then he unfurled his fingers and released her arm. 'My mother is a very dignified woman and far too polite to tell you herself, so I'll do it.'

Steph didn't like the look in Dominic's eye and the way he was standing so close to her; the only way she could move would be to lean back over the banisters. 'I am really sorry about going into the room,' she said. 'I did apologise to your mother.'

'I heard. You may be able to pull the wool over her eyes, but I'm not so easy going, in case you hadn't realised.' He narrowed his eyes. 'Stay out of that room. Got it?'

Steph gulped. 'Yes. Got it,' she managed to say.

Dominic took a step back and smiled warmly at Steph. 'Good. You're a nice girl, Steph. Harry likes you a lot. I wouldn't want to piss him off by having to sack you or anything. And

I'm sure you don't want to lose your job either. The photos sound quite the money-spinner.'

Steph shook her head. 'No. I don't.' She could detect the tremor of fear in her own voice and was sure Dominic wouldn't miss it either. It was true, she didn't want to lose her job here at Conmere, but not for the reasons Dominic thought. She wanted to find out what had happened to Elizabeth Sinclair more than anything now.

'Good,' said Dominic. 'Now, you'd better get on with sorting out the Daffodil Room ready for our new guests.'

He stepped aside so Steph could pass him.

'Oh, Steph,' he called as she reached the top of the stairs. Steph turned to look at him. 'Yes?'

'You haven't heard anything more from Sonia Lomas, have you?'

Steph put on her best perplexed face. 'No. Nothing. Can't think why I would.'

'Someone said they saw her in town the other day. I just wondered if she'd spoken to you. Never quite sure with that woman if she's going to pull one of her publicity stunts or not. We could really do without that. So could Harry.'

'I haven't seen her at all,' said Steph.

'If you do, let me know, won't you?'

Steph gave a shudder as she descended the staircase. She really didn't like Dominic, and if she was honest, he scared her.

Chapter Twenty-Eight

S teph was glad it was her morning break and she could get out of the house for fifteen minutes. Conmere had such an oppressive feel to it; she couldn't explain it, but every time she stepped foot in there she felt uneasy.

She found a quiet spot in the centre of the Rose Garden and sat herself down on the bench which circled the centre-piece rose bush. The smell of the roses was gorgeous and it reminded Steph of her father's funeral and the posy of yellow tea roses she had placed on his coffin. Oddly enough, it was one of the few memories of that day that brought her comfort. Her dad had adored his roses and would spend many an hour lovingly tending them in his garden. It was a happy memory, and seeing roses, especially yellow ones, always made Steph feel that sense of love.

As she sat down she felt the corner of Elizabeth's note-book dig into her leg. She hadn't wanted to leave it in her room and, for peace of mind that she would know where it was at all times, she had slipped it into her pocket that morning.

Sue Fortin

She really should give Sonia a call to make sure she was OK after the accident.

Sonia answered almost immediately. 'Is everything OK?'

'Yes, all fine,' said Steph. 'I was just ringing to see how you were after the other day?'

'A little shaken, if I'm truthful, but I'm over it now. In fact, I'm quite glad it happened. At least that way it proves we, or rather you, are on to something. Whoever crashed into your car was trying to warn you off.'

'Hmm. An anonymous note or phone call would have been sufficient.'

'Someone must know something more about Elizabeth's death.'

'I agree, but it's getting people to talk.'

'You've got to find a way. Please don't give up on me. Or Elizabeth. Please.' There was a fracture in Sonia's voice. 'You're my only hope. Don't lose sight of the fact that this is my daughter's life we're talking about. My daughter was murdered. I *know* that. I *feel* that.'

Sonia's belief churned Steph's heart over and reminded her once again of the lack of connection she had with her own mother. Could you just *feel* things, *know* things, as a mother? 'I'm not giving up. Not yet,' she said, and heard Sonia sigh in relief. Steph continued. 'Did Elizabeth have any friends up here? Someone I could talk to? Someone who might know something that you don't? Someone she might have confided in?'

'None that I can think of,' replied Sonia. 'She only knew the Sinclair family.'

'What about her hairdresser or beauty therapist? Did she mention a salon?' Steph knew she was clutching at straws.

'I don't remember,' said Sonia, apologetically.

'Wait!' Steph almost shouted down the phone. The niggling thought that had been with her since she had rummaged around in Elizabeth's belongings gate-crashed its way forward.

'What is it?' Sonia sounded alarmed.

'You told me Elizabeth had a friend called Camilla, didn't you?'

'Er . . . yes, she mentioned her once or twice.'

Steph thought of the business card with the name Camilla and a phone number. 'I think I might know who she is. That's not exactly true, actually. I think I've found a number for her. I can't explain now, but I'm going to phone her.'

'So you're not giving up on me just yet?' There was genuine hope in Sonia's voice.

'No, I'm not giving up on either you or Elizabeth,' reassured Steph. She stood up and began walking back along the grass path through the roses. 'I'll call you again when there's something to report.'

'Thank you, Steph. Thank you so much.'

'Let's not get our hopes up too much.'

'I know you won't let us down.'

Ending the call, Steph slipped her hand into her pocket and took out the card she'd found in Elizabeth's coat. In her haste to put the coat back in the wardrobe before Pru caught her, she had stuffed the card into her own pocket. It couldn't be a coincidence, not with a name like Camilla. Surely there was a connection. At last she had a lead to follow, one that wasn't a member of the Sinclair family.

She stopped before she reached the edge of the Rose Garden and, using her phone, took a picture of the card which she then emailed to herself as back-up. The card had taken on a new significance and the last thing she wanted to do now was to lose it.

She thought back to her chat with Cameron. The name in the notebook wasn't his name, so could it be Camilla? She flipped through the pages and looked closely at the comment *'Cam . . . 230'*. She let out a deflated sigh. It definitely didn't say Camilla. She studied the writing, which was unusually squiggly, as if written in a hurry. And then it dawned on her. It said neither Cameron nor Camilla.

'Camera!' said Steph, out loud. 'It says camera.' The end squiggle was a dash leading towards the numbers. Perhaps it wasn't significant at all, but the way it was circled, Steph couldn't help feeling she was missing something. She looked at the rest of the list. Immediately below was a phone number, which had been underlined in the same red pen, and then 2206 on the same line, written in the same pen. Again, it seemed important and Steph was sure it was connected in some way.

Steph Googled the phone number. The results shouldn't have been surprising, she thought as she looked at the screen on her phone. The landline number belonged to a company called Jaspers, who were an online audio and visual equipment supplier, specialising in CCTV and monitoring.

She looked back at the notebook. Camera 230 – was that possibly a model number? She tried putting it into the browser but had no luck in finding out exactly what it was. If she could find out what Elizabeth was interested in, then it may help Steph build up a better understanding of what was going on at Conmere. Steph thought for a moment how she was going to do this. A few minutes later, taking a deep breath, she phoned the number.

'Hello. Jaspers Cameras and Accessories. Can I help you?'

'Oh, hello. I'm a personal assistant and I'm just trying to reconcile one of my client's accounts. They're on holiday at the moment so I can't ask them but wondered if you could help me. I'd sooner not trouble them, you see,' explained Steph. 'My client bought some camera equipment from you but, unfortunately, I seem to have just the model number. I know it's a long shot, but could you tell me what it relates to, please?'

'Well, I don't know but I'll give it a go. What's the model number?'

'Two three zero,' Steph offered.

'Is that all you've got? No letter before or after?'

'Just that followed by double-two, zero, six.'

'Hmm. That bit's not the model number. Wait while I input this on our system and see what we've got on our database.'

Steph waited patiently, listening to the tell-tale clicking of a keyboard being tapped. 'I do appreciate this,' she said.

'OK, you're in luck. Here we go . . .' There was a pause. 'It's actually one of our spy cameras. I suppose I'm not breaking any client confidentiality here.'

'No, of course not,' reassured Steph. 'I just needed to know what the item was. A spy camera, you say?'

'Yes. One of our more expensive ones. You can take photos with it, or record moving images.'

'Like a video recording?'

'Yes. It's a snazzy little number. Looks like a TV remote

control. And this particular model uploads the images direct to the cloud as well as storing it on the memory card at the same time.'

'Oh, wow. That sounds very cool,' said Steph. 'Just out of interest, these clouds – are they easy to access? I was just wondering about storing my own files. I've got Dropbox but I can't always link up to that for some reason.'

'For SpyCloud you need a four-digit code, like a PIN you have for your bank card. You can access it from anywhere and the service is very reasonably priced too.'

'Great. I'll have a look into that. Thanks very much for your help.'

'You're welcome.'

Steph hung up. So, Elizabeth had bought a spy camera which looked like a TV remote control. Why? Who had she been spying on?

'What were you up to, Elizabeth?' she muttered.

Steph's phone began to ring, startling her enough to make her drop it on the ground. Fortunately, the grass was a soft landing and Steph picked it up, turning it over to see it was her mother, of all people.

Steph had half a mind to ignore the call. She wasn't sure if she was ready to speak to Wendy right now, but all the same, she felt compelled to answer it.

'Hello.'

'Hello, Stephanie,' came her mother's voice, brisk and chilled as per usual. There was no remorse or contrition in her tone. 'Are you OK?'

Had she heard her mother right? Wendy was asking her if she was OK? She realised her mother was waiting for a response. 'Yes, I'm fine.' Although as she replied Steph conceded that wasn't particularly accurate.

'I think maybe we should talk,' said Wendy, this time more conciliatory. 'Maybe we could have lunch again?'

'Er . . . yes, that would be nice.' Steph was stunned by not only the call, but by the invitation too.

'Good. I'll call you later in the week to arrange it. Maybe Thursday or Friday?'

'Great. I'll look forward to it,' she heard herself saying, before her mum said goodbye and the call ended.

Steph felt both excited and cautious at this apparent development. Perhaps she should have given her mum a bit more credit when it came to understanding her daughter's emotions.

She was still mulling over the phone call as she entered Conmere House, and wasn't aware of anyone else in the hallway until she heard a voice.

'Penny for your thoughts.'

Steph stopped abruptly at the stairs. In front of her was Harry. He smiled at her and his blue eyes sparkled in the sunlight that flowed through the feature window.

'Sorry. I was miles away,' said Steph, feeling herself return his smile, although his friendliness took her by surprise. It was as if they hadn't argued at all. 'My mum just phoned. She's invited me to lunch at the end of the week.'

'That's nice,' replied Harry. 'Where are you going?'

'I don't know. Anywhere you'd recommend?'

'There's the Woodcutters in the village, just a few miles down the road. They do a good lunch.'

'Thanks. I'll mention it to her.' Steph didn't know what else to say and suddenly felt awkward standing there as they looked at each other. She wanted to apologise for not being able to tell him the truth but it would be a hollow apology if she still refused to confide in him. She broke the silence first. 'I'd better get on. Apparently, the clean laundry is coming in today.' She waved a hand in the direction of the laundry room.

Harry pulled a face. 'Laundry duty. That will be fun. I remember having to do that myself when I was a kid.'

Steph raised her eyebrows. 'You did? Oh, I didn't realise you had to do that sort of work.'

'Yeah. My dad said it was character-building and that we all had to start at the bottom and do the worst jobs possible. He said it was the only way to earn the respect of the staff.'

'He probably had a point.'

'Yeah, he did. Put it this way, he didn't believe in anyone being born with a silver spoon in their mouth. His work ethic was probably the only thing I inherited.'

An imperceptible look swept across Harry's face but disappeared as fast as it had arrived. 'And nothing else? Is that all you inherited?'

'All I wanted to,' said Harry, almost to himself.

Steph was both relieved and confused that Harry was speaking to her as if nothing had happened. She went to speak, but Harry beat her to it.

'Look, Steph, I'm glad I've seen you. I was hoping to speak to you later, when you'd finished work, but seeing as we're here now . . . I'm sorry for the way I spoke to you Sunday evening. I know it's no excuse, but I'm finding it hard adjusting to being back here at Conmere, for lots of reasons.'

'I can imagine.' She gave a sympathetic smile.

He looked around the hall and then in a low voice said, 'I really like you, Steph. I don't want what happened here to affect anything between us. If it helps, I'm prepared to answer your questions about Elizabeth, but on one condition.'

Steph's heart threw in an extra beat. 'The condition?'

'It's just between me and you. It's personal and private, so we can maybe take things further but with no taboo subjects. I'm not going to ask you about Sonia or your mum; I'm going to prove I trust you.' He looked intently at her. 'One of us has to give first and I'm willing to do that. I want you to know I trust you . . . then, maybe, you'll trust me.'

Steph nodded. 'I'd like that.' And she would, despite acknowledging that, while this might mean she couldn't publish Elizabeth's story completely, there was the chance that some of it could be used, or at least used to find the truth without betraying Harry's confidence.

He smiled again and her stomach gave a tumble. 'I'll speak to you later – maybe we can go for a drink? Away from here.'

'I'd like that too.' She felt like a traitor to both herself and Harry. She wanted to see him again, no doubt about that. She hadn't felt so drawn to a man in a long time, maybe never, but there was the other side of her who was fist-pumping the air that he was prepared to open up about Elizabeth to her. She might be able to find out something that would be crucial to proving or disproving Sonia's theory.

'I'd better let you go,' said Harry.

'And I've got a date with the laundry room,' said Steph.

'Have fun.'

'Can't wait.'

As she made her way across the hall and to the rear of the house, she didn't need to look round to know Harry was watching her. She could feel his eyes searing into her back. Her stomach gave a little flutter of excitement and she could feel herself grinning broadly.

Conmere, Staff Room, Tuesday, 14 May, 5.00 p.m.

The laundry was as boring as Steph had anticipated and Harry had warned. She spent the afternoon counting in the table linen and napkins, sheets, pillowcases, towels and duvet covers, putting everything away correctly in the laundry room, then going around the various station points in the main house and stocking up the cupboards.

Finally, the afternoon shift was over and Steph was free to do what she liked. She ate tea with Antonio and two other members of staff, Hazel and Eileen. Both women had worked at Conmere for several years. It was a good opportunity to try to get the women on to the subject of the Sinclair family.

'Do you live far away from the resort?' asked Steph, looking at her colleagues.

'I'm about two miles down the road in Conmere village,' said Eileen.

'I'm over at Kendalton, which is about a twenty-minute drive,' replied Hazel.

'Although I haven't always lived there,' continued Eileen. 'I used to live in, here at Conmere House, in the staff quarters.'

'How long ago was that?' asked Steph.

'I've been moved out about eighteen months now.'

'What made you move?' Steph hoped her interest sounded casual.

'A couple of reasons, really. I used to live here with my partner, but we split up and he stayed on working, which made it a bit awkward. Although he did actually leave Conmere six months ago, thank goodness.'

'Good riddance too,' chipped in Hazel. 'Thought he was going to stay forever.' She looked over at Steph. 'He wasn't very popular with the rest of us, in case you hadn't noticed. He was always grassing people up to Dominic for petty things, like being late or having five minutes' longer break, that sort of thing.'

Steph pulled a sympathetic face. 'One of those,' she said. Then, turning back to Eileen, 'What were the other reasons?'

Eileen put her knife and fork together and pushed away her plate. 'It was never the same after Harry left. I used to clean Harry and Elizabeth's lodge.'

'Eileen does all the Sinclair family lodges and private bedrooms,' put in Hazel.

Steph nodded. This was a great way in for her. 'That was awful what happened to Elizabeth Sinclair. Were you here that day?'

'Yes, I was working in the house,' said Eileen gravely. 'Terrible business. There was pandemonium when her body was discovered in the lake. It was Harry who found her.'

'That is awful,' agreed Steph, and she felt a wave of compassion for Harry. 'I can't imagine getting over something like that.'

'I don't think he could,' said Eileen. 'That's why he went off to France six months after burying her. He couldn't cope with being around so many memories of her.'

'Although God knows why,' muttered Hazel. Her eyes met Eileen's and something passed between the two women which Steph couldn't read.

'She wasn't that bad once you got to know her,' said Eileen. 'She just didn't fit in well, that's all.'

'In what way?' asked Steph.

'Oh, I shouldn't really speak ill of the dead.'

'I don't mind though.' Hazel flicked her friend another look and lowered her voice as she spoke. 'Elizabeth was a modern-day woman. She wanted to be involved with the business. She was always floating around telling the staff to do this, that and the other, as if she was our boss. But the brothers and Mrs Sinclair didn't want anyone else involved.'

'Elizabeth wanted to feel like she was useful,' said Eileen. 'It's not quite as cut and dried as Hazel's saying. Elizabeth wasn't like Dominic's partner or Owen's wife. She was ambitious and I don't think the Sinclair family were quite ready for her.'

'She was an awful flirt too,' said Hazel.

'A flirt?'

Eileen answered before Hazel could elaborate. 'She was a beautiful young woman, with a good sense of humour, who was very charming, especially where the men were concerned.'

'A flirt. Like I said. You should have seen her with Dominic. They all got drunk one night and, by all accounts, it was embarrassing for everyone there. Harry and his brother had words and then Harry practically carried Elizabeth back to their lodge.'

'Ladies,' said Antonio, who up until that point had remained silent. 'I don't know if we should be speaking about the late Mrs Sinclair. I'm not sure it's appropriate.'

'Oh, go and polish some silver if you don't like the conversation,' said Hazel, waving her hand at Antonio. 'You didn't even work here at the time.'

Antonio made a grumbling noise and stood up, pushing his chair back. 'You two can gossip all you like.' He looked at Steph. 'And gossip it is. Please don't pay any attention to what these two are saying.'

Once Antonio had left the kitchen, Hazel started up where she had left off.

'Elizabeth was bored here. I think that's why she liked to flirt. It was a bit of amusement for her.'

'So that night, when she got really drunk – did Harry and Dominic have a big falling out?'

'You might as well tell her now you've started,' said Eileen, folding her arms across her chest and sitting back in her chair, whereas Hazel leaned forward, glee plastered across her face.

'Apparently, Harry went out onto the terrace and heard them flirting with each other. He told Dominic he was egging her on and should know better. Dominic told him he was overreacting and he should keep his wife under control.'

Steph raised an eyebrow. 'What a chauvinistic thing to say.'

'Dominic's a bit like that. He's a good-looking man but boy, does he know it. He's had his fair share of lady friends and I'm not sure all of them have been on the market, if you get my meaning,' said Hazel.

'So the brothers didn't have a massive row?' probed Steph.

'No, a few words and then Harry carted Elizabeth off. But the next day they had a proper barney.'

'They nearly came to blows,' said Eileen. 'If it wasn't for

Owen getting in between them and Mrs Sinclair Senior coming in, I dread to think what would have happened.'

'Why did Harry wait until the next day though? You'd think he'd have kicked off when he heard them flirting,' said Steph.

'No one really knows but the story goes that Dominic teased Harry about it the next morning,' said Hazel. 'You see, Dominic, as the eldest, considers himself top dog. He likes to remind everyone of that now and again and flirting with Harry's wife, letting Harry know he could probably wind Elizabeth round his little finger, was his way of reminding his younger brother who was in charge.'

Steph took a moment to digest this information. 'I know Dominic likes to flex his muscles but I didn't realise it extended to his brother. I was under the impression they got on well.'

'As a rule, they do,' said Eileen, getting up and collecting the plates. 'But, like between any strong-minded men, there's sometimes a bit of conflict and a challenge for the role of silverback.'

'If she wasn't off spending money on designer this and designer that, then she was stuck here. Harry was always working. She didn't have anything to do with her time.'

'Didn't she have any friends?' asked Steph. 'There must have been someone she knew.'

Eileen shook her head. 'No. I think the nearest she got to a friend was Natalie, Owen's wife, or one of the girls who worked in the local beauty shop where she got her nails done. Very sad when you think about it.'

'Do you mean Camilla?' Steph said, taking a gamble. She looked at the blank faces of the two women.

'Camilla? Never heard of her,' said Eileen.

'Nope. New one on me,' agreed Hazel. 'Where did you get that name from?'

'Oh . . . I heard someone mention Camilla at the beauty shop on site,' said Steph, trying to sound casual at her lie. She gave a self-deprecating smile. 'I must be jumping to conclusions.'

'Yeah, must be,' said Eileen.

Chapter Twenty-Nine

There was nothing Elizabeth liked better than a party thrown by the Sinclair brothers, especially when Pru was away. It was almost as if the brothers reverted to their teenage years and could let their hair down properly. This weekend Pru was visiting a friend in Spain and, as an early celebration of Owen's birthday the following week, a party was now in full swing.

Between them, the brothers knew a lot of people, although Elizabeth was beginning to realise that Harry had the least number of friends. Consequently, it was times like these that Elizabeth was actually grateful to be surrounded by friends of Dominic and Owen.

With a glass of party punch in her hand, Elizabeth wandered out onto the terrace. It was a particularly warm evening and there were upwards of eighty or ninety people. The music was pumping out via the speakers dotted around, and one corner of the terrace had been turned into a makeshift dance floor, complete with multicoloured strobe lighting.

Elizabeth looked over the edge of the terrace at the swimming pool below. She didn't think it was swimming weather but could imagine some people taking an impromptu alcohol-fuelled dip at some point in the night. Natalie had helped Elizabeth rig up the fairy lights draped across the row of trees which lined the path from the terrace to the pool, giving the walkway an enchanted, almost magical feel in the fading light.

Elizabeth looked back through to the main room of the house. The Sinclairs opened it up for conferences, meetings, large gatherings and functions, and it was ideal for this sort of party. She could see Harry still talking to the group of men she had made her escape from ten minutes ago on the pretence of having seen someone she knew. Of course, she hardly knew anyone but the conversation had been boring her rigid and she needed to get away.

'Now, you look a lonely sight.'

Elizabeth turned to see Dominic at her side. He held up a bottle of champagne.

'Not lonely,' she said, offering up her now empty glass for a refill. 'Just bored, if I'm honest.'

'Bored! Never let it be said that anyone at a Sinclair party is bored.' Dominic gave a look of mock horror and filled up her glass. 'My reputation is on the line here.'

'You might want to tell your brother that.' Elizabeth gestured with her head back to Harry. 'If I was into golf and rugby it wouldn't be so bad. Please, if you're going to talk to me about any of those subjects, then you might as well go now.'

Dominic gave a laugh. 'I would never be so boring.'

Elizabeth raised her eyebrows. 'I only have your word for that.'

'I'm an honest man. I wouldn't make claim to such a thing if it wasn't true. I promise you that.'

'My mother warned me about men who make promises but don't deliver.' Elizabeth finished the glass of champagne and Dominic refilled it without hesitation.

'Where's Lisa tonight?' Elizabeth glanced around the terrace to see if Dominic's girlfriend was about.

'Oh, she's had to go back and check on Saskia. The babysitter messaged over to say that she'd been sick.'

'You've been left to your own devices, then?' Elizabeth looked up at Dominic. She'd always admired his eyes; although all the brothers had blue eyes, Dominic's were almost navy. They looked even darker tonight; maybe it was the strobe lighting but they seemed to sparkle and dance as he returned her gaze.

They were interrupted as Owen bundled into them. 'Sorry,' he slurred. 'Oh, it's you, Dom.' He refocused his eyes on Elizabeth. 'And you, Elizabeth.' He clamped his hand down on Dominic's shoulder. 'I have to say, this is a bloody good party.'

'I'm glad you're enjoying it,' said Dominic. He took the beer bottle from his brother's hand. 'I think though maybe you've had enough tonight.'

'Don't be such a spoilsport,' said Owen. 'I've only just begun.'

'I don't think so.' Dominic's tone took on a more serious note. 'Why don't you have a black coffee and pace yourself? It's only ten-thirty. You're never going to last the night otherwise.'

Owen swayed on his feet a little but managed to stay upright. He took his hand from Dominic's shoulder and wagged his finger at him. 'My birthday. I can get as wrecked as I like. You can't stop me.'

'Hey, I'm not going to stop you,' said Dominic. 'Natalie might though. Here she comes.'

Owen looked over his shoulder at his wife walking towards them. 'Oh, shit,' he muttered.

'Owen. I've been looking for you all over the place,' said Natalie, frowning as she neared, coming to a halt in front of him. 'You're really drunk.' She looked at Dominic. 'How has he got into this state already?'

'I was just wondering the same thing.' Dominic shook his head.

'Stop being so miserable, the lot of you,' said Owen, and with that headed off towards the corner of the terrace to join in with the dancing.

'It's bloody embarrassing,' said Natalie. 'Can't you do something? Say something to him about his drinking? It's getting out of control again. Even your mum has noticed it recently.'

'How bad is it?' asked Dominic.

'Every night. I'm sure he's back to drinking during the day too,' said Natalie. 'I called into the stables the other day and there was an empty bottle of whisky in the bin. I asked him about it and he said he'd caught one of the staff drinking and had tipped it away.'

'Really? He never said anything to me about someone drinking at work.'

'I think he was lying.' Natalie's gaze dropped to the ground and Elizabeth was sure she wiped away a tear. 'It's like he can't go through a day without having some sort of drink. It's the first thing he does when he comes in after work. It's not unusual for him to drink a whole bottle of wine before going to bed. I really thought all that was in the past, but he's slipped right back into it.'

Dominic rubbed Natalie's arm. 'Hey, come on. Don't go getting all upset tonight. Not here,' he said. 'I'll tell you what. I promise I'll speak to him properly tomorrow. There's no point saying anything tonight. Let him get pissed and when he's had enough, I'll get Harry to help me put him to bed. How does that sound?'

Natalie looked up gratefully at her brother-in-law. 'Thank you, Dominic. I'd really appreciate that. I'm going to go back to our place now and let Eileen go home. She was kind enough to babysit for us tonight but I know she doesn't like being out too late. I'll order her a taxi.'

'OK. Goodnight, Natalie.' Dominic gave her a peck on the cheek.

Elizabeth hugged Natalie. 'Don't worry,' she said. 'I'm sure it will all be OK tomorrow.'

'Thank you,' said Natalie again, before hurrying off in the direction of their lodge.

'You're quite a softy at heart, aren't you?' said Elizabeth, treating herself to another look into his eyes. 'All that tough, macho exterior is just a front.'

'There's more to me than meets the eye,' said Dominic with a wink.

'Is that right?' Elizabeth moved a bit closer and swayed a little. 'I see I've got a lot more to discover about you Sinclair brothers than I first thought.'

Before Dominic could continue the conversation, another guest came up. It was a man roughly their age, dressed smartly but with a full tattoo sleeve on his left arm and another in a large tribal pattern down to his elbow on the other arm. His gold earrings sparkled in the strobe lighting. Although he was in a smart shirt and chinos, to Elizabeth it looked as though he would be more at home in jeans and T-shirt, with a bandanna and a motorbike not too far away.

'Evening, Dominic. Nice party,' he said.

Dominic turned to Elizabeth. 'Would you excuse me? I've just got to speak to Mark about something.'

Somehow he didn't look like a Mark, but Elizabeth smiled and nodded. 'Of course.'

Dominic passed his glass to her. 'I'll leave this with you. Back in five.'

Elizabeth leaned back against the balustrade of the terrace and watched Dominic and Mark walk down the steps and cross the poolside before walking around the pool house. She moved position slightly and could just make them out through the glass of the pool house, the festoon lights casting enough brightness for her to see them.

They had a brief conversation and then Mark took an envelope from his pocket and handed it to Dominic. She watched as Dominic looked inside the envelope and then withdrew the contents. She couldn't see clearly but it looked like a wad of notes. Dominic thumbed through the notes before returning them to the envelope, which he then placed in his inside breast pocket. The two men shook hands and Mark walked away, but not back up the terrace steps – he headed off, taking the narrow path which led to the car park.

Elizabeth drank the last of her champagne and, still holding Dominic's glass in her hand, made her way down the steps as Dominic strode back, meeting her at the foot of the steps.

'Has your friend gone?' asked Elizabeth.

'He wasn't a friend, just a business associate,' replied Dominic. 'And, yes, he's gone. What's it to you?'

'Just making sure there were no more distractions.'

'From what?'

'From your champagne. Don't want it going flat,' Elizabeth said, passing his glass to him. As she did so, she stumbled forward and, fortunately, Dominic caught her in his arms.

'Hey, steady,' he said, sounding amused. He took the glass from her hand and swigged it back, while still holding her with his other arm. 'Don't want that going to waste.'

Elizabeth's face was only inches from his. She inclined her head. Her mouth was perilously close to making contact with his.

Dominic jerked his head away. 'Not here,' he muttered, glancing round.

'Sorry, I didn't mean to,' she said, suddenly feeling flustered and embarrassed.

Dominic smiled and nodded at a couple of guests as they trotted up the terrace steps and into the house, laughing together as they went. 'If you're serious, you should come and find me when you're sober.' Elizabeth felt his hand slide down her back and cup her buttock.

'I'm not that drunk,' she said.

'You're not that sober either.' He looked up towards the terrace. 'And here comes your husband.'

'You two are looking very guilty,' said Harry as he approached.

Elizabeth gulped but realised he was smiling at them.

'I was just looking after your wife. Keeping the lecherous wolves at bay,' said Dominic. He gave Elizabeth's backside another squeeze before sliding his hand away.

'And drinking the champagne,' said Harry, nodding towards the now empty bottle.

'Ah, yes, the champagne. Not a bad year.'

'Where's Lisa?' Harry asked.

'Saskia's puked everywhere. I would have offered to go myself but I can't deal with sick.' Dominic grimaced. 'Natalie's gone too. She was hacked off that Owen's got himself pissed so early.'

Harry sighed. 'He's only got one setting – a hundred mph all the time where drink's concerned.'

'I told Natalie we'd scoop him up soon and take him home. I'll have to speak to him tomorrow. It's all getting out of hand.'

Elizabeth stopped listening as the two men discussed their brother and turned her thoughts to the proposition from Dominic. She replayed the conversation to check she wasn't reading too much into the comment or, indeed, misreading it completely, but no, she was certain she hadn't got hold of the wrong end of the stick. It was a very appealing proposition, she had to admit.

She spent the rest of the night keeping one eye on Dominic and being attentive to Harry. She didn't want to arouse his suspicions if she was indeed going to accept Dominic's suggestion. By the time Dominic and Harry had managed to persuade their brother to call it a night, it was gone midnight.

'I'm ready for bed myself,' said Harry, when he found Elizabeth.

'Oh, don't be such a party pooper. The evening has only just started,' she said.

'You've had quite your fair share of booze as well.'

'Who are you? The alcohol police? Lighten up, Harry. Let your hair down and enjoy yourself.' Elizabeth then made a point of hitting the dance floor and throwing herself energetically around to the music.

When did Harry become such a bore? she wondered. He was a lot more fun when they'd first got married. These days he was ready for his slippers and pipe. She thought of Dominic, who seemed a much more exciting and fun proposition altogether. There was a sense of danger about him. It wasn't the first time she'd realized this. She'd always known he was the alpha male of the family, the one who held the power, but it had never seemed as obvious as it did now. Before, when she and Harry were having lots of fun, Dominic hadn't seemed so different, but now there was a growing rift between the two of them.

Harry eventually managed to persuade her to go back to their lodge a couple of hours later. She had partied even harder since Owen was deposited home. She wanted to make the most of it and to make a point to Harry that she wasn't ready to hang up her party shoes any time soon. If he remembered the fun they used to have, he might revert back to his more carefree ways.

Elizabeth flopped into bed and, closing her eyes, turned on her side. Harry was in the bathroom, brushing his teeth. If he had any notion they were going to have sex, he could think again. She was far too tired for that. She knew she'd be asleep before he climbed into bed beside her.

The Dead Wife

Although Elizabeth felt she had only been asleep for a short time, she was surprised to see it was nine o'clock in the morning. She rolled over and saw the bed was empty. Harry was probably organising the post-party tidy-up. She yawned and her thoughts migrated back to last night. Her stomach pitched and she had a sudden and very clear recollection of her moment with Dominic. Oops. She had tried to kiss him right there at the party. And he had groped her arse. She smiled at the thought. And he had told her to call him when she was sober.

Elizabeth tentatively got up from the bed and slipped on her dressing gown. Was this too early to call him? Would he be sleeping off a hangover or would he be helping Harry tidy up? She made herself a cup of tea and, going back up to the bedroom, glanced out of the window. She couldn't have timed it better. There, walking along the path through the trees, were Harry and Dominic.

Elizabeth picked up her phone from the bedside table and dialled Dominic's mobile.

She watched Dominic take his phone from his pocket and after a slight hesitation answer it.

'Hello, Dominic Sinclair.'

'Hello, Dominic Sinclair,' purred Elizabeth. 'This is Elizabeth Sinclair. I'm just phoning to let you know that I'm sober and following up on our conversation from last night.'

'I'm a bit busy at the moment. I'm in the middle of a meeting with my brother,' he replied.

'When do you think you'll be free? I'm off out to do some shopping in a couple of hours. On my own.'

'OK. That sounds doable. I'll meet you in town at eleven clock. I'll text you when I'm there. I shall look forward to it.'

'And so shall I.' And then, just for the fun of it, she added, 'Oh, by the way, I do love the colour shirt you're wearing. The blue really suits you.' She hung up and giggled as she watched Dominic look up towards the house.

Elizabeth continued to watch the two men as they neared and then said their goodbyes. At the sound of the front door opening, Elizabeth hopped back into bed, making sure she cleared her phone history.

'Hiya – you're awake now,' said Harry, coming into the room. He smiled at her and gave her a kiss on the lips. 'How's the head?'

'Surprisingly clear,' replied Elizabeth. 'In fact, I was just about to jump in the shower. I've got to go out in a little while.'

'Where are you going?'

'I've got a massage booked. I thought I'd treat myself to one.'

'In town? I'll drive you in, if you like, and we can get some lunch afterwards.'

Elizabeth balked at the suggestion but quickly regained her composure. 'Oh, normally I'd say yes, but I'm also planning on a bit of shopping for a certain someone's birthday.' She tapped the side of her nose, the lie slipping off her tongue with ease.

'OK, I can take the hint,' said Harry.

Chapter Thirty

Conmere, Tuesday, 14 May, 5.45 p.m.

Steph eventually made her excuses and left Eileen and Hazel in the kitchen, having gleaned quite a lot of background info on the Sinclairs. She wasn't yet sure if it was going to be of any use, but she committed it to memory all the same. The abridged version was that Elizabeth had been a flirt. Dominic was a ladies' man. Dominic also felt entitled because he was the eldest and liked to remind his brothers of this regularly, while Harry was more passive-aggressive and the peacemaker of the family. He was also the one who'd had enough and flown the nest after what happened to his wife.

Steph changed her clothes and decided to go to the lake to call Camilla. She liked it there; it felt peaceful, and the water was comforting. She did a quick scan of the area to make sure she was alone, then took out the business card and tapped in the number.

It was answered after the third ring. 'Hello,' came the voice of a woman.

'Hello, can I speak to Camilla, please?'

'Speaking. Who is this?'

'Hi, my name's Steph Durham. I'm a friend of Elizabeth Sinclair's mother.'

'Elizabeth Sinclair? I'm sorry, I don't know anyone by that name.'

Steph could now hear the very crisp and upper-class accent of the woman and it was hard to place her age, as she sounded neither old nor young. Steph also didn't miss the slightly guarded tone to the woman's voice.

'You gave her your business card. She mentioned you to her mother.' It wasn't quite the truth, but Steph couldn't think of another way to get Camilla to talk to her. 'It's really important that I speak to you.' There was a silence. 'Camilla? Are you still there?'

'Yes, I'm still here,' said Camilla after a moment. 'Thinking about it, I do vaguely remember her. I'm not sure why she'd have my business card though.'

Steph was sure Camilla knew exactly who they were talking about and decided to plough ahead on that basis. 'I take it you know Elizabeth Sinclair died two years ago?'

'Yes, I heard, but then everyone in the area did.'

If Camilla had heard of Elizabeth's death, the chances were she was local too, and Steph jotted that down in her notebook. 'Her mother doesn't believe Elizabeth's death was an accident. I'm trying to help her.'

'Are you a reporter?'

'Not in the way you probably think. Please don't hang up,' said Steph quickly, sensing that Camilla might be of a mind to end the call. 'I didn't know anything about this until last week when Elizabeth's mother contacted me after she found out I was coming up here to cover the opening of Conmere

Resort Centre. I'm not even sure there is a story but I'm making discreet enquires.'

'I can't help you.'

'Please, Camilla, could we just meet for a chat over a coffee? You may not realise you know anything, but if we can just talk I might be able to find something out. It's just that no one other than the family seem to know anything about Elizabeth and I'm trying to build up a picture of what sort of life she had here.'

'I really don't think I'm the one to ask.'

'Then who?'

'I don't know.'

The line went dead. 'Damn it!' cursed Steph. She redialled the number, unperturbed. 'Please don't hang up,' she said as soon as Camilla answered it.

'I have nothing to say,' she snapped.

'Elizabeth kept your card. There must be a reason she did that. Her mother mentioned your name. You may not know it, but you could be important to finding out the truth.'

'I'm sorry . . .'

Steph cut in. 'I don't believe the police know about your card in Elizabeth's coat pocket. I can keep it that way.'

There was a pause. 'Are you blackmailing me?'

'I'd sooner not,' said Steph, injecting a softer tone into her voice. 'Please, Camilla, I just want to ask you a few questions, face to face.'

There was another pause. 'I don't like being blackmailed but you sound somewhere between determined and desperate, and if it will make you happy I'll meet you, but I think you'll be wasting your time.'

'Let me be the judge of that. When and where can we meet?'

'How about this evening? Kendalton Green Hotel. Eight o'clock.'

Steph hesitated momentarily. She was supposed to be meeting Harry tonight. Damn it. She hoped she wouldn't regret her decision. 'OK. I'll be there.'

'Meet me in the bar. I'll be the blonde sitting at the corner table with a pink gin.'

'Great. I'll see you there.'

'Oh, before you go, do the Sinclairs know you're asking questions?'

'No. Like I said, I'm being discreet.'

'If I was you, I'd keep it that way. Have you mentioned to anyone that you were going to call me?'

'No. Not a soul.' Steph was glad the other woman couldn't see her wince at the lie.

'Again, keep it that way. I don't want to end up like Elizabeth Sinclair.'

The line went dead and Steph replayed the conversation over in her mind. It was the only hint in the whole of the conversation that gave Steph any notion Camilla might actually know something worthwhile.

She quickly tapped out a message to Harry.

Really sorry, but I can't make tonight for a drink. Something's come up. Can we meet tomorrow? Xx

She hoped he wouldn't mind and would at least acknowledge her text. While she waited for a reply, she called up the maps on her phone and tapped in Kendalton Green Hotel to double-check the directions. It wasn't exactly on the doorstep and was a twenty-five-minute drive away. Steph closed the app and put the phone back in her pocket, picking up her pace to get back to the house as quickly as possible but without drawing attention to herself. She didn't have much time if she was going to freshen herself up, get changed and drive over to Kendalton.

Cutting across the rear lawn towards the staff quarters, she cursed as she saw Dominic standing at the corner, having a cigarette.

'Hello, Steph,' he said, as she neared him. 'Everything OK?'

'Yes, fine,' she said. 'Just been for a walk.'

'You look to be in a hurry.'

'Not especially. Well, just a bit,' she corrected herself, suddenly wondering if he was going to engage her in conversation if he thought she had nothing better to do. 'I promised my mum I'd give her a call. She hates it if I'm late. You know what mums are like.' God, she was waffling now.

Dominic eyed her appraisingly. 'Yes, I know what mums are like,' he said after a moment. 'They like to chat, eh? Must be something about older women. A bit like Eileen and Hazel. They like to chat, or should I say gossip? Most of the time about stuff they don't know about. I shouldn't pay them any attention.'

'No. I won't,' said Steph. 'Sorry, I really must go.' She gulped as she went past him.

As she got to her room, her phone pinged and she read the text message from Harry.

That's a shame. Tomorrow will be good. Speak soon.

She felt slightly relieved that he seemed to have taken her standing him up relatively well and was happy to meet tomorrow.

Within half an hour, Steph had freshened up, changed and was driving away out of Conmere Resort Centre, and she had to admit the feeling of relief was discernible. She hadn't noticed it while she was there, but a sense of disquiet had grown daily.

Kendalton, Tuesday, 14 May, 7.50 p.m.

Steph took a steady drive over to Kendalton. She parked in the car park alongside the river that ran through the town and, crossing the pedestrian bridge, found herself coming out on the main drag. Kendalton Green Hotel was just down the road on the right.

She could see the flags fluttering in the evening breeze, local county flags and a Union Jack. The hotel stood proudly in the centre of the street, staking its position as the elder statesman of the town. Inside the hotel was very modern-looking, with polished marble flooring and lots of glass and mirrors, giving the illusion of a much bigger building. The bar wasn't too busy and Steph easily spotted Camilla sitting at the table as promised.

Camilla gave a nod and indicated to Steph to join her where two glasses of pink gin were sitting on the table.

'Thank you for meeting me,' said Steph, once they had formally identified each other. 'I do appreciate it.'

'I wasn't initially sure if it was a good idea, but I have been expecting this day to come,' replied Camilla.

'Why's that?'

'After meeting with Elizabeth, I did a bit of digging and found out that she hadn't been entirely truthful with me. However, we had a business agreement and, whatever her reasons for lying, I assumed they were valid enough.'

'Can you tell me from the start what happened, please? How did you come to know Elizabeth?' Steph took a large sip of the gin, which wouldn't have been her normal choice of drink, but she had to admit, tasted rather pleasant.

Steph listened while Camilla explained the circumstances surrounding her meeting with Elizabeth Sinclair. She wasn't entirely surprised, given what she had learned earlier that day from Eileen and Hazel, but all the same, she hadn't quite been expecting what she was hearing.

'So, let me get this straight,' she said once Camilla had finished. 'She hired you to set Owen up, telling you he was her husband, and you were happy to do so for what I presume was a lucrative pay day.'

'That's the long and short of it,' replied Camilla. She looked steadily at Steph. 'You do know what my profession is, don't you?'

'I do now,' replied Steph as all the pieces of information lined up neatly in a row.

'And don't judge me on it,' said Camilla.

'I wasn't. Not at all. I'm not in the business of judging other women.'

'I'm glad to hear it.'

'Do you know if Elizabeth actually did anything with the recording? Did she blackmail Owen? Although I can't think why she'd want to.'

'There are usually two reasons why a woman blackmails a man. One is money and the other is sex. Either Elizabeth wanted some money from Owen in exchange for her silence or she wanted him to leave his wife for her.'

'You think it's that simple?'

'I know it.'

Steph contemplated the scenarios before speaking again. 'Do you think Owen had anything to do with Elizabeth's death?'

'Hooray! The penny is finally dropping. For a reporter you're slow on the uptake.' Camilla smiled and then signalled to the waiter for some more drinks.

'I'll pay for these,' said Steph as a few minutes later two more pink gins were placed in front of them.

'No, these are on me. You're going to need to save your money.'

Steph looked at Camilla with interest. 'Am I?' It was true her finances were pretty dire, but she had a feeling Camilla wasn't referring to that.

'All in good time,' replied Camilla. She checked her watch. 'I need to go soon. I have a meeting with a client in half an hour.'

'If you think Owen had something to do with Elizabeth's death, why didn't you go to the police and tell them what happened?'

'It wasn't any of my business,' said Camilla simply. 'It wouldn't be good for my own business to be associated with the police or for my clients to think I couldn't keep my mouth shut. Not only that, but if Elizabeth was murdered, intentionally or otherwise, I might be putting myself in danger.'

'But if she was murdered, as her mum seems to think she was, surely that's worth more than just protecting yourself?'

'I did say don't judge me.' Camilla's tone took a dip. 'And besides, I'm protecting lots of people, not just me. All my clients expect and receive confidentiality.'

'Apologies. I wasn't intending to sound judgy,' conceded Steph. 'This recording that Elizabeth made, you don't happen to know what she did with it, do you? I know it's a bit of a long shot, but without any hard evidence, all this is just hearsay.'

'The original I assumed she kept somewhere and showed it to Owen at some point.'

'And you think that's what led to her death?'

'It's a possibility.'

Steph pondered this for a moment, but the thought that Owen was a murderer just didn't sit right with her. From what she'd seen of him, she couldn't imagine him having the balls to kill anyone. Then again, what did she know? She needed to keep an open mind about it and Owen's involvement was, at present, just a hypothesis.

'Do you have a copy of the recording?'

Camilla took a long sip of her drink. 'Look, I don't want to get involved with what happened. I don't want to put myself in any danger but . . . there was an incident recently which got me thinking and now, well, I'd like to help if I can. If it means putting away one, some, or all of those Sinclairs, then I'm happy to help.'

'What happened to change your mind after all this time?'

'I had the misfortune of bumping into Owen Sinclair recently, at an event I was attending. I was working, accompanying a businessman, and Owen recognised me. When I went to the toilets, Owen followed me. He attacked me. Said he was getting his own back for setting him up.'

'He attacked you?'

'Attempted rape.'

'Oh, my God! Did you report it?'

'No. I didn't. Like I said, it was attempted. I managed to fight him off but not before he'd ripped my underwear and touched me.'

'Bastard.'

'His brother Dominic came from nowhere and pulled him off me. Offered me money to keep my mouth shut.' Camilla spoke matter-of-factly. 'He wasn't interested if I was hurt or anything, he was just interested in protecting his brother. He assumed Owen had randomly tried it on with me – it didn't occur to him it might be something more sinister to do with Elizabeth, and I wasn't going to tell him otherwise. I did, however, tell him to keep his money. I was angry and upset. I should have taken the money, in hindsight. However, you coming along, it's almost like fate. It's karma. I can get my own back on him without being involved.'

'I'm so sorry,' said Steph, genuinely appalled at the story. Whatever Camilla's profession, a sexual assault was a sexual assault – end of.

'Don't feel sorry for me,' said Camilla. 'I've dealt with worse than that and worse than him.'

'I can't say I liked Owen very much before, but, hearing that, I thoroughly dislike him now.'

'He's pathetic. He's not the one to worry about. Look, I haven't really got anything else to tell you, other than, whatever Elizabeth was doing, whatever her reasons for blackmailing Owen, it was something big. She had a bigger agenda, I'm sure. She didn't confide in me, but I've seen women like her before. They're ambitious. They always want more than what they've got. And Elizabeth, she had a plan to dominate that family and there's only one way you can do that.'

Steph looked at her expectantly, hoping Camilla was going to say more, but she didn't. Steph took a guess. 'Money?'

'Not just money. Power.'

'Power over the Sinclairs?'

'Well done. We got there in the end.' Camilla drained the rest of her glass. 'I need to go. Good luck and be careful.'

'Thanks and thank you for talking to me.' Steph watched Camilla put on her jacket and stand to leave. 'I hope everything works out for you. Take care.'

'Ditto.'

Steph's Room, Conmere House,
Tuesday, 14 May, 9.45 p.m.

Steph looked at the notebook in front of her, confident it had more secrets to yield. It was all there, she just didn't know what she was looking for.

Camilla had been certain Elizabeth's ambition was much bigger than just blackmailing Owen for a few pounds. From what Steph had learnt of Harry's wife, she was of the same opinion. Elizabeth had come from nothing and wanted everything. She was an intelligent woman and wouldn't easily be put off her quest for not just success money-wise, but for power too.

It must have something to do with Conmere; it seemed the most obvious answer . . . maybe something to do with the business itself. Looking at the pages with a fresh agenda, Steph slowly leafed through them, looking for anything that could relate to Conmere.

After several minutes of careful searching, Steph hit gold. It was amazing how something could be hidden in plain sight. Now she knew what she was looking for, it was there, staring right back at her. A couple of months before the last entry in the notebook and just one line, but it was there. The words *'Comp. Hs.'*, followed by a number.

'Companies House,' said Steph, out loud.

She called up the website of Companies House and tapped in the number. It was no surprise at all when it came back with the result of 'Conmere Enterprises Ltd'. Steph clicked on the information, and the directors were listed as Pru, Dominic, Harry and Owen. So Harry was still a director – that was interesting. She was under the impression he had left the business, but obviously he hadn't left it officially.

Steph returned to the notebook and paid closer attention to the entries which followed. She wasn't sure what she was hoping to find amongst the hair appointments, birthday reminders and shopping lists, but she could feel her luck beginning to change.

The next entry which stood out was *'Bovis & Childs. 3m. N. Meadow.'*

Thank goodness for the internet. In a matter of seconds, Steph had searched for Bovis & Childs and been rewarded with a website for a local, but specialist, estate agents who dealt with 'high-end properties' and 'land valuation'.

N. Meadow was probably short for North Meadow, she concluded. The following search for North Meadow took a little longer for Steph to understand, but after just a few clicks the results showed it was a parcel of land at the north of the Conmere estate. The *3m* Steph assumed to be the valuation.

Steph looked at the notebook entry again. There was an arrow pointing to the words *'one vote p/p'* and underneath that, *'letter to BoD sent'*.

BoD? Votes?

'Board of Directors,' she said. Elizabeth had sent a letter to the Board of Directors concerning North Meadow. Steph assumed that the other entry related to the set-up of the BoD. Each director had one vote. If only she knew what the letter had said.

She rattled her pen between her teeth, trying to put together the tiny fragments of information she'd found so far. It was impossible without the letter and the reply. She stopped rattling the pen as an idea began to form in her mind. It was risky. It was unethical. In fact, it was illegal, but it was the only way.

Chapter Thirty-One

Steph stood before the filing cabinet and asked herself if this was one of her better ideas. Suddenly it seemed way too risky. Her heart was pumping harder than it needed to and her fingertips tingled with adrenalin. It had been a long time since she had picked a lock and she wondered if she would remember how. It had been a regular challenge when she worked at the paper with Adam Baxter. Their colleague, Amelia, had been notorious in the office for her penchant for chocolate biscuits and her unwillingness to share them with anybody. So much so that she had taken to bringing in a family-sized box of biscuits and keeping them in her desk drawer. Whenever she was away from her desk, Adam or Steph always dared one another to go and pinch a biscuit without Amelia knowing. What had started off as a small joke had snowballed. One biscuit had become two, two had become three, and not just on the odd occasion Amelia left her desk, but every time. In the end, Amelia had cottoned on to the biscuit theft and had started locking her desk drawer. The challenge to pick the lock was set and soon both Adam and Steph had become experts at getting into the desk drawer.

Steph was now relying on her lock-picking skills to gain access to the filing cabinet in the office of Conmere House.

It was three o'clock in the morning and if she was caught now she'd have absolutely no excuse for being up and about, let alone in the office. Steph held the pen-light she had between her teeth, the small beam directed at the lock. Using a bent paperclip and the clip from a tiepin, bent at a right angle, she jostled with the lock. It was only a case of lining up all the pins inside the lock and then using the tiepin as a lever to turn the lock. She heard the familiar click and the drawer was open.

Steph let out a breath, pleased she hadn't lost her touch. She pulled the drawer open and began fanning through the files. She was looking for anything to do with North Meadow or minutes from the meetings of the board of directors.

She found the minutes folder first but there was only one sheet of paper which looked like a cross-reference list – one column with a date, another with the item and the final column where they were located. Most of the minutes were held on a digital file, according to the sheet. Steph scanned down to around the date that Elizabeth had written in her notebook. As was normal, the minutes had been saved as a digital copy, but for this particular meeting there were appendices, with the word 'SAFE' in the filing column.

Steph looked at the cupboard on her right. She had noticed it when she was in the office with Heidi. Steph opened the cupboard door and there on the shelf was a safe, about twice the size of one of those safes found in hotel rooms. It had an electronic keypad. Steph might be able to open a filing cabinet, but that was where her abilities ended. A digital code was way above her expertise.

Damn it.

There was no way she could guess it, and, even if she tried dates significant to the Sinclairs, it would be a long shot. She turned her attention back to the filing cabinet. Maybe there was something else of interest, although she doubted it. The files held mainly mundane staff details, delivery notes and day-to-day records relating to the running of the estate. She peered into the last drop folder in the drawer, which wasn't labelled. A small black notebook was inside. Steph picked it up and opened it to the first page. It was a list of numbers followed by either the letters A, B or C. Nothing else, just numbers and letters.

'Really?' said Steph, astonished at the simplicity of it. 'This is their code system?' She gave a small laugh to herself. It wasn't exactly high-tech.

Crouching down in front of the safe, she punched in the last code in the book. A green light appeared next to the keypad, followed by the sound of a click. It really was that simple. She was in the safe.

Steph gave a small gasp as she peered inside. On the bottom shelf, neatly bagged and stacked, were several piles of twenty- and fifty-pound notes. It certainly exceeded any petty cash Steph had seen before. What was it all doing in there when such a large sum would be better off in the bank? But then, that would mean having to declare it to the taxman. She couldn't help wondering who knew about it. Conmere operated on a cash and card basis, and she suspected most of their clients would use their credit or debit card; she couldn't imagine large amounts of cash would pass through the till, and besides, almost everything was paid for in the all-inclusive price tag.

Money laundering. The alternative crept up on her. Were the Sinclairs laundering money through the business and, if so, where from?

The idea sat uneasily with her as she considered who would know about it. She assumed Pru and all three brothers had access to the safe. She did a rough calculation of how much money was there – somewhere in the region of ten thousand pounds, she thought.

A noise from somewhere in the building startled her and she stilled, listening for another sound. Her heart beat furiously and her mouth dried. She listened even harder, but there was nothing.

Steph took a deep breath. This snooping-around lark was certainly not for the faint-hearted. She had a sudden urge to get out of the office as quickly as possible but she knew this was probably her best chance of finding something about the letter Elizabeth had sent.

On the shelf was a reef of files. Steph took them out and inspected the labels. She found the one marked 'Minutes Correspondence' and with shaking hands opened it and withdrew the wodge of papers. She flicked through, looking for Elizabeth's letter. There it was, neatly printed out and addressed to the board. Steph scanned the letter, taking in the contents.

Dear Board of Directors

I would like to make an official request for a meeting with the Board of Directors of Conmere Enterprises Ltd to discuss some personal information I have in my possession relating to members of the Board which could prove detrimental to the standing of the company. I would confirm that I am willing to come to a mutually satisfactory arrangement concerning the handling of this information and trust the Board are open to discussions in this respect.

I look forward to hearing from you.

Yours faithfully

Elizabeth Sinclair

Paperclipped to the back of the letter was a reply on Conmere headed paper, signed by Pru.

Dear Elizabeth

Thank you for your letter.

The Board would be willing to meet with you on Monday 7th October to discuss the information you hold. The meeting will take place in the Boardroom at Conmere House.

We trust until such time the information will remain confidential.

Yours sincerely

Pru Sinclair

Director

Taking out her phone, Steph hurriedly took photographs of

the letters. There wasn't much to remember, but at least now she had some evidence of the correspondence, just in case the originals went missing.

She looked through the remaining papers and there, towards the bottom of the pile, was a letter from the valuers, Bovis & Childs.

Dear Mrs and Messrs Sinclair

It was a pleasure to meet with Dominic Sinclair today and to visit North Meadow, situated at the edge of the Conmere grounds.

In accordance with your instructions, we have appraised the piece of land known as North Meadow, Conmere Estate, and are pleased to enclose our valuation report herewith.

Steph scanned the rest of the letter and then skipped to the report. It was five pages, mainly dealing with the legalities and technicalities of its findings. It was the last page which interested Steph, quoting the land to be worth in excess of three million pounds if sold with the consent of planning permission for a small development of houses.

Steph checked the date of the reply – it was the day before Elizabeth had been found unresponsive in the lake. Whatever information Elizabeth had had, this must be the lesson she had been going to teach them that Cameron had mentioned. Had this letter cost Elizabeth her life?

It seemed odd that Elizabeth would be communicating in such a formal way with the Sinclairs, but maybe she wanted some sort of traceable record to be left. Perhaps Elizabeth had known she was playing a dangerous game and the written correspondence was her security? Which was all well and good if the police had been playing fair.

Steph's heart dipped. Poor Elizabeth, she hadn't stood a chance.

Steph took a photograph of the report. Elizabeth must have been after the land. She'd wanted North Meadow sold so she could have access to the funds. A cool three-quarters of a million pounds for each shareholder, less any costs. Steph put the paperwork back in the folder and placed all the files back on the shelf of the safe, arranging them in the same order in which she'd found them.

Taking care to make sure the safe was closed properly and everything was returned to the filing cabinet, Steph closed the drawer and with her makeshift lock picks repeated the process in reverse, leaving the filing cabinet securely shut, and with any luck no one would be any the wiser.

Her palms were sweating and all Steph wanted to do was get back to the safety of her own room. She checked her watch and was surprised to see she'd been in the office for nearly an hour. Soon the breakfast chefs would be getting up to start their shifts.

Steph gave the office a final sweep with the torch beam and, ensuring no one was about, sneaked out and back up to her room. She closed the door and let out a long sigh of relief. A dizziness washed over her and her arms, neck and face were clammy. It was probably the adrenalin rushing around her body, Steph thought. She went into the bathroom and ran the cold tap, splashing her face with the water before wetting her flannel and applying it to the back of her neck. Gradually, she felt her body temperature lower and the giddiness disappear.

As Steph brought her head up and looked at her face in the mirror, it took a moment before she realised something was wrong.

'Shit!' Her hand flew to her ear. One of the drop-pearl earrings was missing. She frantically looked all around the bathroom and retraced her steps back to the bedroom door, but it was nowhere to be seen. Oh, hell, what if it had fallen out when she was in the office?

Chapter Thirty-Two

Two Years Earlier,
Travelodge, Near Kendalton, 24 September, 12.30 p.m.

Elizabeth slipped back into the double bed next to Dominic, who was looking at his phone.

'Sorry,' he said, glancing up. 'Just got to reply to this email. Don't want anyone to think I'm slacking off.'

Elizabeth snuggled up to him and trailed a finger across his chest. 'I don't think anyone can accuse you of slacking off.' She gave a satisfied sigh.

'Never let it be said that I don't give something my all.'

'No regrets?'

He stopped tapping at the screen and looked down at her. 'Bit late now for regrets.'

Elizabeth propped herself up on her elbow. 'I haven't got any, but tell me, what makes a man want to sleep with his brother's wife?'

'Odd sort of question.' Dominic carried on with his email.

'I'm just interested.'

He put the phone down. 'Because I wanted to. Because

you wanted to. It's Harry's problem if he can't stop you from looking elsewhere.'

'You're very cut-throat about it,' said Elizabeth.

'Pot. Kettle.'

'I have my reasons but they're probably different from yours. I don't find Harry a threat, I just find him boring.'

'Harry – a threat? I don't think so.'

'Then why?'

Dominic gave an impatient huff. 'Because he pisses me off at times, the same way he used to piss our dad off. He thinks he's better than everyone. Even as a kid, he used to give this aura of being a bit . . . removed from us. Not really a Sinclair. I'm like my dad, so everyone says, and I'd be inclined to agree with them. I've got the business brain. I'm a tough but fair boss. I expect my staff to be loyal and I'll treat them right. Harry never showed any interest in the business, everything was done begrudgingly, and that's one of the reasons Dad got cross with him.'

Elizabeth had, of course, heard Harry's side of the story and it wasn't dissimilar. 'Yeah, he's said in the past that he didn't get on with his dad and would try to spend as little time with him as possible.'

'He just made life more difficult for himself. I hate to say it, but in that respect Owen had more brains than Harry.'

'What do you mean?'

'Harry would go out of his way to annoy Dad, but Owen did everything he could to make sure he kept Dad happy. He kept a low profile but in a good way.'

'Harry said your dad was heavy-handed.'

'His reality, not mine. Sure, we used to get a clip round

the ear if we were cheeky or did something wrong, and there's nothing wrong with a bit of tough love, but Harry was so belligerent, he used to make it more difficult for himself. Once when we were getting a telling-off from the old man, we were all lined up while he was bollocking us and then he cuffed the three of us. Me and Owen weren't stupid and kept our heads down, but Harry, he had to be defiant, and I could see out of the corner of my eye, he kept his head up. It was like a challenge to Dad. Anyway, he earned himself an extra cuff on both sides of the head for that.'

'Your dad sounds like a bully.'

'He was harsh, but he loved us.' Dominic rolled over and straddled Elizabeth. 'Anyway, no more talk of my dad or my brothers; it's not exactly a turn-on.' His gaze raked her body. 'You, on the other hand . . .'

Chapter Thirty-Three

Conmere, Wednesday, 15 May, 3.00 p.m.

S teph had finished work for the day and, despite her text messages with Harry the day before, she hadn't heard from him about meeting up that evening. She found herself deeply disappointed and checking her phone far more often than necessary to see if he'd been in contact. She hoped he wasn't having second thoughts about talking to her.

She looked at her watch; maybe he'd call later when his own working day was finished. She needed something to distract herself from thinking about him. Outside, the sun had broken free from the clouds, bathing the trees in a deep golden light which would make for some great photos.

Without giving it too much consideration, Steph picked up her camera and, slipping it into her rucksack, decided to head out for a walk. She could do with some fresh air to clear her head and taking photos would be a good way to keep her mind from dwelling on Harry. She felt caged inside the house, and the thought of being outside and capturing the images was never more appealing.

Steph walked briskly through the resort, passing the lodge

she had stayed in at the weekend, and carried on along the path which threaded itself through the woods, only then realising she was heading towards the lake. She had been right about the light. The golden rays dipped into the water and sent a white, sparkly sheen across the surface. She spent some time taking various shots, some straight at the light and others from different positions around the south side of the lake. There were three little boats tied up about ten metres from the shore, which Steph assumed were currently off-limits. She wondered how the boats were brought to the pontoon so people could use them – maybe someone came down with a paddle board or perhaps even swam out to them.

Steph's gaze stretched out across the water to the north edge and immediately her thoughts were filled with images of her and Harry in the bird hide. She walked round to the other side and followed the same path Harry had shown her before. It was so different in the sunshine than in the rain and she found herself repeating the shots she'd taken before, but this time in the glorious rays of the sun. After a few minutes scrambling up the path, Steph reached the bird hide, which, as before, was empty. She stood with her back to the construction and looked out across the water, surprised to see that, despite the sunshine, this corner of the lake was as dark and murky as before. It was almost as if the light couldn't reach this part and the water was forever a dark and never-ending mass. She stepped nearer to the edge and tentatively leaned forward to look down the bank and into the water as if some magnetic force were pulling her towards it. It would be almost impossible to scramble up the sides if you fell in here. She suddenly swayed and stumbled to her right, but managed to regain her balance.

The sound of a text message on her phone startled her and she stepped quickly away from the edge. She blew out a long breath. It would be as easy as that to fall in.

The text message was from Harry.

So sorry but I've been trying to sort out a problem at work all day and now I've got to meet with Dominic and Owen. Definitely meet tomorrow though?

Steph couldn't deny her disappointment at this. She had found herself increasingly looking forward to seeing Harry.

It was her turn to message back saying it was a shame but she'd look forward to seeing him tomorrow.

She looked back out across the water, the compulsion to take more photographs having now vanished. Steph sat down on the ground, her eyeline level with the top of the bushes and brush which bordered the edge of the path. It was so lovely to feel the warmth of the sun on her face, feel the gentle breeze on her skin, to listen to the birds chirping around her and the water lapping at the edge of the lake. She closed her eyes and tilted her face up to the sun. It was absolute bliss.

It was after a few minutes that she became aware of the sound of a car engine somewhere in the distance. The lake must be closer to a road than she imagined. It took a few seconds for her to realise the lake wasn't anywhere near a road.

From her position on higher ground, she could see a car

making its way along the edge of the water, heading towards a small boathouse she hadn't noticed before. It was too far away to see what type of car of it was, but it looked like a silver-coloured 4x4. Steph lifted her camera and looked through the lens, adjusting the focus to zoom in on the vehicle. Dominic was driving, and a man she didn't recognise was in the passenger seat. More out of habit than a conscious decision, Steph clicked the button on her camera and took several shots. She lowered the camera and followed the car with her naked eye; it was still heading for the boathouse, slowing down and then pulling up alongside it.

Steph raised her camera once more and again zoomed in. She could see Dominic's face clearly, as if he were standing right in front of her. He climbed out of the car and looked around, before closing the door. He said something to his companion, who was also out of the car, and the two men went to the boot. Steph couldn't see what they were doing but she kept the camera fixed on the activity. She didn't know why, but something told her this was no ordinary visit to the boathouse.

Dominic now walked over to the boathouse and disappeared around the corner, reappearing a few seconds later as he pinned open the door. Steph shuffled onto her knees to get a better position and, still looking through her camera, watched as Dominic and the man began ferrying several large boxes from the rear of the car into the timber construction. Judging by the way they were carrying the boxes, the contents were relatively heavy but not so much so that they couldn't manage a box each. They moved quickly and within five minutes Dominic was closing the door and making his way back to the driver's side of the car.

It was then he halted and looked up towards where Steph was sitting. He seemed to look directly into the camera, his gaze making contact with her own. She gave a small gasp and jolted back, throwing herself off-balance. She put her hand out behind her to balance herself.

There was no way he could have seen her. She was hidden by the bushes. She was too far away, surely, and yet he had looked straight at her. Slowly, Steph poked her head back above the bushes. The car was driving away, dust kicking up in its wake, before disappearing from sight.

Steph stayed where she was, watching the other side of the water, where she presumed the track would come out, and, sure enough, the 4x4 reappeared on the south side of the lake and headed towards the resort. She remained where she was for a minute or so, to be certain it wasn't returning.

'Are you all right, dear?'

A woman's voice from behind Steph surprised her so much, she nearly toppled over as from her kneeling position she twisted round to see who was there. 'Oh, Mrs Sinclair,' she said, in relief. 'You scared me.' Steph got to her feet and dusted down her trousers.

'Sorry, I didn't mean to,' said Pru. She turned and called over her shoulder. 'Girls! Come on! Here!'

Within a few seconds Pru's three dogs appeared at the head of the path and excitedly ran up to Steph. She stooped to make a fuss of them before they lost interest and scampered off further along the path. 'I was just taking some photographs of the scenery,' explained Steph, holding up her camera. 'The light today is amazing.'

'Oh, yes. Harry told me you were a photographer. He said he'd asked you to take some pictures.'

'I'm not officially a photographer. It's just something I like to do in my spare time.'

'Harry seems to think you have a flair for it. He said you had some photographs in a gallery for sale.'

Steph felt flattered that Harry had taken the time to tell his mother. 'That's right,' she said. 'My friend has a gallery and I do sell some prints from time to time.'

Pru came to stand next to Steph. 'From what I can tell, Harry thinks a lot of you,' she said.

Steph's stomach gave a small roll. What else had Harry told his mother? 'We get on well,' she opted for saying, avoiding looking at Pru by paying close attention to fitting the lens cap into place.

'I'd like to see him happy,' continued Pru. 'After what happened to Elizabeth, I'd like to leave this world knowing my son was able to live again.'

Steph felt a little uncomfortable, unsure what to say. She stole a glance at Pru, who was looking wistful. Steph wasn't sure if she was even addressing her any more. 'I'm sure he will in time,' Steph offered by way of comfort.

'Hmm, I hope so.' Pru continued to look thoughtful for a moment and then seemingly shook herself out of her trance. 'Oh, before I go, you might like this.' She unzipped her pocket and felt around for what she was looking for, before holding it out to Steph and dropping it into the palm of her hand.

Steph's heart nearly leapt into her throat as she looked at

the drop-pearl earring in her hand. 'M-my earring,' she stammered.

'Thought it was yours. I remember admiring them the other day when you were in Elizabeth's room.' Pru arched an eyebrow. 'I found it in rather an odd place, though. The office. Not sure how it got there.'

'I . . . er . . . didn't realise I'd lost it,' said Steph, trying to hide her shock. 'Maybe someone handed it in to the office and it got knocked on the floor?' It sounded plausible, but only just.

'Maybe that's what happened,' said Pru, in a tone that didn't sound entirely convincing. 'Right, well, I'd better get on and catch up with those dogs.' Then she broke into a gentle jog.

Steph watched as Pru disappeared over the rise, heading in the direction of the boathouse, and couldn't help admiring how fit Pru Sinclair looked for her age; she was in her sixties, and the active-wear certainly looked good on her. She remembered the photograph in Harry's lodge of Pru in her wetsuit. Pru Sinclair was evidently a woman of determination and stamina who loved her family dearly.

Steph took a moment to replace her earring, uncertain whether Pru's finding it was a good thing or not, but at least she had it back now. She supposed it was better that Pru had found it than Dominic or Harry – they would probably have wanted a better explanation as to how it had got there. Hopefully, Pru would forget all about it and not mention it to them. She took one last look at the boathouse. Ideally, she'd like to go down there and have a little nose around, but with Pru about it wouldn't be wise to do so. She resolved to come back later when it was darker.

Conmere, Wednesday, 15th May, 8.45 p.m.

Steph hadn't heard anything from Harry since his earlier text and more than once her finger had hovered over her phone as she argued with herself whether it was a good idea to text him or not. In the end she had decided not to and to use the opportunity to sneak out to the boathouse, hopefully without being missed. She grabbed a quick bite to eat in the staff kitchen and then made herself scarce by staying in her room. She hoped that it would be a case of out of sight, out of mind where the rest of the staff were concerned.

Now it was dusk and the sun would soon be setting, Steph dressed in some dark clothing and a fleece. She tied the laces on her trainers and, armed with just her phone and a torch, hurried out of her room, making sure the door was locked. Fortunately, the front desk was unmanned, so no one witnessed her exit.

Deciding to make out she was going for an evening run, Steph jogged through the grounds and out beyond the last row of lodges. It was already dark amongst the trees and she was glad of the torch to light the way.

It wasn't long before she came through the trees and out onto the track which ran alongside the lake. The sun had sunk behind the hills which surrounded the water, and with no lighting along the path it was particularly dark and, if Steph was honest, ever so slightly creepy. The water looked like a black hole in the ground, and the only indication it actually was water was the gentle slopping sound it made against the shoreline.

Instead of taking her usual route up to the bird hide, Steph jogged round in the opposite direction. It was too dark to see across the lake, and the cloud which had come in during evening was obscuring any light from the moon. Every so often she found herself startled by a rustle of the trees or bushes but reassured herself each time that it was only the wind and possibly some wildlife, like a fox or a badger.

Before long she was nearing the boathouse. The dark grey form of the weathered structure stood out in the dwindling light. Steph raised her torch beam and swept it across the building from side to side, before extending it in an arc around the boathouse to ensure there was no one about. She knew from her vantage point earlier that afternoon, the doors of the boathouse could not be seen from any other point around the lake, and she relaxed slightly at the thought.

The double garage-like doors were locked with a heavy-duty chain and padlock, passing between two bars which ran from top to bottom in front of the doors and looking to be fixed into the framework of the building. The doors could only be opened if these two bars were removed. The doors themselves were also locked with a more traditional locking mechanism.

Steph stepped back and looked up at the building. There were no windows on the front at ground level, with just a small window above the doors which she assumed was the first floor. Steph moved round to the left-hand side of the building but there were no windows or doors there. The right-hand side was more accommodating. There were two ground-floor windows and a boardwalk about a metre-wide which ran the length of the building out into the water. It looked as if it went around the corner of the boathouse to the back, where, Steph recalled, there was a roller-type door. She assumed this was where boats could go in and out.

Steph walked over to the first window and, with her torch pressed against the pane of glass, she peered in. There wasn't much she could make out, but the opposite side of the wall looked to be kitted out with hooks and shelving. There were several paddles hanging along the wall, and life jackets on hooks. There were also two steel boxes pushed up against the wall. In the middle of the floor was a large shape, but Steph couldn't quite work out what it was. Maybe it was a boat with a tarpaulin covering it. She wasn't sure. She moved along to the second window to try to get a better look, but this window was blacked out.

Steph eyed the boardwalk. It looked sturdy enough to take her weight and tentatively she shuffled along, keeping close to the side of the building. The water didn't look particularly deep here, although it would have to be enough to allow kayaks and small boats to gain access to the boathouse, and it looked clear of weeds. She reached the corner and moved round until she was facing out onto the lake. Again, the blackness of the water was hard to comprehend. It was amazing how it could feel so sinister in the darkness and yet somehow there was a strange and dangerous attraction to it.

She turned away and looked at the roller door. If she could lift it up just a little, she might be able to scramble underneath. The bottom of the door disappeared below the waterline, but Steph pulled up her sleeve and, crouching low on her knees, ran her hand downwards. The water was colder than she'd expected, but not unbearable. The bottom of the roller door was only a few inches below the water level. She cupped the edge with her hand and tried to yank it upwards on the off-chance it wasn't locked from the inside. She gave it several attempts but it wouldn't budge.

She sat up and flicked the water from her hand and forearm. She couldn't see a way in, not without breaking the glass, which would then alert Dominic to the fact that someone had been there.

As she took a moment to ponder her dilemma she became aware of the sound of a vehicle approaching, and not just at a steady speed – it was coming in fast. Her heart missed a beat and her stomach flipped. The car engine grew louder as it raced towards her.

She stood up, switched off her torch and pushed her back flat against the end of the building. If it was Dominic returning, she hoped to God he wouldn't have any reason to come out to the back of the boathouse.

Steph made a conscious effort to control her breathing and listen hard to the sound of the car. It was slowing. She could see the bright beam of the headlights swing round, lighting up the bank and the water. They were flicked to full-beam, enhancing the lake still further.

A car door opened and then closed.

'Steph! Steph? Are you there?' The voice was loud and clear in the quietness of the evening.

Steph froze.

It was Harry's voice.

He called out again and this time he sounded closer. Steph hugged the wall even further. She couldn't think straight. Was he friend or foe?

'Steph. Stop hiding. Come out.'

He sounded really close now. As if he was at the other end of the boathouse. Then she heard his footsteps on the boardwalk. He was coming down the side of the building. How was she going to explain what she was doing here and, more to the point, why she was hiding?

Self-preservation took over. She had only one option.

Steph slid down the wall and dangled her legs over the edge of the boardwalk and into the water. She had to forcibly quell the yelp which wanted to escape at the shock of the coldness. Slowly she lowered herself into the water. She was hip-deep before she made contact with the muddy bed of the lake. She felt her shoes sink a little way into the squelchy mud but fortunately no further than an inch or so. She was beyond the point of return. She could hear Harry's footsteps getting closer. Her phone was in the zipped breast pocket of her jacket and there was no way of avoiding its getting wet.

With just a second's hesitation, Steph took in a big gulp of air and submerged herself fully under the water. She kept her eyes closed and allowed her hands to find the way as they groped for the bottom of the roller door before she propelled herself underneath. The gap was just big enough for her to swim under. She was conscious of making ripples and splashes in her wake, and pushed her feet into the lake bed. Two or three seconds later she was inside the boathouse. She stood up but stayed perfectly still so as not to cause any more disturbance to the water. Very carefully she unzipped her breast pocket and took out her phone. She dared not check it and was grateful she'd put it on silent before she'd left her room. Her torch was in her other hand. She had no idea if that would still work.

She listened carefully to the sound of Harry's booted feet on the boardwalk. She knew he wouldn't be able to see her from the first window, as she was too far back in the building and the one behind her was blacked out. If he had keys and came in through the front doors it would give her time to swim out and maybe hide along the bank.

Harry's footsteps came to a halt at the end of the boardwalk.

'For Christ's sake,' she heard him mutter. For a long time he didn't move and she could only imagine he was standing there, scanning the water looking for her. Then, with another curse, he marched back along the boardwalk. She could hear the car door slam and the engine start up. She waited until she was certain the car had moved off, and even then she didn't move. She wanted to hear it disappear into the distance.

Shivering now, Steph turned on her torch and, after a flicker or two, it illuminated the space in front of her. There was a small rib on the right, moored up to a wooden platform. The space next to it was empty and Steph waded through the water, heaving herself up onto the pontoon. She shone her torch further into the boathouse and could make out an interior door which she assumed went through to the dry dock. She turned the handle and the door opened with a creak.

In this part of the boathouse was the tarpaulin covering what she had assumed was a boat when she had peered through the window. She lifted the corner of the heavy-duty plastic and shone her torch to reveal the upturned hull of a small boat. She let the plastic drop back down and, casting the light beam around the room, she saw the toolboxes and workbench. In the corner was a wooden ladder reaching up through a small trap hatch. As she looked closer she could see that the dust in the centre of the rungs had been dislodged. She took a deep breath as she looked up into the blackness. This must have been where Dominic had gone.

Tentatively she climbed the ladder, and as she reached the first floor she poked her head up through the hatch and shone the torch around. Again, there looked to be lots of old boating equipment, most of which was stacked somewhat haphazardly around the edges of the room. Her torch light picked up the gleam of something metal at the front of the loft, underneath the small square window. It was the only thing that looked out of place. Steph heaved herself into the loft area, once again noting that the dust on the wooden flooring had been disturbed, leaving a path directly across the room to the metal storage box.

On top was an assortment of open boxes which contained various tools and boating accessories, all of which looked to be old and covered in dust and grime – they certainly hadn't been used in a long time. She noticed that the top of the storage box was also covered in dust but there were scuff marks where the boxes had probably been slid off and on the unit.

Steph balanced the torch on the window ledge and, taking hold of the first box, placed it on the floor. She repeated this with the other three boxes and then after a little manipulation was able to lift the lid on the storage box. At first she just thought the unit was filled with more boating equipment, but as she moved a few items from the top she saw the packages that Dominic had transferred from his car earlier.

She hauled out one of the packages, which was wrapped in brown paper and sealed up with parcel tape. The package was heavy and compact, but the contents didn't feel solid; it reminded Steph of a bag of flour.

'Shit,' she heard herself whisper as it dawned on her what she was holding in her hands. It couldn't be anything else, it had to be drugs of some description, and her money was on cocaine. Funny, if she hadn't seen Dominic here earlier, she would have been certain this was Owen's doing, but it seemed both brothers were involved. She couldn't help wondering if that meant Harry was too. She didn't want him to be. He'd said he wasn't and she wanted to believe him, but why would he have been up here just now? The only reason must have been because he didn't want her to find this stash. And, let's face it, she told herself, this stash wasn't just for personal use. There were six packages like this altogether; she had no idea how much that was worth on the street. Her heart plummeted at the thought of Harry's potential involvement.

And then another thought struck her. Had Elizabeth been involved in this? Or, worse still, had Elizabeth discovered what was going on? Had she threatened to go to the police? Had this led to her death?

Panic washed over her as the muddy lake water had earlier. She needed to get out of the boathouse before anyone came back. As quickly as she could, she stuffed the package into the storage unit and threw the other contents back on top to hide it. Then, forcing the lid into place, she replaced the boxes, taking care to put them in the same space as before and not disturb any more dust.

Keeping a grip on her panic, Steph left the boathouse the

way she had got in, only this time wrapping her phone in a cloth and plastic bag so she could pass it under the roller door quickly and place it on the boardwalk before she swam underneath. This way her phone would be in the water for even less time. Once she was out of the boathouse, she ran as fast as she could back round the lake, through the trees and towards the main centre of the resort. It was only when she reached the swimming pool that she slowed down to a jog, hoping once again not to attract any attention. It was dark and no one would notice she was wet; all she had to do was make it through the house and to her room without anyone seeing her.

Fortunately the way was clear, and it was not without a great deal of relief that Steph closed her bedroom door and locked it. She slumped down on the floor, catching her breath, and took her phone from her pocket. She unwrapped it from the protective layers and was relieved to see it was still working.

With her legs bent up, she rested her elbows on her knees and held her head in her hands as she took time to process what she had just discovered. As much as she wanted there to be some other explanation or some way that Harry wasn't involved, she couldn't find one. She had to be careful now; she was in more danger than she had thought. This wasn't just about Elizabeth's death, it was also about drug-dealing and blackmail. She began shivering and knew she needed to get out of the wet clothes and take a hot shower.

As the water pummelled her bare skin, she felt the blind panic from earlier clearing. She had to think straight and work out what she was going to do next. Was there anyone she could trust? Was her mother really involved more deeply than she thought she might have been? What if Wendy had known about the drug-dealing? Had she been on the Sinclair payroll? God, it sounded like a bloody gangster movie – she could hardly believe she was seriously considering this as a plausible explanation.

As Steph stepped out of the shower with a towel wrapped around her body and another around her hair, there was a sudden and loud banging on her door.

'Steph? You in there? It's me, Harry.'

Steph froze for the second time that night at the sound of his voice.

Chapter Thirty-Four

Conmere, Wednesday, 15 May, 10.30 p.m.

Harry was certain Steph was in her room – he'd heard the shower running just a little while ago. He thumped on the door with the heel of his hand. 'Steph! Open the door.'

A door further down the hall opened and a head poked out. It was a staff member from the stables. Harry gave the lad a glare which the stable lad clearly understood, as he then hurriedly disappeared back into his room.

Harry drummed his fingers on the door. He didn't want to carry on shouting, but, by God, he'd get her to answer the door – either that or he'd get Security to open it for him. Then he heard her reply.

'What do you want?'

Harry took a deep breath. 'I need to talk to you,' he said, into the door jamb. 'It's important.'

'I'm about to go to bed,' she replied.

He allowed himself a moment to consider the idea of Steph in bed, but quickly scrubbed away the thought. 'Please,' he said, this time more gently.

'Wait a minute.'

He waited patiently for the door to open. When it did, Steph was standing in her pjs with a dressing gown wrapped tightly around her, fastened with a belt. 'Thanks,' he said. 'Can I come in?'

She opened the door wider and allowed him into the room. 'This is like déjà vu,' she commented, closing the door, but not moving away. Harry didn't miss the slight wobble in her voice.

He smiled to reassure her. 'I just wanted to check you were OK,' he said. It sounded like a feeble excuse.

'You could have texted.'

'I did but it didn't go through. Got a non-delivery notification.'

'Oh?' Steph glanced across the room at the bedside table. Harry followed her gaze and saw her phone there. He went over and passed it to her. Steph inspected it and frowned. 'It's dead. Must need charging.' She slipped the phone into her dressing-gown pocket. 'Anyway, as you can see, I'm fine.'

'You sure? Only my mum said she'd bumped into you up by the lake. She said you seemed distracted and a bit jumpy.'

'Really? Well, I only jumped because I didn't know your mum was there, and prior to that I was just looking out across the water. It's mesmerising.'

'I saw you out running about an hour ago.' He watched her face carefully for a reaction but there was none. He carried on. 'You looked like you were heading for the lake.'

She gave a shrug. 'Yeah. I like to run in the evenings; it's quieter and gives me more thinking time.'

'Did you go to the lake?'

'Yeah. Ran around it and back here to my room. I didn't see you.'

He looked down and noticed a pile of wet clothes on the floor. Running gear. 'You got wet?'

She looked a little uneasy this time. 'I tripped,' she said. 'Along the edge of the lake.'

He wasn't sure he believed her but he couldn't disprove what she was saying either. 'So you're OK, then?' he asked finally.

'Totally.'

'Look, I'm sorry about cancelling earlier tonight.'

'It's fine. We're even now,' she said with a smile.

'It wasn't tit-for-tat.'

'I know. I was joking.'

Harry pinched the bridge of his nose. It had been a stressful day and it had reminded him of all the reasons he hated working at Conmere. Dominic had been on his back again about Steph, and when his mother had said she'd seen Steph up by the lake Dominic had gone off on one, repeating all his reasons why he didn't like or trust her. He had seemed particularly agitated that she'd been at the lake at all and no amount of reassurances from Harry that she was simply taking photos had made any difference. Sometimes, you just couldn't tell Dominic anything once he'd made up his mind about something. Stubborn bastard – just like their dad.

'I'll walk over hot coals to make sure we get that drink. How does Friday sound? I'll definitely be free then,' he said. 'Although I think I should at least upgrade it to a meal.'

'That will be nice. I'll look forward to it.'

Not without a good deal of effort, he forced himself to

say goodnight. As he walked down the hallway, he found himself wondering how on earth he could pacify his brother about Steph. He had a bad feeling about what Dominic was thinking, and his instinct to protect Steph was overwhelming.

By the time he'd reached the ground floor, he'd made up his mind. It probably wouldn't go down too well with Steph, but it was the only way forward.

He went into the office behind the reception desk and, switching on the laptop, he called up a password-protected file.

It had been a long time since he'd read anything in here – two years, in fact. It contained all the information he'd received about Elizabeth's death, from a list of people dealing with the case to the official findings and scanned documents relating to the enquiry. There was another folder with more pertinent information – death certificate, coroner's report and suchlike – but that was kept in a safe-deposit box at the bank. He took a deep breath and clicked on the folder icon, before locating the contacts list and the name he was looking for. There it was – the telephone number for DCI Wendy Lynch. Beside her name was the police-station number, her work mobile number and her home number. It was the latter he was interested in.

It was late to be making a phone call but Harry couldn't wait until the morning; he wanted answers tonight so he had time to work out what to do next.

Wendy Lynch answered the phone on the third ring. She sounded alert. 'Hello.'

'Wendy Lynch?'

'Yes. Who is this?'

'Sorry to ring this late at night. It's Harry Sinclair.'

'What do you want? You do know how late it is?'

'Yes, I'm sorry, but I need to speak to you.' He paused to gather his thoughts. 'It's about your daughter, Steph Durham. Nothing has happened to her, she's perfectly well,' he added hastily.

'What is it, then?' There was caution in her voice, and if she was surprised he knew who her daughter was, she didn't show it.

'Steph's here from her travel company to report on the resort,' said Harry. 'But I think there might be an ulterior motive. Another reason why she's here. I'm concerned she might be getting herself involved in something that's not in her best interests.'

It was Wendy Lynch's turn to pause. 'Are you threatening my daughter?'

'No. Not at all,' said Harry. 'I know she's been talking to Sonia Lomas, my ex-mother-in-law, and Sonia has been here at the resort, and, of course, I now know Steph is your daughter. She's been asking some questions concerning Elizabeth's death.' It wasn't quite true but Harry thought if he laid it on a bit thicker, it might go some way to Wendy opening up. 'Do you know if she's looking into my wife's death?'

'Is my daughter in danger?'

'Probably not. I'm just covering all bases.'

'You don't sound very convinced,' said Wendy. 'Did she tell you I had a brick thrown through my window on Monday?'

'What? No. She never mentioned it. Do you know who did it?'

'No. I played it down as kids, but I'm not totally sold on that idea. Was it you? Was it a warning?'

'No, it wasn't me!' said Harry, realising he'd raised his voice indignantly. 'I don't know anything about that.'

'I've warned her not to go poking around. I've told her it will only cause trouble. It seems she hasn't listened to me. Did she also tell you that she was run off the road by a black 4x4?'

'No! She said she lost control on a bend and hit a fence.'

'That's not true. Sonia Lomas phoned me today. She was in the car with Steph at the time. She's been worried about her ever since. You really don't know anything about that?'

'Absolutely not,' said Harry. His mind raced back to Steph's car and Dominic's explanation.

'Now if I was to ask you again, do you think my daughter is in danger, what would you answer?'

Harry's mouth went dry. He swallowed hard as he processed the implications. 'Maybe she is. I'll speak to her tomorrow.'

'She's very stubborn,' said Wendy. 'I'm not sure talking to her will change anything, unless you tell her what she wants to know.'

'There's nothing to tell,' said Harry, not hiding his impatience. 'You investigated Elizabeth's death. You know that.' Wendy didn't answer and this made Harry feel uneasy. 'You're the one who said it was an accident.'

'That's right, I did,' said Wendy, eventually. 'There was no evidence to suggest otherwise.'

He didn't like the way she said that. It sounded too textbook. Too rehearsed. 'I'll look after Steph. I'll do everything I can to make sure she's safe.'

'And I'm supposed to trust a Sinclair?'

'You have my word.'

'That doesn't reassure me.'

The line went dead and Harry was left staring at the receiver. Why the hell hadn't Steph said anything about being run off the road or the house brick? She obviously didn't trust him. Shit. This wasn't good. He slammed the phone down in the cradle and slumped back in the chair.

'Knock, knock.' Pru tapped the door lightly with her knuckles and looked round into the office. 'Oh, it's you, Harry. I wasn't expecting to see you here. I saw the light on and assumed it was Heidi. Is everything all right?'

Harry forced a smile to his face and sat forward, closing the file on the computer. 'Yes, everything is fine, Mum. I was just checking up on a few things. Nothing to worry about.' He rose from the chair.

'Are you sure? Only both Dominic and Owen seem a little preoccupied at the moment. In fact, Dominic was particularly bad-tempered this morning.'

Harry gave a shrug. 'If it was important I'm sure they'd have told you, and Dominic was probably just in a bad mood. I shouldn't pay any attention to either of them.' Harry hoped he had soothed his mother's concerns.

'He said something about Steph still being here. I don't think he likes her very much. Unlike you.' She gave him a pointed look.

Harry held in a sigh of frustration. Dominic really should keep his thoughts to himself, especially in front of their mother, who never missed anything. 'OK, I like her,' he admitted, as there was no point trying to pretend otherwise.

'But it's complicated. She's based in the UK and I'm based in France.'

'Why doesn't Dominic like her?'

'Honestly, Mum,' he said, aware of the irony of his opening word, 'I don't know. And I don't really care what Dominic thinks. She is none of his business.'

'I found an earring belonging to Steph.'

'You did?' Harry sensed there was more to come.

'I knew it was hers, because it's a beautiful drop-pearl. Quite expensive, I should imagine, not throw-away tat. I found it in here, actually. On the floor by the cupboard.'

'In here? That's an odd place to find her earring.'

'That's what I thought, especially as I found it first thing in the morning after the cleaners had been in last thing the night before.'

Harry met his mother's gaze. No words were needed. Harry understood the implication perfectly. 'What have you done with the earring?'

'I've given it back to her.' She continued to hold his gaze. 'Maybe Dominic has got reason to dislike her.'

The idea troubled Harry as much as it irritated him. 'Dominic doesn't know what he's talking about. He needs to calm himself down.'

'He's only looking out for you.'

'No, he's not minding his own business,' snapped Harry. 'And you wonder why I moved to France.'

He regretted the words as soon as they had left his lips and he saw the hurt in his mother's eyes that followed.

'I don't want to argue,' she said.

'Neither do I. I'm sorry,' said Harry. She smiled and patted his arm in a conciliatory way, which made him feel a complete shit.

'Let's not, then,' said Pru. 'Life's too short for petty squabbles.'

Her words knocked the air from him. Such a loaded expression. 'Are you OK?' he asked, wanting not only to change the subject but also to try to coax his mother into telling him about her health.

'Me? Yes. Couldn't be better. I was just heading up to bed,' she said. 'Not that I'm tired; I was watching the news, but it's all doom and gloom – far too depressing for me.'

He put his arm around his mother's shoulders and shepherded her out of the office and into the hall. 'Do you want me to take you to your room?'

She gave a tut and a small chuckle. 'I'm not that old and frail yet,' she said. 'Next you'll be bringing me cocoa and a shawl for my shoulders.' She gave him a peck on the cheek. 'I'm fine. I'm going to read my book for a while, and I have the girls to keep me company.'

Harry looked at the three bichon frises which had appeared from the living room to find their mistress. 'Fair enough. Sleep well.' He watched as the dogs trotted off up the stairs and reflected on how the outside world didn't matter to his mother. As long as everything in her own Conmere House world was all right, she was happy.

Chapter Thirty-Five

Kendalton, Thursday, 16 May, 3.10 p.m.

From the very beginning of the day, the usual oppressive atmosphere which weighed heavily in and around Conmere House seemed to have intensified with every passing minute. When it came to three o'clock and her shift had ended, all Steph wanted was to get as far away from the place as possible. She hadn't seen Harry at all that morning, but had now and again seen Dominic from across the hall, and Pru had crossed paths with her as she had gone to stock up the laundry station at the pool house.

'Nice to see the earrings are back where they should be,' she had said as she passed Steph, on her way for a swim. A perfectly innocent comment but one that still managed to send a shiver down Steph's spine.

Having gone up to her room after her shift and changed out of her uniform, Steph was now in her battered car, speeding away from Conmere. As she drove out of the gates, she could feel the tension ease from her body.

With no particular destination in mind, Steph was surprised to find herself in Kendalton, and for a reason she couldn't explain she drove to her mother's house and parked on the driveway. She wasn't sure why she'd come here, and acknowledged it was an odd thing to do. She never normally came unannounced but Wendy hadn't been in touch as she'd said she would, and there was something about the call that had left Steph unsettled with a nagging feeling she couldn't quite get a hold of.

Wendy's car was on the drive and the upstairs bedroom window was open, so Steph knew her mother must be in. Wendy would never leave the house without first making sure all the windows were securely shut. Still, Steph had to ring the bell twice, the second time more insistently, and then rap on the door with her knuckles.

Puzzled at Wendy still not appearing, Steph crouched down and called through the letterbox.

'Mum! You there? It's me, Steph!'

She was convinced she could hear voices and peered through the letterbox. She was able to look right through to the kitchen at the end of the hall and could see the bottom half of Wendy, but there was someone else with her. The back of the kitchen chair was just visible and, although her view of the other person was partly blocked by her mother, Steph saw them move to Wendy's right. She couldn't see who it was but could see they were wearing a waxed cotton Barbour jacket or coat. Steph had only caught sight of them for a second but she heard the back door close and saw Wendy rest her hands on the kitchen table for a moment.

Steph stood up and pounded the door again. 'Mum! Open the door!' She held her finger on the doorbell and could hear the persistent sound of the buzzer from inside the house.

It seemed an age before Wendy finally opened the door. 'Stephanie, what are you doing here?'

Under normal circumstances Steph would have inwardly sighed at her mother's greeting. She'd always fantasised that one day Wendy would open the door, smile broadly, open her arms and exclaim what a lovely surprise it was to see her. Today, however, she didn't have time to indulge in such fantasy.

'You took ages to answer the door – is everything all right?' Steph looked over her mother's shoulder and down the hallway. Wendy didn't move.

'Of course. Why wouldn't it be?'

'Because I've been ringing the bell, knocking on the door and shouting through the letterbox. Have you got visitors? I can come back if it's inconvenient.'

'I was upstairs in the bathroom, if you must know,' said Wendy. Her eyes weren't looking at Steph, though, but at something behind Steph in the street.

Automatically, Steph turned to look back over her left shoulder to see what had attracted Wendy's attention. She heard the noise of a car as it passed and quickly looked in the other direction. A black 4x4 accelerated down the road.

'Who was that?' demanded Steph.

Wendy's face was a picture of confusion. 'How do I know? Anyway, why are you here?'

Steph gave another look down the road, but the 4x4 had disappeared out of sight now, and she turned to face her mother again. 'I just thought I'd call in. You seemed worried about me the other day. Can I come in or have I got to stand on the doorstep all afternoon?'

Wendy barely supressed her sigh and opened the door to allow her daughter in. 'Do you want a cup of tea?'

'Yes, please.' Steph trailed Wendy into the kitchen and discreetly cast her gaze around the room. She didn't know what she was looking for, just something that would give her a clue as to who had been here. There was nothing, but as she casually moved towards the back door with the pretence of looking out of the window at the rear garden she got the tiniest whiff of either perfume or aftershave. She couldn't work out which, but it smelt familiar. She tried to pin down the smell and where she'd come across it before, but the memory was too far out of reach.

'Are you going to sit down?' Wendy placed a cup of tea on the kitchen table and a cup of black coffee for herself on the opposite side. A symbolic gesture, even if an unconscious one, thought Steph as she sat down facing her mother. There was no mistaking the chill in the air despite the warmth of the sun shining in through the window. 'When are you going back to Brighton?' asked Wendy.

'Not sure yet. Maybe at the weekend.'

'If it's money stopping you going home, then I can give you petrol money and some extra cash to keep you going.'

Steph almost choked on the mouthful of tea she was in the middle of swallowing. She gulped it down and disguised her surprise with a cough. 'Went down the wrong way.'

'Yeah, of course it did.' Wendy eyed Steph across the table. 'I've got enough cash in my purse for petrol. I can send the rest by bank transfer. If you leave in the next couple of hours, you'll be home before midnight.'

Steph put her cup on the table firmly to underline what

she was about to say. 'I'm not leaving today.' She met her mother's gaze with equal intensity. 'I have money to get home, but I'm not leaving yet.'

'I think you should.'

'I know.'

The clouds had shifted in the sky and the sun was hidden, casting a shadow across Wendy's face, which darkened with her mood. 'I want you to go. Today.'

'I don't know why you don't want me here,' said Steph. Wasn't it just the other day her mother was phoning to see how she was and suggesting they go for lunch? Now it was as if that had never happened and they were back to square one with each other. 'I can't make up my mind if it's because you're frightened of what I might discover or if you just really can't bear being in my company for too long.' She rose from the table. 'Your call wasn't because you were concerned about me. It was because you wanted to see if I had left. Well, I'm sorry to disappoint you, and I'm sorry I cause you so much discomfort and displeasure.' She waited for Wendy to say something, to deny her accusations, to ask her to stay, but she did nothing. She remained in her seat and continued staring straight ahead. 'I'll text you when I leave, just to reassure you that I've gone.' Steph's words were bitter, maybe more so than she had intended, but it was that or break down and cry in front of her mother, which was the last thing she wanted to do. She wasn't going to give that woman the satisfaction.

'Wait!' Wendy rose from her seat.

Steph stood still. 'What?'

Wendy motioned for Steph to sit back down and, in what

was possibly their first act of synchronisation in anything, both women lowered themselves onto their chairs in unison.

Wendy laid her hands flat out on the table in front of her as if bracing herself and then uncharacteristically fiddled with her wedding ring. 'You're more like me than perhaps I realised or you'd like to admit,' she began. 'Stubborn. Determined. Unflinching.'

Steph had never considered herself anything like her mother, but put like that, she couldn't really deny it. 'So it would seem.'

'What I'm about to tell you is strictly off the record. I could still get into a lot of trouble for telling you this but . . . I'm going to because I'm concerned about you.' She couldn't quite meet Steph's gaze and focused on her wedding band again. 'When I began investigating Elizabeth's death, I asked questions that the Sinclair family didn't like. I didn't take it at face value that her death was an accident; I wouldn't have been doing my job properly if I didn't look at all possibilities.'

'What was your gut feeling?'

This time Wendy looked her daughter straight in the eye. 'My gut feeling? It wasn't as straightforward as the Sinclairs were making out. They were hiding something, but I didn't know what. I didn't know if it was directly related to Elizabeth's death or something else.' Wendy paused before speaking again. 'I was called before my bosses and told in no uncertain terms that my findings were to conclude it was an accident.'

'But I thought you were asked to leave because you handled it wrong?'

'I was set up. I was being squeezed from all sides. Basically, I was a pain in the arse and they wanted rid of me.'

'But why are you so insistent that I don't stir anything up? I'm not doing anything illegal. The police can't arrest me.'

'I think the Sinclairs put pressure on my bosses. I've said before they are very influential, but it's not just that. They're dangerous as well. Everyone at Conmere was under suspicion, especially the husband.'

'Harry?'

'You're on first-name terms with him already, but don't be fooled by him or any of them. Blood is thicker than water, as they say, and it certainly applies to that lot. Basically, they closed ranks and put up this wall of silence which was impregnable. And still is.'

'Wow, so Sonia Lomas is right to be suspicious.' Steph sat back in her chair as she digested what her mum had told her. It sat uneasily with her that Harry was essentially the main suspect, but she tried to offset her disquiet with the notion that it didn't fit with the Harry she knew. She just couldn't see him murdering his wife.

'Do you know anything about a video recording that Elizabeth might have made?'

Wendy couldn't hide the surprise on her face. 'How do you know about that?'

Steph shrugged. 'It doesn't matter, but you've answered my question anyway.'

'Don't waste your time looking for any recording,' said Wendy, pre-empting Steph's next question. 'All I can say is, if there was a recording, it was probably destroyed. I'm sure the Sinclairs wouldn't have left anything like that lying around.'

Steph felt deflated. The one thing that she was sure held the key to the truth no longer existed. 'Are you just saying that?'

'No. I know for a fact. You're living in cloud cuckoo land if you think you'll find anything.'

Steph stopped and looked at her mother as a sudden bolt of realisation hit her. She jumped up from her chair. 'Thank you, Mum,' she said, a broad grin spreading across her face.

'Thank me for what?'

'Cloud cuckoo land – you're a genius.'

Wendy shook her head. 'What are you talking about?'

'I've got to go. I need to check something out.' She could barely contain her excitement. There was still a chance of finding that recording.

Conmere, Thursday, 16 May, 4.15 p.m.

Safely in her room, with the door locked, Steph took out her laptop and switched it on. As soon as it sprang to life, she went onto the camera shop's website and after a bit of searching found the link for their SpyCloud. She typed in Elizabeth's email address from the information Sonia had given her when they'd first met. It then asked for the four-digit PIN. Steph checked the notebook and input the numbers written in red alongside the camera shop's phone number – 2206. It made sense now: it was Elizabeth's birthday, 22 June. Holding her breath, she pressed the enter key and waited. The egg timer appeared on the screen for a few seconds and then the screen went white and three movie icons appeared in front of her.

She was in.

They were labelled Diary Entry One, Diary Entry Two and Diary Entry Three, all in movie format. Steph clicked on the first one.

Straight away the screen was filled with Elizabeth settling back on her bed, having just started the recording. Steph was struck by the beauty of her, with her lovely blonde hair which fell in soft waves down to her shoulder. Even though it was only a half-body shot and Elizabeth was in casual clothes, she still looked stylish. Steph was sure she herself never looked so glamorous when she was in jeans and a T-shirt. She couldn't help wondering what Harry had seen in her when he obviously had much more sophisticated tastes. It wasn't without a little dip in her heart that she acknowledged she probably didn't mean a great deal to him. She shook thoughts of Harry from her mind as Elizabeth began to speak.

'My name is Elizabeth Sinclair. I'm making a series of recordings, as I've found out some things here at Conmere which are troubling and knowing these, I'm now in danger. I'm hoping no one ever has to see this recording and I'm being paranoid, but just in case I thought I'd do this.'

Her diction was clear and crisp, every syllable and every vowel pronounced with precision. Elizabeth paused to take a sip from the wine glass she held in her hand.

'I'm married to Harry Sinclair, the middle Sinclair brother of Conmere Resort Centre. We've been married for two years and things haven't exactly been great lately. I'm not

trying to excuse my behaviour or anything, I'm just stating the facts. I'm very bored here at Conmere; there's really nothing much to do and I haven't made any friends. I'm not proud of the fact, but I've had one or two indiscretions – shall we say? – where men are concerned. Nothing serious, just a bit of fun to alleviate the boredom. Harry spends all day working and leaving me alone with nothing to do except update their website or send out a few posts on social media! I've tried getting involved with the business but it's such a closed shop, no one will let me, least of all my mother-in-law, Pru. Now, she's a force to be reckoned with.

Wisely or not, I've been having a little affair with my brother-in-law, Dominic Sinclair. It's been going on for a while, and during that time I've learnt some interesting things about him. One of them being, he's a drug dealer. He stores the drugs here at Conmere up by the lake in the old boathouse.

You may wonder how I know . . . well, let's just say, there's a constant supply of cocaine and I may have partaken in some recreational use at one of the parties. Dominic supplied me with the stuff and told me about his little sideline. It seems I'm not the only Sinclair who likes to indulge. Owen is quite fond of it himself but, unfortunately, isn't able to limit his use.

So, what's the problem, you might ask? Why do I think I'm in danger? Well, Dominic wants to end our relationship and, if I'm honest, I don't. I'm still having way too much fun and the thought of going back to Harry and his boring ways really doesn't appeal to me, not yet anyway. Dominic has threatened to tell Harry about my other affairs if I don't let him end our relationship. He's got another thought coming if he thinks he can just use me whenever he wants and there are no strings attached. I've told him as much. I've told him if he thinks he can just fuck me and then fuck me off, I'm more than happy to pass on some incriminating evidence to the police. He has far more to lose than I do. I could walk away with a divorce settlement. What could he walk away with? A jail sentence, that's what.

Needless to say, he's not very happy about that and we are at a bit of a stalemate. But it was the look in his eye and the way he spoke which frightened me. Now I'm not sure if he is planning something else to shut me up for good. That's why I'm recording everything here. If something does happen to me, then Dominic will be responsible. I guarantee it.'

Steph didn't immediately open the next file; she paused to take a moment to reflect on what she'd just seen and heard. It was unsettling seeing Elizabeth alive. The recording humanised her. Elizabeth was no longer the daughter of Sonia Lomas or the wife of Harry Sinclair – she was a real person. It sounded crazy, because of course Steph knew she was real, but the recording brought Elizabeth into clear focus. Steph felt a wave of compassion for this woman whose life had been cruelly taken.

A noise outside her room startled Steph. She sat very still and listened for another sound. A wave of fear washed over her as she remembered the night at the lodge with the intruder.

There it was again. Another noise – the tread of feet on floorboards?

Very slowly, Steph moved off the bed then stood up and crept across the room. She put her ear close to the door, trying to hear any other sounds. Carefully she turned the lock and, squeezing the handle, took a deep breath and then snatched the door open, hoping to catch the eavesdropper.

There was no one there. She looked up and down the hallway. Empty. As she looked down to the end of the hall again, she could see a light on in the communal bathroom. She gave a sigh of relief. She'd probably just heard another member of staff getting up to use the bathroom.

Steph closed the door. She was about to lock it, when something made her change her mind. Patiently she waited, listening for the sound of the bathroom being vacated. She didn't have to wait long before she heard the door open and then close, followed by footsteps coming down the hall.

Steph opened the door and looked out.

'Oh!' She let out a small cry of surprise at the last person she'd expected to be there.

'Everything all right, Steph?' asked Pru Sinclair.

'Yes. Sorry. I . . . wasn't . . .' she faltered.

'Wasn't expecting to see me?' Pru smiled. 'No, I don't suppose you were. I was just checking the bathroom. Someone reported the tap to be dripping. I thought I'd have a look before sending Maintenance on a wild-goose chase. Looks like it just needed turning off properly.'

'Oh, I see,' said Steph, not really sure what to say.

'Anyway, I'll be off now. Bye.'

Steph closed her bedroom door after watching Pru head

off down the stairs. How odd that she should come up here herself.

She didn't dwell on it any further, the lure of the remaining documents on the SpyCloud being much greater. Steph made sure the door was locked and this time she plugged her earphones in and settled down to watch the next clip.

'I've done something very stupid tonight, very stupid indeed.'

This time the Elizabeth sounded more concerned. She was speaking quietly with a nervousness that hadn't been there before.

'I've had an argument with Owen about changing his mind about voting on the sale of North Meadow. He said he wasn't going to. He said he was going to call my bluff as he didn't think I had the balls to tell Natalie or his family about his heavy drinking, gambling and sex with the prostitute . . . I mean, escort, or whatever she was. Anyway, we had a terrible row out on the terrace, one of those hissed rows where you want to shout but you can't because there are people about. Yeah, one of those. Well, I was so mad that as I marched off I couldn't help myself . . . I shouted back to him that he was going to be sorry when his bare arse was splashed all over social media, and I didn't realise but Natalie was there. She looked all concerned and I was so angry that I actually said to her something like, you'd better ask your husband what he was doing at Kendalton Green Hotel, and while you're at

it get yourself tested for an STD because I don't think he used a condom.'

Elizabeth buried her face in her hands for a moment, before looking up and flicking her hair back from her face.

'I can't believe I said that. Natalie looked mortified. As for Owen, well, he practically launched himself down the steps at me. If it wasn't for Dominic appearing from nowhere and somehow getting between myself and Owen, I'm not sure what would have happened. Then Harry turned up, demanding to know what was going on. Natalie was crying. Dominic was still bundling Owen out of the way, telling Harry to take me home, like I was some sort of child! And Harry didn't even stop to question his brother but just dragged me in the other direction!

'Me and Harry have just had the most awful row. I've tried to play it down for Natalie's sake really. I said me and Owen argued and he called me a gold-digger and I pretended I made that up about Owen sleeping with a prostitute. I'm not sure Harry believes me. I've texted Natalie and said as much but she hasn't replied. The look on Dominic's face . . . he glared at me with such hatred . . . he really despises me. I honestly don't know why I did it. I really am sorry. It seems I've managed to upset the entire Sinclair family.'

She blew out a long breath, looking down at her hands. and then after a moment it was as if she'd had a realisation, and she cocked her head and frowned. Steph continued to watch.

She sensed there was more to come from Elizabeth. And she was right.

'Do you know what? I think I might have had enough of the bloody Sinclairs. I actually think they are more trouble than they're worth. I'm certainly not flavour of the month around here. Might be time for me to get a pay-off, from all of them, and leave. Yes, leave before it's too late.'

Elizabeth's bravado faded and apprehension filled her eyes.

'I should probably get out while I still can.'

The recording ended.

'Wow,' muttered Steph out loud. Elizabeth was like a hand grenade when it came to the Sinclairs.

She clicked on the final file and this time the recording cut to a hotel room.

Here we go, thought Steph. She watched as the woman, whose face couldn't be seen, but obviously Camilla, came into shot, standing in front of the recording device as she pressed the record button. Steph cringed as the scene unfolded on her laptop. She fast-forwarded it, giving the recording the merest of glances as she made her way to the end. She took her headphones out of her ears. Seeing was bad enough, without having to listen to Owen too. Finally, the recording ended and there was nothing more on the card.

For good measure, Steph made a copy onto the hard drive of her laptop and onto a spare memory stick before taking out the memory card and hiding it.

She lay down on her bed, still fully dressed, and pondered what she'd found out. There was definitely motive for more than one person of the Sinclair family to want to silence Elizabeth, but who was the most capable of murder?

Chapter Thirty-Six

Two Years Earlier,
Conmere, 24 September, 3.00 p.m.

Elizabeth pulled up on the driveway to her and Harry's lodge and was unsettled to see Harry's car under the car-port, as she had been under the impression he was out with Owen today looking at some new horses.

As she parked she inspected her face in the vanity mirror on the sun visor, grateful she had reapplied her lipstick after leaving Dominic less than an hour ago. The red mark on her chin from where his stubble had grazed her skin was still visible, but she was sure Harry wouldn't notice, although if he did she'd blame it on some reaction to a new moisturiser.

She took a deep breath before getting out of the car. Her clandestine meeting with Dominic had started well and the sex had been amazing as always but after that it had rapidly gone downhill.

'Time to call it a day,' he said so casually as they dressed that at first she wasn't sure she'd heard him right. He repeated himself, slowly and clearly.

'Just like that?' She felt insulted at his careless manner. She wasn't some piece of trash.

'Wait . . . you didn't think . . .? Oh, Christ, you did, didn't you? You thought this was going somewhere. Jesus, Elizabeth, I didn't take you for being that naive.'

'You're a bastard, you know that?'

'It's been said before.' He gave a don't-give-a-fuck grin at her.

Elizabeth wanted to rush round the other side of the bed and slap that conceited, smug smile right off his face. If he thought he could just chuck her away when he'd had enough, then he had another think coming. 'Don't flatter yourself. I'm not looking for anything more than a bit of fun and excitement from you, but despite what you might think, I'm not cheap. There's a price for me tottering back home to Harry without a word of this.'

He stood up as he buttoned the cuffs on his shirt. 'Really?' He gave a dismissive snort.

'Yes, really. I'd say you've got far more to lose than me. Don't forget I know all about what happens up at the boat-house for a start.'

Ha! That wiped the smile off his face. He wasn't so smug now.

He walked around the edge of the bed and pointed his finger so that it was almost in her face. 'Don't fuck with me. You'll be sorry.'

'Oh, I'm frightened,' said Elizabeth, determined not to let Dominic see she was intimidated by his unexpected aggression.

'You get yourself back home like the good wife you're supposed to be. That's if you know what's good for you.'

Elizabeth was still fuming when she arrived home but she knew she was kidding herself really. Yes, she was angry at Dominic, but she was also scared. There had been something in Dominic's eyes she couldn't quite read. It wasn't anything she could put her finger on, but there was some underlying intent, something evil just below the surface where Dominic was concerned.

'Where have you been?' demanded Harry as she walked through the door.

'Out, shopping.'

'Where are your bags?'

'I didn't see anything I liked.' Elizabeth dropped her car keys into the bowl. 'What's with the interrogation?' Harry was becoming increasingly suspicious about what she did with her time and it was not just annoying her, but it had begun to worry her a little too. She might be able to convince him to forgive her an indiscretion but she wasn't sure he'd forgive her if she said the indiscretion involved his brother. She remembered he wasn't supposed to be home. 'I thought you were out with Owen all day?'

'Change of plan. Sorry to disappoint you.'

Elizabeth sighed. 'Honestly, Harry, I'm tired of all this.'

'All what?'

'Living here. I'm bored. You're hardly around, which I think is by design. I wish we could start again somewhere else.' She didn't really, not with him anyway, but she wasn't in the mood for another row, especially if it meant he would catch her out. She went over to him and, leaning over the back of the chair, slipped her arms around his shoulders, running her hand down the buttons on his shirt.

He shrugged her off and jumped to his feet. 'Fucking bitch,' he said, his eyes blazing with anger.

'What?' Elizabeth had no idea what Harry meant by that.

'You might have fixed your hair and done your make-up but you forgot to wash the smell of aftershave off you.'

Elizabeth felt her knees weaken. She rested on the back of the chair for support. 'Don't be silly,' she said after a moment. 'I've been in the department store, testing out new aftershaves for you.'

Harry shook his head. 'Bullshit.' With that he stormed out of the house, slamming the door hard behind him.

Elizabeth dropped into the chair and held her head in her hands. What a mess! She really needed to leave but she hadn't managed to squirrel away nearly enough money to do so. She felt unexpected tears sting her eyes and, feeling in need of some kind words and a shoulder to cry on, she phoned her mum.

It went to voicemail. Elizabeth almost hung up, but she felt compelled to leave a message.

'Hello, Mum, it's me. Look, I'm sorry to call like this and leave a message. I really wanted to speak to you in person but . . . things aren't too good here. I've got myself into something and it's way above my head. I don't like it. I have a bad feeling about it all. I need to come home. I'm going to leave this place. Leave Harry and come home. I'm not sure when, but it will be soon, just as soon as I've worked a few things out. Got to go. Love you.'

She sat back in the chair, wiping a stray tear from her face, and wondered if Sonia would call back soon. It would be nice to hear a friendly voice for a change.

'Hello, Elizabeth, is everything all right?'

392

Elizabeth spun round in her chair to see Pru standing in the doorway. 'Sorry, I didn't hear you there.'

'I did knock. I was worried. I've just seen Harry storming through the house in a foul mood and I was concerned. I know things are a bit tricky between you two at the moment.' She gave a sympathetic smile. 'I don't mean to pry. I can leave if you prefer.'

'No, it's fine. Do come in,' said Elizabeth, feeling emotionally tired from all the stress. 'Would you like a coffee?'

'You sit there. I'll do it.'

Elizabeth watched as Pru busied herself in the kitchen making them both a coffee. She placed the cups on the coffee table and sat down in the chair next to Elizabeth. 'Thank you,' said Elizabeth.

'You know there's a lot of pressure on people these days to live the perfect life,' said Pru. 'We are constantly fed images of how we should be living, and there's always some expert from somewhere banging on about how to be happy and content, but you know what? Real life isn't like that. It's not a fantasy life from something out of an old Doris Day film.'

'You can say that again.' Elizabeth took a sip of her coffee.

'You know, when I first met Max I was well and truly charmed by this good-looking Englishman. He only had to speak and I would have killed just to listen to that accent.' She laughed. 'It's an American thing – we love the English accent. Anyway, we did fall in love that summer, but that wasn't the only reason I ended up coming over to the UK and setting up home with him.'

'No?' Elizabeth was surprised at this candidness from her mother-in-law.

'Not at all. You see, we made a good team on a number of fronts. The most prevailing one, which has stood the test of time, has been Conmere.'

'Sorry, I don't understand.'

'Max had the house, the grounds, the land, and he had a vision, but he also had a tremendous amount of financial liability in keeping the place running. Cue a wealthy American heiress.' She tapped her chest with her finger. 'I had the money he needed to make a go of the place, to realise his vision of running Conmere House in the black for once. It was an arrangement that suited us, and the fact that we were rather fond of each other helped too.'

'It was certainly a good coming together,' said Elizabeth.

'It wasn't plain sailing, and as the years went by the love did peter out, but we knew we worked well together as a team. I could have left Max at any time, I knew he had a wandering eye, but I decided to stay because I knew I could gain a lot more from staying than I could from leaving.' She placed a hand on Elizabeth's knee. 'The grass isn't always greener on the other side. I know I'm biased but you have a good man in Harry and it would break my heart to see him unhappy. I know he wants to leave Conmere but if you're here and you're happy here then he'll stay. It's as simple as that.'

Now the penny dropped. Pru wasn't particularly concerned about Elizabeth but she was concerned that Harry was happy and that Harry didn't leave. Pru felt Elizabeth was key to that. An idea was slowly forming in Elizabeth's head. 'I think I know what you're saying,' she said. 'But I think I deserve something in return.'

Pru arched her eyebrows and took her hand away. 'Right, let's get down to business. What is it you want?'

'I want a share in Conmere. I want to be able to vote on matters concerning Conmere.' There, she'd said it. She could tell by the look on Pru's face, she wasn't expecting that. What the hell? Elizabeth had had enough, waiting for Owen to sort this out, and if she could get Pru to agree, well, she could use that video evidence against Owen in some other way if and when the opportunity arose.

'A share in Conmere in addition to Harry's?'

'Yep. I want an equal stake.'

'Impossible.'

'Nothing's impossible.'

'I'll never give a share of Conmere to anyone else.'

'That's fine. I can just walk away and probably take Harry with me. I can also take down what you've spent years building. I know enough about all three of your sons to discredit them and to have at least one of them arrested.'

Pru looked at her for a long moment. 'I underestimated you. My fault.' She tapped her knee with her finger as she pondered some more. 'I actually admire you. I thought you would be easy to manipulate. I do like you, Elizabeth, and now I think I like you even more.'

'So?'

'So, I'll need a formal request in writing from you. Something I can take to the board – in other words, my sons. I'll need to convince them it's a good idea. I'm sure we can come to an arrangement.'

'Great,' said Elizabeth. 'And just so we fully understand each other, I'm deadly serious about it.'

'So am I.' She smiled. 'Maybe just let your mum know you're all right. I didn't mean to eavesdrop, but I heard the message you left. I'm sure she'll be worried. Give her a call or email to let her know you're OK.'

Chapter Thirty-Seven

Conmere, Friday, 17 May, 7.00 a.m.

Steph woke the next morning not to the sound of her seven o'clock alarm, but to the sound of her mobile ringing. It took her a moment to work out it was her phone and when she looked at the screen was surprised to see it was her mother. Steph contemplated ignoring it. After yesterday, she wasn't sure she wanted to speak to her mother for a long time.

'Hello.'

'Good, I've caught you before you've started work.' Wendy got straight to the point. 'I need to speak to you before you see any of the Sinclairs. Are you awake properly?'

'Yes. What's going on?' Steph swung her legs out of bed and planted her feet on the floor, pulling her fleece jacket around her shoulders. 'I'm wide awake. What's up?'

'I didn't say anything before but I had a phone call from Harry Sinclair. He's concerned to say the least that you're getting too involved with Sonia Lomas and the death of his wife.'

'Oh, for goodness' sake.' Steph pushed her hair from her face.

'He had every right. It's his business and you're causing problems.'

'If I'm causing problems it's because they're hiding things.' Steph pushed her arms into her jacket. 'Look, Mum, I've found out a few things about the Sinclairs.' She lowered her voice. 'I found out that Dominic Sinclair is dealing in drugs.'

'What?'

'I saw him and then I went and had a look for myself. He's storing them in the boathouse. I don't know what do to.' For some reason she held back from telling Wendy about the recording.

'Now, listen to me, Stephanie. You are not to tell the police. You are not to get involved in anything. I want you to pack your bags and go straight to Brighton, like I said yesterday.'

'I can't do that,' said Steph, annoyed her mother was still trying to tell her what to do. 'Did you hear what I said? There are class A drugs, a lot of them, on the Sinclair premises. Owen is a user. I saw that for myself. Both he and Dominic are involved. I can't ignore that.' She hesitated before she added, 'And if they're involved, then I wouldn't be surprised if Harry is too.' She hated herself for saying it but it seemed a logical thought process, even though it hurt her. It would mean she couldn't have anything to do with Harry, not now – no matter how she felt about him, she wasn't about to get involved with a drug dealer.

'They are dangerous people,' replied Wendy, with an insistency Steph hadn't heard before. 'Do not do anything to upset them. Leave there immediately.'

A feeling of dread walked its way up Steph's arms, causing goose pimples to pucker her skin. Her stomach clenched and her heart threw in an extra beat as a tiny voice in the back of her mind started to push its way to the fore. She didn't want to acknowledge it – she had tried to ignore it, to reason it away, but there was no shutting herself off from it now. She swallowed hard as she prepared herself to speak.

'Mum,' she said slowly. 'Are you involved in any way with the Sinclairs? I mean, do you or did you work for them? Have they paid you to help them?' She hadn't been able to bring herself to say the actual words, but she knew her mum, if guilty, would know exactly what she meant.

'I don't know what you're talking about.'

'What about Cameron from the pub? Harry attacked him. He said the charges were dropped because there wasn't enough evidence. He said the investigating police officer wasn't interested and played the whole incident down.'

There was a silence before Wendy spoke. 'Are you suggesting what I think you are?'

'Please, just answer the question.' Steph was surprised by the tears which filled her eyes. 'Were you on the Sinclair payroll? Are you still? Did you know what Dominic was up to? Is that what Elizabeth had found out? Is that what got her killed? Did they pay you not to investigate Elizabeth's death?' She gulped down a sob. Of all the things she thought her mother was, a bent police officer was not one of them, but the words of Rob, her mum's old work colleague, came flooding back. Wendy had been asked to leave the force; she hadn't retired.

'I can't believe you've just asked me that!' Wendy almost shouted down the phone. 'How dare you?'

'Is it true?' asked Steph, swiping away a stray tear.

'I'm lost for words!' exclaimed Wendy. 'I'm stunned.'

'You're not denying it, are you? Mum . . . please?'

The line went dead.

Steph dropped back onto the bed and allowed the sob to escape untamed. She rolled onto her stomach and buried her face in her pillow. She felt betrayed. Wendy had been a shit mum, she had betrayed Steph on that level, and in all that time Steph had held on to the fact that her mum was a good police officer. She could justify her mother's behaviour towards her on the basis that she was committed to her job, but now, to realise Wendy had been a corrupt police officer, she felt betrayed for a second time. Steph felt so unworthy. It was one thing Wendy not loving her because of her job, but it brought it to a whole new low that she didn't love her because she loved her corrupt job more. Steph had never wished more in her life that her father was still here. Someone to comfort her, to put his arm around her and tell her it was all right, that he loved her and he would take away her pain.

The sound of her alarm going off brought Steph from her heartbreak. Her anguish was now turning to anger. If that was what Wendy was really like, then she didn't care if she never saw her again. She scrolled through her contacts list and, reaching Wendy's number, blocked it. That woman would never contact her again. If Steph never spoke to her again in her life, she wouldn't care.

Chucking her phone on her bed, Steph dressed quickly. She needed to be at work in ten minutes and the sooner she got her shift over with, the sooner she could decide what to do. She needed some thinking space. If her mother was corrupt, it probably wasn't a good idea to go to the local police. What if the police were still in the Sinclairs' pockets? No, she'd have to go to a different police force, she supposed. Maybe she could ask Adam? She mulled this over as she brushed her hair. Adam had warned her to stay away from the Sinclairs, too. Was he the right one to go to? The Sinclairs might be able to influence a local paper. No, she decided, she'd have to go to a national paper with this. What she needed to do was to gather all her evidence together.

She stopped in mid-brush. What evidence? OK, she had seen Dominic's drugs stash but if she alerted him too soon that she knew about it, he could easily move it. She'd have to take some photos, which would mean going back to the boathouse. That would solve the drug-dealing problem, but what about Elizabeth's death? She had evidence from the SpyCloud that Owen would have a motive to kill her – after all, she'd been blackmailing him with the sex tape. Elizabeth had also recorded her fears that her life was in danger from Dominic, that she had discovered what he was up to. Well, it didn't take a genius to work out that it was probably drug dealing, but it still wasn't unequivocal proof.

Steph finished tying up her hair and straightened her uniform. She'd have to get a confession out of one of them. Did Harry know? Did he have anything to do with Elizabeth's death? If he knew Elizabeth was having an affair with his brother, was that enough for him to want to kill her?

Whichever one it was, she was certain that they were all covering for each other. Sticking together. Dominic was the kingpin, Harry, she liked to think, was the reluctant one, and Owen the easily led one.

What she needed was some sort of confession. So that left either Dominic or Owen. She decided Owen was the weak link. If she was honest, Dominic scared her and she was pretty sure he wouldn't talk, but Owen . . . she could use the sex tape maybe.

Unwittingly she realised she was now in the exact same position she imagined Elizabeth had been in, except unlike Elizabeth, who was driven by greed, Steph was driven by the truth and by justice for Elizabeth and peace for Sonia Lomas.

Conmere, Friday, 17 May, 2.05 p.m.

Steph had managed to keep well out of the way that morning, preparing the lodges on the far side of the resort.

She closed the door on the final lodge and made her way over to the small laundry room nearby to store away the cleaning products and deposit the used bed linen, which would later be collected by someone with the laundry cart. It saved the housekeeping staff having to lug cleaning products and bedding around the resort with them. She locked the door and, using the pushbike provided for staff, she cycled back to the main house.

'All done?' asked Heidi as Steph handed back the keys. 'Looks like you timed it right for the weather.' Heidi nodded towards the window, through which they saw that a black cloud had settled in the sky.

'It was quite cold cycling back,' admitted Steph. 'I wished I'd brought my coat. Anyway, what do you want me to do now?'

Heidi checked her watch. 'Why don't you take your lunch break? This afternoon I want you on the pool house team. We want to give both wet and dry side a good clean today, ready for the weekend.'

'OK. I'll see you later,' said Steph. She left the housekeeping office and decided rather than spend an hour in the staff kitchen having lunch, she'd sooner be by herself and avoid any possibility of Harry coming to look for her. She still hadn't made up her mind what to do about the recordings Elizabeth hade made. Part of her wanted to speak to Harry so he could tell her how he wasn't involved at all, but another part of her was more cautious, telling her she should play her cards close to her chest.

As she crossed the main hall, Pru Sinclair came out of her private living room. She was dressed in casual trousers, a T-shirt and fleece. 'Oh, Steph, just the person,' she said, smiling at her. 'I need some help down at the lake. A couple of the rowing boats have gone adrift. I saw them this morning when I was out with the girls. I would have rowed out and got them in myself, but I couldn't leave the dogs on their own. You wouldn't mind coming out with me now to get them?'

'Er, yeah, of course,' said Steph, not sure it was a great idea.

Pru didn't miss her hesitancy. 'I would ask one of the boys but Dominic and Owen are both tied up over at the stables this morning, and Harry . . . well . . . let's just say, Harry isn't in the best of moods today.'

'It's fine, honestly,' said Steph, wondering what exactly had put Harry in a bad mood. 'I don't mind at all.' And she didn't, now she thought about it – it would be a good opportunity to try to get some information out of Pru, but she knew she would have to be careful about it. 'I'll need to grab a coat,' said Steph, moving towards the stairs.

'Oh, I'm sure there's one in the office you can borrow,' said Pru. 'Wait there.' She returned almost straight away with a waxed cotton jacket. 'It's Harry's. He won't mind. And here are some boots – you look about the same size as me. Size five?'

Steph nodded, taking the jacket and eyeing up the boots. 'I'll be OK in my trainers.'

'Wear the boots. We'll have to wade out to the first rowing boat. Your shoes will get ruined.'

Steph took off her trainers, which Pru whisked up and put in a holdall she had hooked on her shoulder. 'Good. Let's go.'

Obediently Steph followed Pru out of the house, through the centre of the resort and along the now familiar path down towards the lake. Pru walked briskly, chatting to Steph about how she'd used to come down to the lake every day when she was younger and take an early morning dip.

'I used to try to get Max to join me, but he never would,' she said. 'In the end I gave up asking him. He was never really an outdoorsy type of person. He was much more the engine room of the business side of Conmere.'

'It sounds like a good partnership,' said Steph. 'A good balance.'

'Yes, it was,' said Pru, with a small smile. 'I do miss him, despite his being a bit cantankerous at times.'

They had reached the edge of the lake now and Steph could see the two rowing boats drifting in the middle. She couldn't remember if there had been two or three boats out there when she was last down here and these looked further out than she recalled. It wouldn't be that easy towing two boats behind their one. She followed Pru into the water and they waded out to a lone rowing boat tied up to a buoy.

'Do you want me to row?' asked Steph as Pru climbed in first, putting the holdall in the front of the boat.

'I'll row out; maybe you can row back,' said Pru, holding out her hand to help Steph climb into the boat. 'You save your strength for the return journey.'

Chapter Thirty-Eight

Conmere House, Friday, 17 May, 2.45 p.m.

Harry was in the office, going through the bookings for the forthcoming weekend. His mother had accused him of being in a bad mood earlier and, although he had denied it, he was well aware he was grumpy. He hadn't been able to see Steph for the last couple of days and it was pissing him off. God, how had she got under his skin so deeply and so quickly?

He needed to take some paperwork in to his mother to sign and attempted to push his bad mood aside, although that was easier said than done.

He knocked on the door to his mother's private living room and went in but the room was empty. There was a strange smell hanging in the air. Harry took a couple of sniffs. It was a burnt sort of smell but plasticky at the same time. He wondered if it was something electrical but as he looked round the room for an obvious source he noticed a candle on the sideboard with molten black drips down the shaft. He went over and felt the wick between his fingers; it was still warm. It looked as though his mother had been melting something. How odd. He looked over the surface of the sideboard and, noticing a black drip on the edge of the wood, he allowed his gaze to trace its way to the floor. He bent down and picked up a small semi-melted square of plastic and, holding it between his finger and thumb, tried to work out what it was. There was a waste-paper bin to the side and Harry reached over for it.

In the bottom he could see more melted pieces of plastic. He fished them out. It didn't take a genius to work out that this had once been a memory card of some description. He turned over a piece in his hand and immediately recognised the small fraction of handwriting that remained. The fancy and elaborate capital letter *E* written in the gold-ink pen his wife had loved so much was as clear as the day she had written it.

A noise behind him made him look round. Dominic was standing in the room, his hands in his pockets as he watched his brother. Harry stood up and held out his hand with the remains of the memory card. 'This was Elizabeth's.'

'Hmm. Yes. It was.' Dominic walked over to the drinks tray and poured himself a whisky.

A hundred different thoughts crashed their way around Harry's mind, bumping and bouncing off each other so fast, he couldn't pin a single one down to examine closely.

Harry squeezed his eyes shut and opened them; standing straighter, he pushed his shoulders back and glared at Dominic. 'What the fuck is going on? Why were you burning it? What was on it?'

'It doesn't really matter now.'

'It matters to me.' Harry barely recognised his own voice, such was the snarl to his words.

Dominic downed his drink and placed the glass on the tray. 'Elizabeth was trying to do a deal with Mum. She wrote a formal letter to the board requesting a meeting. She said she had information which, if released, would put the company and all the directors in difficult positions. Basically, she had dirt on all of us to cause a mini-scandal.'

'How come I didn't know about this?'

'I don't know why your own wife wouldn't tell you, but I know Mum didn't want anyone to find out. She decided she was going to handle this herself.'

Harry frowned at Dominic's comments. He couldn't describe the emotion hitting him in the gut right now. Disappointment? Betrayal? Indignation? His wife and his mother had been striking a deal and he knew nothing about it and yet Dominic did. Harry chucked the pieces of plastic into the fireplace. 'Is this why you've been so jumpy all week? Because you were worried Steph was going to uncover the scandal?' He emphasised the last word to underscore his disdain.

'It's so much more than a scandal. And for once I wasn't just covering my own arse. But I tell you now, Steph needs to stop digging. Either you stop her or I will.'

'You stay away from her,' warned Harry, clenching and unclenching his fist. The anger was surging through him, mixed with fear for Steph. And then the thought he'd been trying to ignore, the one that had been lying dormant in the darkest recess of his mind, the one he denied airtime to, rose up like a tsunami and swamped him. He stared at his brother, seeing him for what he was.

'What's wrong, Harry? You look like you've seen a ghost,' said Dominic, with more than a hint of nonchalance.

'You. It was you.' Harry's pulse throbbed in his neck. He was shouting now. 'You wanted Elizabeth out of the picture, didn't you?' He slammed his fist down onto the sideboard, making Dominic jump.

'What the fuck are you on about?' Dominic raised his own voice and met his brother eye to eye.

'Elizabeth's death – you had something to do with it, didn't you?' He grabbed his brother by the lapels and yanked him towards him until their faces were only inches apart.

Dominic struggled, trying to prise Harry's hands from his jacket. 'Get off me! You fucking idiot!' he yelled. 'What the hell are you doing?'

Harry was aware of the door flying open and someone running into the office.

'What the . . .?'

It was Owen. He tugged at Harry. Another pair of arms wrapped themselves around Harry's shoulders and he was pulled backwards, releasing Dominic as he did so. It was then he realised Antonio had rushed in with Owen.

Harry was being hustled up against the wall, Antonio standing in front of him, his hands slightly raised, ready to make a grab for Harry if he moved again. Owen was pacifying Dominic, who was calling Harry a variety of names, none of them complimentary.

'I'm all right,' said Harry to Antonio. 'Honestly, I'm fine.'

Antonio didn't look convinced, but a nod from Dominic and he left the room.

'Just what the hell is going on?' asked Owen.

Dominic straightened his jacket. 'You need to ask that idiot over there.'

Owen looked to Harry for an explanation.

Harry's gaze fixed on his older brother. 'Was it you?'

'Don't be such a prick,' said Dominic, smoothing down his hair. 'You don't get it, do you? It wasn't *me*. Yeah, I like this place. I earn a good living from it. It's a family business, but Conmere is not my blood group. If you cut me, I wouldn't bleed Conmere.' Dominic flicked a look to Owen and then back to Harry. 'None of us in this room would.'

Harry looked in disbelief as the reality of what Dominic was saying hit him. He shook his head. 'No. It . . . it can't be.'

'It can be and it is.' Dominic sat down.

'Would someone like to tell me what you two are going on about?' chipped in Owen.

His brothers ignored him. 'Look, Harry,' said Dominic. 'I'm only trying to protect her. She's not strong enough to deal with this now. I'm sorry. I really am. I didn't want it to end the way it did, but what's done is done. It's better this way.'

'No!' Harry heard himself shout. 'It's not. It's not better.'

'Of course it is,' said Dominic, his eyes narrowing. 'Unless, of course, you want to see our mother spend the rest of her life in prison. Unless you want to see her die there, because that's what will happen. She's not strong enough to withstand a trial. She hasn't got the luxury of time. Now get that into your head.'

'Someone, please—' began Owen, only to be cut off by both Harry and Dominic telling him in unison to shut up.

'You know how much she loves this place. It means everything to her. It means more than any one of us, singular or plural. Conmere really does run through her veins. You can't do this to her.' Dominic blew out a long breath. 'Now, go find that girlfriend of yours and warn her off, before I have to.'

Harry looked defiantly at his brother. What the hell was he supposed to do? Could he really tell Steph the truth? But what about Elizabeth? She didn't deserve this, nor did Sonia. 'All this time you've known,' he said.

'I was at the boathouse. I saw it happen.'

'And you cleaned up for her.'

'I had no choice. The same way you don't.'

'Well, fuck you,' said Harry, before storming out of the room.

Chapter Thirty-Nine

Conmere Lake, Friday, 17 May, 2.50 p.m.

Steph pulled Harry's coat tighter around her. It was colder out here on the water but the drop in temperature extended further than her physical symptoms. The atmosphere in the boat had shifted; something had changed. There was a look on Pru's face that she could not determine but it was sending shock waves to Steph's nerve endings. Suddenly, she didn't want to be in the boat with Pru. She felt vulnerable and in danger. 'Are you sure this needs to be done today?'

'Positive.' Pru pulled hard on the oars and Steph was surprised by the older woman's strength. 'I wish Harry didn't live in France,' said Pru unexpectedly as she began to hit her stride with the rowing. 'But he has his reasons.'

Steph resisted the urge to say she wished that too, but then again, she wished a lot of things about Harry and his not living in France was just one of them. 'Did he ever want to move to France when Elizabeth was alive? Did Elizabeth like living here on the resort?'

'She wouldn't have wanted to live in France,' said Pru, with a distaste that surprised Steph. 'She liked it here too much.

Harry spoiled her.' She tutted. 'He treated her like a princess and she behaved like a slut.' Steph looked up at Pru, who met her gaze with a defiant look. 'I know it's not the done thing to speak ill of the dead, but she caused trouble with my sons.'

A beat and then another passed.

Suddenly, Steph could see everything in twenty-twenty vision. The inexplicable danger she had felt moments earlier was now explicable.

'What trouble was that?' she said, trying to keep her voice even, while scolding herself for being so blind to the truth. She had been so convinced it was one of the brothers who had been behind Elizabeth's death that she hadn't even tried to look elsewhere. She had been fooled by Pru. She thought it was only her own mother who put everything before her own children, but it wasn't. Pru did exactly the same and Steph had missed it through her own prejudices towards Wendy.

'Haven't you worked it out yet? I thought you would have done by now, especially with your connections.'

'Connections? What do you mean?' Steph's mind was racing. She needed to think fast to try to find a way out of this without alerting Pru to the fact she had worked out the truth.

'With the newspapers, of course.' Pru smiled one of the warm, motherly smiles Steph had seen her use when talking to guests.

'Oh, yes, newspapers. Er, well, I'm a features writer, not really a journalist.'

'Ah, but don't try to tell me you wouldn't jump at a story

if there was some scandal to be revealed.' Pru yanked on the oars harder.

'Is there a scandal, then?'

'Not if I have anything to do with it.'

Steph looked beyond Pru's shoulder; they were only a few metres away from the other boats now, but Pru seemed to be heading around them. 'Don't we need to get closer to the boats?'

Pru didn't answer but just eyed Steph, a small smile turning the corners of her mouth upwards. 'Change of plan,' she said.

'What do you mean?'

'You're not really very good at lying,' said Pru, adopting a carefree tone. 'And don't say you don't know what I mean.' Pru brought the boat to a halt. She was barely out of breath despite the exertion. She pulled the oars into the boat and then began undressing.

'What are you doing?' asked Steph in alarm as Pru took off her coat, followed by her shoes and then socks. Pru lifted the holdall and began putting her clothes into the bag.

To Steph's surprise, Pru was wearing a wetsuit underneath her clothing.

'I thought I'd take a swim,' said Pru. 'But not until you have first.'

Pru began rocking the boat.

'Stop!' Steph gripped both sides of the boat with her hands. There was no need to second-guess Pru now, whose plan was quite clear, but there was no way she was going to end up the same way as Elizabeth. 'You drowned Elizabeth!' she shouted.

Pru laughed out loud. 'Of course I didn't drown her. She

drowned all by herself. You know, she was a terrible swimmer. Hated the water. I didn't have to drown her, just get her in the water.'

'You pushed her in,' said Steph. 'You're responsible for her death. And I was stupid enough to think it was one of your sons.'

Pru stopped rocking the boat and her eyes hardened. 'My sons are many things but they are not murderers. They haven't got the stomach for it, they haven't got the balls. They left me no choice. I did it for them.'

Steph felt stunned. She had underestimated Pru Sinclair by a long way. The woman was insane. She'd killed Elizabeth to protect her boys and now she wanted to do the same to Steph.

She needed to think of a plan, but out here in the middle of the lake her options were limited. She had to keep Pru talking while she tried to think of something. She had her phone with her but it was in her pocket, underneath the coat Pru had given her. She pulled it out and looked at the screen. No signal.

Pru laughed again. 'You might as well throw that in the water. No use whatsoever out here.'

'Why did you have to kill her?' Steph fumbled with her phone. She wanted to hear Pru say it herself.

'She had an affair. She cheated on Harry,' spat Pru. 'But she couldn't be content with just having an affair with anyone, it had to be his own brother – Dominic.'

'Why didn't you just tell her to stop?'

'It was too late. She was going to leave Harry. She was blackmailing Dominic and Owen. She would have destroyed all of my sons, and not only that, it would have been the end of Conmere. I wasn't going to let that happen. With her out of the way, my sons would be free and the resort would be saved.'

'Did Harry know?' She felt a compassion for Harry that she hadn't been expecting. 'Did he know she was cheating on him?'

'He suspected. He even confronted Dominic, but he denied it. Owen was there at the time and he told me about it. That's when I knew I had to do something.'

'Couldn't you have paid her off?' Steph sensed the confession was coming to a close. She ripped off the heavy waxed jacket and pushed it under the seat, before dropping her phone on top of it.

'And have her blabber-mouthing about it to everyone? No. Absolutely not. Either that or she would have just kept coming back for more and more money. She couldn't be trusted. The same way I can't have you telling your story.'

'What makes you think I know anything?'

'I'm not stupid. I know who your mother is. I know everything that goes on around here. I make it my business and I know you've been poking your nose in where it doesn't belong. I tried to warn you. Tried to warn your mother and Elizabeth's mother, but no, you wouldn't take the hint, would you?'

'You? It was you in the car and you with the brick?'

Pru rolled her eyes skyward. 'Ten out of ten. And now it's your turn to take a swim.'

'You won't get away with this.'

'Oh, goodness, can't you think of anything original to say?'

scorned Pru. 'You're going in the water. So am I, but I get to swim back to shore and put on my clothes.' She tapped the holdall. 'My dry bag will ensure my clothes are still dry and then I can raise the alarm that you've fallen in the water trying to get the boats for me. I'll be distraught, of course. I won't be able to imagine another death in the lake. No one will suspect me of being out there. I'm in my sixties, I'm dying of cancer, I can't swim that far.'

Steph gulped. 'You're dying of cancer?'

'Yes; I have nothing to lose really. I'll be dead in six-to-twelve months but I don't care. I will have saved my beloved Conmere and my sons.'

'You're mad, you know that?' said Steph.

'Oh, shut up and get in the bloody water,' snarled Pru.

Steph shook her head vehemently, her hands gripping the wooden seat. Still, the speed with which Pru moved took her by surprise, and before she realised what was happening Pru had yanked her to her feet. 'Get off me!' grunted Steph as she tried to pull Pru's hands from the neck of her jumper.

Pru was stronger than she looked and Steph was fighting hard to keep her balance as Pru tried to tip her overboard. The boat lurched to one side and then the other. Steph's footing was momentarily dislodged, and as she attempted to re-establish her balance her foot slipped on the waxed cotton coat. Pru seized the opportunity and threw her weight into Steph, sending them both flying out of the boat and into the water.

Chapter Forty

As Harry stormed out of the living room, he was greeted by the sound of more raised voices. This time two women's. He looked up and was surprised to see Wendy Lynch standing there, in the middle of a heated debate with Heidi.

'I just want you to ring my daughter or call her on the walkie-talkie or whatever system you use,' Wendy was demanding. She looked round as Harry stepped into the hall. 'Right, you. Where's my daughter?'

Harry shot Heidi a look. 'Where's Steph?'

'On her lunch break, but she's not in the staff kitchen – I've just come from there.' Heidi looked at her watch. 'She should be back in about ten minutes.'

'Any idea where she might have gone?'

At that moment Eileen came through from the main doors, and she stopped in her tracks as she took in the worried faces in front of her.

'Have you seen Steph?' Harry asked, trying to keep the anxiety from his voice.

'A while ago, yes – I saw her walking with Mrs Sinclair.'

'Where?' he demanded, barely before Eileen had finished her sentence.

'Through the resort.' She pointed in the direction of the terrace and pool.

'Did you see where they went?' Harry's heart was hammering inside him.

'Just saw them go down the terrace steps,' said Eileen. 'Mrs Sinclair didn't have the girls with her.'

Harry didn't bother to answer; his only concern was for Steph. He went to grab his coat from the hook on the back of the door, but it was missing. Instead, he picked up a lightweight waterproof jacket and hurried after Wendy, who was already storming her way out of the building. His stomach churned with anxiety and his heart thumped with fear. Steph was with his mother and they were heading for the lake. He clenched his hands as panic began to surge through him. He couldn't let history repeat itself. He couldn't let anything happen to Steph. He had to get to the lake and fast. He stopped, spun round and grabbed a key from the reception-desk drawer.

'Wait! Wendy, just wait a minute,' said Harry as he caught up with the former DCI. 'I'll get one of the resort buggies. We can cover the grounds quicker. This way – they're behind the pool house.'

'Hurry, we need to find her, and quickly.'

They raced round to the pool house and Harry used the key to start the electric buggy, which was basically a quad bike but with a bench seat and a steering wheel. 'Ready?'

Harry steered the buggy round the pool house and along

the path which filtered through the trees, past the first tier of guest lodges and then into the denser woodland. 'I know what happened,' he shouted above the noise of the engine. 'And I know Steph must have worked it out.'

'I spoke to her this morning on the phone. She said she'd discovered the cocaine your brother has been dealing. He's got a haul of it hidden away in the boathouse.'

'What?' Harry turned his head to look at Wendy. She was deadly serious.

'Look out!' yelled Wendy.

Harry yanked the steering wheel to the left, narrowly missing a tree. 'A drugs haul?'

'Yes. Just keep your eyes on the track,' said Wendy, raising her voice to be heard. 'Where are you going exactly?'

'Down to the lake. My mother likes to go there. Steph likes the lake. It's where . . .' His words trailed off. He didn't need to tell Wendy it was where Elizabeth had drowned.

He could feel Wendy's gaze on him and he took a sideways look at her. He couldn't read her expression, but in just a quick glimpse he had seen guilt and fear. 'You know as well, don't you?' he said. The buggy jolted violently to one side as it hit a root but stayed upright and he steered it along the woodland path, opening up the accelerator.

'Elizabeth found out too many secrets about your family and she was holding them all to ransom,' said Wendy, eventually. 'She made enemies of just about everyone and she knew it. She was playing a dangerous game.'

'She was difficult to get on with in the end,' said Harry, thinking back to how, in the last couple of months of her life, they had practically been living separate lives and he'd been planning for a new life ahead as a divorcee. He hadn't spoken about this with anyone, not even his brothers, and after her death it had seemed pointless. It was only heaping more misery on everyone, especially her mother, Sonia. He wondered now if Elizabeth had confided in anyone. No one had spoken to him about it, no one had mentioned it or even hinted at it. He didn't know if, like him, they felt it was irrelevant after her death.

'She was making life difficult for all of you,' said Wendy. 'Her death was very convenient.'

Harry shot her a look. Convenient? That was one cold-hearted way of describing it. He concentrated on the path ahead as they reached the descent towards the lake.

The buggy trundled down the hill, swaying and dipping as it covered the uneven ground. Within a few minutes they were at the side of the lake.

Harry scanned the shoreline, and there, sprawled out on the muddy water's edge, was a figure. He brought the buggy to a halt, stalling the engine, and jumped off, running across the stones. He threw himself down on the ground beside the limp body. It was his mother. She was wearing a full wetsuit. Beside her was a dry bag.

'Mum! Mum!' shouted Harry, turning her over onto her back. He pressed his ear to her face. He could feel her breath on his skin. It was faint, but it was there. He pulled his phone from his pocket and dialled for an ambulance, before taking off his jacket and covering his mother with it. He stood up and looked out across the lake.

There were three rowing boats in the centre of the lake that shouldn't have been there. One was slightly more adrift than the others. He squinted some more. There was a dark shape floating by the boat. Fear gripped his throat.

'Ambulance service. Is the patient breathing?' came the response of the emergency-call handler.

Harry forced himself to answer. 'Yes. She's collapsed though. She's been in the water. Swimming. I've found her by the edge of the lake. It's my mother, she's sixty-eight.'

He waved his arm frantically to Wendy, pointing out across the lake. He was torn between answering the operator's questions and diving into the water himself. Wendy, however, had no hesitation. She was battling against the water, wading towards the nearest rowing boat.

Harry looked at his mother and back at Wendy and then out at the body in the lake. His indecision was relieved as a car came speeding up along the track and skidded to a halt. Dominic jumped out and started running towards them. Harry threw the phone at his brother.

'You deal with this. It's the ambulance service.'

With that he turned and ran into the water, shouting at Wendy to wait for him. Fortunately he'd kept himself in shape, and years of wild-water swimming with his mum were about to pay off. He dived into the water, wishing he'd taken time to kick his shoes off as he powered his way to the rowing boat.

Reaching the edge of the boat, he hauled himself in and took the oars from Wendy, pulling harder and faster than he'd ever done in his life. He had no idea how long Steph had been in the water. It might already be too late.

Memories of Elizabeth flooded back to him, images of her lifeless body in the hospital, tubes down her throat, wires attached to monitors. The beep-beep of the heart monitor and the sound of the ventilator wheezing. All the machinery which had kept Elizabeth alive but had not been able to save her.

Please, God, no. Not again. He wasn't a man of faith, but if there was ever a time to convert, then it was now. If there was ever a time to believe in some force, some being, some entity that was able to perform miracles and was able to offer some ray of hope, then it was now.

'Faster! Faster!' urged Wendy, who was kneeling at the front of the boat. 'We're nearly there. Steph! Stephanie!' The desperation and anguish in her voice wrenched at every fibre in Harry's body. Despite what Steph had thought about her mum, she was wrong. This woman loved her daughter. There was no doubt about that. Whatever had gone on before was irrelevant, as in this moment all Wendy cared about was Steph.

From the depths of his reserves, Harry found a renewed burst of energy as he powered the rowing boat towards Steph. He guided it alongside her and, as Wendy leaned over to grab her daughter, Harry helped lift Steph up onto the side of the boat.

He could see Wendy's police training taking over and she began to perform CPR on Steph's lifeless body. He needed to get them all back to the shore. He knew his efforts were best used in rowing them back, but the wind had picked up and the current across the water was strong. He hoisted himself back into the boat and immediately took up the oars.

His arms and legs burned, his back was on fire, but he pushed through the pain, as his sole focus was getting Steph to shore. He watched as Wendy continued to pump at her daughter's chest and then duck down to give her mouth-to-mouth. Again, he found himself offering up a prayer of mercy, that Steph be spared the same fate as Elizabeth.

Harry glanced over his shoulder; there was an ambulance by the lake and what looked like a paramedic car. Thank God! A spluttering and vomiting sound snapped his attention back to the boat. Wendy was rolling Steph on her side, who was throwing up lake water. She groaned and vomited some more. Then her eyes opened and she looked up at her mother, taking a moment to understand what was going on.

Wendy leaned over her daughter, cradling her head in her hands. She was crying. 'Oh, Steph . . . oh, thank God,' she was saying over and over again into her daughter's wet and matted hair. Wendy held her daughter tightly. 'It's OK. You're going to be OK.'

Harry didn't take his eyes off Steph. He could hardly believe Wendy had managed to revive her. Steph's gaze found its way to Harry and they looked at each other for a long moment, before Wendy was engulfing her daughter again.

Chapter Forty-One

Kendalton General Hospital, Campbell Ward,
Friday, 17 May, 4.30 p.m.

Steph opened her eyes at the sound of footsteps approaching her bed. She was surprised to see her mother standing there.

'How are you feeling?' asked Wendy.

'All right, actually. The doctor wants me to stay in overnight just to check I haven't got concussion and there's no water lying on my lungs. I'd sooner not be here, though.'

'It's the best place for you. I've had no end of phone calls from the press wanting a story from you.'

'I hope you told them where to go.'

'I most certainly did. Besides, you can't comment about an ongoing police investigation, which is what this will be now.'

'Sonia will be happy.'

'She is. She phoned me,' said Wendy. 'She'll speak to you herself, she said, but for now just wanted to pass on her utter and complete thanks. She said she can't put into words how grateful she is to you.'

Steph gave a small smile. 'I hope she gets the result she wants.'

'I'm sure she will.'

Steph fiddled with the edge of the sheet as a small silence fell between them. She knew if she didn't take the opportunity to say something now, the moment would disappear. She looked up at her mum, whose green eyes seemed a little softer than usual; in fact, Wendy's face seemed softer. The tight-set jaw was relaxed and there was no furrow in the brow. Wendy sat on the chair next to the bed, her hand in her lap. Steph reached out and Wendy allowed her to hold her hand. 'Thank you,' said Steph. 'Thank you for saving me.'

'It wasn't just me,' said Wendy. 'I'm not sure I could have done it without Harry. You need to thank him too.'

'I don't suppose he'll want to see me now,' said Steph. 'How's Pru?'

Wendy dropped her gaze before looking back at Steph. 'She's in a bad way. She suffered a heart attack from the effort of swimming back to shore. She had another in the ambulance. I haven't heard any more.'

Steph couldn't help feeling deflated at the news. Despite the woman trying to kill her, Steph's empathy was with Harry. His mother had betrayed him on so many levels and now she was critically ill. He probably had so many mixed emotions about her right now, and who could blame him?

'Have the police been to see you?' asked Wendy.

'Yes, they've just gone, actually. They took a preliminary statement.'

'What did you tell them?'

'Everything I knew. They took my phone.'

'Your phone?'

'When I was in the boat with Pru and I realised I was in

danger, I tried to phone you, Harry, anyone, but there was no signal out on the lake. I thought I was going to end up the same way as Elizabeth but I was damned if it was going to be put down to another accident.'

'What did you do?'

'I switched on the recording app. It recorded pretty much all of Pru's confession.'

'Oh, my,' said Wendy, with a smile. 'What a clever girl you are.'

Steph looked up at her mother, whose voice and face were filled with pride and admiration. Steph wasn't sure she'd ever been the cause of either in Wendy before and her heart swelled with unexpected love.

Wendy leaned closer to Steph. 'I'm sorry I've let you down.'

For the first time in her life, Steph could see tears in her mother's eyes. She squeezed Wendy's hand. 'It's OK, Mum,' she said. 'Don't cry.'

Wendy wiped at her tears. 'There's something you need to know,' she said evenly. 'In fact, there's a lot you need to know.'

Steph could see the steely look resurface in her mother's eyes, but she could also see fear and uncertainty. 'What is it?'

'When you met Rob at the house earlier this week and he told you I was asked to leave the force . . . he was telling the truth.'

'I don't care about that any more.'

'But you should, and it's important that you know the truth. It's best you hear it from me first, before you read about it in the papers. I've never told you any of this because I wanted to protect you. That's all I've ever wanted to do. I know I'm not very good at showing my emotions, but there was a very good reason. You won't like what I'm going to tell you and you may need a few days to think it over.'

Steph sat herself up further in her bed. 'What do you mean?'

'I'm likely to be arrested in the next twenty-four hours or so and this is why I need to tell you now.'

'Mum, you're scaring me.'

'Don't be scared. Just listen.' Wendy took a deep breath before speaking. 'Your father used to drive for Max Sinclair from time to time. You were only young, still at school, and we needed the money. I was a young police officer then and financially we were struggling. Anyway, I'm not really sure how it came about, but one day your dad came home and announced he had an evening driving job for Max Sinclair.'

'I remember him going out driving,' said Steph.

'He used to drive Max about a lot. Sometimes he'd run errands for the Sinclairs, pick stuff up for them, drop things off. Your dad didn't know what the packages were, he just did it. He told me not to ask questions. He didn't ask questions, so I shouldn't, and besides, the money was good.' Wendy paused for a moment. 'And then one day he came home and said he'd been involved in something really bad with the Sinclairs. He'd been stopped for speeding on one of his collections and the police had searched the car. They found the parcel and it turned out to be amphetamines. Your dad was in line to be charged for supplying. Anyway, Max Sinclair knew someone in the force and they had the charge dropped.

Don't ask me how, but it was dropped. The only trouble was, your dad was now in their debt.'

'Bloody hell,' uttered Steph. She couldn't believe her father had been involved in criminal activity. He just wasn't the sort. Not her dad. 'What happened after that?'

'I had to turn a blind eye to what your dad was doing. I was torn between a sense of duty and not getting your father arrested. I mean, what would I do then? I had you to look after. I couldn't afford for your dad to be arrested and I didn't want the disgrace. My career would be picked apart and looked at in minute detail, they would be certain to think I was involved somehow and, to be honest, just knowing would be enough to make me lose my job.' Wendy looked out into the middle distance. Steph waited silently for her to continue. 'When Max Sinclair died, I thought that would be the end of it and we would be free of that family. Your father and I argued a lot about it. He said that it was too late, Dominic was already running the show and he was much more conniving than his father. There was no escaping them. Dominic made sure of that.'

Steph felt her hand tremble. She couldn't believe the dilemma her mother had been put in. 'What did Dominic do?'

'He paid money into my account, even though I didn't want him to. He said it was insurance, to make it look like he was paying me. He said he was going to pay it in every now and then, just enough to make it look suspicious if it was ever investigated.'

'Why didn't you report it?'

'We were already in too deep, what with your father and Max. And Dominic has a sadistic streak, like his father. He implied that something might happen to you if I didn't do what he said.'

'He knew about me?' whispered Steph.

'Yes. He'd seen you out with me one day and then again at your dad's funeral. And, of course, over the years the Sinclairs had made it their business to know all about us. It's their way of keeping control.' Wendy closed her eyes at the memory. She took a moment before continuing. 'I knew about the drug smuggling but I turned a blind eye.'

'Oh, God, Mum.' It was getting worse by the minute and Steph knew there was more to come.

'When I told you about being asked to shut down the investigation into Elizabeth's death, I didn't tell you quite everything.' Wendy bowed her head, her shame obvious to Steph.

'What else?' Steph realised she had always known Wendy was keeping something from her. A little fact that would be the last of the puzzle pieces.

'I wasn't just put under pressure from my bosses to hush things up, I was put under pressure by the Sinclairs. When Elizabeth died two days after the incident at the lake, Dominic said I was to make sure the investigation found it to be an accident. He said that I was in no way to implicate anyone in her death. I'd been asking questions and, although I couldn't prove anything, when he came to me and said that, I knew her death couldn't have been an accident. I mean, how could it if he was telling me to make sure that was what the investigation concluded?'

'He knew it was his mum.' It was a statement rather than a question.

'He knew all right. Or at the very least, he suspected. So did I, but what could I do? I couldn't do anything for Elizabeth any more. She was dead, but I had to protect you. He made a barely veiled threat that something nasty could happen to you. I didn't know whether to believe him or not, but I wasn't going to call his bluff. I couldn't let him do anything to harm you. I needed to keep you safe. You were all I had. You are still all I have.'

Steph lay back against her pillows. She was having trouble taking all this in. Her dad was a criminal who had basically worked for a drugs gang. Her mum had not necessarily perverted the course of justice, but she hadn't looked into the death of Elizabeth fully. Wendy had certainly failed to perform her duties diligently. She had covered up the murder of Elizabeth to protect . . . Steph paused in mid-thought. Wendy hadn't done any of this for her own gain, she had been caught up in this because she'd wanted to protect Steph.

Oh, the irony. All this time Wendy had kept Steph at arms' length because she didn't want her getting involved. She had pushed her away, both in an emotional sense and in a physical sense to protect her. Even when Steph had thought her dad was so wonderful, so caring and so loving, that her dad was the good guy, Wendy had let her believe that to protect her.

Tears filled Steph's eyes and she once again reached out for her mother. 'Oh, Mum,' she said, and her face crumpled as the tears spilled over.

Wendy leaned across the bed and held Steph close to her. Steph couldn't remember the last time they'd had so much physical contact. Her mother was actually comforting her. Steph could feel the love surging from Wendy like she'd never known before. More sobs came, sobs of joy and relief. Her mother loved her, there was no denying it.

It was a few minutes before Steph was able to put another coherent thought together. She was acutely aware now of the sacrifice her mother had made, not only in what she'd done in the past, but also in what she'd done today. She wished there were another solution but she knew Wendy had to step forward and be accountable for her actions. Wendy owed it to Elizabeth Sinclair and to Sonia Lomas.

Steph thought of Harry and what he must be going through right now. Did he know what his mother had done to Elizabeth, or was he just praying she'd pull through and at that moment able to forgive her anything?

Steph wasn't sure how she felt about Pru Sinclair herself. The woman had tried to kill her. She shuddered. She didn't remember much else after going in the water, except Pru slipping in beside her. At first, in her confusion, Steph had thought Pru was going to save her, but then she'd realised she was trying to hold her down. Some primitive instinct in Steph had surfaced and she remembered thrashing around, trying to get away from Pru.

The last thing Steph could remember was Pru grabbing a handful of Steph's hair, right at the scalp, and then slamming Steph's head against the side of the boat.

Steph touched the gauze dressing on her head. She had a gash but other than that, no real damage. Thankfully.

And then another memory punched its way through to the fore of her mind. The waxed cotton jacket she'd seen through Wendy's letterbox.

'Who was at your house yesterday when I came over?

There was someone in your kitchen.' She halted, hardly daring to utter the name on the tip of her tongue. 'Was it . . . was it Harry?'

Wendy shied away, giving Steph an old-fashioned look of disbelief. 'You think Harry was at my house?'

'I don't know . . . whoever it was, they were wearing a waxed cotton jacket. I saw it.'

Wendy's face relaxed. 'I think all the Sinclair family own waxed cotton jackets.'

'It was Pru, wasn't it?' asked Steph, suddenly remembering the smell in her mother's kitchen the day before; it was the perfume that Pru always wore. She scolded herself for not realising this sooner.

'It was Pru,' confirmed Wendy. 'She came to threaten me. She said you weren't listening to any of the warnings.'

'Which is why you phoned me.'

'I'm sorry,' said Wendy. 'I'm sorry I was never the mother I should have been. It has been my biggest regret, but I didn't know how else to deal with it. I thought if I could make you hate coming to visit me, then you would stay out of all this. I thought it was the best thing to do but, when your life was in actual danger, I realised it was wrong. It wasn't your poking around into Elizabeth's death that led to you nearly coming to the same end, it was me. I am responsible for everything. I should have left your father as soon as I found out what he was doing. I should have left him and taken you with me and that would have broken the cycle, but I stayed and I allowed myself to be used.'

'I don't know what to say.'

'I'm sorry,' Wendy whispered again.

Kendalton General Hospital, Campbell Ward,
Friday, 17 May, 6.00 p.m.

Steph had convinced Wendy to go home and get some rest. The police hadn't been back since taking their preliminary statements earlier.

'I expect I'll get a visit from someone higher up sooner or later,' Wendy had said before leaving.

She had seemed resigned to the idea, and for the first time Steph felt she was seeing a fragility in her mother she hadn't seen before. Wendy was tired from the years of turning a blind eye and from the years of being under threat from Dominic Sinclair. Did Wendy think the years of pushing her daughter away, covering for her husband and neglecting her duty as a police officer had been worth it? Steph wasn't sure. Wendy should have just come clean right from the off and then none of this would have happened. She felt uncharitable thinking like that, but it was the truth.

Steph was just about to close her eyes and try to get some rest when, to her surprise, she saw an unexpected visitor coming through the doorway.

'Adam! What are you doing here?'

'Come to see you, of course. Now that you're famous.' He leaned over and gave her a kiss on the cheek, his beard tickling her face, and then dropped several newspapers onto her lap.

Steph looked at them, scanning the headlines of the articles Adam had outlined with red felt-tip pen.

SINCLAIR CASE TO BE REOPENED

SINCLAIR DROWNING:
LOCAL JOURNALIST FINDS NEW
EVIDENCE SUGGESTING MURDER

UNDERCOVER JOURNALIST FORCES
POLICE TO REOPEN CASE

'Wow. I am famous,' said Steph, without much enthusiasm. It was strange, now she had made both the local newspapers and one national; the excitement she had anticipated just wasn't there. Instead, all she could think about was Harry and what a bloody tragedy this must be for him, together with Sonia and what a bloody relief it must be for her to finally have some sort of closure.

'So, now we've established what a fantastic journalist you are, how about an exclusive?' said Adam.

'Never one to beat about the bush,' said Steph with a wry smile.

'Is that a yes?'

'No! No, it's not.'

'We can pay you. I've been given an open chequebook.' He shrugged at Steph's doubtful expression. 'OK, not totally open, but we can pay.'

'Honestly, Adam, it's not about the money. I don't want to sell my story.' She looked away. She hadn't consciously come to that decision until that very moment, but she suspected it had been there all the time. It would somehow feel disloyal to Harry. She didn't want to cause him any more pain than he already had to deal with. Her integrity as a person far outweighed her ambition to make it in the world of journalism.

'Oh, come on. As a favour to me. Say yes. I'm going to be fired on the spot if I don't come back with a yes.' Adam pushed his hands together in prayer.

'Have you got the contract with you?' Steph asked.

'Of course!' Adam produced the paperwork from his bag with a flourish worthy of a magician pulling a bunch of flowers from a top hat. He thumbed through to the final page and, together with a biro, thrust it into Steph's hands. 'Just sign there.'

Steph picked up the contract and, with equal flourish, tore the paperwork in half and then half again. 'Sorry. Not sorry.'

'Oh, man!' groaned Adam.

'Look, I've had all sorts of offers. But I can't say anything, not until the case has been looked at again.'

'I think that knock on your head must have knocked your senses out at the same time.'

'Nope. Knocked some sense into me, I'd say.' She looked ruefully at her ex-colleague. 'And don't think you're going to get any information out of me either, so don't bother even talking to me about it.'

Adam picked up the pieces of torn paper. 'Oh, well, I tried.'

He stayed a little longer and Steph managed to keep the conversation off-topic, even though she knew Adam was itching to turn it around. Much as it was nice catching up with him, she was relieved when he finally left, the effort of being on her guard sapping her energy.

Steph rested her head back against the pillows and closed

her eyes. She was exhausted and now the adrenalin had evaporated she was feeling the effects of her near-death experience. A wave of emotion surged and the desire to cry overwhelmed her. She snatched at a tissue from the box on the bedside cabinet and wiped her face. She had nearly drowned. Pru Sinclair had tried to kill her. The enormity of the events battered her, causing more tears to fall.

It was a moment or two before she became aware someone else was in the room. She was shocked to see Harry standing just inside the door. His face was drawn, his eyes puffy and red-rimmed. Steph swallowed hard and fought against her tears. She looked at Harry, who returned her gaze without saying a word.

It took a moment, but all at once, Steph understood.

'Oh, no,' she said, flinging the covers from her and slipping out of the bed. Her bare feet pitter-pattered across the cold, sterile floor. She reached him, went to put her arms around him and then stopped, conscious that she might have misread the situation or that he might not even want her to hold him.

A tear escaped from the corner of his eye and his shoulders slumped. Steph had no hesitation this time – she threw her arms around him, and even though he had to stoop, she held the back of his head as he rested his forehead on her shoulder.

'She's dead.' Harry's words were muffled.

'I'm so sorry for you,' said Steph. She wasn't sure how she felt about it herself. The bloody woman had tried to kill her but she felt so much empathy for Harry. He was truly heartbroken at his loss.

She led him over to the bed and they perched side by side

on the edge of the mattress. Steph put her arm around his shoulder and held his hand.

'Her heart just wasn't strong enough in the end,' he said, after a while. He cleared his throat and sat up. 'She was dying anyway. She had cancer. It had gone into her bones and vital organs. She only had a matter of months to live.'

'Did you already know that?'

'Only found out last week when I came home. Dominic told me.' Harry looked up to the ceiling and blew out a long breath. Then he stood up. 'I'm sorry, Steph. I shouldn't have come. It was really insensitive of me.'

'No, I'm glad you did.' She reached for his hand again. 'And I am genuinely sorry for your loss.'

'You're a better person than me. Jesus, Steph, I don't know how you do it. She . . . she tried to . . . she tried to kill you.' He looked away towards the window. 'She killed Elizabeth.'

'Try not to blur the lines,' said Steph, standing next to him. 'Grieve for your mother, allow yourself to do that, and keep any other thoughts about what she did separate.'

'I don't know if I can.' He looked back at her. 'I always knew I came from a rotten family and I blamed my dad for that, but it seems the rot ran deeper and came from more than one source.'

She rubbed his arm with her other hand, not knowing what else to say. It was something he had to work out for himself. 'Don't rush anything,' she said in the end. 'Take it a day at a time. Have you spoken to the police yet?'

'Briefly. Someone from CID is coming to see me tomorrow.'

Steph nodded, as much to herself as to Harry – the wheels had already been set in motion. Soon she'd have to hand over the details of the SpyCloud and Harry would find out what his wife was really like. She couldn't have him find out from the police. That would be too awful, too humiliating.

'There's something I need to tell you before you speak to the police,' she began. 'Elizabeth recorded a sort of video diary.'

'I know. My mum had it but she destroyed it.'

'It was automatically backed up to a cloud. I have the details. I accessed it,' she said carefully. 'She said she knew things about your family that could get her into trouble. She was scared.'

'Fuck.' He frowned. 'What aren't you telling me?'

'In it, she admits to having an affair,' said Steph with even more care. She saw Harry's chest swell as he took in a deep breath and then it gradually deflated.

He ran his hand through his hair. 'Is there anything else I should know?'

'Maybe I should give you the details to access it,' said Steph. She picked up the rucksack Wendy had brought back from Conmere and wrote out the details on a piece of paper from the notebook, before handing it to Harry.

'Did she say anything about my mother on it?' he asked, taking the paper and giving it a cursory look before folding it in half and tucking it into the pocket of his jeans.

'Oh, no,' said Steph, surprised at Harry's question. 'No, she didn't. It was more about what Dominic was up to.'

'The cocaine, right?'

'Right.'

'I swear to you, Steph, I wasn't involved in that. I didn't even know it was going on. I knew Owen had a problem, but I didn't for one minute suspect Dominic was the supplier. God, what a tangled web of lies and deceit. What a fucked-up family I have.'

'You're not alone,' said Steph. 'It's a long story but apparently my dad, the one who I adored and who was my superhero, turns out was a bit of a phoney on the superhero front. He drove for your dad.'

'I do know that. Dominic told me the other day.'

'Did you know Dominic told my mum to make sure the verdict on Elizabeth's death was misadventure and if she didn't something would happen to me?'

'I can't believe what I'm hearing.'

'She did it to protect me. That's why she shunned me. Not because she couldn't bear the sight of me, but because she loved me and wanted me as far away as possible, somewhere Dominic couldn't touch me.'

'It's like some sort of nightmare.' Harry dragged his hands down his face. 'I can't believe I'm going to ask this, but . . . did your mum know the truth about what happened to Elizabeth, that it was my mum?' He almost choked on his words.

'She never fully investigated,' said Steph softly. 'But that doesn't mean she didn't suspect something, and that in itself makes her guilty of not carrying out her duty as a police officer.'

'Did my mum tell you what happened? Did she actually say she killed Elizabeth?' Steph looked down at the floor. She couldn't meet his gaze. It was just too painful. Harry swore under his breath. 'She did, didn't she? She told you because she thought it was safe to. She thought you weren't going to live, so she told you the truth.'

Abruptly, Harry broke contact with Steph, and then took another step away, putting distance between them.

'I'm sorry,' he said. 'I need time to get my head round everything.'

'Sure,' said Steph. As much as she knew it was the best thing to do, her heart tugged in her chest. Something told her he was about to walk out of her life, probably for good.

'I wish I hadn't come, but I'm glad I did in some sort of perverse way. I needed to know the truth.'

'I wish I could have told you something different.'

Harry rested his hand against the door jamb and patted it twice, as if trying to come to a decision. He turned back to her. 'There's something on that recording that you're not telling me. What is it?'

Steph gulped. How could she tell him about Dominic? 'I . . . I don't think so.'

He appraised her before speaking again. 'Was Elizabeth having an affair with Dominic?'

This time, Steph's throat was too dry to gulp. She opened her mouth to speak, to deny it, because that was what he wanted to hear, but the words stuck in her throat. She tried again. 'I don't know,' she managed to choke out.

'You're a crap liar,' said Harry. He walked back to her and gently cupped the side of her face with his hand. 'Take care, Steph.'

She looked at him, tears blurring her vision. She managed a nod and leaned her face into his palm. 'You too.'

Chapter Forty-Two

Harry's Lodge, Conmere, Wednesday, 5 July, 1.20 p.m

Harry looked at the letter in his hand. Had he known it was from Sonia Lomas before he'd opened it, he might have been tempted to throw it away without reading it. However, it was in his hand, a single sheet of white bond paper, her neat handwriting gracing the page.

Dear Harry

I hope you find it in yourself to read this letter for it is not sent with any kind of malice and I hope it is received in the way it's intended. I know we haven't been able to speak to one another for some time now and I feel this is the best way.

Firstly, I want to extend my condolences to you for the loss of your mother. This is said not because of how I feel about what Pru did, but to you as a man who was once my son-in-law and who as a son is grieving in the most difficult of circumstances.

I know deep down you are not a true Sinclair, not in your heart, and I take comfort from that. I know

442

you loved Elizabeth once and that your feelings were genuine and that my daughter was probably not deserving of such love. She was a complex person and if it's any comfort to you, I know she did love you too but for Elizabeth love was never enough. She always wanted more. Despite her gregarious nature, underneath it all, she was insecure and never had the courage to acknowledge her background or to be proud of her roots. She felt it was a weakness and she turned her back on it, believing she'd find fulfilment in material things and power. My only regret is that I wasn't able to teach her to value herself and those who loved her more highly.

In a strange sort of way, I can understand how your mother felt. That's not to say I understand how she reacted but I understand the love she had for Conmere and her family. I would go to the ends of the earth to protect my loved ones. Whatever the outcome of the new enquiry, I know I have made peace with myself and with my daughter. I have found strength from my faith, having returned to it in recent months, as I look towards some sort of forgiveness. I'm not there yet, but I'm making progress. And you must try to do the same. I hope you find a sense of peace and I hope you find love because that is the strongest gift a person can receive and give. That's what makes us human and that's what gives us purpose.

Take care and may God bless you.

Sonia

Harry's eyes swam with tears. He wasn't sure he deserved such humility from her. He reread the letter several more times and each time it touched his heart a little bit more.

Chapter Forty-Three

Kendalton, Thursday, 6 July, 11.33 a.m.

Steph folded the flap on the last packing box in Wendy's house, taped it down, then marked it 'Living Room'. She slid it over with the other boxes neatly stacked up in the corner.

'That looks about done,' she said, looking up as Ria came into the room.

'Here, have a cup of tea.' Ria placed the tray she was carrying down onto one of the boxes.

Steph picked up her cup and with a sigh looked around the room. 'Strange to think my mum's life amounts to half a dozen cardboard boxes. I know she's not particularly sentimental, but this is all she wants to take with her.'

'She's moving to a small apartment. What do you expect?'

'I hope she's doing the right thing. Devon is such a long way away from everything she's known for the past thirty years.'

Ria gave a sympathetic smile. 'I'm sure your mum knows what she's doing. Besides, it was where she was brought up. Maybe that's the draw.'

'Ignore me,' said Steph, shaking her head. 'I'm just being over-anxious. I need to stop worrying about her.'

The sound of the doorbell startled both women, who exchanged a look.

Steph went over to the bay window and moved the vertical blind a fraction. She let out a gasp and darted out of sight, pinning her back to the wall.

'What's wrong?' Ria crossed the room.

'It's . . . it's Harry.'

Ria nearly spat her tea out but managed to swallow it without choking. 'Harry Sinclair?'

'Yes!'

'What's he doing here?'

Steph steadied her nerves. She hadn't spoken to or heard from him since the day at the hospital. She genuinely believed he had walked out of her life. The doorbell rang out again, this time with a more insistent buzz, followed by a rap of knuckles on the glass. 'I'd better see what he wants,' said Steph, reluctantly pushing herself from the wall. She smoothed her hair with her hands and brushed herself down.

'You look fine,' said Ria with a smile. 'I'll make myself scarce upstairs. I'll clean the bathroom. Just shout if you need me.'

Steph went to open the door as Ria disappeared. She felt rather more apprehensive than she had imagined she would. She couldn't think for the life of her what Harry was doing here. Maybe he wanted Wendy for some reason. Yes, that must be it. She opened the door but there was no look of surprise or shock on his face.

'Hello, Steph,' he said. 'Sorry to doorstep you like this, but I thought if I asked you to meet me, you might say no.'

'I might have done,' she said, although Steph knew in her

heart of hearts, she wouldn't have. 'Do you want to come in? Ria is here, but she's busy upstairs.'

'Actually, I'm just popping out to the shop,' said Ria, coming down the stairs. She picked up her handbag and, giving Harry a smile, she went on her way.

'Do you want a coffee? I haven't packed the kettle yet.' He didn't answer as he stood in the middle of the room looking very uncomfortable. 'Are you OK?' she asked gently.

'It was Mum's funeral last month.'

'Yes, I know.' Steph found herself going to comfort him, but stopped herself at the last moment, instead rubbing his upper arm with her hand. 'I would say sit down and I'll pour you a stiff drink, but as you can see, we're down to sitting on the floor or packing boxes.'

'How have you been?' he asked with a tenderness that reminded her of their time at the lodge. She found herself yearning for those moments again.

'Getting by,' she said. 'You?'

'Much the same.'

They both went to speak at the same time and stopped abruptly. 'You first,' said Steph.

'I was just going to say that we've decided to sell Conmere.'

'Sell it? Wow. I didn't think you'd do that.'

'I want out whatever. Owen wants to run his own stables and riding school. He's talking of moving to Norfolk. That's where Natalie's parents are. He wants a clean break. To start again without any baggage. Personally, I think he wants to get as far away from Dominic as possible. He's been in rehab the last four weeks.'

'I hope it works out for him. And Dominic?' By rights, he

should have been locked up for drug dealing but by the time the police had searched the resort and the boathouse, there had been no evidence to find.

'He's talking about going into business with his friend, property developing.'

'And you?' she asked tentatively.

'I know about Elizabeth and Dominic,' said Harry, not answering her question.

She couldn't meet his gaze and looked down at her feet. 'I'm sorry.'

'Don't worry about it. It wasn't a complete surprise, if I'm honest. I was already suspicious of Elizabeth, and as for Dominic, he always wanted to spoil what I had. Goes way back to when we were kids. I thought he was over it as an adult, but clearly I was wrong.'

'You sound very magnanimous about it all.'

'I might do now. It's amazing how dropping your brother with one punch to the jaw can work wonders for your anger.'

'You didn't?'

'Yep. Afraid so.'

'He deserved it. And more.' This time she did meet his gaze. 'Wish I'd been there to see it.' They exchanged a smile.

'How is your mum?' asked Harry, shifting the conversation on. 'I hear she's moved away. Devon?'

'That's right. She's already in her new apartment. I take it the police told you that they had reviewed the original investigation?'

'Yeah. They found no evidence of her failing to perform her duties diligently.' Harry blew out a breath. 'I'm still getting my head round that one. I still don't really know what to believe.'

'She was told not to dig too deep,' said Steph, feeling she wanted to defend her mother and yet knowing Wendy had done wrong. 'But you know why and it won't do any good going over that again. I am sorry.'

'You don't have to be sorry. You've done nothing wrong. All you've done is give Sonia Lomas some sense of closure. It may not be exactly what she was hoping for, but I think she's taken some sort of comfort from Mum's death.' He said the words with no malice as he looked around the room.

'I'm just here packing up the last of Mum's things,' explained Steph. 'She didn't want to stay around to do it herself.'

'You weren't tempted to move with her, then?'

'It's early days between us,' admitted Steph. 'There's a long way to go before I think we're at that stage. There's a lot of damage to repair, now the honeymoon period of our relationship is over.'

Harry nodded. 'I'm glad you've found each other finally. You hold on to that, Steph, because it can be taken away from you when you least expect it. Don't be too hard on her. No one is perfect.'

She could see the pain in his eyes. 'You don't have to feel guilty about anything.'

Harry shrugged. 'So, what are you going to do with yourself now?'

'Go back to Brighton, I expect. I don't want to stay around here; it has too many sad memories.' She was surprised when her voice caught in her throat.

'Whatever your dad was, whatever he did, from what you've

told me, there was never any doubt he loved you,' said Harry. 'Don't let anything taint your memory of him.'

Steph went to speak but found the lump in her throat too big to swallow. She nodded instead, which dislodged the unexpected tears from her eyes. Harry thumbed away the tears and let out a sigh. 'Don't cry.'

Steph wrenched in the emotion. 'I'm being silly and you're being so kind.'

'I haven't finished being kind yet,' said Harry. 'I wanted to thank you.'

'For what?'

'For not going to the papers with your story.'

'I didn't want to do that to you. I didn't want to exploit your pain for my gain.'

'You could have been offered that dream job at a big national.'

Steph shrugged. 'Turns out I don't really want that anyway. I'm going to focus on my photography. That's what makes me happy.'

'Sometimes it takes more than things to make someone happy.'

'True. You never answered my question,' said Steph, looking up at him. 'What are you going to do now?'

'I'm going back to France,' he said, and then somewhat unexpectedly, 'Come with me?'

It was said so simply, as if he were asking her if she wanted to go for a walk or a drink at the pub. She looked at him as a seismic swirl of emotions sped through her – amazement, temptation, realisation and finally disappointment. 'I can't. How can I? How can we even contemplate it when our lives are so intricately entwined for all the wrong reasons?'

'I don't know,' he replied. 'In my world, it would be just you and me.'

'But in the real world . . . God, I want to say yes but I . . . I don't know, Harry.'

'You don't have to commit. You could just try it. See how you like it.' He gave a smile. 'There are some pretty cool places in France to photograph.'

'Oh, God, why can't this be in another six months' time? I've still got things to sort out. There's my mum – I can't just leave her, not now when we're trying to patch things up.'

'France isn't the other side of the world. You can jump on a plane and be in Devon in three or four hours.' He let out a long breath. 'Six months, you say? OK, I can wait.'

'I just need a little more time.'

'Like I said, I can wait.' Harry dipped his head and kissed her very lightly on the mouth. It was brief but said so much. Once again, he wiped her tears with his thumbs as he cupped her face. 'Take care of yourself, Steph.'

'You too.'

'Oh, before I forget.' Harry took an envelope from his pocket. 'Sonia sent this to Conmere. She asked if I could pass it on, said she didn't have your address.'

Steph took the envelope, unable to look at Harry for fear of crying. He left without another word, leaving her alone in the middle of an empty room, bar a few packing boxes. Her heart felt as empty as the space she was standing in.

She opened the letter.

Dearest Steph

Now that everything has settled down, I wanted to take the opportunity to write to you. I know I could phone or email, but to someone my age it would seem inadequate and would dilute what I want to say, so forgive me for being old-fashioned with this letter but do know it comes from my heart.

I cannot begin to thank you for all you have done for me and Elizabeth. For all the things Elizabeth was or wasn't, she was always and will always be my daughter and I can rest easy knowing I shall never have to fight for justice again. You showed a faith in me that no single other person did. You believed me and were willing to take a chance, and for that I shall be ever grateful.

Now it is your turn to find what you are looking for. I know you never talked about it, but I always had a sense you were looking for something that was missing in your life. In my experience, the only things that we truly want are to be loved and to love, but to do that we must first forgive. Don't be harsh on yourself or on others.

Go out there and grab life with both hands. As they say, life is for the living.

Fondest regards

Sonia

X

Ria appeared in the doorway. She gave Steph an appraising look. 'So?'

'So?' repeated Steph.

'So, what are you waiting for?' She glanced out of the window. 'He's just about to get in his car. If you run, you can catch him. I'm sure he won't mind postponing his flight for a few more days while you sort the rest of your mum's things out.'

'You know?'

'Sure. He just told me.' Ria held out her hands in exasperation. 'Go on! Go!'

Steph looked at Sonia's letter and then back at her friend. She could feel a broad grin spread across her face. She hugged Ria. 'I bloody love you.'

'You're saying it to the wrong person,' said Ria. 'Now go!'

Steph ran out of the house and almost flew down the path. She could hear a car engine start. She was out on the pavement. 'Harry!' she yelled, waving her arms wildly, as his car pulled away from the kerb. 'Shit! Harry!' The car moved on down the road. Steph raced out onto the road, watching as the BMW continued away from her.

Then, just as it reached the junction, it stopped. The white reversing lights came on as it retraced its journey, stopping within a few feet of her.

Harry stepped out from the car and looked expectantly at her.

Steph suddenly felt nervous. She took a deep breath. 'Could you condense those six months into six days?'

Harry walked over to her. 'It would be my pleasure.' He enveloped her in his arms as he kissed her.

The letter crumpled as Steph returned the embrace. Life definitely was for the living.

Acknowledgements

Whilst Conmere, Conmere Lake, Con Point Hills and Kendalton are all figments of my imagination, I can only thank the Lake District and its beauty for providing me with the inspiration. I'd thoroughly recommend the Lakes as a holiday destination if you love getting out and about in the countryside. For those of you who are familiar with the area, it's probably not too difficult to work out roughly where I imagined Conmere Resort Centre to be.

As always, huge thanks to the wonderful HarperCollins team who make my dreams possible - especially to Charlotte Ledger for her immeasurable support and advice throughout my writing career. I would also like to thank my two editors, Emily and Laura, who have worked so hard on my manuscript and pushed me to make it the best book I can.

A shout-out to the NaNoWriMo gang of 2018 who with their support and unflinching encouragement made it possible to write such a huge chunk of the book in one month. Also, to the Strictly Suspense writing group who are always at the other end of the computer for cheer-leading and shoulder-crying.

I'm extremely lucky to have wonderful writing pals and I

really appreciate the friendship I've found in the writing community. In particular, I would like to say a big thank you to fellow writer, Nicky Wells who read an early draft of *The Dead Wife* and, as always, gave me her honest and invaluable feedback. To Laura E. James and Catherine Miller for helping me thrash out plot issues while we were on our writing retreat in France and then later over our frequent writerly chats. Thanks also to Facebook friends and Twitter mates who often come to the rescue with answers to my research questions.

Last but by no means least – a heartfelt thank you to anyone who has read any of my books, shared their enthusiasm for my stories in real life and/or via social media, for the wonderful reviews and messages I have received and for all the super supportive book bloggers out there. It really does mean so much. You're all amazing!